a gathering storm

A Gathering Storm begins in a small University town in the South when a gay college student is beaten. As the young man struggles to survive in a hospital, the residents of the town and the University find themselves at the center of a growing media frenzy as the crime reverberates through the local and national consciousness over the following week. Using details and elements from actual hate crimes committed against gay men, author Jameson Currier weaves personal and spiritual layers into a timely and emotional story.

a gathering storm

a novel by

JAMESON CURRIER

Chelsea Station Editions
New York

A Gathering Storm
by Jameson Currier

Copyright © 2014 by Jameson Currier.

Cover art by Duane Hosein
Book design by Peachboy Distillery & Designs

Published by Chelsea Station Editions
362 West 36th Street, Suite 2R
New York, NY 10018
www.chelseastationeditions.com
info@chelseastationeditions.com

Hardcover ISBN: 978-1-937627-19-5
Paperback ISBN: 978-1-937627-20-1
Ebook ISBN: 978-1-937627-53-9
Library of Congress Control Number: 2014939405

First Edition

About the Novel

While assembling material for a collection of my nonfiction writing, I was searching through my old computer disks for an essay that I was certain I had written in October 1998 in the days following the beating of Matthew Shepard, a gay college student at the University of Wyoming who was beaten, tortured, tied to a fence and left to die near Laramie, Wyoming. I had participated in the October 19, 1998 rally against hate crimes and the impromptu demonstration down Fifth Avenue in Manhattan and I was sure that I had written about the experience.

What I stumbled across, instead, was the manuscript of a novel I had begun in the aftermath of Matthew Shepard's death. Writing the book had been both a rewarding and painful experience, but I had chosen to forget about my novel because of the personal disappointment I had attached to it.

Like many gay Americans I was moved by the tragic fate of Matthew Shepard, and in the days following the crime I struggled to pull together portraits of the victim and the assailants from the emerging news. One reason why I decided to write *A Gathering Storm*, a novel about a hate crime against a gay man, was because I felt what was missing from the news were the details and stories of the individuals involved—the crime was analyzed and politicized but oddly not humanized. We did not know who these young men were, what they were thinking, what were they doing, why had they been where they were when things went wrong. We only had their generic representations in the media. The national focus on the issue of hate crimes seemed to overwhelm the personal stories.

I finished writing the *A Gathering Storm* in early 2001 and

I submitted the manuscript to my editor at the publishing company that had published my first novel and had an option of first refusal on my next one. My contract called for a six-week response, but because I was an unagented writer the manuscript languished at the publishing company, never generating any attention or a formal rejection until my editor casually informed me that he was leaving the press to begin another career.

In spite of this I secured the services of a literary agent to represent the novel, who shopped the manuscript around without much success, and, in my estimation, without much enthusiasm on his part, so I began shopping it around myself to additional publishers and editors. After I found a British publisher who was interested in the novel, the agent declined to act on my behalf, and interest faded away when the British publisher—who saw *A Gathering Storm* as a commercial thriller and not a literary novel—was concerned that I did not have another thriller ready to go as a follow-up.

By then Matthew Shepard had been the subject of too many movies, plays, books, and dramatizations. One editor at a mainstream house declined the manuscript stating "the Shepard murder was discussed and dramatized and debated in the media so much that this novel may have a hard time finding an audience." *A Gathering Storm* was both too similar and too different. My novel was fiction that read like fact. I had consciously changed many details, including moving the location to a college town in the South. During the aftermath of the Shepard murder, the town of Laramie, Wyoming, where the beating and murder occurred, fell under tremendous scrutiny. News reports and other works based on this crime focused sharply on the town. It was my intent to step aside from this location and show that this type of crime could happen anywhere. In choosing to locate this story in the South, I was also able to draw from many of my own experiences and memories and to write it as a story I felt I could tell.

During the course of writing the novel I had also rewritten many details about the Shepard crime and the characters involved with it, weaving in details from other hate crimes against gay men. More importantly, however, I was peering inside the emotional lives of the characters who were living inside my mind, not just presenting the facts. Fiction can oftentimes carry more emotional weight than a news story or a nonfiction account and it was my intent with this work to present a more human face to this tragedy than what was emerging through other works, both in terms of understanding the deep suffering of the victims as well as looking into the psychological motivations and backgrounds of those behind the crimes.

And I had made a conscious decision to write this novel in a different style from the long, complex sentence structure I had favored in my first novel, *Where the Rainbow Ends*. *A Gathering Storm* is a deconstruction of a crime and this time my prose was purposely short and choppy, like a screenplay. I wanted the visuals to rise immediately off the page and to do so I had, in fact, studied many screenplays and true crime narrative accounts and the way they presented both dialogue and action. And since I was deconstructing the crime, I also wanted to deconstruct the narrative structure of the novel, presenting it as linear, circular, *and* fragmented.

Sometime in 2003 I formally severed ties with the literary agent and abandoned the manuscript to pursue other projects. I never expected the novel to be published and had been so upset by the experience of both writing the book and not finding a publisher for it that I had stored all the notes and drafts of the novel into a box and hid the box at the bottom of a closet in my apartment, out of sight and incapable of wounding me any further. But there it was, *A Gathering Storm*, always at the top of a list of my completed work that I keep on a bulletin board above the desk where I write, ignored and overlooked until I *saw* it there again while I was looking for my Shepard essay. Even as I copied the manuscript files of the novel from the floppy disk to my laptop to archive it, I did not anticipate publishing the work because I felt it was surely outdated, even though other authors had revisited the Matthew Shepard crime and had published recent books about it.

What I discovered when I sat down to reread *A Gathering Storm* was a densely absorbing work full of purpose, a novel that I cannot believe I walked away from and I cannot believe I did not find a publisher for. My faith in it had been shattered by the kind but continued rejection of it. One editor who turned down the manuscript remarked on its "enormous integrity" and found it "refreshing to read a manuscript that is informed by such passion." Another called it "a shocking yet timely story that truly gets to the heart of gay hate in America." Still, no one offered to publish it.

I see now that this novel is a bridge to other themes in my later writings, particularly the gay-themed ghost stories that I would publish later in the decade. But I also see it indicative of the evolution of the gay novel during the first decade of the twenty-first century—how it fell victim to mainstream publishers only wanting commercial blockbusters and how smaller publishers decided to mimic this desire—and how during these years gay authors such as myself, because of our gay themes and narratives and characters and the choices of our fictions—had to find other publishers and other ways and outlets to continue to be published and to find readers. I began Chelsea Station Editions to publish work that was overlooked and ignored by other publishers, worthy gay-themed literature that needed to find its way into print, and I am grateful for the advances in technology, economics, and business and trade practices that have allowed me to do so. I have never been a writer who has chased financial or critical success, only a place to publish what I have wanted to write and what I felt needed to be written and shared. I never expected to be a publisher or a bookseller. But I am extremely proud to say that I have created the perfect home for *A Gathering Storm.*

Jameson Currier
July 2014

a gathering storm

In memory of those lost by hate.

Death cannot kill what never dies.

William Penn

1

Tuesday

Headlights stretch across the black pavement of the road. It is just a road, black concrete with a broken white line painted at its center. Patches of tar fill the cracks. Nothing discernible on either side. This story could happen anywhere.

This particular road is a long, straight, country road. The neon signs of the small town have disappeared. Gravel and limestone pebbles look gray in the headlights. It is after midnight and the landscape is dark. All that can be seen from the front seat of a pickup truck are dead leaves tumbling across the road or grassy weeds as beams of light travel across their skins. Inside, the dashboard casts an eerie glow. Three men are traveling together in the front seat of a pickup truck.

The first blow brings disbelief. A young man shields his face to fend off the next one. He is conservatively dressed. A college boy, handsome but short. Blue eyes and floppy hair with blond streaks. The taller guy, the one driving the truck, laughs as the blow hits his passenger. He twists his neck to watch the college boy bend down in the seat, leaning his chest over his knees, to protect himself. A high-pitched "stop" rises up like a bubble, as laughable to the driver as a child being chased by a bee. The one riding by the door, the one with the thick hair and big ears, clutches the college boy's neck with his hand and pins his face against his leg. This one is short, too, but he is taller than the one he pins. He has a face that looks ridiculous with glee.

"Looks like the college boy is a pussy," A.J. says. He is the big-eared one by the door. His brow is large and high. His eyes are deep set, lost in the shadows of the night. He lifts Danny upright by the neck and punches him again in the face. Danny is the short, conservatively dressed one in the middle. Danny feels the punch push the flesh of his cheek against the metal braces on his teeth. The taste of blood in his mouth makes him cough. "Don't," he says weekly, his hands come up to his face again. He tries to use his elbows to dig his way out of this predicament, but it only provokes another blow from A.J.

"College boy is afraid of a little blood," the one driving says. His name is Rick. He has a stubble of beard, unshaved for two days, dark brown hair cut close to the scalp. His eyes are blood shot from the lack of sleep, too much crank, or both.

"That's because the college boy is a pussy," A.J. says. "Let's see what you got."

Again with one hand A.J. pins Danny's neck against the seat of the truck and with his other hand digs into his back pocket for the wallet. He shakes the wallet open. A college ID card hits Danny's leg and falls onto the floor of the truck. A photo of the student stares back at him.

"Twenty bucks," A.J. says. "Twenty fuckin' bucks." A.J. takes the money out and tosses the wallet onto the floor. He shoves the money into the front pocket of his jeans.

"College boy's gonna have to pay since he doesn't carry cash," A.J. says.

The college boy is still bent over. His head throbs with the pulse of fear, a crackle of lightning that waits to play itself out in thunder. He sees A.J.'s free hand move beneath the seat and retrieve a gun, a barrel so long it looks like a rifle. It occurs to him that he might die. He waits to be shot, waits for his head to split open, darkness envelop him.

What happens is worse: The butt of the gun lands against his back. The force surprises him, makes his lungs airless, as if he has plunged underwater and an unexplained weight is preventing him from surfacing and breathing. Slowly, like the concurrent rings of a splash, pain travels across his body. When his breath comes back to him he hears the sound of wheels moving over dirt and pebbles. The grip is back against his neck. He is yanked out of the truck and pitched to the ground. A boot hits him in the groin. He folds his body in pain. He's done nothing to deserve this. Why is this happening to him?

He had only asked for a ride home. He had met the two guys at the bar, talked to them a few minutes, felt at ease as they crossed the parking lot together to the truck. As he doubles himself up in pain, he realizes the mistake. The one with the big ears seemed too willing to leave the bar, too eager to have his friend drive his truck. The toss of the keys between the guys in the parking lot should have been a giveaway. A change in routine. A plan of attack. The other one had played it cool, even when he had difficulty getting the truck into gear.

But there had been no perceptible sign of disgust in the bar. He had talked openly with the two guys. Explained to them he was gay, in his first year at the University, that he had attended a meeting before coming to the bar to help plan a gay awareness event on campus. "The best thing that happened was when my parents found out," he said. "It made it much easier to go on from there."

The cool one had shook his head, his eyes wide and agreeing. "I could never tell my old man about being gay," he said. "He'd beat me to shit."

Now it comes to him that it was a deceptive sneer on his face and not a grin. The big-eared one had rocked back and forth on his heels, said, "Yeah, it's great that we have a place like this to hang out."

Then, inside the truck, after the cool one had eased onto the highway, an odor of loathing erupted, fumes enveloping them like a poisonous gas. "Guess what, college boy," the big-eared one said. "We're not gay. And you just got jacked."

On the ground the college boy clutches at the dirt, draws up a handful in his fist. They have stopped where a trail begins behind the old church cemetery. The cool one shuts off the lights of the truck. Behind him, a split-rail fence follows the road, bleached gray by the weather. Up a short hill, a white clapboard church soaks in what light there is, its sharp steeple looming over the valley, the windows and door frames black and gaping in shock.

The college boy lifts himself up on one leg but the big-eared one rams the gun against his face. He falls, catching his weight with his wrists. Another blow on his back sends him to the ground. At the back of his throat is a taste of vomit and blood. The night is raw: chilly, windy, a storm is gathering. He understands his danger now. But his body is losing its impulses. He knows he must flee but pain is controlling his movements. He does his best to scream, but fear and constrictions in his throat only make a short sigh, almost like a taunting laugh.

Somewhere he finds the energy to stand and run. He makes it only a few steps, kicking up gravel. The tall one snags him by the coat. He wiggles out of one sleeve, then the other, makes it a few more steps till the tall one must tackle him to prevent his escape. They land on the ground together. Again, no wind in his lungs, another roar in his ears.

For a moment they are face to face, arm in arm, till Danny presses his face into the crook of Rick's neck, as if a moment of intimacy between them might bring forgiveness. There is a flicker of recognition in Rick's eyes. A rich, mossy scent rises up into his nostrils. A cough of Danny's blood frightens him to his feet.

A.J. grabs the college boy by the shirt, the coat hangs on his body by one sleeve. He slams the pistol against his face again. The college boy drops to his knees, his head bowed as if in prayer. A.J. drags him through the dirt toward the truck. The coat falls away, his credit card slides from the pocket onto the ground, coins roll and scatter in the dirt.

"Get the rope out of the back," A.J. says to Rick.

"Come on, let's go," Rick says, instead of obeying. The blood on his jacket has changed his mood. "That's enough. He looks pretty bad."

"Shut the fuck up," A.J. says. He swings the gun against Rick's face, splitting his lip.

"You fuck," Rick shouts back. He walks away, back toward the truck.

"What's the matter, wus? Faggot got your dick?" A.J. shouts at Rick.

"Shut the fuck up," he yells back.

"You a faggot lover too?"

"Shut the fuck up," he yells again.

"Go get the rope," A.J. says. There is an authoritative sneer to him. Crime has made him the leader.

The tall one walks to the truck, steps up onto the bed, looks around, finds a rope. He looks back, watches the big-eared one drag the college boy to the fence. He doesn't think about what the college boy feels. Only that his own lip is busted. And how he is going to get back at his friend.

The big-eared one holds the college boy against the fence as the tall one ropes his wrists together behind his back and around the post of the fence. The tall one draws the rope tight, remembering the knots he learned in scouting. Now he thinks they can go. He doesn't imagine that the college boy can't free himself. That he is a prisoner. He only thinks about getting drunk. Or maybe high.

"We've got to teach this faggot a lesson," A.J. says. "This ain't a faggot town. We've got to make all those faggots aware this ain't no place for them. Faggot awareness."

A.J. takes the watch off of Danny's arm, looks at it. "Junk," he says. He tosses it to the ground. "Take his shoes," he says to Rick. He is finished with the rope. "So he can't walk back to town."

The tall one takes the college boy's shoes off of his feet. Blood has dulled the polished patent leather. The tall one does not want to touch the blood, but it has dripped onto the laces. He takes a shoe by the heel, yanks it off the foot, then the next. The college boy seems to crumble without them. He slowly slides down the post till his weight rests again on his knees.

"How are you gonna get out of this one, college boy?" the big-eared one asks.

The college boy opens his mouth. It is full of blood, looks like an apple. He feels the blood on his face, running along his neck, making him itch. It is impossible for him to see out of one eye. This can't be real; it can't. But it is. He looks at the big-eared one, then the tall one, then out at the road. The horror has made the night as vivid as day. His good eye falls onto the license plate of the truck a few feet away. Slowly he reads the digits aloud.

The big-eared one becomes frenzied, a rage magnified by his own fear and contempt. He takes five deep, energizing breaths, like a kung fu expert concentrating before slicing a cement block. He brings the handle of the gun against the back of the college boy's neck in three swift strokes. Thump. Thump. Thump. Savage, merciless blows. Each as brutal as a gunshot.

2

Monday

He struggles with waking. His body senses the assembling clouds: the dark, puffy, popcorn-like cumulous, the slow moving higher cirrus, weaving into one another for the possibility of rain. Fall already seems like a memory, or a dream that was over too quickly. Winter inches its way through the walls. He feels unprepared for any of it.

He burrows deeper into the blanket, seeking out the warmth his own body will generate. He hears an alarm clock go off, a high-pitched electronic tone like a cellular phone. He knows it is not his own. The sound echoes through the building and wakes him anyway. He turns on his side, looks at his own clock on the windowsill.

It is 7:30. He wishes it were Tuesday, not Monday. Tuesday lets him sleep later. No early classes that day—like a vacation, a Saturday, at the beginning of the week. But it is not Tuesday. It is Monday. He thinks about skipping his Political Theory class. He finds it tedious, a burden. He only goes because it is a prerequisite. He wanted to jump into something deeper, more philosophical, right away. But he couldn't get around the course. No way to hop over it, exempt it. He feels things are going so slow. But he has promised his parents to try to finish the term.

He sits on the edge of the bed, waits for his head to clear. He is, as usual, tired. Even though he'd been sleeping hard up to the last few minutes. He coughs, testing the congestion in his lungs. He's been battling a cold the last few days. Surprisingly his lungs are clear, only phlegm caught in his throat today.

Another day begins. Full of challenges. Standing, he

realizes he is already battling loneliness. As he makes his way to the bathroom, he wonders if it was wise to live off campus. Not to have tried the dorms. He exempted the on-campus living requirement because of his age. But the truth is he isn't sure this will work. Like a test, he knows he will either pass or fail. He's failed loneliness, he thinks. He decides it was a mistake not to live in the dorm. Even if he is different, not just older. But fate has made the difference stronger.

He pisses in the toilet, flushes, watches the yellow swirl away in the bowl. He thinks about his health, pushes it aside. He doesn't like this apartment. Everything seems old and large—the high ceilings, the white stone walls, the exposed radiators that have yet to shed any warmth. Even the dark colors he has collected—for the bedroom, the bathroom, the couch—haven't made the place feel warmer, friendlier to him. He looks at himself in the mirror, flattens his hair with his fingers, then watches it rise back up into an overnight cowlick. His hair is short on the sides, recently cut. He has a long neck, tunnel of an Adam's apple, high cheekbones, makes him look sorta pretty. He smiles, disappointed by the gray metal atop his teeth. He sees a pimple growing on his right cheek. It makes him depressed. When will it ever stop? He's twenty and they still torture him. He rubs the small blisters on his chin, now fading, then thinks he feels another, working its way out. What does it matter anyway? He doesn't see himself as aging. Ever.

In the bedroom he turns on the TV set, checks the temperature outside—forty-two degrees—then thinks about changing the station to CNN. He decides he is not yet ready for the day, turns the television off. The room floats back to silence.

In the kitchen he opens the refrigerator door, withdraws a bottle of soda. His cat, Chloe, recognizing the sound, dashes into the kitchen. He picks her up off the floor, drawing in a reluctant welcome from her before he gets her food. She squirms in his arms. He drops her to the floor. She lands, begins to rub her body back and forth against his legs, mewing.

He lifts her bowls from the floor. Runs water from the spigot into one. He rattles her box of food, using the sound to tease her. She looks up at him, sits, waits. Then she jumps up and noses the bowls as he returns them to their place on the floor. She ignores him as she eats the dry food, cracking the small wafers into smaller pieces at the back of her mouth.

He pours himself some soda. He uses a glass this morning instead of drinking straight from the bottle. He still has a boy's desire of food—sweets, hamburgers, French fries. He doesn't eat any breakfast. The carbonation and the sugar from the soda expand in his stomach. It will be enough to last till he meets Leah for lunch. Even if he knows it isn't any good for him.

Back in the bathroom he contemplates shaving. There is not much of a beard to him. He can often go days without any stubble. He decides his neck feels scratchy this morning. He lathers his face, then goes to the bedroom, turns on the stereo. He programs a CD of dance hits his friend Walt gave him. But the bass sounds too loud to him. He wants something softer. He finds the Reba CD he likes best, puts it on.

In the bathroom he sings along. Shaves slowly. Looks for nicks, blood. The music brings him loneliness again. He rinses his face, dries, finds his medicine in the cabinet. He smiles again, trying to overlook the braces but he can't. He pops a tiny blue tablet into his mouth, using the water from the faucet to chase it down.

In the shower he tries not to let the day overwhelm him. He has four classes, lunch with Leah, promised last week to take Walt to the movies tonight, to celebrate his birthday. Already he feels anxious, ready for a nap. The water drains him of energy, till he hears the pipes shake in the wall and the warm water disappear.

The cold water startles him, makes him annoyed. He curses the building again. Wishes he lived somewhere else. He turns the water off, reaches for a towel, his teeth clench from the chill.

In the bedroom he can't decide what to wear. The season is slipping away, becoming something else. He turns the CD off, hoping to clear his head. Chloe scampers into the room, sits in her usual spot on the windowsill, watches him move around.

He decides on the long sleeve blue shirt, button-down, preppy-looking. Before he gets it from the closet the phone rings. He slips a white T-shirt quickly over his head, grabs the phone before his answering machine picks up.

"It's Leah," he hears. "Just calling to check in, hon. How's it going?"

"Fine," he says. The sound of his own voice disappoints him. He wishes it were deeper.

"Did you call your mom and say you're sorry?" she asks.

"Not yet," he answers. Last night, on the phone, he had fought with his mother over the credit card bills. The bank account overdrafts. He hates being on an allowance. A budget. She had only called to let him know that his friend Mark, from St. Clare's, had passed away. It was in the paper. She wasn't aware that the news would shake him like it did. She doesn't know the real story, the story he's never told her. In the ensuing panic, he had called Leah as a sympathetic ear. Leah is old enough to be his mother, runs a bed and breakfast near campus with her partner Naomi. Naomi is always worried about money, about how much things cost, what they are spending. Leah believes things work themselves out in the end. She had calmed him down about the news about Mark, reminding him that he had told her that he had been sick for some time. And was his ally about the money problems. "I'll call her when the rates go down," he says. "Or maybe e-mail my dad from school."

"Naomi told me last night that if I want to get a better car I have to find a way to pay for it," Leah says. "I told her that it wasn't safe driving that old lemon anymore. What if I'm stranded? Her response was to start in on me about the new boots I bought."

"Which you need because you can't drive anywhere," he adds. "My mom is the same way. She pays more attention to my money than hers."

"Are you going to class today?" she asks. Leah takes one class every semester at the University, "to keep my mind alive" she told him when they first met.

"I think so," he replies. "If I fall behind, they'll just bitch at me some more."

"I'll meet you at the cafeteria," she says.

"Okay," he answers and hangs up.

He runs the towel through his hair, drying it more, combs it in front of the mirror, refusing to smile. He puts on khaki pants, the blue shirt, his favorite black shoes. When he straps the watch on his wrist, he thinks about his mom again. The watch was expensive. More than anything else he owns. He told her he bought it to cheer himself up, to make himself feel better. She didn't understand that. She never understands.

From the hall closet he gets his navy blue sports jacket. He knows it makes him look older. He's tired of looking like a kid. He wants people to take him seriously now.

3

Tuesday

There is not death yet, but there is a darkness. Evil has left a wound in the night which howls from injury. The night does not recognize this. Its sounds continue beyond the human violence it has absorbed: The wind rustles the fur of a rabbit, a swirl of dirt rises into a funnel and disappears, a single, brown leaf crosses the road more skittish than a deer. The temperature has fallen below freezing. There is no sound that registers it. Only the cells of a plant have thickened in protection; a ground squirrel has nestled deeper into its burrow for warmth.

Winded, beaten, and betrayed, a young man has been roped to a fence like a scavenging fox, butchered and nailed up to warn others like him to stay away. But he is not conscious of the grass at his feet, nor of the field behind him, not in these minutes, nor of the cold that is beginning to chill and dry the blood on his clothing. Only a few seconds lie between his last words and consciousness, but instead of sleep or dreams, the tissues of his brain tumble through an abstract blackness. His brain cells have become depolarized, their neurotransmitters fire in an unhealthy cascade of chemical chains. His moments are indefinable, elusive, a random energy of memory.

He is not fortunate but he is not without hope. His heart continues to beat. Blood flows from his wounds. Eighteen blows to the skull has left bruises and gashes. Blood vessels beneath the skin, broken and still bleeding, have begun to swell the flesh purple. Other wounds—a gash behind the left ear, a slice in his scalp—have started to clot and close themselves up. The blood which fully covers his face, protects him now like another skin.

24

And his flesh is still warm. In fact, he is sweating. His face and body twitch as muscles go through spasms. His kidney and bladder continue to function. In his stomach, a slice of cherry pie eaten hours before is being digested; the alcohol from three beers is being absorbed into his blood.

But his body is not without battles. In the assault a tooth was chipped and has slipped into his windpipe. A metal wire of his braces broke free, slashed the inner cheek in his mouth. Somewhere between being drug across the dirt and roped to the fence he urinated down his leg. His pants absorbed the fluid first, then dampened his skin, and like his shirt has now taken in the cold.

Three ribs have been cracked. His nose has been broken in two places. Two fingers are also broken. Portions of his upper spine have been shattered. He suffers internal bleeding. Blood has collected at his wrists from the pressure of the ropes, unable to make it into his hands. And the alcohol, moving into his bloodstream, counteracts the effects of the drug his physician had prescribed, altering his heartbeat as dangerously as his attackers.

But his lungs have not abandoned him. His breathing continues, rising and falling, even if the swelling and the pressure and the lodged, chipped tooth distress his windpipe. Somehow a bubble of air has been trapped in his stomach and a spasm of a muscle sends it up through the cavity of his chest, squeezes it out of his mouth. The movement is enough to bring him suddenly back to life, send a moan out into the night as the air passes across his vocal chords. And then the fear of death, the hope and will to live, make him hyperventilate, sending enough gasps of air to recreate a consciousness to his brain. When he surfaces he finds the night again, recognizes the cold and the pain that is now blinding him.

At first he sees only the dark socks still on his feet, then the grass around him, then closer, the small pebbles of blood which have dropped from his face. At the corner of his vision—out of the eye that still sees—he notices his watch on the ground, face down in a patch of dirt, unable to tell him the length of his misery. He wants to apologize to someone but he doesn't understand what crime he has committed. Does he apologize for being such a ready target? Does he say he's sorry because he has been shamed and humiliated? Or does he apologize for his own rising anger of his disfigurement? The wind rises around him. The cold makes his eye tear.

And then everything is black again. He exists only as energy.

As the night progresses the land does not offer him answers, nor does it offer to defend him. There is no sanctuary nor respite from his pain. The minutes play out as years to his body. Time moves so slowly that he becomes simply a vertical figure on the horizontal beam, quietly resting on the flesh of his wrists, not yet departed.

4

Tuesday

Rick feels a chill as the truck edges up onto the road. He is driving again. Pebbles scatter as he turns the truck back toward town. He wants the evening to end. The gash in his lip burns. He twists his shoulder and arm toward his lip so his coat sleeve will soak up the fresh blood. His arm feels numb. He wants to thump the veins. "You shit," he says to A.J.

"I didn't like the way he looked at me," A.J. says. He is breathing hard. Like he has been sprinting. He is defensive, ready for another fight. Something still remains unfinished to him. "Why the fuck did you tell him we were gay?"

"You think he wanted to fuck you?" Rick yells. "Are you fucking crazy?"

"He was fuckin' with us," A.J. snaps back. "He could fuckin' turn us in."

The road has brought them to the edge of town. Rick brings the truck to a stop for a red light. On the corner is a gas station, the fluorescent tubes glowing in the night even though the station is closed. The night is empty. He's been up for four days straight. Started a bag on Friday night. His head is cranked up again, this time from fear. Full of a thousand moments. It freezes on an image of the college boy's hands, bound by the rope to the fence, his skin as bright as the station light. Then it jumps to A.J.'s swings. Swift as a guillotine blade. Thump. Thump. Thump. The driver dabs his lip against his shoulder again. "We're gonna be in big shit," he says. "You didn't have to fuckin' kill him."

"Did you see the way he spoke to me?" the big-eared one says. His eyes are black, dilated, wild. "Like I wanted to like him."

A.J. can't sit still. His skin is scratchy. He punches the dashboard. Rocks violently back into the seat. The bloody shoes on the seat beside him jump like they're dancing. He's still not finished. "He fuckin' tried to make me," A.J. says. "Did you see that fucker? That college boy was fuckin' trying to make me."

Rick wipes his hand down his neck. He has frozen on the image of the college boy's lips pressing against him. He wipes his hand against his jeans. He feels dirt under his nails, a gummy sweat under his arms. He wants to shower. Get out of here. But there are too many things to do.

He pulls the car over to the curb. Stops along Hogan Street. He wants a drink. Or a hit. Something right away. To mellow out. Or get out of this shit. There is too much stuff crashing in his brain. He reaches into the pocket of his jacket for his cigarettes. He feels an unfamiliar sliminess, looks down, notices there is blood on the front of his coat. "Jesus," he says, wiping his hand on his jeans again. The tied hands, the hammer blows freeze in his mind. "We gotta get rid of this stuff," he says. "What happens when the cops come lookin'?"

"Nobody's gonna know unless somebody tells," A.J. says. His words are like spits, hisses of a rattlesnake. "Who's gonna miss a faggot anyway? We got the money. It's enough to get a bag from Baffer."

"Fuck Baffer. We gotta think this through," Rick says. "The coat he was wearin'. And the gun. Where's the gun?"

A.J. doesn't answer him right away. Rick spits out his question again. "Where's the fuckin' gun?"

"It's in the back, you fuckin' wus," A.J. replies.

"We gotta fuckin' get rid of it," Rick says. His eyes have glazed over with terror. He has lost his sense of place. He hops out of the car. A.J. tries to stop him, but his reflexes are slower, more focused on himself. He jumps out of the car on the other side. The doors bang like gunshots in the empty night.

"You can't fuckin' mess with that gun," A.J. says.

Rick is leaning into the bed of the truck. A.J. is behind him. He yanks Rick down by his coat. He shoves him at the shoulders, sending him back a few steps.

Rick shoves A.J. in the chest, takes a few steps forward, grabs him by the collar of his coat. His eyes are nervous, jumpy. "Don't you understand anything, you fuck? We gotta get rid of it. It's got his blood all over it."

"Stop calling me a fuck, you shit," A.J. spits back. He tries to send a knee to Rick's groin, but Rick gives him a shove that sends him staggering back a few steps.

"You queers better watch out," a voice yells from across the street. "Cops are circling. Lookin' for trouble."

"Stay the fuck out of it, faggot," A.J. yells out to the street. His eyes are black again, full of rage.

"Who you callin' faggot, asshole?" a voice lobs back at him. Low buildings line the block, shop fronts on street level, apartments upstairs. Only safety lights are on in the store windows. A faint lamp glows above the telephone wires. Across the street two figures, silhouettes, stop. Their clothes appear baggy in the legs and shoulders, hanging low at the waist. One wears a cap. The other looks to have a shaved head.

"Looks like nothing but trash in this side of town," A.J. says.

"Then what you bitches doin' here trying to pass?" the one wearing a cap says.

"You fags better get out of here," he yells back.

"Fuck yourself, man," the shaved one calls back. "Just 'cause you can't get laid."

A.J. steps onto the bed of the truck, leans in, retrieves the gun. He jumps back down to the curb, walks briskly to the other side of the street, the gun hidden behind his back. "You want to say that too my face, faggot?" he yells at the one wearing a cap. Rick follows a few steps behind him. Dust glows around the lamp light. The cap is red. The guys are young, lean. The shaved one wears an earring, his nose crooked, like it has been broken before.

The two guys stand their ground. When he is a few steps away from them, A.J. pulls out the gun. The shorter of the two, the one with the cap, darts to the left, like a cat being spooked, yelling, "He's got a gun."

The other one, the skin head, raises his hands to shield himself. Or surrender. A.J. steps up, swings the butt of the pistol at him, cracking him in the side of the head. The guy takes two steps back, clasps his hands against his skull. His words are muffled, lost in his disbelief.

A.J. turns to walk away, gives a wicked laugh as if showing off to Rick, when he feels a thud against his own head. The other guy, the one with the red cap, has pulled an iron club from his jacket, cracked it over A.J.'s head. The force of the blow knocks him to one knee. The pain slices his head like a knife. Rick charges after the one with the club but he disappears around a darkened corner. When Rick returns the other one has disappeared too. A.J. is back on his feet, shouting, "What the fuck! What the fuck!" His hands are bloody. His head is heavy, full of needle-like stings. "I'm gonna kill those faggots." Again he picks a fight with Rick. "Why didn't you fuckin' stop him?" he yells. "Where the fuck were you?"

He swings the gun at Rick. But he is weakened, sluggish, frustrated, in pain. Rick steps out of range, yells, "Get rid of the fuckin' gun."

The gun is still in A.J.'s hand a few seconds later when the police car pulls onto the block. A.J. and Rick dart out of the street, hide behind the truck, crouching out of the range of the squad car's lights, hoping not to be spotted. A.J. slips the gun behind a tire of the truck, out of sight. The police car comes to a stop. An officer jumps out, walks over to the truck. Another one remains in the car, visible from the dashboard light.

When it is clear to them the cop intends to check the scene, they both run. A.J. goes west, toward Old Union Highway and the railroad tracks. Rick runs north on Market Street.

Rick makes it behind a building. He looks out, hears the cop chasing A.J., their footfalls on the street. He sees the second officer get out of the car, run in his direction. Before he turns away, he hears the muffled sound of a tackle, a high-pitched, frustrated grunt that can only belong to A.J.

He runs west now. As far as he can go.

5

Tuesday

He knows a lie, but he does not write that in his report.

The suspect says he was jacked. Two guys approached him, swearing, swinging a metal tire jack, cracked it over his head. For no good reason. Just because he was out here.

If he was jacked so easily, why's he still got his wallet? He cuffs the suspect to prevent him from running, looks through his wallet. He keeps the suspect on the ground. Face down. He reads the name on the driver's license. Asks the suspect if that's his name.

The suspect says yes and he helps him stand up. They return to the squad car. The officer notes the suspect's clothes are bloody, too bloody for the cut in his scalp. But the cut worries him. The suspect says his head hurts, everything looks yellow. A second later he leans over, vomits onto the ground.

He tells his partner to call for a medic. The second suspect was unapprehended. His partner is already running a trace on the truck.

This officer is tall, bushy eyebrows, nicotine-stained fingers. His name is James Pearce. He's lived in the county all his life. Been on the force twenty-two years. His body is soft through the middle, limbs more muscular but not especially long. This is what he sees: A suspect, male, appears to be late teens or early twenties, thick black hair, long, wide ears, wound behind the left ear. Mild complexion, dirty nails. Clothes covered with what appears to be blood, possibly flesh.

The clothes are what disturb him.

"Why'd you run?" he asks the suspect.

"Don't want any trouble," he responds.

There is a sneer to him that the officer doesn't like. His partner is out of the squad car, examining the pickup truck.

This officer is younger. Mid-thirties. Clean shaven, short, stocky. His name is Bill Rivers. He carries a torch light. He runs the light over and around the truck. This is what he sees: black pickup truck, Ford F150, old boxy style before the redesign. He makes a sweeping inspection of the vehicle. Small dents in driver's door, fender lopsided. Wheels in good condition, body covered with dust. Trailer hitch covered with dirt, grass. In the back he notes: red jumper cables, yellow plastic tool box, car jack, spare tire, dark sports jacket, one sleeve inside out.

The officer examines the label inside the coat with his torch. Size 20. Boys. Could fit the suspect. Maybe not.

He examines the pockets. Empty. He examines the breast pockets, inner and outer. Empty. He returns the coat to the back of the truck.

He shines the torch through the side window of the truck. On the seat he sees a pair of shoes. He opens the car door. Shines the torch. Keys in the ignition. Candy wrapper underneath driver's seat. Empty soda bottle, carpet fragments near the peddle. Passenger side: a card is on the floor. He shines the light on the card. It is a student ID for the University. Photo and name belongs to someone other than the suspect. He sees a wallet kicked beneath the seat. He retrieves it. He finds a bank card, a voter registration card, a dry cleaning slip. Same name as the ID. He returns the torch to examine the shoes again. They appear to be size seven. Men's. Black patent leather. Polished. New. Except for smudges around laces and toes. He shines the torch closer. Notices it is blood. He does not touch anything. He will wait for another investigator.

He walks back to the squad car. "Looks like we might have a possible burglary," he says calmly to his partner. He tells him about the wallet, the student ID.

"You know this fella?" James Pearce asks the suspect. He repeats the name his partner discovered on the student ID card.

"Never heard of him," the suspect answers.

"What size shoes you wear?" Bill Rivers asks the suspect.

The suspect hesitates. "Don't know," he says. "Not sure."

"Looks like you got big feet to me," the officer replies. "What about your friend?"

"What friend?" the suspect says.

"The one that got away," he says.

"Didn't see anybody else," the suspect says.

Bill Rivers leaves the suspect to answer a radio dispatch. When he returns he tells James Pearce the name of the owner of the truck. The suspect responds without being asked. "He's my uncle," he says. "He knows I borrowed the truck tonight." Bill Rivers tells his partner the suspect is waiting sentencing for another crime, a robbery, three months ago.

The officers notice a vehicle turn onto Hogan Street, a new pair of headlights move toward the squad car. It is the ambulance arriving without a siren or strobe. As the ambulance positions itself on the other side of the black pickup, Bill Rivers notices something lodged behind a wheel of the truck. He walks over, kneels down, shines the torch under the body of the truck.

This is what he sees: the barrel of a gun. Long, about ten inches. Black steel case.

He waits until the medics have unloaded a stretcher and the suspect has been transferred into the back of the ambulance. He tells the ambulance driver to wait. Then he shows James Pearce the gun.

James Pearce identifies it as a .357 Magnum. About fifteen years old. Blood covers the casing, the barrel, the butt. More blood than the suspect's cut could have caused. So much blood James Pearce knows there is another crime somewhere. Yet to be discovered.

James Pearce smells the ground near the gun, trying to detect if it has been fired. There is no scent of it having been fired recently.

He returns to the ambulance. The suspect is in the back, on a stretcher, his eyes glassy, weepy from the pain. He has a fresh bandage around his head, pink where the cut above his ear lightly bleeds.

"Seems we might have a crime scene," James Pearce says. "You ever seen that gun that somebody hid behind the wheel of your uncle's truck?" James Pearce asks the suspect.

The suspect responds again in the negative. He turns his head away from the officer, looks at the side of the van. His head feels thick, like a rock, like someone trying to chisel through it.

"Your friend ever seen this gun before?" James Pearce asks.

"Can't answer that either," the suspect answers. He does not attempt to move his head, meet the officer's gaze.

"That gun ever been fired, you think?" the officer asks.

The suspect ignores him. Like he is a blank slate, something is being hidden. "Don't know," he says.

"You think this gun's been fired tonight?" Bill Rivers asks the suspect.

The suspect lifts an eyebrow lightly. A taunt. He answers, "I don't think you'll find anyone with a bullet in them."

6

Tuesday

At first she believes it is the baby coughing. Then she hears the sound again: a throaty cough as if an animal were choking on a bone. She hears the toilet flush and she gets out of bed. She is still a teenager. Overweight. Her name is Chase. She is round and soft and has a moonlike face, drab, mud-colored hair. She wanted to get married but was afraid of pushing her boyfriend away. Her baby is now three-months old. The three of them live together in the trailer park in the southwest part of town.

The bathroom door is closed. She twists the handle, pushes the door open. The light and the smell hit her at the same time. She takes a step back. Rick is at the sink. The faucet is running. He is dabbing toilet paper at his lip. When he pulls it away, she sees the cut. A black crack. "Jesus, Rick, what happened?" she asks him.

He leans his head into the sink. Douses his face with water, rubs his hands tightly across the skin. Then he starts crying. "I couldn't stop him," he says. She barely understands him. His voice lost in the water and his hands.

She picks up his shirt from the floor. She notices the stain, then notices it is blood. She sees he has thrown his coat into the bottom of the shower. Something he has never done before. He always leaves the coat in the kitchen. Why is it on the floor of the shower?

"Jesus," she says. "Are you hurt?"

He washes his face again. She notices the blood on his T-shirt. On his jeans. His shoes. "I knew I should stop him," he says. "But I couldn't."

He turns the water off. Reaches for a towel. Dries his face

and hands. "I think A.J. killed somebody, baby," he says. "I couldn't stop him."

She knows there is only some truth in this. He is always exaggerating about something. It's always something bigger than the truth to him: This is the best job I've gotten, baby. This is the biggest raise yet. This is my biggest high all day.

Something is different now.

He feels he needs to explain more. "He fuckin' hit me in the lip." He reaches for the toilet paper again. Presses a wad against his lip. Brings it away. There is less blood then before.

She reaches to his face. Examines the cut. The red edges are beginning to swell. She moves around him, reaches into the cabinet behind the mirror. "I can put some iodine on it," she says. "It'll sting."

He flips the lid down on the toilet. Sits down. Looks her over. Her nightgown is unappealing. Flannel. Shapeless. Makes her look like an old woman. He thinks she's gained too much weight since the baby. He hates the way she wears her hair piled up on her head, half of it falling down. When she moves her face close to his with the iodine stopper his mind freezes again. He is on the ground. The college boy beneath him. He moves away from her. She says, "It won't hurt that much."

He sits back down. Remains still for her. Cusses as the iodine hits his skin. He stands. Kicks the toilet. She says, "Keep it down. You'll wake the baby." He hates the trailer they live in. Hates the way their life has become. He's always poor. She's always nagging him to work more.

He goes into the kitchen. He finds her cigarettes. He keeps the lights off. He looks out the window of the trailer. The lots are dark. Weeds bend in the wind. He notices a dog sniffing at the engine parts in front of another unit. He watches the dog lift his leg, urinate, move on.

He lights the cigarette, inhales, blows toward the ceiling. She stands behind him. Waiting at the doorway. "What happened?" she asks. She hasn't seen him since Friday. Four days ago. She doesn't care too much about his story.

"Something horrible," he says. "We were just going to rob

him. It got out of hand."

"A.J.?" she asks.

He nods. He takes another puff. "We went to this bar. On Market. We were out of money. A.J. was itchy. He'd been doing crank since Friday and he was coming down. He wanted to get drunk. There was this guy at the bar. Rich kid. We thought he was gay. A.J. thought we could pretend to be gay and rob him. We took him out to Upper White Chapel. A.J. thought he was coming on to him. He just wanted to beat him up bad enough to teach him a lesson. Not to come on to straights. We left him out by the cemetery."

"Where's A.J.?" she asks. She is twisting a strand of hair around her finger. It makes her look childish. Her eyes have welled up with tears. She doesn't know this man in front of her. Why is this happening in her home?

"We drove back to town," he says. "Some punks jacked us in town. They got A.J. in the back of the head. I got away when the cops showed up. I think they got A.J."

She is speechless. Her mouth forms an "O." Then her lips pinch forward and her eyes focus, as if trying to read something far off in the distance. "Were there any witnesses?" she asks.

"Just the two guys that started it."

"No," she says. "The other one. The college guy."

"Probably some at the bar."

"Did you tell him your name?"

"Just Rick," he answers.

"Could he identify you?"

He laughs a bit, takes a final drag of the cigarette. "I don't think so," he says. "Not what A.J. done to him. Like I said, A.J. beat the shit out of him."

"Get out of those clothes," she says. There is a command in her voice, authoritarian. She is taking charge. She is standing in front of him. Her eyes are wild. Like A.J.'s earlier.

"What the fuck why?"

"We're goin' to hide them," she says. "You were never there."

"But A.J.'s gonna tell them," he says.

"I don't have to look out for A.J.," she says. "I ain't letting this happen in my home. It's time you started helpin' out here. I have to use stamps to get food for that baby of yours. You ain't goin' to jail and leavin' me with nothin'. Get out of those clothes."

She steps closer and tries to tear the shirt off of him. He pushes her back. She lands with a thud against the kitchen counter. Her eyes widen in disbelief. Pain travels down her spine. She is just about to tell him to leave when he starts to take the shirt off. The pale skin of his chest soaks in the light, makes him look boyish. He is not yet a man.

He sits down and unlaces his boots. Takes them off one at a time. She collects the clothes from the bathroom floor, puts them in a plastic garbage bag. "I can't do this to A.J., baby. He's been a good friend to me."

"He's a crankhead, Rick. Just like you. He's a crankhead who killed someone," she says. "What kind of a friend is that?"

"What about Kelly?" he asks. "I thought she was your friend, too."

"Kelly's got to get out of her own mess," she says. She finds her sweater on the back of a chair. She pulls it over her nightgown.

She is outside putting the garbage bag in the trunk of the car she drives—a red Buick—when she hears the phone ring.

She runs to catch it before Rick does. Before the baby wakes. He beats her to it. When she comes inside the trailer, he is stretching the phone out to her. "It's Kelly," he says. "I don't know what the fuck to tell her."

7

Tuesday

He blunders in, headed toward the register, but his legs are too big for his body. He laughs at himself, thinks it's funny—rubbery legs, like a cartoon character. He has no control of his mobility, his legs move away from him like they are on wheels. He raises the gun and points it at the girl behind the counter. The barrels extend toward her. Again like a cartoon. He laughs, likes the way he looks with a smile. He thinks the girl looks like his wife. Then decides it is Kelly. She laughs at him. Thinks he looks ridiculous with legs too big for his body. She tells him his ears are growing and his legs shrinking. He looks down at himself. He doesn't like the way she is laughing at him. He wants to slap her with the gun. His anger rises. His eyes blur. Suddenly the gun is in his mouth. Someone is shoving it into his throat. A guy. A guy in a jacket. Deerskin. Smokey. Belt buckle open, slapping his knee. His throat is tightening. He wakes gagging, as if he were suffocating.

A.J. is alone in the room. A glass of water is on the stand beside the bed. The door is open. His head is bandaged. The bandage feels heavy, solid, like it's made out of plastic. Or lead. His head hurts, like a headache. His mouth is dry, lips sticky. He gets up to leave but he loses his energy. His temper rises because he cannot control his movements. He thinks this is unfair, unjust. He feels trapped. Someone has trapped him. Done something to make him slow, lazy. They've drugged him. Made him a prisoner.

He lies back down. His eyes move rapidly around the room, looking for ideas for escape. He has no idea what time it is. They've taken his clothes. He's dressed in a white hospital gown. Kelly will bring him something. If she can get her fat ass out of the chair. She can get a ride here. She can call Chase and Rick. Rick will drive her here. If she can just get her fat ass moving.

Then he remembers the fight. The club striking his head. He touches his scalp. Feels pain shooting like needles. This is Rick's fault, he decides. Rick got the drugs. Rick got the beers. Rick stopped the car. This is all because of Rick.

They should arrest Rick. He thinks about telling someone. His eyes search the room again. There's not even a TV. He notices a camera mounted to the wall, pointed at the bed. He hates being trapped. He hated his mother for locking him in the basement when he was a kid to keep him out of trouble. He hates people looking over his shoulder, telling him what to do, what is and isn't right. How the fuck do they know? How do they know what is right or wrong *for me*?

He hears voices outside the room. In the corridor. He lies, listening, his heart beating heavy. Everyone wants to rat on him. Even when he's not around. Suspicion bleeds from him like a wound. Since he was small. It was always his fault. Even when it wasn't.

He closes his eyes. He will pretend to sleep until Kelly comes. He doesn't want to answer any more questions. Questions about the gun. Questions about the coat. The shoes. The college boy's ID. The wallet in the truck. Where they came from. No one will ever know the answers he knows. They'll never find the college boy. He'll turn to dust before he's found.

He snaps his eyes violently open. He can get out of all of this by blaming Rick. Rick stopped the car. Rick bought the drugs. Rick paid for the beers. When Kelly brings the clothes they can pack and go to California. Pick up some cash on the way. They could have better luck in California. Live there cheap. They won't make any of this stick. It was Rick's fault.

He wonders why Kelly is not here. They didn't call her. They're trying to scare him, make him confess. There ain't nothing wrong with beating up a faggot. It's in the Bible, after all. They got the wrong guy here. This is all Rick's fault. He'll tell them the truth when Kelly gets here.

8

Tuesday

Another country road. The headlights are lower. The grass and weeds are different. There is no fence along the side of the road. Instead, swirls of leaves. A canopy of trees. Gusts of wind occasionally rock the car.

Disbelief carries her at first. How could she love a man who acts like this? How could he let a friend kill someone? How could he become so irresponsible? Dangerous? Bring this into their lives? This is not the same guy she knew at school. He's changed. Things have gotten out of hand.

Chase looks at him through the rear view mirror. Rick is riding in the back seat with the baby in his arms. He has showered, smells now of soap and shampoo. His upper lip is broken in two, red and swollen at the cut. She had thought about doing this on her own. Without him. But she didn't want to leave the baby behind with him. It wasn't that she was afraid. It was because he had become someone she did not know.

The tension has made her sleepy, strained. She can feel the puffiness in her face. She feels insecure, vulnerable. Still in her nightgown and sweater. In front of her the road is a dizzy black line. He leans forward, asks her to turn on the radio.

"No," she snaps. "This is not the time."

She wants him to know what's at stake here. Their lives. Her sanity. The baby's future. She thinks the drugs have gotten out of hand. At first it was okay. The high. The partying. They weren't talking about living together. They were escaping. Escaping school. Parents that mistreated them, abandoned them. They'd build fires behind the football field. Roast marshmallows. Get high. Set off firecrackers. They'd cuddle.

He'd talk about his father leaving the family when he was two. His mother's death. A botched hysterectomy. Moving in with his Granny. She described her parents' fights. Her mother's black eyes. Their divorce. Moving into an apartment on Old Union with her mom.

But he's changed since then. Even if he still has his looks. She fell for the way he looked. He was the cutest boy in class. He had that nose. Those dark eyes. He wasn't a redneck. Or a hick. Or a hillbilly. He was someone different then. She thought he would make something of himself. He went to church. He was a scout. Working to become an Eagle. He got his last merit badge cleaning the cemetery on Upper White Chapel. His picture was in the paper. She was proud of him. They looked happy together. They'd sit out by the fires. Dream about going to Florida, starting a business.

She loved him, she said. She liked the way he held her hand in public. Made her seem special in front of others. Sex was okay to her. But she was afraid of becoming serious with him. Said she wanted to go to college. She didn't want to end up living her mother's life. Cleaning motel rooms, frying hamburgers, drinking too much. She wonders if she held him back. Made her dreams change his because they became a couple. He called her every night. Took her out. They went dancing at the bars. He wanted her to get pregnant. He said he wanted a family.

She didn't get pregnant until she knew she would graduate. By then she was ready to get married. They decided to move in together first. Wait on the rings, ceremony, until they had some money in the bank. The only thing they could afford was the trailer park. She was willing to settle because she was happy. And he seemed to be too.

But things changed. The drugs got out of hand. At first it was pot. Stoned all the time. Stoned when he went to work at the bowling alley. Stoned when he came home. Then he started construction. He was straight for a while. Till the weather was cold. Then he started the crank. He said it kept him warm. Made him work better. He started snorting one gram a week.

Then started doing half a gram a day. Started missing days of work with the contractor, even when he knew there was a baby due.

She thinks it is A.J.'s fault. They weren't friends in school. They only started hanging out together when he started working for the contractor. They went out for beers. Cruisin' in that big pickup truck of his uncle's. She found out A.J. was trying to be a dealer. She tried not to worry. Till Rick's became a habit. Then he started trying to deal on the side himself. But he smoked and snorted away whatever money he seemed to earn. Buying an eight ball every few days. Hoping to turn around some cash. Ending up worse, broke, trying to get straight but not really wanting to. That's how the jacking started. The robbery. They were always broke. Money to sell drugs. Drugs to stay high. They were never going anywhere. Dreams disappeared. He started jacking up cashiers. Hoping he could get away with it. All this has gone on too long. It has to stop. It's time for her to get out of this.

When she gave up the idea of going to college she became depressed. Ate too much. But only what they could afford to buy. With the stamps. Or what she could afford to buy from the money his granny gave them. He never gave her any of his. He never pitched in. It was always her money and his granny's money that fed the baby.

"Where you goin'?" he asks her from the back seat.

"There's some dumpsters behind where Granny lives," she says.

"That far?" he says.

"I don't want anyone to find this stuff," she says.

There is nothing else from him in the back seat. She checks the mirror to make sure everything is okay. She watches him looking at the baby. He looks up, meets her eyes in the mirror. She looks back at the road, scared. A strip mall has come into view. She thinks about dumping the garbage bag of clothes there, then decides again on the lot behind his granny's house.

"What did Kelly say?" he asks.

Again she glances through the mirror. His face looks more disturbed now. His thoughts are back to the crime.

"She didn't know anything," she says. "She was waitin' for his uncle to show up. He called her and told her A.J. was in the hospital. That's all she knew."

"The hospital?" he says. "She say what was wrong?" There is surprise and alarm in his voice.

"No," she says. "She was just waiting. She thought you'd know. I told her you'd been home all evening. She knew I was lying. But she didn't say anything."

She turns at the stop light behind the strip mall. She follows the road to a set of buildings off another road. She turns, takes this road a bit slower. It doesn't occur to her to ask him where they left the college boy, that he might still be alive. It doesn't occur to her that they should go help him. Call the police. 9-1-1. That the blood on the clothes she is trying to get rid of belongs to someone else. She doesn't think about the college boy at all. His pain, his struggle. Not now. Only about what trouble Rick has brought home. Where she must dump the clothes. What lies they will have to tell. How they must get out of this. "I don't understand any of this," she says, finally, her mind a jumble of thoughts. There are tears in her eyes. She thinks she should stop driving but she continues.

He doesn't answer. Looks out the window. At the road and the darkness. Anxiety washes over him. He wants another cigarette. Or a drink. He wishes he had brought a beer. He swallows, feels a roughness in his throat. He thinks he might throw up. He holds the baby away from him, presses his face against the glass of the window, takes a deep breath. The coolness seeps into him even as his lip responds to the pressure and pain shooting across his face. He thinks he might have some stuff in his pockets. He searches them. They are empty. He feels his lungs contract with disappointment. He'll smoke another cigarette when they stop. Maybe they can find someplace open to get a beer.

She parks the car behind a building. The windows are dark. Everyone is asleep. The night is dark around them.

He makes a move to get out of the car. "Stay with the baby," she orders. She leaves the door open, the light in the roof of the car makes him squint.

She gets the garbage bag out of the trunk. She closes it quietly. Runs across the pavement to a dumpster that stands like a war tank guarding the back entrance of a building. She creaks open the lid. Tosses the bag inside. She runs back across the parking lot to the car. Jumps into the seat and closes the door. She has not turned the car off. She puts the car in gear and they leave.

She looks at him again in the back seat. His eyes are black and vacant. She doesn't know this man. And he is someone she no longer wants to know.

9

Tuesday

"Don't understand what got into those boys," Ray says.

He is driving Kelly to the hospital. She only knows about the stitches and the concussion. Other details have not been related to her. She does not know of the bloody gun, the wallet belonging to someone else, the small black shoes, the coat found in the rear of the truck. "We don't know anything," she says, though she knows there is more to know than what she has been told.

He looks ahead at the road, thinking it's best to keep her out of it. "Officer said they haven't got a clue about the two fellers who attacked him."

"Are they even looking?" she asks. She is a short, sallow faced, ash-blond haired girl, not yet a woman, though cigarettes and drugs have given her a hardened appearance, make her seem older than her years. Her hair hangs down in her eyes, which she thinks looks sexy, but to others gives her a mistrustful appearance. There is anger in her response. Not because of the police but because bitterness has infected her life. She harbors other hates than what she determines as the inefficiency of the police.

"Now don't go getting yourself all tied up in knots," he says. "It's not gonna do that baby any good."

She is seven months pregnant. She is forty pounds heavier than she has ever been in her life. She cannot recognize herself in the mirror. She is awake in the middle of the night. She is unhappy because she is being dragged into the misery of a man she no longer loves. "What about Rick?" she asks. "They were drinking together earlier, I know that. Even though that lyin'

46

Chase says he's been home all night."

"Well, we can't be too concerned with Rick right now," he says. "We got to think about A.J. first. He's family, after all." Uncle Ray's skin is yellow from the lights of the dashboard. He's about fifty-two, same face as his nephew but without the big ears: broad forehead, thick hair, though his is gray and cut short. His skin is thicker, muscles fattened, a gut from beer and food. Family is a habit for him. He watches over his wife, son, nephew, now Kelly. He has a good rapport with the outside world but it puts more pressure on him. Which he holds inside.

"I bet Rick is part of the answer," she says. She tries to calm herself but she can't. She begins crying. She knows he must think she is crying about A.J. and his predicament, but she is not. She is crying because of her hate. Her hate for Rick. She is sure her baby is not her husband's. It belongs to Rick. They had been having an affair for almost a year before she got pregnant. It wasn't difficult to get around A.J. Or Chase. He was stoned. She was pregnant and worried about having a miscarriage.

She hates him now because he has failed her. Broken his promises. When they first started sleeping together he told her he wanted to break up with Chase, move with her to Florida, start a new life. Get out of the rat hole he had fallen into here. But it changed when Chase became pregnant. He said he would break up after the baby was born. Give him some time. He would do it. He promised her.

But when she told him she was pregnant, he broke things off. "You can't prove that it's mine," he said. He was annoyed, disgusted with her, like it was her fault she was the married one. "And if you tell A.J. about us he'll kill us both."

So she lost him and gained the weight. She didn't want an abortion. She wanted the baby. She thought somewhere along the way it would pull them together. But now when he comes over and does a hit with A.J. he doesn't even say hello to her, not even a wink of acknowledgment. Now she blames him for the misery he has left behind for her—A.J. becoming wilder, the drugs getting out of hand, the robbery they staged together three months ago.

"Cop was asking me about a college boy named Danny," Uncle Ray says. "Asked me if I knew anything about a guy named Danny. You know anyone by that name?"

"Could be anyone," she answers. She thinks about smoking a cigarette. She hasn't smoked in four months. She wants a drag bad. Anything that could take her away from this. Even if it were bad for the baby. Fuck the baby. She can't take much more of this.

At the hospital she follows Uncle Ray through the lobby and into the elevator. She has brought along a change of clothes for A.J., a razor and shaving crème, even though she knows he will not use it. He thrives on looking like some kind of wild beast. It used to turn her on. Now it just bores her. Everything bores her. She wishes the baby were born so she could be doing something else except carrying all this extra weight around.

"You want to wait out here while I go in first?" he says to her. She hates the way he treats her like a child. She is not a child. She is a child *carrying* a child. "No," she answers. "I'll follow you in."

In the room A.J. is sleeping. He looks harmless to her, a white bandage around his forehead, the white sheets on the bed. It finally hits her that something is wrong. She feels uncomfortable, like the baby has twisted into the wrong shape. Like a fist is punching the lining of her stomach. She tries to take a seat but can't. She walks back and forth, pushing her hands against her lower back, as if the baby has kicked her kidneys. She decides she wants some water and goes out into the hall.

Outside the room she feels better. She walks down the corridor to the water fountain and takes a long sip. When she returns to the room she finds Uncle Ray talking with an officer. Uncle Ray introduces her.

The officer's face is young, thin, seems too small for the wide body of his dark jacket. He asks her when she's due and she gives him the exact date her doctor told her. He flips open a notebook and asks her if he knows where her husband might have gone earlier in the evening.

"I'm sure his friend Rick could answer that," she says. "Far as I know he was hanging out with Rick. They were together earlier at the apartment. Then they went out together in the truck. You should talk to Rick. Bet you could find out a lot of things from him."

10

The nightmare wakes her. Her neck is clammy, moist, as if she wanted to yell but couldn't. She was dreaming that her older son was homeless, abandoned, not telling her that he had lost his home because he had stopped paying the rent in order to save money. Danny was standing outside a door—a red door—waiting to see if someone would let him inside.

She gets up out of bed. Paul, her husband, does not move, his sleep undisturbed. She finds her way by memory to the kitchen, the digital clock on the microwave glows: 3:27. She turns on the fluorescent light above the sink. It ping-ping-pings into brightness. She catches her reflection in the window above the sink, straightens her hair. Her face wears her emotions easily. Her skin is dry; her eyes watery. Her confidence is weak, strength mostly uncertain.

She opens the refrigerator door, looks inside at the items on the shelves, then on the inside racks. They need to eat the hamburger meat within a day or so or it will go bad. They are running low on orange juice, eggs, and the cream Paul uses for his coffee.

She is a list maker. She sits at the kitchen table. She begins recopying the list of items she needs from the grocery store tomorrow that she has taken off of the front of the refrigerator, the one held in place by a carrot-shaped magnet. To the side of this list she adds another list of other items she does not want to forget. Change light bulb in basement. Clean out upstairs hall closet. Take the old toys to the Salvation Army. Call Danny. She will call her son to check up on him. Will tell him not to worry about the money. She will get more from his father. She

50

worries that he has become a loner at college, even though he mentions his new friends in conversations. He harbors too much inside himself, like her. His brother, her younger son Luke, is more like Paul. Active, outward, social. A head for finances and figures. Danny won't even balance his checkbook. Luke budgets his money. Danny is uncertain about college. Luke already sees a law degree in his future.

She returns to copying the list. The image of Danny on the street from her dream returns. She recalls that there was a wound on his head. Blood, dried, forming a scab. She sends her mind through her past, locating an image of Danny as a boy, only a decade ago, when they he had gone on a camping trip with the scouts to Vancouver. She decides that her dream, her nightmare, was a revisit to not being there when he fell and broke his leg, scraped his forehead, and has nothing to do with him now, as an adult, trying to make it on his own. She wishes he had chosen a place closer to home—to Seattle. She feels that he is too far away from her to exert her influence the way she wants. Perhaps that is best—he needs to be out on his own, testing himself. But he is so unlucky. Things happen to him that shouldn't. Trouble is always right before him.

She tries to stop her worrying. Then thinks that maybe she won't call him in the morning, first thing, but will wait till later in the day. She'll call and check up on him in the afternoon. She decides to give him more space to grow. She is forty-one years old, struggling to understand her empty feelings. Her sons are growing up, not growing away. Still, she fights the feeling of being abandoned.

11

She is calling to apologize. She wants to make sure he knows she is only trying to help him. His bouts with depression worry her. She thinks he needs counseling, not just medication.

She's surprised she gets his answering machine. She knows he likes to sleep late on Tuesday, but he should be up by now. She wonders if he went to a bar last night, if he is sleeping off too much booze or drugs. (Or perhaps, good fortune.) Maybe he met someone and isn't back home yet. Or not yet ready to answer the phone. It would do him good to date someone steadily. Give his life some stability. A partner. Give him a better attitude about things. Make him calm down some.

Her next thought is a panicky one: What if his depression overwhelmed him? What if he took a handful of pills like he had said he might do if things get worse? What if he really attempted suicide, not just talked about it? What if he really *is* depressed and not just talking about it, hoping to get attention?

She hangs up without leaving a message, wonders if she should call his landlady. Worries follow her through the rooms. She stops in the common room, the room they let guests smoke in, watch television, drink coffee, hot chocolate. She straightens a doily that hides a stain on the coffee table. Rearranges magazines. Then decides to wash the ashtray. Heads into the kitchen with it. They had gone together to a bar in Richmond last weekend. He had rented a limo, an indulgence that seemed unnecessary to her. She had offered to drive. That old lemon of hers would have made it. She doesn't drink and the trip was under an hour. But he said he wanted to treat himself—both of them, really—to make them feel special, like it was a special occasion (which it wasn't). He thought the limo was a better, more reliable, flexible plan. She thought it was just plain extravagant.

She rinses her hands in the sink. Dries them on a towel hanging through the handle of the refrigerator. She opens the dishwasher. A warm mist floats into the room. She begins emptying the contents, putting the dishes and glasses used for breakfast away. Her thoughts wander again to the weekend trip. The evening had started out fine enough. Pop's silver limo had picked her up first at eight. She had worn black jeans and a black T-shirt, felt underdressed even though they were just going to a bar in another city. Pop had rung her doorbell, opened the door for her as she stepped into the stretch. Treated her like a guest.

She hadn't felt comfortable, though, like a guest. She leaned forward and talked to him in the front seat during the drive to Danny's apartment. She had known Pop since he, his wife, and his sister had worked at the bakery in town. He had retired after his sister's death, sold the bakery, started the limo company. She remembers him telling a reporter for the local newspaper that the reason for the change at age sixty was because he wanted to "get out of the oven and see what was cool in the world." She'd always believed Pop was an honest and trustworthy man in a town where they were difficult to find.

She places the dishes that need to be re-washed by hand into the sink. She feels a sharp pain in her shoulder. Thinks it is from arthritis. She closes her eyes, practices her breathing, slowing it down. Wills the pain away. She is fifty-seven years old. Same height as Danny but twice his size: broad hips and shoulders, no waist. A figure like a sack of potatoes. She keeps her gray hair cut short, long enough to still look feminine. Refuses to color it like Naomi. Her arthritis started in her early forties. Joints stiffening. Riding injuries harder to forget. Which is why she found it so strange she would go dancing with Danny. All that jumping around.

They picked him up outside his apartment. Ate at a

Chinese restaurant he had heard about, his treat, said he liked doing this kind of things for friends. (He always complained that for a college town there wasn't one decent Chinese restaurant near campus.) They had invited Pop to join them. Dinner conversation had been mostly questions and details about Pop's business—he had just set up a Web site and was asking Danny advice. Danny had purposely talked above Pop's head—throwing out terms like "servers," "cookies," and "encryption" which Pop made him slow down and explain. Then the conversation had drifted into anecdotes about Pop's riders—the married English professor who liked to use him to pick up his girlfriend from the airport, the country band that always wanted to moon other drivers, the drug deals that he had to pretend he didn't see. "I just play dumb," he said in his thick Southern drawl. "I see plenty of things I don't see."

After dinner they had gone to the club. It was still early according to "gay time." (Danny's phrase. Translation: You know, *late* arrivals). "Nobody ever shows up till midnight," he said. "I don't understand why it all happens so late. It just does."

She looks at the clock above the sink. Wonders if she should try calling him again. Or wait. She decides to scrub the dishes that didn't get clean in the dishwasher. She fills one side of the sink up with hot water, detergent. Lets the dishes crusted with bits of cereal, eggs, soak.

They had sat outside at a white patio table in a courtyard between the two buildings—a smaller one that housed the bar and the other, a warehouse type of structure, where the dance floor was. It was a warm, Indian summer night—unusually mild for this time of year. White Christmas tree lights were strung along crisscrossed wooden trellises. He said it made it look like they were "sitting inside the stars." He seemed relaxed then, not straining to be liked. She liked him however he was, always thought of him as a child watching the circus from the bleachers, wanting to be inside the center ring, instead, *performing*.

Pop had stayed inside. At the bar. He didn't find the place

intimidating. He said he would hang out for a while, maybe take a nap in the limo if he needed. They could find him by paging him. She ordered a cranberry juice. Danny was on his second beer. (He had ordered a drink at dinner.) There wasn't much other activity at the bar. Except for a guy who kept circling where they sat, eyeing Danny. "It's way too early to be hittin' on someone," Danny said. "I'm not ready to hook up with someone yet."

She asked him if there was anyone in his classes that he wanted to date. He told her, no, not really, a few guys he had crushes on. Probably weren't gay. He said there was a guy named Gary he had been e-mailing back and forth, since the summer. An eye doctor in his thirties. Lives in D.C. The guy said he would drive out to the campus. Danny was hesitant about it. "I'm not sure if I want a long distance relationship," he said. "I get sucked in real easy. He sent me his photo and he's pretty good-looking. But I'm not sure I want to get so obsessive about someone right away. I've only been here a month. And I really don't feel like getting dumped."

She laughed at him. She hadn't meant to and she tried to joke about it. Told him they should get together. Hook up. Just to see. "You complain about not meeting anyone, that you don't have a boyfriend, then there's a guy hovering around you here and another one who wants to meet you and you avoid all of them and say you don't want to be serious and can't go through with it. You're defeating yourself both ways."

He pouted. That was his response. He hadn't been angry then. "So I'm choosy too," he said. "I bet Naomi wasn't your first lover."

She hears Naomi upstairs now. Walking on the wood floor. The light tone of her voice drifting through the walls, pipes, the hollows of the old Victorian house that they converted into a bed-and-breakfast inn. Naomi is always working: cooking, washing clothes, lifting, replacing, repairing. She sings while she works, her strong little fingers drumming phrases on an imaginary keyboard, her feet practicing steps for the organ pedals. Naomi is still in her forties, a few inches taller than

Leah, watery blue eyes, no eyelashes to speak of, fluffy red hair that waves around her face like rolls of cotton candy. Her skin is fair, cool, wonderful. So sensitive it doesn't stand any makeup at all, inflamed by colds, food, emotions. Work has toughened her hands but she has kept the unconscious ease and grace of herself, keeping guests charmed, engaged, something Leah cannot do as well herself. Or on her own. She must be changing sheets, Leah thinks.

She finishes the dishes. Dries her hands again. Looks at the clock one more time. Wishes she were outside, that it were spring, so she could be working in the garden. Or riding.

"I had to go through a lot of guys and a real bad man before I got to Naomi," she said to Danny, looking at the white lights behind him. "I wish it had all happened a lot earlier than it did, but the way it turned out is all right with me, too."

"You're so lucky. I wish I had someone like that."

The subject changed. She didn't want to tell him she didn't always feel so lucky that way. She didn't want to admit that she felt guilty leaving Naomi behind at the house. (Even though she had no desire to join them at the bar.) Instead, they talked about why she didn't want a stronger drink. (She used to like gin but had gotten drunk on it one night and had never wanted to have the taste again.) The music was good. They both agreed on the music. A speaker was mounted above one of the trellises, the music from the disco piped out into the courtyard. It was a late Seventies disco weekend. Bubblegum sound with a solid bass and drum track. When a song that Danny particularly liked came on—a Village People hit—they went inside and danced for a few songs. Till she had to tell him she needed to stop. Out of breath, sweaty, tired. They ordered more drinks. Sat in the courtyard again, dabbing at their faces with cocktail napkins.

"Did you ever go through a drug phase?" he asked her. They hadn't been friends for long, just since the summer, when he stayed at their guest house while looking to find an apartment near campus. They discovered they had a lot in common even though they were years apart in ages: the same birthday, baptized at the same church. She knew she aroused the mother-son relationship in him without the genetic liability. It worked vice versa.

"I did all that stuff," she said. "Before I was your age, even. I just didn't feel I was being me. I felt like I was someone I didn't know and if I met her, I wouldn't like her."

"I could take a handful of pills and no one would miss me for days," he said.

"That's not true," she said. She tried to keep it light. Like he was joking with her. Pretending. "I'd miss you. Who'd I complain to about Naomi?"

Again she looks at the clock above the sink. What if he had done it? Taken the pills. She decides to walk outside to get the mail, clear her mind. She isn't sure why she feels so panicky today.

She waits another hour before trying him again at his apartment. They hadn't planned to meet for lunch today. She lets the phone ring six times. Waits for the message to begin. Hesitates again about leaving a message. Hangs up without saying anything. She decides that if she doesn't reach him in another hour she will look for him in the café where he sometimes studies. She hopes he's not avoiding her. She'll find a subtle way to apologize if that's what it needs. Maybe she should step back from this mothering role a bit. Perhaps that is what is smothering him.

12

Monday

Little things pull him down, like frustration over wasted time. He doesn't mind the walk to campus—the car he bought with the money his parents gave him feels too big to him—like driving a boat. And trying to find a parking space on campus is too difficult. As long as it isn't raining, he doesn't mind the exercise. He enjoys the walk. The campus is bucolic. Bathed in fall colors. Giant trees shedding leaves. But today he's worried a bit about the weather. He looks for the wind. He takes along a collapsible umbrella. The extra weight in his backpack annoys him, makes him break out in a light sweat, makes him think he might catch a cold.

The walk gives him a chance to make a mental list of the things he wants to do once he gets to the school. But today he is running late. He is annoyed by the slow pace of his fast steps, annoyed having to wait to cross the street because of traffic, annoyed he has to rearrange his route because the custodial crew has decided to repave the sidewalk steps at the west entrance.

He triggers an alarm as he enters the library—he has brought a library book by mistake instead of his Political Theory text. The library book is overdue. A security guard says he must either return the book or renew it. This morning there is another student with a similar problem. He waits in line while the student argues with the librarian over the amount of the fine. His frustration begins to show on his face. His spare time before class is being eaten away by someone else. As he counts the minutes away—seconds, really, his impatience makes them seem as long as years. He thinks he must make a choice what to do in the time remaining before his class: either send an e-mail from the computer lab or check for his snail mail at the campus post office. He doesn't have time to accomplish both. He decides on the e-mail. He wants to send a note to his father to give his mother. And send a note to Gary, suggesting he bring a warm jacket—the weather will likely change before this weekend.

The librarian makes him pay the fine before he renews the book. When he pulls his wallet out, he realizes he needs to go to the bank before lunch. He feels his time being robbed from him, more than the money. He decides he must do the e-mails before anything else. He'll cash a check on the way to meet Leah for lunch.

At the computer lab all the terminals are in use. He asks the student behind the counter when he thinks one will be free. The guy's impartial shrug sends him huffing back out into the hall, down the steps and outside. He wishes he had sent the e-mails from home. Now it has to wait. Has to be remembered. He races across campus to check his mail. His legs just don't seem to move fast enough. But he slows his pace down, not wanting to look like a nervous, foolish geek.

At the post office he finds his box empty. He asks the clerk if the mail has been sorted yet. She answers the regular guy is out sick today. It will be another hour before the mail gets into the boxes. He rolls his eyes. She offers an indifferent apology. He runs back out of the building, across the green lawn of the quadrangle to make his Political Theory class.

He finds the lecture today boring—the evolution of government constitutions. He had hoped this would be his favorite course—he thinks he wants to be a political science major—but the professor seldom lets students express opinions. When they are allowed to speak, they are merely called upon to answer a question, not to offer their own theory. He listens half-heartedly, feels his eyelids becoming heavy, scribbles doodles in his notebook, makes a list of groceries he needs to buy before Gary comes to town. He looks at his watch slowly ticking. Things move so slowly when he wants them to be faster.

His next class, Mathematical Reasoning, keeps him more occupied even though he feels he has no use for it. It is only something that he must take to fulfill another University requirement. He likes the instructor, however, a graduate student who wouldn't look so bad if he exercised his waist, cut his hair short instead of trying to look like a time transplant from the Sixties. His sideburns work. Sexy. He'd do it with him. If he asked. If he wanted it.

He makes it through math—today they are doing problem solving—then walks with his friend Andrea across campus. She tells him she's going to write a paper on C.S. Lewis for the mid-term assignment for their writing course. He tells her that he might try to talk to the instructor—another graduate student—and see if he will let him do a rap song for the project. He says he thinks the idea will be nixed because the instructor must get approval for him to do it.

"What do you know about rap?" she says. She has a light, mocking laugh.

"It's just poetry speeded up or slowed down, that's all," he says. "But nobody thinks it's got any academic merit. I want to do something different, you know, not just a *paper*."

"You realize he would probably make you do it in front of the class," she says.

This hasn't occurred to him. "I could do it," he says, even while he's imagining a case of stage fright.

They walk past the ivy covered walls of the bell tower, the leaves yellow and red, dropping in the wind at their feet. They say goodbye when they reach the Administration Building. He climbs the steps, thinking now he will abandon the idea of the rap song. He goes inside to cash a check. Then he walks quickly to the east campus to meet Leah for lunch at the cafeteria. She is already there when he arrives and she has ordered a chef salad and a diet soda. He knows he should start eating healthier than he has been. But he decides to order a cheeseburger and fries and join her at the table.

"Did you see what the Love Bandit did last night?" she asks

him.

"No," he answers. His word is high-pitched, strung out, filled with a child's curiosity. "Where is it this time?"

The Love Bandit is a campus graffiti artist who strikes at night, tagging the sidewalk in front of a campus building with a spray-painted stencil of "L-O-V-E." So far the tagger hasn't been spotted. The tags have turned up everywhere, from the dormitories to the student center. "He did the sidewalk in front of the Alumni House," she says.

"The Alumni House?" He smiles at her. "I wish he'd target a few places off campus."

They talk some more about where the tagger will strike next. He is convinced it is a guy. A student. Leah is not so sure. They have, like everyone else, invested his or her targets with a meaning: an introspective prejudice that needs correcting. He says he hopes the Love Bandit will start doing a couple of the homophobic spots in town—the card store on South Main, the gas station on the Old Union Highway. She gives him an uncomfortable response, asks why, these are places she goes to all the time.

The subject shifts. She asks him about his plans for homecoming weekend. He avoids giving her any definite answer about whether his friend Gary will come into town. He remains vague, replying, "I'm not sure yet."

He asks her if he can try her bleu cheese dressing. She says he better use his own fork, shows him the side to eat from, explaining she feels a cold might be coming on and Naomi thinks she is getting something too. She doesn't want to pass it along to other people.

Next, she says to him, "Naomi says she has a friend who sees a psychiatrist in town who treats gay people. I got his name for you."

"You've haven't been telling people I need a psychiatrist?" he asks. His voice is wobbly, worried, upset.

"No, of course not," she answers.

"Oh God," he sighs. "Everyone's gonna know it's me who's looking for a therapist. How many new gay friends do you have that are in therapy?"

Leah and Naomi don't refer to themselves as lesbian. She says it's because people in this town will treat them different, strange. Naomi says they will lose business, credibility. They are out as lesbians only to a close circle of friends, mostly those in their church choir. Leah has no problem talking about her friends who are gay to other gay people, as though it was not a problem to be openly gay in this town. Which it is.

"This is crazy, Danny," she says. "You're paranoid. You asked me if I knew someone and I said I would ask around. One minute you ask for my help and the next you beat me up for it. Do you want the guy's name or not?"

"Let's just drop it," he says. He fills his mouth with fries, drinks his soda with a straw, looks out into the room, away from her, thinks she has no understanding of what he is going through.

"I'm just trying to help," she says.

"Let's just drop it," he says again. "My head is about to explode."

13

Tuesday

He will not shave this morning. Nor shower. He will not clip his nails, comb his hair, take a piss or sit on the toilet. He will not feel embarrassed of his braces. He will not drink any soda. He will not talk to Leah on the phone. He will not choose the black shirt to wear, hoping to draw the attention of the guy who works in the student union office. He will not listen to the disco CD, nor the Reba one. His cat will grow anxious as the hours pass. Not at first. At first Chloe will lie in the window, mindful of his absence, then lap at water in her dish and roam between the legs of the table.

He will not make it to the library today. He will not go to Political Theory or Mathematical Reasoning (but that is because on Tuesdays there are no scheduled classes for them). Still, he will miss his Writing Center appointment. He will not show up at the language lab to do the next set of French tapes. He will not have a chance to talk with the tall guy named Geoff.

He will not get his mail. He will not try to cash a check, use his credit card, or make a trip to the bank. He will not log on to a computer, will not send his father an e-mail message, will not chat on-line with a stranger, will not get the message Gary has sent asking him what time he should arrive on Saturday. He will not have to worry about whether he carried an umbrella with him when he left his apartment because he will not be there. He will miss a phone call from Steve Connor, asking if he wants to be an usher for the string quartet recital next week, and Bob, the carpenter he met last week at a bar who still has his phone number in his pocket and wants to hit him up for money. He will not learn that his grandmother called, at the urging of his mother, to remind him that he should plan to spend his Thanksgiving break with them, even though it's over a month away.

He will not decide to be healthy today, change his diet, order a chef salad. He will not stop at the vending machine in the English building. He will not buy gum or chocolate or the sweet and sour chewies that get caught between his braces.

He will not have a sore throat or the beginning of a cold this morning. He will not stay home from classes and watch TV. He will miss a cheating couple on Jerry, dating tips on Oprah, makeovers on Sally Jesse, and a musical production number on Rosie. He will not read *Variety*, *Billboard*, or the old issue of *Entertainment Weekly* that he sneaked out of the library that has a picture of Tom Cruise on the cover. He will not watch MSNBC or CNN. He will not pick up the day's issue of the student newspaper, where the top story is whether or not a skateboard park will be approved.

He will not hear the news about the school building a new dormitory on the east campus. He will not see that the physical plant has already painted over the Love Bandit's tag in front of the Alumni House. He will not see that the bandit struck again the evening before, this time leaving his mark at the steps of the Administration Building.

He will not drive his car, will not have to hunt for a parking space. He will not walk to campus. In fact, he will not walk at all today. Instead, his heart will beat, his lungs will fill and collapse with breaths, his blood will flow, thin, thicken.

Time will not pass quickly for him today. His skin will register the warmer temperature; his body temperature will rise. First, when the outside temperature reaches forty degrees. Then fifty. His body will begin to lose more moisture as it rises above sixty, water evaporating through his skin, keeping his shirt ironically cooler than his body. Only the back of his neck will be harmed by the sun as it breaks through overhead clouds. By late afternoon, when it is almost seventy, the reddened skin, drained now of moisture, will swell to a sickly bluish tint. His fever will rise above one hundred degrees.

By afternoon, the solidity and hardness of his body will seem to melt. The boundaries of himself, his body, will lose its edges. A feeling of fluidity will envelope him. Water will run from his eyes. His nostrils and mouth will dry. The warmth of his body will begin to seep away as the sun passes behind the mountain range. His feet will lose their warmth first as his body loses the ability to oxygenate itself. The circulating peptides will alert his nervous systems that his own ecosystem has become endangered. Heat will concentrate only around his heart. Life is in the act of extricating itself from his protoplasm.

Today, there will be no traffic on the trail where he has been left. No riders from the nearby stables. No joggers trying to shed their first winter pounds. No hikers will make their way down the path. No picnics will be held on the chapel lawn. There will be no one throwing Frisbee with their dog. There is no postal route for this road. Today, the minister who works at the chapel will visit a patient at the University hospital, before stopping off at a retirement home south of the University to see another. There will be no workers arriving at the cemetery to rake leaves, tend the grass, pull the weeds away from the flowers. No amateur genealogists will wander through the old tombstones in search of their potential ancestors. There will be no one walking the perimeter of the farm land or alongside the fence.

He will not be alone, however. His blood will draw him company. Flies will orbit him, land, crawl across his shirt, then leave, worried that their wings are becoming wet. Bacteria will sway on blades of grass, circling him, like Indian warriors surrounding a caravan of settlers. They will wait in their attack, not yet ready to announce the moment they will strike. Then move in closer. And closer. A spider will run rapidly up a crease in the bark of the fence. A crow will join him late in the afternoon, peering at him first from the telephone pole on the other side of the trail, then flying down to the fence beside him. The crow will not approach any closer than his shoulder—the breeze fluttering the long bangs of his hair will keep the bird nervous, the flapping hem of his blood-stained shirt worried.

The clouds, too, will keep him company, darkening and lowering, as if to offer him a blanket. He will not be aware of winter moving in. Or know of the cold front from the Midwest headed his way as the strong coastal winds move inward. But the wind will entertain him for a while, as though a pet standing watch at his side, ready to flap and bark and offer him distinction, when and if someone arrives.

14

Tuesday

He hates hospitals. And he has been to this one too many times.

He is here today as a favor. His neighbor, Ray, has called him about his nephew, A.J., being assaulted. "Things are tough enough for him, Teddy," Ray said. "We're trying our best to get him off that robbery charge so that he don't have to do any time, what with the baby coming and all. Now he's laid up in the hospital with a fractured skull and a concussion. I need some help with the boy."

But it is not Ray's nephew he has come to visit. He has read the statements A.J. gave to the officers on duty: Someone assaulted him around one a.m. at the corner of Market and Hogan. There were two guys, maybe three. One of them carried a long, thin club—like the iron rod used in a tire jack.

He is here to see another victim. A young man has been admitted with a fractured skull and a head wound that required twenty-two stitches. His mother and friend filed a complaint this morning. The victim supplied additional details by phone and to an officer on duty at the time in the hospital.

The corridor is long. The floor is slick and shiny. Doors are cracked open, one after another. He tries his best not to look inside, not to be swept into other stories. He finds the room number on his folder. He knocks lightly on the door with his middle knuckle. Looks inside.

In the room he finds a young man, age seventeen, in a hospital bed. His head is shaved, a thick, long scar travels across the side of his skull, like the way an interstate highway is denoted on a roadmap. From his notes he knows the boy is black, slightly under six feet tall, weighs in at 170 pounds, his name is Troy. In the bed the young man is wearing a white T-shirt instead of a hospital gown. On his right forearm a tattoo is visible: a circular design of barbed wire.

Beside the hospital bed, in a chair, sits a woman who appears to be forty, maybe more. She is short, overweight, dark black hair pulled into a ponytail and bright white teeth. When he enters the room, he introduces himself. She stands, shakes his hand, says, "Thank you, thank you," too many times.

He is about the same height as the boy would be if he was standing, but he weighs in almost sixty pounds more. His name is Ted DeWitt—everyone calls him Teddy—most likely because he has a benign, bearish look about him. He is closer to fifty than he is to forty, and has a thick, wide mustache that in good, sunny weather looks a shade lighter than the thinning, brown hair he wears in a crew cut. He has something of a belly and wears his pants low, beneath his waist. He is pigeon-toed but his slow gait is deceptive. He is a man who sees everything from a height.

The boy is watching TV, attempting to ignore the man who has walked into the room. A commercial is on, an animated one about a robot. "I hope that little cut you have on your head don't make it too hard to laugh," Teddy says to him. He hates making chit-chat. He'd much rather get right to the question on his mind. Twenty years of detective work have led him to believe it's easier to get information by bonding first. Go slowly toward the information.

"I'm gonna beat the shit out of him when I get out of here," the boy says. His tone is angry, bitter, not entirely from the scar.

"I see it has," Teddy replies dryly. He opens his notebook, flips through a few pages, looks down at the boy, says, "You don't mind if we go over some of the details on this report?"

This one doesn't like chit-chat either. "You get the guy yet?" the boy asks.

"No," Teddy answers. "Not exactly. We got some ideas though. But I need your help. That's why I'm here. Unless you rather I go."

There is no answer from the boy. He continues to watch the TV. His mother stands, says, "Of course, we'll help you."

She slaps her son's arm near the tattoo. Troy remains stubborn, closed off.

"I hate competing for your time," Teddy says. He reaches for a remote control for the TV, flicks the set off.

"Ain't you got his license plate number?" the boy asks. "He was right there. I saw the cops pull up. Or is this one of those race things? Since he was a white boy."

"Well, we got a guy who was beside the truck," the officer says. "But there seems to be some things missing in this report. You say it was about one o'clock in the morning. He assaulted you with a gun. Where were you headed at one a.m. in the morning?"

"Me and a friend were just hanging out," he says.

"Hanging out," he repeats. He notices when the boy turns toward him that his nose is crooked. Broken bone from before. In his left ear an empty hole, where an earring might have been. "There's been a couple of reports about slashed tires in the area. Over on South Main. The officers who were in the area were responding to a call someone made about a car alarm going off."

"I ain't done anything to get jacked like this," Troy says.

"So you think this other fella was out slashing tires by himself?" Teddy asks.

"He won't by himself," the boy says. "There was another guy, too. White boy."

"So we got four guys on this scene," Teddy says. "What were you boys talking about for him to crack you on the head like that?"

"We weren't talkin' about nothing," the boy says. "We just walking down the street. Them two guys were fightin."

"Fighting?" Teddy asks. He thinks he might be getting something. Not what he expected. "What were they fighting about?"

"Shit, I don't know," the boy says. "They both looked like faggots to me. Real short dudes. Whities. Both of them. We went up to them and told them to watch out."

"Watch out for what?" Teddy replies.

"The cops," the boys says. His expression shows his exasperation. "They told us to fuck off and started talkin' trash."

"Trash?"

"Faggot, bitch, shit like that," Troy says. "Calling us shit. So we yelled back at them."

"So you thought these two might be homosexuals?"

"They were acting queer," he says. "Like they were fightin' over someone or somethin'. They were callin' us a bunch of queer names and then the shorter one just up and cracked me on the side of the head with that gun."

"He had the gun in his hand?" he asks.

"No," the boy says. "He got it out of the truck."

"This short guy—the one you hit," Teddy says.

"I ain't hit him," the boy says. "He hit me."

"The one your friend hit," Teddy says. "Can you describe him?"

"He looked like a retarded sort of guy," the boy answers. "Big head, jug ears, big hair. Like it was all too big for his body."

"If I showed you a photo of the guy, do you think you could identify him?"

"I'd know that motherfucker anywhere," he says.

Teddy takes a photograph of A.J. out of the folder he is carrying. It was taken three months ago when A.J. and his friend Rick were arrested for robbing the Red Lobster at gunpoint. The one at the highway exit. "Does this look like the guy?" he asks.

"That's him," Troy answers. "That's him. I hope you put that son-of-a-bitch away. He tried to kill me."

"And this guy," Teddy says, pulling out another mug shot. This one of Rick. "Was he the other guy?"

"That looks like him," the boy answers. "Hair was shorter. The other dude is the one for sure."

Teddy puts the photos back in the folder. "I couldn't help

but notice that another officer issued you and your friend a warning about a month ago. Same place."

"We weren't doing anything," the boy answers. He is defensive now.

"Trying to score some drugs, is what I hear," he says.

"I ain't done none of that shit," the boy answers. His eyes roll over to his mom. Back again.

"But you both were drinking," he says.

"That's it," the boy says. "That's all we done. We had a drink. That's it. We were clean that night. We weren't doing any drugs. Or looking for anything."

"One thing's not clear," Teddy says. "Why were you carrying a club?"

"For protection, man," the boy laughs. "It was late. Lots of dudes lookin' to rob you for no reason at all."

"One more question and then I'll let you get back to your television," he says. "You friendly with any college students? Anyone you hang out with at the University?"

"No," he answers. "Not really. Them all rich white dudes over there. I don't know many of them over there I want to like."

"Anyone named Danny?" he asks. "You know a college kid named Danny?"

"No," the boy answers. "Is he one of them, too?"

Teddy doesn't answer the boy. He writes in his notebook. He looks up, casts his eyes back down to the bed, nods and says, "Thank you" to the boy. His hand rests for a moment on the mother's back and then he turns to leave.

"You gonna arrest that guy?" the boy yells at him. "I want to press charges."

Teddy turns, says, "I'll see that he gets what he deserves." He nods again at the boy and his mom, makes his way down the hospital corridor swiftly, trying to catch the elevator before it leaves for another floor.

15

The road is familiar now. He drives by rote, instinct. His Jeep takes a pot hole uneasily. Inside, things jitter: coffee cup holder, keys, glove compartment lock. He clutches the steering wheel tighter.

Teddy thinks he is a poor choice to help A.J. He knows too much. Not about this crime. He knows a few things about A.J.'s childhood, facts, rumors passed along by the boy's uncle, aunt, neighbors, his own son.

There was the boy's mother—Cindy—who locked A.J. in the basement to keep him out of trouble. Ray had always complained about his sister, saying she had an attitude problem—a chip on her shoulder as if the world was against her—that seemed to manifest itself when she was drinking. Then there was the alleged abuse—after A.J.'s father left the house, Cindy went through a string of boyfriends. She no longer locked him in the basement. But she also couldn't keep the boy out of trouble. At ten he was taken from the house when Cindy discovered that the boy was being sexually abused by Bryce, her boyfriend.

Problems continued when he came to live with Ray and his wife, Marybeth, after Cindy's death, after she crashed her car, drunk, into a telephone pole. The neighborhood boys picked fights with him, called him "shrimp," held him captive in headlocks, ridiculed his big ears. Teddy remembers returning home from the station, seeing the boy crying in the corner of the garage, trying to remain out of sight of the other neighborhood kids. He tried talking to the boy, making him feel that because he was different—an orphan—he was special, trying to get him interested in a hobby, bringing him books about war, model racing car kits, decals from space flights—none of which he seemed to work.

Then the boy discovered the use of weapons, small things at first—sticks, rocks, water balloons. Then progressing through a series of more serious ones: b-b guns, pocket knives, razor blades. At twelve, he flunked seventh grade. A year later he was expelled when he tried to slice another student's finger off after an argument in the school cafeteria when the boy tried to take a bag of potato chips from him.

Teddy wants to believe that A.J. never came to violence naturally. More out of self-defense. There was the matter of his being shorter than most of the guys his age. There was his looks that got him taunted—the big ears, the mildly retarded look because of his wide brow, the sunken eyes. And there was something else about him—some kind of sensitive, effeminate trait that made him try to overcompensate his lack of muscularity with violence. He'd never been good with guns (he had once gone elk hunting with A.J. and his uncle, only to find the boy more noisy and self-absorbed than in wanting to learn to hunt) and he'd never been athletic. His uncle had tried to get him involved in football or skiing but without success. Even in shoplifting he wasn't very agile. (Although he was persistent—he had been caught almost a dozen times since he was fourteen.)

And then there were the rumors. He'd heard from his own son—Ethan—that the boy was queer, willing to do things to other boys to keep from being beat up. Teddy didn't believe too much of it—it was just his own son spouting off after he was caught hitting A.J.—but he'd hesitated about passing that kind of information along to Ray. A few years later Ray confided to him that A.J. had hit a difficult age—there had been some sort of confusing situation with one of his cousins—they'd been discovered fondling one another in the bedroom when Marybeth had walked in to get the boy's dirty clothes for washing. They'd shipped the boy to a detention center in town, a choice Teddy didn't feel had been a wise one to pursue. They welcomed his advice, his concern, his friendliness, but not his solutions.

Then there was the robbery. A.J. and the other guy he had started hanging out with about a year ago—Rick, a co-worker at the roofing company where A.J. worked—had surprised the night manager at the Red Lobster. Tied her up and got away with a couple of thousand dollars in cash and gift certificates. The girl, Debbie Fowler, seventeen, required five stitches in her scalp after being hit in the head with a wrench. She still had her hands tied when she dialed 9-1-1. The county officers—Larry English and Chris Santini—had called in the canine squad. They had used a dog to track west from the restaurant as far as a parking lot off Emmett Street, next to the entrance of the apartment building where A.J. and Kelly lived. The girl had easily picked A.J. out of a line up. Ray had hinted then that there was a problem with drugs. The boys were trying to pay off some debts. Ray had hired a lawyer in town—Kurt Vong, a guy who handled some of the town's business cases—to help A.J. get a reduced sentence—a fine—because of Kelly's baby being due.

And other things about A.J. From other officers. Sources. Rumors of dealing. Dope. Meth. Speed. Nothing that he can pin down. But he sees what's happening. The town becoming unhinged. They've caught kids dealing in the parking lot outside the grocery store on Gatewood. Last week they raided a crank house on Raven, just north of the Stadium. Windows sheathed in tinfoil. Ephedrine being cooked up in the kitchen. The five they arrested were rail thin, paranoid, said the police were trying to kidnap them.

Ray mentioned nothing to him about the crank. About whether A.J. was doing crank the night of the robbery. Or this morning when he cracked the black boy in the head with a gun. Or even where they were, where they went, before it happened. Who was their source.

He thinks again the situation might be because A.J. is different from the other guys—that some kind of fear of who he is might be making him lash out at anyone who crosses his path. Maybe A.J. needs counseling. Needs detox. Some kind of intervention. When he talked with Ray, he asked if the girl A.J. was living with was working out. Ray said his nephew was still going through wild sprees—always coming over, wanting to borrow his truck and a gun to go out shooting tires at the recycling center, telling his uncle he needed to get his rocks off and all, what with Kelly knocked up like a balloon.

Teddy thinks there are too many "what ifs" to make A.J. the victim this time. There are the details in the officers' reports. There is the blood on the gun, the student ID in the truck, the coat that doesn't seem to belong to anyone—not A.J., not the taller boy in the altercation. Something doesn't seem finished here, even though he wants to believe A.J.'s story. Too many missing links.

He passes the parking lot on Emmett Street, turns down gravel road that leads to the southwest section of town where an unfinished housing development lies in a swampy field that once used to be farmland. He adjusts himself in the seat to handle the rocking. The trailer park is not far from there. Maybe another half-mile down this road.

16

Rick thinks so much it is painful. It's as if he exists only as a mind. Thoughts. No body. Only what to do. What next. What could happen. He thinks about going to jail. He thinks about never seeing Kelly again. He thinks about Chase and the baby on their own. He thinks about the college boy. Then tries to stop thinking about him.

He feels pressure in his chest. His back. Shoulders. Neck. His stomach is filled with liquid. His guts boil, travel to his veins. Should he confess? Wait? Run? Turn himself in? Would it make a difference? He doesn't think about the college boy still being tied to the fence. Or of his wounds, his broken bones, his swollen organs. Only of the boy in his mind. The easy smile when they met. Taunting him. Then blood on his shoulder. Clothes. Everywhere.

He wonders if A.J. will talk his way out of this. This is all his fault. He should have stopped him. A.J. is nothing but a loaded gun.

He thinks their chances of getting off light for the robbery are over. When they find the boy. Chase told him that he could get off with probation because of the baby, in spite of the other arrests—the one for drunk driving in January. The other for resisting arrest last year. He wonders again about his options—whether he should call the lawyer who's bargaining for him and A.J. and confess to this other crime. This new problem. He wonders if he's got the guts to kill himself—at least it would be a way to get rid of all of these thoughts. Stop his head from exploding.

He slept till noon. Not a sound sleep—he spent the night

76

restless. Slipped away for an hour or so once the sun came up. But he continued to toss in bed. Not knowing where to go. What to do. When something will happen. When he got up there was a note from Chase saying she had gone to his granny's for a while.

In the kitchen he opens a beer. If they come for him now he will at least be drunk. Sober he would be too scared. Drunk he could pretend he doesn't care.

He finishes the beer quickly. Opens another bottle. Sits at the table, thinks about calling Kelly. If A.J. answers he could hang up. If he doesn't, he could ask her about what has happened. What the police have been asking. What happened at the hospital. How A.J. is doing.

He punches her number into the phone, thinking now of Chase, wondering if he could run, leave her and the baby behind. While the phone rings he wonders if Kelly would run with him. He thinks of himself on an island. On the Gulf side. Palm trees. Striped beach chair. Rubbing a cold bottle of beer against his chest. Not a care. Never a worry. Money just happens. Things don't have to be planned.

He lets the phone ring and ring and ring, expecting someone to answer. He looks out the window of the trailer, out at the semi-circle of lots. He hears a car moving across the dust and gravel of the road, an engine cutting dead in front of his trailer. He hangs the phone up and looks through another window, crouching. He sees a Jeep. A man gets out—a tall guy with a gut, brown mustache, wearing a tie. He raps on the trailer's door.

He straightens his posture, stretching his back. Takes another swig of beer. He knows the guy is a police officer. He can tell. Smells like trouble. He thinks he can bluff his way out of this. Pretend not to know anything. He won't give himself away. If anything happens to him, it won't be his own fault.

17

Teddy remains outside the trailer. On the lowest step. "Thought I stop by and ask a few questions," he says. "Heard a friend of yours is in the hospital."

"Hospital?" the guy answers. He stands in the crack of the door. T-shirt shivers in the breeze. Unshaven, dark stubble, maybe three days' worth. Cowlick at the back of the head, like he just got out of bed. Fat scab on his upper lip. "Someone's in the hospital?" He opens his eyes wider, shakes his head.

He can tell it is an act. "A.J.," he answers. "Your friend A.J."

"A.J? Is he hurt?" The guy lets his mouth hang open. "Is he gonna be okay?"

"I think he'll recover," he answers. "Thought I might ask you a few questions about him."

He takes another step toward the door. The guy does not move back, clearly doesn't want him inside. "We can talk here or at the station. Your call."

The eyes grow a bit wider. The door cracks open. He climbs the last step. Walks inside the trailer.

It's warm inside, sour. Smells of sweat. Beer. He notices the empty bottles on the table. Dishrags in the sink. Baby powder on the counter. The guy reaches for a pack of cigarettes, book of matches. He keeps his distance so that he doesn't overwhelm the guy. He's twice his size. He can feel the weight of the floor buckle beneath him.

The guy says, "We've met before. Over at Ray's. You're Ethan's dad. He was two years behind me at Walton. He's a sweet kid."

The "sweet" hits him hard. There's a mock in the way it's

said. Like a taunt for a change of subjects. "That's right," he answers. "Knew you and A.J. were pretty tight. That's why I came over here, you know. Knew you might know some things about A.J."

"That A.J.'s a wild card. What's he done now?"

He watches the guy light the cigarette, blow the first smoke up toward the ceiling. "Nasty cut on your lip," he says. "How'd you come by that?"

"Work," the guy answers.

"Must have bled a lot," he says.

"Not as bad as it looks," the guy answers. "Except when I touch it."

"You see a doctor?" he asks. "Might need stitches."

"Don't have that kind of money," the guy answers.

"Company won't pay for it?"

The guy narrows his eyes, like he thinks he's being tricked. "Not mine," the guy says. He cracks a window open, taps the ashes of his cigarette off. "A.J. over at the University?"

"Yeah," he answers. "That's where they took him."

"What happened? An accident? He bust up that truck again?"

"Nope," he says. "Some trouble over on Hogan last night. Four guys got in a bit of a fight."

"He's got a big temper," the guy says. "He's gonna get in trouble some day because of it."

"Lot of people concerned about his temper," he says. He shifts his weight from one shoe to the other. The Formica tabletop between them is scarred with water rings. He glances around the trailer, canvassing for clues. The room seems tragic, pitiful: a mustard-colored sofa, covered by a plaid blanket, a small TV with a broken antenna, shoes scattered on a rug. Another sour smell hangs over the room. Like dirty diapers. Nothing hits him as strange, except the cut on the lip. "Why don't we start this by you telling me where you were this morning? About midnight to two a.m."

"You understand that I can't answer that," the guy says. Mischievous smile. Almost a smirk. "My wife and all. Don't want it to get back to her."

"You understand I can make you answer that," he says.

The guy tries not to fluster. He shakes his head again. As if it were a habit. A tick. "I was out with a girl," the guy says. He shrugs his shoulders, opens up empty palms. "I was spending time with a girl."

"You want to give me her name?"

"Can't do that too easily," he says. "She's got a husband. This all got out, shit would hit the fan, ya know?"

"It's already hit, so it seems," he says.

They stand regarding one another. Awkwardly. He shifts again to break the stalemate. "I got a few people who are saying you were out at Hogan about that time," he says. "I'm sure this girl could clear that all up. Why don't you give me her name? I'll give her a call. Maybe stop by and see her. I'll keep it confidential."

The guy becomes nervous, stubs out his cigarette. "No need. Let me talk to her, okay?" he says. "I'll have her come talk to you. Clear things up. I was with her last night. I just don't want this to get too deep. What with my wife and a new baby and all."

He plays the fool. The stupid cop. Only because he knows it's too soon to play rough. "Well, that sounds fine," Teddy says. "Don't want any more trouble than we already got. Thank you for your time. You give me a call and let me know when I can talk to her."

"Will do, officer," the guy says.

He stops at the door. "You know many kids at the University?" he asks.

"Not many," the guy answers. "Why?"

"You know a guy named Danny?" he asks. "Short fella. Small. Sorta like you and A.J. Maybe even smaller."

Blood drains from the guy's face. He touches his scab. Squints. A line of sweat is visible beneath his arm. He shifts his eyes away from the officer. "Naah," he answers. "Don't sound too familiar to me."

"Wore nice shoes, I heard," he says. "We'll be talking."

"Sure," the guy answers. "We'll be talking."

18

Tuesday

He is thirty-eight years old, has a long face, lots of dark hair, somber eyes which seem ready to roll down his cheeks like giant tears. He is the pastor of the small chapel that sits atop Skyline Mount. He is a man who believes God is good, even though God has not been kind to him. He is a refugee from tragedy. His family—his wife, three year-old son—drowned in a flood when a hurricane hit five years ago near the coast. He has learned to think about great things and found that he is not so great. He was sent to the chapel to heal. His name is Peter Fletcher. Reverend Peter Fletcher.

Reverend Fletcher wants to be a teacher of faith, not a student of it. He wants to explain the way the world is, no longer experience its sorrows himself. He thinks about this all the time. He thinks about this in his office at the chapel. He thinks about this at his small apartment above the hardware store in town. He thinks about this driving in the car, which is where he is now. Right now he is thinking about the last chapter of Deuteronomy, the graphic tour of the promised land, the view from Pisgah, eastward from Jericho. The view was all that one could desire and deserve. "I have let you see it with your eyes but you shall not go over there," God told Moses. Moses died where he was, not where he was going. Why did God let it end this way? Why did Moses not reach his promised land?

The minister sorts out his reasons. He thinks about beauty, desire, what God intends for us to do. Reverend Fletcher thinks there appears to be something unfair, unjust about God not letting Moses reach the promised land. Was Moses being punished for his temper? Or was this the arbitrariness of God? Is there a stronger metaphor at work here—that we struggle to the top of the mountain only to see a future into which we cannot enter? Or a future that isn't there?

Peter Fletcher is originally from Atlanta, grew up in one of the suburbs, in a two-story ranch house not much different than many here. He did not know poverty, hunger, crime or sorrow. His father was an engineer, prosperous. His mother was a homemaker, the family and house her life. His wife was a good companion, his son filled up their empty spaces. His decision to work in the church was not a calling but a happy challenge. Until the tragedy. Until he had to question his losses. Until he was forced to relearn every lesson of faith he thought he understood.

Now he finds problems with the beauty of God. This town is beautiful, picture perfect, two hundred year-old apple trees, mossy rocks at the bottom of waterfalls. Quaint Southern charm. Beauty overwhelms the real truths. Children from the hills arrive at school barefoot. Divorce rates are up. Depression consumes his congregation. He is witness to confessions of drug abuse, alcohol consumption, quarrels that turn violent. Some people here say that hate arrived long before the ante-bellum homes and neoclassical architecture: the Indians hated the colonists, the slaves hated the landowners, the hillbillies hated the scholars. And on and on.

He looks out of the car window, sees two workmen washing store windows filled with local crafts: quilts, baskets, whimmy diddles with painted propellers. Tourists arrive to photograph old wooden shacks as if they are quaint, unaware of families inside passing down clothing from generation to generation to save money. It doesn't seem fair: the rich admiring the beauty of poverty. This is a landscape of denied opportunities, an inheritance that will never be collected, a future that will never be enjoyed by all.

He struggles with comparisons. He drives without a notebook at his side, without a pen within his reach. He wants his heart to sort it out first. The land into which Moses looked was filled with both promise and peril. The book of Joshua and those that follow show that the promise was not easy, the land flowed not only with milk and honey but also arrived with obstacles and problems.

Is there such a thing as a promised land? The perfect place on earth? God's beauty is evident here in the white clapboard churches with picket fences, the streams that fall from the mountains, the small creeks or "cricks" as locals call them. But legend has it known that the stench of Hope Creek comes not from the pollution of the cement factory wandering into the valley waters, but from the undiscovered remains of Hattie Jane Boyd, a seven year-old girl who has been missing for more than thirty years. Rumor has it that she was kidnapped, raped, tossed into the hills. Never found.

He drives along Bridge Street, crosses the river, stops before turning north on Upper White Chapel Road. This spot used to be farmland. The best in the valley. Now a subdivision remains unfinished. A muddy road leads to nowhere. Construction stopped because the developer went bankrupt. Hulls of houses sit unfinished. A blight, no sign of life. This was supposed to transform this area of town, hide the trailer park that lies over the small ridge. Is this missed opportunity or the will of God? To leave the blight for all to see. To wreck what is perfect, beautiful.

He turns and follows the road to the chapel. Beauty overwhelms the view. The yellow leaves of the sugar maples are so light it seems as if God is shining through them. He parks his car in the lot behind the chapel. Outside, before entering his church, he casts his eyes back down to the valley. Is life unfair because few of us can orchestrate the conclusion of our lives? That most of us will die with our work undone? Our dreams unachieved?

He breaths in the light air, struggles with faith, His message. Beauty clouds his mind, hides from view the horror of a boy's struggle only breaths away. God is not ready to involve him with these brutal facts. Like other things, this path is not clear to him. It remains unknown, a mystery. He does not know how to look *beyond* the beauty. To *discover* the truth. This is not yet his challenge, his newest lesson.

19

Tuesday

The lights have been on all day. The sun, for most of the afternoon, hidden behind clouds, emerges with a scorching vividness. Something about the day has kept her cold. Kelly has lingered mostly in the kitchen, as if she wants to turn the oven on, send a toasty comfort back into the room. Sounds of cars come in from the road, sometimes makes the walls shake, like when a truck passes by. His knock at the door startles her.

"You shouldn't be here," she says. A screen door lies between them. The neighborhood outside is gray, strewn with junk. A slight buzz emanates from the power lines.

"We've got trouble," Rick says. "Can I come in?"

She doesn't move to let him in. He could easily break through the wire, but doesn't. She notices his cut lip, his cowlick, the stubble around his neck. "You look like shit," she says.

"That's a fine way to greet me," he says.

"I can't do anything for you," she answers.

He opens the door. She takes a few steps back into the kitchen as he walks inside. She takes a sweater off the back of a chair, drapes it over her shoulders. She is colder, frightened. She feels a short pain in her stomach, wondering if it is the baby kicking.

"How's A.J?" he asks. His eyes move in circles around the room. Cabinets, dirty dishes, ashtray filled with amber-colored stubs, fluorescent light above the sink on. He leans his butt against the counter, his arms folded across his chest. His eyes search hers. They meet. She deflects his gaze.

"They're keeping him at the hospital for more tests."

She moves away from him but remains in the room. He approaches her and she lets him advance. He kisses her first on the forehead, then on the lips. Her features soften for him. Her blue eyes become brighter. His arms draw around her. He smells of cigarettes, stale smoke caught in fabric. She is self-conscious of her weight. He is drawn to placing his hand against her stomach. Which makes him smile. His fingers are chapped, nails crusted with dirt. "They don't have anything on me," he says. "Cop came to visit but I said I didn't know anything."

"Nobody knows anything," she says. She has hardened again. "Or so I hear. Chase called here looking for you."

His response is to kiss her neck. She responds by pushing him away. "I need your help," he says.

"I can't do anything for you," she answers. "Cause I don't know what's going on."

Again he circles her with his arms. She feels frustration tighten his body. "A.J. killed a guy," he says. "It was A.J."

She wobbles her head. Struggles in his arms. "I don't know nothing about this," she says. She twists herself away from him. "I don't know nothin' about somebody being killed. All I know about is the guy with the bump on his head that A.J.'s taking the rap for."

"He hit the guy," he says. "But that ain't nothing compared to what he did to this other guy. College kid."

"I don't know nothing about that," she says. She backs away from him. Retreats to the table.

"It's gonna get worse," he says, following her. "I can't go down for A.J. He murdered that guy. I need you to tell them we were together last night."

She lifts an eyebrow in disbelief. "But we weren't," she says. "You ain't been around to see just me for a while, you know."

"That don't mean I ain't been thinking about you," he says. He approaches her again. She pushes against his chest with her hands. It is a mock push. Not much behind it. He knows it. "I need you to do this, baby," he says. "When this all blows over, we'll go to Florida. You always wanted us to go to Florida. We can get a place in the south. On the Gulf, maybe."

"And what about Chase?" she says. "What you gonna do about Chase?"

He doesn't want to think about Chase. He frowns because she is there, part of the conversation, part of the problem. "Chase and me don't get along too good no more," he says. "She don't love me. I know that. And I don't love her. Not like I do you. We got a history going—you and me. I need you now, Kelly. You can't let this happen to us. Don't you love me?"

"A.J. would kill you and me both if I did this," she says.

"They're gonna put him away," he says. "Don't you understand that? Maybe not today. But soon. Think about what happens when he explodes and it's against you. Or the baby. We gotta get out of here. How's A.J. gonna kill us when he's in jail?"

"What if the college guy says you were there too?" she asks.

"I don't think he's goin' to be doin' any talking," he answers. "Far as I know they ain't even found him yet."

20

Tuesday

It is close to four when Leah calls the police. She has come back to the apartment after grocery shopping and tried his phone again: There is no answer. She tells the man who answers the phone at the police station that she is worried about a friend. She wants to know if there have been any reports filed. He is a University student. He didn't show up for classes today. He isn't answering his phone. No one has seen him. She doesn't tell him that he is fighting depression, possibly suicidal. She holds back that information, as if her worry will bring some kind of recognition from the voice on the other end.

"We've had nothing on a person with that name," he says. "Is this a husband or a boyfriend?"

"Just a friend," she answers. "Well, my best friend, really. I'm worried about him."

"Can you give me a description?" the officer asks.

"He's real short," she says quickly, then realizes her answer is not full of enough details. "Five feet, two inches," she adds. "Barely over a hundred pounds. He's got blond hair. Or blondish hair. It's kind of streaked. He's cute, boyish looking. Blue eyes."

"How old is he?" the officer asks. His voice is methodical, expressionless.

"Twenty," she answers. "But he looks a lot younger."

"Any distinguishing characteristics?" he asks. "Like a mole or a tattoo or a birthmark? Something obvious."

She wants to say, "Well, he's gay," but she holds it back. It flashes through her mind that she has always thought he looked gay. But she doesn't want to describe him as effeminate—that wouldn't be right at all—and then there would be all sorts of questions from the officer about whether he was gay or not. That could possibly hinder her chances. And his. "He wears braces," she answers, after a pause.

She waits while the officer looks through some reports. When he comes back on the line, he says he hasn't heard of anyone who fits that description. She gives him her name and phone number in case a report comes in. When she hangs up, she decides she will call the campus security office. She goes to the kitchen to look for her University guide with departmental phone numbers.

She gets a colder treatment from campus security. "Nothing's been reported," a security guard tells her. "Except that the Love Bandit tagged the Administration Building."

She hangs up, decides not to worry anymore. Maybe he went to Washington for the day to meet the guy he was e-mailing. Or Richmond again. She thinks about calling Pop, to see if he has heard anything, took him out somewhere. She puts the thought aside, doesn't want to bother him. She's tired of chasing him.

She sits at the table for a long time reading the small print in the University manual—as if it will calm her—until she decides to read the papers she copied in the library yesterday for her research paper.

The phone rings about a quarter to five. Her first thought is that it is Danny, calling to let her know his whereabouts. Instead, it is the police department. Another officer, not the one she spoke to originally, wants to ask her a few questions about the friend she reported missing. He tells her his name is James Pearce. He asks when she last saw him.

"For lunch yesterday," she says.

"Do you know what he was doing after that?"

His voice sounds full of courtesy, suspicion. "Is he in some kind of trouble?" she asks.

"Not that I know of," he answers. "We've got a few cases on our desk we're trying to unscramble, that's all. Just checking to see if any of your details might match our own."

"He was going to go to the movies with a friend," she says. "But I think he might have backed out of it."

"Why do you think that?"

She hears other voices behind him, can't make out their words. "He had a test he had to study for," she answers. "He might have gone to the student union or to one of the bars near campus for a drink. He likes to stay up late."

"Any particular place he likes to go?" the officer asks.

"No special place," she says. "He's been trying a bunch of different places to see which one he likes best."

"Do you know who any of his other friends are?" the officer asks.

"There's a girl in his math class that he's friendly with. And Walt, the guy he was going to go to the movies with."

"Do you have a number for him?"

"No," she answers. "But he lives in one of the dorms. I'm sure the University switchboard will have him."

"Are there any people in town who might not like him?" the man asks.

She thinks it is a strange question. "No," she says. Her heartbeat catches in her throat. "He's a sweet guy."

"What about a friend named A.J. or Rick?" he says. "You know if he has a friend named Rick?"

"No," she says. "That doesn't sound familiar to me."

He runs by two other names for her to see if she recognizes them—Troy, Jamie—but she doesn't recognize them either. "Will you call me if you hear anything?" she asks.

"Yes," he answers. "Is there anything else you think I might need to know about him?"

She knows her hesitation is revealing, but she feels she must make some effort to maintain his privacy—in case it's simply Danny being difficult and moody. "No," she answers. "Nothing that I can think of."

21

Tuesday

She had tried to convince him to take the day off. The training was starting to get to her—she wasn't as obsessive about it as he was—and the drop in temperature today had aggravated the muscles of her knees. Now, with all this constant exercise, she is worried that she is developing tendonitis. Jerold had agreed that they could skip the Deer Mountain run today. She is relieved not to have to try to navigate the highway, watch out for the trucks. But at three he said he still wanted to go out today—somewhere: Why don't they do a smaller loop from campus out to Upper White Chapel and the Fancy Gap Trail?

It is more than ninety minutes later before they set out. (He had taken a call from one of his students who asked if he knew if there was an English translation of one of the German texts listed on the course syllabus. Then she made him wait while she stretched her leg muscles and wrapped her knee.) She has on her tights today, the first time she has put them on since May. He wears khaki shorts over knee-length spandex briefs and a short-sleeve coolmax shirt. She has a long sleeve shirt and a wind shell on (which comes off almost as soon as they head out of campus).

She isn't as fond of mountain biking as he is. She would have much rather gone cycling on a paved surface and at a slower pace. But most of the trails on the west side of town are not paved—more for horse riding than cycling. Helmets and padding are as essential as a water bottle. She never enters the competitions—she leaves that to him to do alone—which is what all these daily excursions are all about. Or so he says: "I have to get ready for the 10K" or "I have to be able to do the two-part mountain run."

The knee stills bothers her as they take Clifton Road down to the Old Union Highway so that they can cross the river at Bridge Street. She hates holding Jerold back on these rides. She always feels like she's holding him back, even when her leg is functioning perfectly. But he's always trying to show off by racing ahead of her, letting her know who has the strength. The truth is, he'll peter out soon enough, slow down because he's a fifty year-old man trying to pretend he's still a teenager. But she does not try to rob him of the pleasure these runs give him. And he seldom rides without her, says he prefers her company more than Professor Bosewell, the chemistry professor who sometimes fills in when she's decides she's really had enough of it.

They walk the bikes across the old one-lane bridge, the river gray, shivery waves catching the sunlight. They bike beneath the highway underpass, turning onto the old dirt trail that leads to the Upper White Chapel. To the west, suburbs roll over hills resembling seashore dunes. She looks at the new homes being built at the edge of the big meadows here: huge five and six-bedroom houses. She thinks they are too large, out of place for this small town. Houses which have video rooms and saunas which few can afford here. An easy ticket to bankruptcy. Unless they're bought by the bureaucrats fleeing Capitol Hill, thinking they belong here.

The Fancy Gap Trail starts not far after that—a small climb up a hill, that flattens for a space as it begins to circle Skyline Mountain. It follows an old split-rail fence along a stretch of farm land. As the elevation rises toward the chapel three kinds of weather can be seen at once—dark bellied clouds against the eastern mountain range, visible at the end of the horizon, clear sky above her head and to the north, and the white clusters of cumulus that travel inland, hanging over the valley on the east, sun breaking through in beams to shine against the University dorms. The wind is now harder up here—the chill works its way into her hands.

She has only done this loop maybe twice before. (He prefers

the longer, tougher terrains.) But this trail is rougher than Deer Mountain—and the going is slower than she remembers. She has to constantly look at the road ahead of her, judging the rocks and holes and sticks in her path. She has to fight to keep the handlebars steady.

The deeper they ride the trail the nastier she finds the weather—the wind is brisk now, the sky lost. He rides well ahead of her. She keeps her pace steady as the elevation climbs. When she takes the decline of a small hill, she thinks she feels a drop of rain. She tries to look up, but can't. She has broken a sweat, her concentration focused so intently on not falling off the bike.

He finds an easy path, bolts far ahead of her as the trail circles the cemetery that stretches behind the chapel. She imagines he will slow down soon. She will catch up with him when they reach the downhill terrain on the other side of the church. (He has a blister on the instep of his left foot that has been bothering him for three days. She knows he has difficulty taking the uphill paths.)

She is about a thousand feet behind him now. She sees him pump up a small dune, start down the other side when the bike slides away beneath him. A crow, which must have been sitting on the fence, flies up, swoops to a telephone pole on the other side of the trail. She thinks the pebbles must have scattered beneath the weight of Jerold's wheels sending him off balance. She looks up quickly, trying to tell if he is hurt. All she sees is him standing, brushing the dust off his legs.

His eyes follow the bird first. He notices the scarecrow, thinks it's doing a poor job of scaring the crow away. His own fall did much better. He stands, brushes his legs, looks off at the big meadow filled with tombstones behind the chapel. His next thought is that it is an odd place to hang a scarecrow—what is he guarding?—lost souls? It must be something children in one of the new houses put together. Halloween's not far away, popular in the valley. He's just about to yell over his shoulder to Jill to look at the scarecrow that some kids put together, when something—a flap of a shirt—catches his eyes. He thinks they did a good job with the hair. It actually looks real—the color of straw. Long and loose—like it had once been on a doll.

Then he notices the dark, rusty patches on the shirt, the russet-colored face. And then the features—the broken nose, the blistered mouth. They swim up to him, behind the color. He turns and waves Jill to stop.

"Turn around and go call the police," he says, when she comes to stop beside him.

She is about to ask why when she sees a figure behind his shoulder, a scarecrow tied to the old fence.

He steps in front of her line of sight, to purposely block her view. "Try the chapel. Tell the preacher there's a body out here. Tell them we've found a body."

She turns the bike around without trying to look around him, but the image of the scarecrow has been burned into her mind. She tries to deconstruct it as she pedals faster. It all comes vividly back to her—a little boy—the hair, the shirt, the bruises, the blood.

She feels an urgency with every pedal. Pain from her knee shoots up into her thigh. She takes a path that cuts behind the fence. Seconds seem like hours. She feels like she is moving into warp speed while everything around her slows down. Time passes in images: the rut in the trail, the pothole before the paved street, the dark color of the cement, the clear windows of the chapel, the red front door. She leaves her bike in the driveway, runs to the door, trying to calm herself. She tries the door but it is locked. She looks around, runs to the side of the chapel and to another door. This door is locked too. But she sees a doorbell. She pushes a buzzer and waits.

A man answers that she recognizes—the preacher who oversees weddings at the chapel. Her words tumble out. She tries to keep them coherent—a body, a boy, beaten, tied to the old wood fence along the trail just at the end of the cemetery. Can she call the police and report it?

He nods his head, of course, waves her into the back rooms, his hand coming momentarily against the small of her back. He leads her this way through a room of steel office furniture into another where there ceiling expands into dark A-framed beams. He pulls a portable phone off its cradle, dials 9-1-1, hands her the phone. When a voice comes through she finds it hard to make her voice and thoughts connect. She hands the preacher back the phone. She is breathless. He says, "Hello?" into the receiver for her. After a pause he says, "I'd like to report an accident. We've found someone out on one of the trails. A body. A boy."

She waits while he listens. Moments drag. She finds herself focusing on the pores of his skin, the size of his earlobe, the small black hair protruding from his nose.

When he pulls the receiver away from his ear, he asks, "Was he still breathing? Do you know if he was alive?" the images of the boy again topple through her mind. For a moment she thinks she has fainted—everything has blacked out in front of her except the slow motion of the wind lifting the edges of the blue shirt. "Yes," she answers, not knowing if her answer is the truth. "Yes," she repeats. "I think I saw him breathing."

22

She is the first officer on the scene. This is what she finds: two bikers standing beside their bikes, a man and a woman, both appear middle-aged. The woman is wearing a parka around her waist, her helmet is off, her complexion is red, her eyes wide. She looks as if she has been crying. The other biker still has his helmet on. His hands are on his hips, as if he is waiting, impatient. Another man is present. He is middle-aged, black-haired, dressed in jeans, gray sweatshirt. It is 6:04 p.m. when she stops the squad car. It is still light, but overcast. The ridge of mountains is a faint blue haze. A wind, about ten miles per hour, blows from the chapel, across the cemetery. Except for gusts. Reaching maybe thirty miles per hour. The two men and one woman wait at the edge of a dusty, unpaved part of the Fancy Gap Trail.

Across the trail on a wooden fence appears to be a body tied to a post, male, slumping to the ground on his knees. As she approaches she thinks it is a boy. A crow circles broadly overhead, lights on the fence post when she reaches the victim.

She is immediately surprised by his condition. His body is small. Like a thirteen year-old. Blood has dried on his face, streaks erasing the rusty color where there appeared to have been tears. She thinks first of her own son. Jesse. Four. Then breathes and concentrates on this boy. "Baby boy, baby boy, I'm so sorry this has happened to you," she says.

Her duty is not to look for evidence yet, search for any clues of the crime, but to see if the body, the person, this boy, can be saved. She checks his eyes. One is dull, lifeless.

The other is damaged. His breathing is shallow. His lungs sound like they are full of fluid. She looks at, memorizes the details of the injuries on his forehead. The back of his neck. He is unconscious. There appears to be massive head injuries. Possibly fatal. There is no response from the boy to the sound of her voice.

She sees blood on his shirt. His legs are folded beneath his body. His hands are pulled behind him, tied behind a post. His wrists are bound together as though they were handcuffed. She looks at the rope, memorizing the way it is tied. She tries to detect anything foreign—fibers, threads, that might belong to the assailant. Nothing registers to her except the need to get the boy comfortable. She tries to untie the rope. The knots are tight. His skin is swollen. She is unable to get the rope to budge.

She stands, takes a boot knife from her pocket, kneels beside him again, uses the blade to cut his hands free.

She holds his body upright as his hands relax to his side. She has to take a deep breath to maintain her composure, adjust to his weight. Like carrying a baby in her arms. Which makes her think of Jesse again. And makes her breathe deeper. Concentrate. Relax. Do her job.

She checks his breathing, unfolds his legs so that he sits on the ground. The man in the sweatshirt crosses the street, says, "Can I help?"

Something about the man's voice is familiar and she places him somehow with the Chapel. She shakes her head no, saying, "I got him. It's okay folks. I'll get him comfortable. I need you to stay back from the area."

The boy's body now bends slightly forward. She notices his breathing has stopped. She leans his right shoulder and chest down to the ground, brings his legs into a reclining position. Fresh blood, new red liquid, spills out of his ear, into the dirt. Behind her she senses the woman wince. They have crossed the trail and are close behind her, watching.

"You folks might want to stay back," she says. "Don't want to disturb the scene." She tries not to display her own fear. She has blood on her hands, wipes them into her uniform. Against her pants.

She tries to get the boy comfortable but she is aware of the woman, now back across the trail, crying. It makes her upset as well, knowing she must divorce herself from the boy before her—see him not as a person but as a victim who needs to be attended to. She opens his mouth, notices he wears braces. Again she thinks of his age. Her son. The blood. She thinks he is too young, too small to be found in this type of condition. She feels her back tensing, her body reacting to the thought of pain the boy must have felt. She clenches her hand into a fist, releases it, forcing the tension out through her hands. When she thinks she has his breathing stable again, she returns to the squad car, radios to make sure an ambulance is on its way.

She returns to the scene with a camera from the car, searching the ground now for clues, things that might have been left behind by the perpetrators—footprints, tire tracks left behind in the dirt, something lost in the grass. About twenty feet to her east she sees where the tire tracks stop, a rupture of dirt and grass against an embankment just below the fence. Not far from there she finds a watch, overturned on the dirt. She bends down, looks at it closely. There is no inscription on the back. She notices the change and the card covered with dust. She doesn't lift the card. She moves it with her keys. Reads the name imprinted in the plastic. In the dirt she sees something that looks like a caterpillar. She bends down, looks, decides it is a carpet fragment. She stands, photographs the change, the card, the fence, the carpet fragment, the boy lying on the ground. She returns to the car. "Possible identification of the victim," she says into her radio transmitter. She tells the dispatcher the possible name of the victim. Before she disconnects she sees the crow fly up into the air. When she turns, she notices the flashing lights of the ambulance headed in her direction.

23

Monday

Lunch has made him sleepy. He finds himself daydreaming at the Writing Center. Thinking about Gary's visit. Thinking about sex. Maybe he shouldn't be too subtle. Maybe he should just go for it. Ask him to stay over, sleep in the bedroom.

His eyes flip down to the paper. Words blur, focus, blur. His head feels light, heavy, light. The assignment today is to read Turgenev's essay, "The Execution of Tropmann," write a three paragraph response to the crime and its punishment. Andrea groaned the minute the sentence left the instructor's lips. "Why can't we do anything decent?" she whispered to him. He shrugged, drifted off again.

He loses his concentration somewhere around the third section. The description of the limping dog. He rereads it, fades again when the author quotes Pushkin. He hates having to do these assignments. If he had stumbled on this essay on his own he would have no problem analyzing it. The teaching assistant is tougher than the instructor. Trying to show off. Look good. He sits at the front and watches them read, giving the class a smug expression, leaking a wicked smile.

He finishes the essay but doesn't write a direct response. He outlines his thoughts on the state's current stance on capital punishment. Writes: *Violates human rights. Mistakes happen. Race issues.* He draws boxes on his paper, connects them with lines. Finds a new sheet and begins to write. "*No*," he scribbles hurriedly, glancing at his watch. "*We should have matured from the days of 'an eye for an eye.' Capital punishment does not deter crime.*"

It is still cloudy when he walks across campus with Andrea,

but patches of sunlight suggest the day might turn out warmer than forecast. The outside steps leading to the main floor of the Administrative Building are crowded. Students study notes, watch the traffic across the quadrangle. On the lawn, others stretch out optimistically on the grass, convinced that it will not rain. Five guys wearing blue jerseys with Greek frat letters wear shorts instead of jeans. A girl lying on a marble bench on the pathway tilts her face skywards as if it were her last chance to catch the sun.

When they reach the walkway that creates a short-cut to the library, he asks Andrea what she thinks about doing a project on Jack Kerouac. Or something about the way literature invents new words.

She says, "That sounds more like what he wants." Meaning the writing instructor. She leaves him to go to the library. He wanders to the left path, to the language lab, which travels between two rows of hickory trees which have not completely shed their browning yellow leaves. He senses, from the smell of the soil, and the coolness of the shade, the seasons changing. He thinks about shopping—deciding he will buy some flannel shirts this year even though the patterns make him look short. Shorter. Maybe if Gary comes they can kill time shopping. If he decides he wants Gary to come. Doubt still crosses his mind. He knows he has not made it official, not sent the e-mail about where to meet. He tries to think of a way to remember to do this. At home, he will do it from home.

In the language lab, his laziness returns. The physical plant has turned on the heat in this building—or turned off the air-conditioning. The air is stagnant, warm. After repeating the second line of conversation—*Est-ce qu'il fera beau demain?*— he is lost in the lesson. He keeps hitting the repeat button, trying to find a way back in—the gap he has missed. Out of the corner of his eye he sees Geoff arrive, bend and place his knapsack on the ground, sit on the monitor's stool behind the counter.

He straightens his posture. His attention is sharpened. He repeats the line again. Another line skips by without his repetition. He studies what Geoff is wearing today. Geoff is tall, thin, has short black hair with a wave sticking up in front. Brown eyes. Good bones in his face. Thick forearms, intricate hands. Dark hair at the knuckles, wrists. Makes him look older, wiser. He is wearing a striped T-shirt (crossways, long sleeves), jeans (Levi's, blue), high top sneakers (Nike, white). Geoff reminds him of Craig, a boy he met his junior year in high school when his family moved from Portland to Seattle after his father got a promotion and a relocation. He had begged his mother to let him finish his last two years of high school in Portland, to not make him move till then. She was strict about wanting to keep the family together, said she had no intention of leaving him or his brother Luke behind.

So he started his junior year in high school depressed. An outsider again, a loner. Stirred by a feeling he was different. Not just because he was the new boy in school. A posting on the cafeteria bulletin board changed his course. A flyer, announcing tryouts for *Bye, Bye Birdie.* He had been in the chorus of *Li'l Abner* in Portland, had loved the experience. He would have rather been in a band, singing country or pop songs, tight harmonies. But he also liked the idea of being one of the dancers, thought it might be a way to make new friends.

He was small and boyish enough to be cast as Randolph MacAfee, the younger brother of Kim, the female ingénue who falls for Conrad Birdie (a fictional depiction of Elvis Presley). He was disappointed he was not in the large, dancing production numbers, but during rehearsals he found every line he said produced a laugh, was thankful for the featured role. Rehearsals lasted for two months. Two nights a week. And outside of classrooms, in hallways. Besides lockers.

He developed a crush on the guy who played Hugo, Kim's boyfriend. That was Craig. Craig was a senior. He was dark-haired, dark-eyed. Danny thought he was better looking than the guy playing Conrad. He wanted to know everything about Craig. He made Danny's heart race, made him avert his eyes. He was able to keep his obsession hidden, until Craig talked to him during those long waits for their scenes. Their eyes would lock. Danny would blush, stutter, backing away a few steps, giggling like a girl. He would try to correct himself by making Craig laugh. Or smile. The smile was wide, toothy. Something to fall for.

Est-ce que je vous dérange?

He repeats the line, waits for the answer to be announced. He lifts his eyes up from his text book, watches Geoff talking to a girl carrying a blue knapsack. He is better looking than Craig, probably in better shape, too. But Craig was Craig. Craig was his first infatuation. A confusing thrill. Back home in his bedroom he replayed and rehearsed his past and future conversations with Craig. In his mind they were becoming fast friends. His first inkling of erotic feelings emerged. He imagined Craig wandering down the street, knocking the door of his house, saying, in a whisper, he was thinking about him, too. And wanted to become as close as possible.

It never happened that way. Why not? Why not? He curled himself up into the sheets alone, feeling as if he were far, far away from Craig. Why couldn't they fall in love? Why shouldn't they? Love and sex and friendship were intermingled in those days. He was a quaking romantic. Even if things so easy felt so difficult to understand.

Combien est-ce que cela fait? This seems so long ago.

He had known about sex since seventh grade, when Dana, a tall, skinny boy in his class, had told him about "making cream" on their walk home from school. He had only vaguely understood that the stiffness that would overcome him in class was supposed to be a desire that linked an attraction toward girls. Dana had not offered a demonstration, but he had described the sensation with such earnestness, such glee, that the news had shocked him, sent him upstairs to his room to examine himself. He touched, taunted, tortured himself till it happened to him, too. Made cream. But he hadn't realized the secret life he harbored inside his mind until Craig came along.

They had long conversations about Elvis's later career, the

102

right way to execute a dance step. But nothing about their own bond, their behavior. This crazy infatuation continued until the cast party. Danny, giddy from the punch someone had spiked with a rum, began singing to Craig, "one boy, one special boy," exactly as Tina, the girl cast as Kim. They were seated in a corner of the cafeteria, transformed by low lights, crepe paper, into a party. They were seated where the music—CDs and tapes being blasted from a portable sound system—was not overpowering. They were leaning into each other, deep into revelations about their favorite type of music, when Danny began his serenade.

This sudden expression of infatuation was too much for Craig to accept. He said, "That's not funny," pushed Danny at the shoulders when he had tried to kiss him.

The disturbance went unnoticed by most of the cast. Those who saw it called it an accident. The force of Craig's push tilted Danny out of his chair. He had been able to look like he had lost his balance because he was drinking. He hadn't been physically hurt—a bruise on his forearm where he cushioned his landing—but his pride was wounded.

Permettez que je présente.

Out of the side of his vision he notices Geoff removing his T-shirt. His head disappears first, a patch of hair along his stomach appears, then the head reappears. He pulls his arms out. A short white T-shirt is underneath. It shows his rib cage, his triceps break through the arms. Danny stares till he stares too long. Then looks away.

Je suis les Etats-Unis.

In the days after the cast party Craig avoided him whenever their paths crossed. He grew unhappy, discouraged. He knew his mistake but could not tell the reason to anyone. He began to watch himself better, knowing he was different. Craig was civil to him till graduation. But they were never friendly—close and friendly—again.

He finishes the French lesson, lets the tape play itself out. He replaces the guide and the cassette into the folder, gathers up his knapsack, approaches the counter. He thinks Geoff is out of his league. Too tall. Too good-looking to be interested. He doesn't even know if he is gay. He finds his perception of other gay men—his gaydar—is all out of sync on campus. He can't tell who is or who isn't here. All he knows is a handsome face when he sees one.

He returns the folder to the front counter. He loses his nerve of introducing himself when Geoff hands him his student ID card back. Geoff doesn't give him any hint of wanting an introduction. He shoves the card into his wallet, thinking: *He didn't even look to see who I was.*

24

Tuesday

Kelly finds him at the house. She has gone to Ray's for dinner, walked across the lawn while Marybeth is cooking to speak with Mr. DeWitt. Knocked on the front door instead of the back. Keeping her visit slightly formal.

Teddy answers, invites her in. Motions her into the front room, the one only used for guests. He tells her to sit down, get more comfortable. She says it's more comfortable to stand right now. What with the baby and all.

The room is white. White sofa. White carpet. Antique white coffee table. Round, framed mirror hangs over sofa. She smells oil frying, thinks they must be having chicken. Or fish. She notices he is impatient, agitated. Not as easy going as other times. The room seems too pretty for him. Makes him look out of place, like a wet dog ordered to sit, not track mud through the kitchen. She says she wants to clear up some things she told another officer. "Rick is not the other guy you are looking for," she says.

"He seems to think that too," he answers. His hands are folded across his chest. He doesn't sit down either. Keeps the authoritarian air intact. Remains in charge. In control. What with this clearly not a social call and all.

"He was with me last night," she says.

He does not show surprise. He does not know about the college boy being found. The news has not yet reached him. Or her. "And about what time would that be?"

She notes that he is not writing anything down. Wonders if that is important. If what she says will stick. He is acting like he doesn't believe her. "From about eight on," she says. "While

A.J. was out."

"That's what his girlfriend is saying too," he answers. "Chase said he was with her. I spoke to her on the phone. Earlier today. Found her at his grandmother's place."

She keeps herself steady and focused. Rick had told her not to fluster in front of him. "She's just trying to cover up for him because he wasn't home," she answers. "She doesn't know where he was. She doesn't want it to get out that he might have been, you know, with someone else."

"And is there anyone who might have seen the two of you together last night?"

She wants to explain about the baby. That it might be Rick's. But she holds herself back. Something stops her about talking too much. In case stories have to change again. Or again. "We've been seeing each other for a while," she says. "A.J. don't know. Chase don't know. We don't want either of them to find out. Rick ain't the guy you're looking for. A.J.'s got a lot of friends, you know. He could have been out drinking with any of them."

"But you know we are looking for another guy?"

"That's what I heard," she says. "Police said there were four guys knocking each other up."

"I don't have my notes here with me," he answers, "but I seem to recall you telling an officer at the hospital that he should check with Rick. Rick was the key to this."

His mind floats elsewhere. Away from her. Away from the case. He has his own troubles inside. In his home. His life. He thinks about the argument he walked away from in the kitchen, the words between Ethan and Emma. Ethan did not come home last night. Came back this morning without any explanation.

She holds herself steady. Looks at the mirror over the couch. She can't see her reflection. Only the side of him, his nose, his mustache, the top of his belly. "We had an argument last night," she says. "I was angry at him. That's why I said that."

"Well, you know I'd like to believe you," he says. "But I got a lot of conflicting stories here. I got two guys in the hospital with a few holes in their heads, both of whom say the other started it. And on top of it, I got a victim who says your friend Rick was the other perpetrator. He identified the photo we got on file for him for the robbery a few months ago. Now I'm not sure whom I should believe here. Why don't you tell me why I should believe you?"

"Well, the thing is, you know. A.J. and I are married. Rick and Chase ain't. I'm telling you because I know you're friends of A.J.'s family and all. I know that Rick wasn't involved in splitting that guy's head open. I just don't want it to hurt Chase, you know. And A.J. gets crazy sometimes. You know that. This is all A.J.'s doin'. A.J.'s done got us all in a big mess. If A.J. finds out I said that to someone, he's gonna take it out on me."

He takes a deep breath. He doesn't want to continue, knows he must. "You realize your statement could be putting you in jeopardy," he says. "If you're covering up something. You realize you could lose custody of that baby before it's even born."

"I know," she says. He watches the news sink into her skin. She looks defeated, but continues. "Rick won't there," she says. "He was with me. We want to get out of this place together. We've been planning on Florida. Finding a place in Florida after the baby is born. And we can get the charges cleared on that Red Lobster thing." She senses that she's not making any headway, so she trembles her head, makes her eyes tear, tries her best to be feminine, vulnerable. "A.J. don't love me. Chase and Rick been having problems. We want to start over, you know. Clean slate. Rick ain't the guy you lookin' for, Mr. DeWitt. I know that. We're planning to leave this town as soon as we can."

25

He does not move until the ambulance leaves, until the boy has been taken away. The light is growing dimmer. He walks over to the officer, offers the church as a source of light to help the investigation, but they discover, once the outside lights are turned on, that it is too far to cast anything more than shadows. So he drives his car (Lexus, gray, leased) and parks it on the path, leaves the headlights on.

By the time he is parked more officers have arrived. The crime scene is roped off with yellow plastic tape. The female officer recounts discovering the boy. There is blood on her uniform where she wiped her hands. The cyclists answer questions. Why they were biking the path. He explains his own part in the tragedy—calling 911, how the boy looked when he arrived at the fence. The police have also positioned their cars to cast their lights against the fence. The gravel path is photographed some more, combed for evidence. A bar of the fence is removed, wrapped in plastic sheeting, positioned into the back of a police van. The night closes in around them. He casts his eyes over the ground, thinking he will find imprints of the boy's life.

Another officer approaches him. Asks him his whereabouts during the day. He explains that he helps out some mornings at the retirement home not far from his apartment. He ran errands after that. And at the chapel you cannot see this portion of the fence because of the slope of the hill. He knows the officer is trying to absolve him of any guilt, but he feels the guilt already. He should have seen the boy. He should have found the boy. Even though, as he tells the officer, the cemetery grounds are only tended when the leaves obscure the tombstones. A man from the valley does that. Another officer remarks that technically the boy was not found on the chapel property—the land at this point belongs to Parker Mahonen—the woman who owns the horse farm on the southwestern slope. The two officers talk a moment about Mahonen—her nephew used to attend Walton High with one of the officer's daughters. The same officer mentions his daughters used to be in day care here. Back when Lois Thompson and Reverend Drake were at the chapel. It's a pity they took all that equipment down. He means the old tire swings that used to hang from the branches of the trees. He doesn't tell them they weren't taken down. The ropes rotted a season ago. The burns are still on the tree limbs. Where the bark has worn away.

The questions do not stop. Another officer arrives. Wants to know more answers. Finally, he makes his way back to the cyclists, offers to store their bikes in a back room at the chapel and drive them into town. They follow him, pushing their bikes up the slope. Around the cemetery stones. They are quiet now, reverential. He tells them he will be at the chapel most afternoons. Gives them his number to call to pick up the bikes. They walk back down to the path. At his car, an officer offers to take the cyclists back to town. It is the female officer who found the boy.

He watches them drive away. Soon the car lights are shut off. The yellow tape remains. He drives his car back to the chapel parking lot. He goes inside the chapel, walks to the windows on the south side of the building. He looks at the darkness outside, tries to imagine if he could have found the boy. Guilt has not yet left him. Another tragedy has arrived.

26

The facts are what stun him. The magnitude of the injuries. A college student beaten and tied to a fence. Left to die. Outside. Overnight. The dispatcher reaches him at home around 6:45 p.m. Teddy is eating dinner. His wife frowns when he excuses himself, takes the call.

This is what he hears: A credit card found on the crime site links the victim found beaten to the items discovered in the truck belonging to A.J.'s uncle. He wants to believe that there is another story other than what is unfolding. That A.J. wasn't involved in this. That at least the other incident removes his involvement with this one.

But it doesn't. The facts match too closely. In his gut he knows this is true. The truth mixes uneasily with his dinner: the chicken, baked potato, vinegary dressing on the salad. And the family argument has made his appetite disappear.

On his drive to the hospital he tries to unravel the motive. Self-defense hardly seems plausible in this instance. The report said the victim is barely over a hundred pounds. Smaller than A.J. If A.J. were defending himself he wouldn't have left the boy strung up to a fence. Doesn't make sense.

He tries to convince himself that it is drug-related. Maybe the college boy was selling drugs. Or buying. So far there has been no evidence to support that theory—no drugs were found on the site. No money. The victim's wallet was in the truck, not at the fence.

He thinks about the others involved: Kelly, hiding something. Her visit a few minutes ago makes that clear. Did she know about this? Is she hiding something else? Covering

110

up for A.J.? Rick? Or is she hiding something from A.J.? Or from his wife, Chase? And Chase, too. Is she covering up for Rick for some reason? And how are the other two kids picked up on Hogan linked to this? What were they doing with the college boy? Or were they even there?

What is clear to him is the blood and the gun and the card and the victim and A.J. What is clear is that they have been waiting for a crime to be discovered. And now it is here.

As he makes his way through the hospital lobby, he sees John Eaton and Steve Mulford, two officers from the county force. They shake hands and wait for the elevator. As they step inside, John says, "Jesus, I can't believe this guy is still alive."

There are already two other security guards on the floor. At the nurse's station John hands some paperwork to the nurse on duty. Then the three officers walk down the hall to the room.

This is what he remembers: his shoes squeaking, stopping, the boy in the emergency room, blood still seeping through the bandages, the sound of machines trying to help him breathe, a huddle of doctors by the door, one of them describing his chances. ("Slim, slim, very slim.")

Outside the emergency room the officers compare notes. Instead of waiting for the elevator, they decide to use the stairs.

They find A.J. in the room alone, looking at a magazine—*Field & Stream*. His eyes widen with recognition, narrow into thin lines as John begins to read him his rights. Teddy still wants to believe that such a crime is not possible by this young man. But the facts are what they are. And he can't be lenient. Not because his neighbor is his friend. His job is to find the truth. Stand behind it.

"I didn't do it, Mr. DeWitt," A.J. says. The officers wait till A.J. is dressed, then cuff his hands behind his back.

"This hurts me, A.J.," Teddy says. "Your uncle's not gonna understand this at all."

27

Tuesday

He does not suffer, though suffering surrounds him. His body is eliminating the nonessential. He breathes only to survive. Pain is felt by others around him, uncomfortably imagining the source of his wounds. The medic in the ambulance who sat beside him in the ride to the hospital will not look at his body for more than a few seconds at a time because of the damaged, mangled eye; the intern who responded when he first arrived in the emergency room will draw back with an audible gasp because of the discolored, pale condition of his skin and its swollen bluish-red patches; the nurse who washes his face and hands while a doctor searches his body for a response will imagine the discomfort the broken rib cage must have caused as it was crushed against his lung. The doctor, Chung-E Tseng, a forty-seven year-old physician who has worked at the hospital for twelve years, examines the cuts and wounds, the rising welts on his body. He disbelieves the report that circulates around the room—that the young man was discovered beaten, tied to a wooden fence out on Skyline Mount. The injuries he finds are more in common to those sustained in an automobile crash. The neck and head wounds disturb him the most because the boy is still alive, which must have meant that the damage was not swift and merciless, but lingering. As she helps the doctor administer a series of tests to determine the young man's physical reaction to pain, the nurse, fifty-two year-old Mabel Schoenbrot, cannot disassociate herself from the hatred that must have been directed at the patient. One side of his head is beaten in several inches. What could have caused something so vile and intense? She steadies herself by drawing in a series of long, moist breaths through her face mask, before she tests the area around the patient's Achilles tendon.

A sexual assault examination is performed. Hair and fingernail samples are collected; swabs gather cultures from inside his nose, ears, and lips. The cotton sticks are dropped into plastic bags, labeled, left on top of a counter. The tests no longer matter to him. They are of his physical form. He will fail them all. His brain stem is seriously damaged. His vital functions—heartbeat, breathing, temperature control—are critically impaired. It is impossible to operate to save him. There are no signs of reflexes, no response to external stimuli. His body has begun a journey even though others still struggle with the fear of it. He is moved into a curtained room. The lodged tooth in his windpipe is discovered, removed. An incision is made in his throat, a tube is inserted to keep the airway open. His breathing is regulated, monitored. He encounters strange machines with blinking lights, whirling discs, digital readouts, even as the rush of his own deterioration continues. His blood is more acidic. Bacteria begins its invasion. His body accepts that it cannot walk, cannot swallow, that it is helpless, dependent on others. Another physician, examining the condition of his skull, will insert a drain to reduce the pressure caused by his swollen membranes against the bony encasement, the tissues folding and cramping against each other, even as his thoughts, his emotions, his sensations move to another plane of existence.

He does not feel a sense of betrayal, nor of hate, nor of a need for revenge. He has begun a journey beyond his sense of self, beyond the personal level of his consciousness. He has progressed beyond the turbulence, the chaos that surrounds him. He has moved beyond his denial, anger, depression. There is an empty fullness to him in his physical form, a turning inward, a quality of radiance that Mabel will notice first, a strange opalescence as his body empties its energy into his soul. It reminds her of when her sister died. When the cancer could no longer be stopped. And fate was accepted.

But he has not yet surrendered. He is not empty of hope.

Hope is what remains in him. He is not finished, yet, with hope.

28

Tuesday

The wind rises. Leaves beat, flap, like wings that can't fly, dropping to the ground as they are yanked, sucked from branches. Up goes a breeze and down again, rising like a flock of birds disturbed. The sky over the valley is both light and dark, shapes spectral, the meadow silvery. Far off the familiar sound of a car stops on a gravel path.

It is late when the officers reach the trailer. When Chase comes to the door, Teddy, the taller of the two, apologizes for waking her. He informs her that he is here on official business. He inquires where her boyfriend is.

"He's not here," she says. Her voice is tiny, small, full of knowledge.

"Do you know where we might find him?"

"I haven't seen him since this morning," she says. She touches her hair, face. Worry comes to her. "I know he didn't show up for work today, either."

He does not think she is hiding anything, but notices she moves back from the light. "We have a few more questions for you as well," he says. "We can do them here if you like. Unless you think you can find someone for the baby."

"Is there a problem?" she asks. Her face is confused, tired. She seems hollow, like the wind is blowing through her.

Something has left her. Teddy notices that. Some quality she wishes returned. "Yes," he answers. "There's a problem."

Inside, she sits on the couch. He remains standing. She looks up at him. "He was here with me," she answers.

"Well, so far we have four other sources who can also identify being with your boyfriend at that time last evening.

May I remind you that if any of your answers are found untruthful, you face the likelihood of losing custody of your child. Now, I'll ask you again. Do you have any knowledge of where your boyfriend might have been about midnight to two a.m. this morning?"

She slowly bows her head. Her eyes well up with tears. She wishes his granny was here. Guiding her. Taking charge. Someone to help her out. She doesn't understand how any of this trouble came to her. "They went drinking," she says. "I was only trying to keep him out of trouble."

29

Tuesday

Later, she will recall this as the beginning of her own journey. Her memory is vivid of when the news came to her. She knew something had changed. She was sitting at the vanity upstairs in her bedroom. She had started to put on lotion—her hands were chapped from cleaning in the kitchen—but she had not actually reached out to grab the bottle. She had noticed the dust on the mirrored surface of the table, thought about cleaning it. Then noticed the way the light of the lamp in the left corner highlighted the dust on Naomi's collection of ceramic angels. She had collected them since she was six. There were close to thirty small figurines assembled on four tiers of shelving. Naomi could detail the place and date she had acquired each angel. It wasn't a religious obsession. More like a hobby, like collecting Christmas ornaments. Things that looked pretty together. A band of angels bearing musical instruments. Trumpeting beauty: physical, faithful.

She had never considered herself a religious woman. She went to church twice a week, sang in the choir since she was seven. It gave her a sense of belonging, something her marriage had not. It was where she had first met Naomi, twenty years ago, when she came to be the new organist. She didn't consider it an act of God that they met this way. That would be foolish. She considered herself more practical, grounded. Not so spiritual.

But something she couldn't explain was at work that night.

What caught her attention first was the dust on the seated angel playing a guitar—in the light, the white collar looked grayish. As she was reaching out for it, she noticed dust collected in the harp strings of another angel. More at the base of the horn of another's long trumpet. Something, she will later say, made her reach to the angel Naomi referred to as Gabriel, the one with the trumpet. She stroked her thumb over the frame of the horn and the phone rang. She knew Naomi would not answer the phone. She was downstairs, making muffins to serve the four guests in the morning.

She thought it was someone calling to make a reservation, then realized that couldn't be the case—the reservation-line only rang downstairs in the office space Naomi had assembled in the kitchen, not in the bedroom. Her next thought was that it was Danny. She made her way across the room, barefoot on the carpet, thinking about saying to him: "I thought you must have gotten lucky with someone," or "I was just about to try the FBI next."

The news lasted only a few seconds. It was the officer she had spoken to earlier in the afternoon, calling her to tell her information about her friend. She made only a few words out. A wave of noise seemed to overcome her as she clutched at words: hospital, beating, Danny, coma.

She does not remember the sweater she chose. Or that she left the house without her wallet. She does not remember the drive to the hospital, or that the car stalled on Clifton and that she had to pull over and restart it. She remembers instead waiting at the bank of elevators, waiting for what seemed like a interminably long time since the hospital seemed empty, inactive.

What she remembers most was the moment she entered his room. She felt a presence of energy—a pulse of light or a spark of radiation—even before her eyes found him in the bed. The energy, the spark, the light, the pulse seemed to recognize her. And then it was gone, as if a bird had been disturbed and taken flight.

His body was covered by a white sheet. His forehead and hair disappeared behind a wide, white bandage. Closer, she could detect small cuts above the bridge of his nose, along the cheekbones, the slope of his jaw to his chin. His nose was bluish. His eyes were closed. One eye seemed enlarged, his eyelashes disappearing into the swollen flesh. He was on a respirator. IV tubes ran into needles and into the veins of an arm. Tubes ran in and out of his throat. A monitor registered his heart, sent an electronic beep into the room, created an unwelcomed suspense.

She would remember the qualities about him more than the actual damages. She would recall the room seeming to glow again, as if a spirit returned to the room. She will swear that she saw his face move into a small smile when she began speaking to him—silly, nonsensical things like, "Oh hon, things will be okay."—while stroking the flesh of the arm that was exposed above the sheet. At one point she closed her eyes to gather her own strength. In her mind's eye a brilliant light dawned, like an eclipse of the sun at the moment when the eclipse is almost over. When she opened her eyes she thought his skin looked radiant, as if some divine force were with her. Or within him.

30

Tuesday

The specimen is taken in the emergency room. Tuesday. When the patient arrives at the hospital. From the bright red blood which drains from his ear a syringe is used to extract a few drops. The drops are placed in a test tube and capped. The nurse, Ellen Chu, places a white adhesive strip with a series of numbers on the tube. The numbers are the code which identifies the patient. She does not remain in the emergency room, though she lingers longer than she would under normal circumstances. Something about the facts being revealed make her stay, see if there is any hope in reviving him. Is it true he was left there overnight? Is it true he was conscious when he was tied to the fence? Is it true he might have not been unconscious after the beating, that time and pain were played out to him in heartbeats?

When she can take no more she leaves the room. She has been on duty since one o'clock that afternoon. She walks the test tube to the nurses station. She fills out a request form. She wraps it around the tube, secures it in place with a rubber band, twisted around the glass shaft. She places the tube in a brown cylinder, leaves it in the out box to be picked up.

An hour later, Emilio Montano, a runner, picks up the cylinder along with other items: envelopes, bills, magazines, which are to be delivered to other floors of the building. Or to other buildings on campus. Or elsewhere. To other cities, states. Emilio picks up other items from the ground floor. The cylinder stays on the cart. He takes the elevator in the old wing, makes deliveries and pick ups on the second floor. He does the same for the next floor. And in a room on the third floor—37D.

There he leaves the cylinder in a refrigerated unit. He picks up the outgoing mail from a wire basket.

The cylinder remains in the unit for another hour until Mohammad Bari, an intern, logs the specimen on a record which is kept on a clipboard at the front desk of the lab. Mohammad doesn't evaluate the specimen, or even open the refrigerator unit to see if it is still there. His job is paperwork. The cylinder waits another fifteen minutes until Radu Ariton, a student technician, arrives. Radu, from a village outside Madras, India, is on a scholarship exchange program, a senior biology major who works part-time in the hospital. A grant from his department and the school of medicine has set up this lab. He takes a sample of blood from the vial, places it in a cartridge. He places the cartridge into a centrifuge. He sets a timer for ten minutes, lets the centrifuge run. He knows nothing about the identity of the patient, only what he is looking for inside the blood.

The centrifuge stops. He takes the cartridge out, checks the color of the sample. He records the result next to the log which identifies the patient's hospital number. The results are positive. He repeats the process one more time. Blood sample, cartridge, centrifuge, timer. Ten minutes later, the blood result is again positive.

He writes the result of the test on the form which arrived with the blood sample. He places the form in an interoffice envelope, writes "RUSH" in bold, red letters. Places the envelope into the lab out box. He places the unused blood sample in the refrigerator unit. Thirty minutes later Emilio makes a pickup from the department. He stops at other departments, mailboxes, other floors. Even though he carries an envelope that reads "RUSH."

An hour later the envelope with the results is delivered to the nurses station of the emergency room.

Another nurse, Bill Chainey, logs the results of the test onto another form. The form is inserted into a patient's file. It will be another five hours before a physician reads the result. Thirteen hours will have passed since the sample was first taken from the patient. It has become another day.

The diagnosis will not reach the patient first. Or his family. First, a doctor will make a phone call to the police station and ask to speak to the sheriff. He will find the sheriff at home. Only then will he reveal the results of the blood test indicate that the patient, the victim found earlier the evening before, is HIV-positive. He will suggest that anyone who made contact with the victim be put immediately on a drug. "As a precaution," he says. "To keep the virus from infecting."

31

Wednesday

The moment is best in the minutes just before sunrise. He can work quick, efficiently, his technique down to swipes across the stencil. They expect him to strike at other times. In the darkness. In the night. Not just as people are rising, moving clumsily out of sleep. If any light still burns it is someone cramming in the last minutes before an exam, rime of frost on the window refracting the beams. Not seeking him out. Eyes travel down the lines of print, not outside to the lawns.

He is a sophomore. His name is Geoff. He is from Oklahoma City. Or a suburb near there. He is planning to declare his major next year. Finance. Or marketing. He will probably work in real estate. Like his father.

This morning he uses red paint. He always uses red paint. He knows he will soon have to start buying paint in different stores. Or in another town. Or stop for a while. The security department is looking for him. The local police are involved. They think him a criminal. A vandal.

He sprays the sidewalk in front of the hospital entrance. He crouches, like he has dropped coins, pulls the can and the stencil from his jacket, paints. Swipe, swipe, swipe. There are security cameras. A guard. But they will not see him. They do not expect him here. Or now.

L-O-V-E. Block letters. Times New Roman type face. Height: six inches. Each letter four inches wide. Red. Bright red. The stencil folds easily, hides in his jacket. The spray can harder to disguise. He carries it in a plastic shopping bag.

Some say that he is defacing property. Others call him a hero, a visionary. He sees himself only as someone caught up in something other than what it was intended to be. The meanings others attach are not his. He is not who they think he is: a religious fanatic, a frustrated student, a radical free-thinker.

It started as a message for his girlfriend, Holly. He wrote "L-O-V-E" on the steps of her dormitory so that she could see it from her third floor window the next morning. Her birthday. In bright red paint. He called her, asked her if she saw the message. Explained why he did it. L-O-V-E.

The next night she left him a message. She swiped a red "L-O-V-E" back for him. She worked quickly, in the dark, the technique and timing not perfected. She left her mark on the sidewalk in front of the men's dorm. She hid in the bushes after she painted, frightened someone might discover her.

It would have ended there had it not been for the student newspaper. A front page story, with photos, commending and berating the prank. University officials demanded that the "bandit" come forward, confess. Absolution would be complete.

But the next day "F-E-A-R" appeared on the wall of the Chemistry building. In silver letters. That was not their doing. It was a statement from someone else. The security department painted over the letters—just like the notes they had left for each other—but that night the two of them, dressed in black, wrote "L-O-V-E" in red paint on the steps in front of Chemistry building. To show it wasn't them. That this was their signature. Their tag. Not something else. No other meaning implied.

He continued on without her. Writing "L-O-V-E" on the path she took through campus. He chose the places for her. So that she would see them. He skipped days, worked sporadically, which kept her guessing when she would discover the next one.

This is what happened: She grew worried he would be discovered. They fought. He told her to stop acting so righteous, pious. She threatened to turn him in. He told her that she could be expelled too. She was in on it. From the start. Warning signs were posted around campus. The student paper ran a story that the crime was a misdemeanor, punishable by up to six months imprisonment and/or a fine. If the damages continued, the fine could escalate. Ten years imprisonment. He was sought after. He became an icon. A campus legend. Everyone wanted to know who he was. They wanted him found.

She told him she would not see him until he stopped. This had gone too far.

L-O-V-E. This is what he thinks. It hurts. It frees. It transcends arguments. If she loves him she will not back away. She will stand by him. Isn't that love? Or does love mean he will change for her? Does he wait for her to come back? Or does he stop to go back to her? How strong is love apart from love?

As he leaves the hospital steps he feels a pang of loneliness. Something he has not felt before. He has not seen her for five days. They have not talked to each other either. He feels a desperation enter him. His eyes grow heavy. He misses her. He sees her before him: her hazel eyes, the heart-shaped face, the long lines of her neck, legs, the bones of her pelvis. He thinks he will go back to the dorm and sleep. Then call her. Who else would love him after they learned of this? He only wants her to know what he is thinking. L-O-V-E. That's it. That's all. He wants her to know that he loves her.

32

Wednesday

She has not spent the evening thinking about the crime, the beating, or who could have possibly done this to him and why. That happened her first moments at the hospital—with the staff on duty, a policeman standing outside the room, with a detective she spoke to on the phone. She no longer worries about what pain he might feel—the blood soaking through his bandages, the damaged eye, the fact that his rib cage and skull have been crushed into pieces.

She has cleared the questions from her mind, regained her composure, thought of herself as his friend, someone to keep him company until family arrives, someone to stand beside him in a crisis. To pass the time she has read aloud items from the local newspaper, articles from *Time* or *People*, magazines she found in the hallway. For a while, in the early hours, she napped in the chair, awakened only by the movement of a nurse or an intern into the room to check his status. Awake, she sits and breathes with him when she is not reading, adapting her own rhythm to his and the ventilator. She stays with him till early morning, when his aunt and her boyfriend arrive from Knoxville.

Roxy arrives with a clacking of her heels on the slick floor of the hospital. She is short and blond, has an aggressive temperament that a generation removed softened into Danny's more inquisitive consciousness. His features are reflected in hers: The cheeks are fuller, the eyes green, not blue, the apple-like shape the same, a dimple splitting the chin. Her boyfriend, Wayne, seems from another world. He is tall, lanky, a cowboy who reeks of stale smoke and beer. He is her quiet half.

She hugs Roxy when she arrives at the room. They kiss. Squeeze hands. Shake heads. Re-introduce one another. She as the girl who kept the stables in order years ago; Roxy as the red-haired girl with the palomino jumper—Ironic. Wayne stays in the background. Silent, removed.

Roxy is too agitated to remain in his room. She looks at him once in the bed, goes out into the hall. She positions herself in front of the nurses station in the middle of the hall. Wayne follows, leans against a wall, his thumbs hooked through the belt loops of his jeans. Roxy keeps asking "But what are his chances?" of a succession of staff, moving with an increasingly shrill voice from one person to the next with, "Well, who can tell me then?" until a man arrives from another floor who identifies himself as Dr. Donald Carberry, the hospital's program coordinator, the person who handles administrative matters with the University's medical school. He walks with her toward Danny's room. Wayne stays in place, his eyes following them.

Dr. Carberry is not who she wants to talk to. He does not know all the details of the case, where the fractures and broken bones and ruptures are, why his breathing is impaired, why he is unconscious, what has been discovered about her nephew. She wants his doctor, his surgeon, his brain specialist. The person who is supervising his care. Someone who can give her facts. Chances. Not him. But he has sought her out. He reaches out to touch her at the elbow, thinking it will ease the tension. "There are reporters calling me for details," he says to Roxy.

"Reporters? What the hell for?" she asks. Her eyes dart back and forth. She wants answers, not complications.

"The hospital should release a statement about the patient. There have been questions from reporters over whether this was a hate crime," he says. His voice is not soothing, more business-like, severed.

"Well, of course it is a hate crime," Roxy says. Her back has stiffened. Her eyes are glassy, as if she is annoyed by the continual questioning of a child. "What kind of friend would do this to him?"

"You don't seem to understand," he says. "They are questioning his sexuality—whether it could have been motivated by some kind of bias—some kind of anti-gay sentiment?"

"Anti-gay?" she answers. Her hand finds the necklace at her throat. She twirls the icy green stone between her thumb and first finger. Behind her an orderly pushes a cart of supplies. Another doctor passes by without noticing them.

"They seem to think since Danny was gay the beating was hate-motivated," he says. He straightens his posture, as if stress has been applied to his spine. One hand is squeezed around a clipboard. The other hand hidden in the pocket of the white hospital jacket he wears.

"I don't think this should be discussed outside of the family," she says. "This is not a matter for reporters. Or the media."

"But there's been a quote from a member of the gay campus group that says he was a member," he says. "He was at a planning meeting earlier Monday. A girl from the campus newspaper has already called asking for confirmation that he is gay."

"This is personal information," she says. Her hand falls away from her neck. She twists her head back and forth, throwing glances at Wayne. "This is not for the media to report."

"But if this is a hate crime," he says. "The issue will have to be addressed at some point. It's only fair."

"Fair?" she says. "Do you think the trash who beat him thought they were being fair to his mother and father, his brother, to us?" She folds her hands across her breasts as if she is being forceful. "This should be his mother's decision," she adds. "Not mine. We're not agreeing to releasing any statement like this until she arrives."

Leah has overheard the exchange. She stood by the door when she heard them talking outside. She hadn't been convinced herself that the beating could have been due to Danny's sexuality. Not until now. She steps out of the room into the hall, breaking the space, the tension, between Roxy and Dr. Carberry. "He often talked about how he wanted to fit into the community here," she says.

Roxy shifts toward her. Dr. Carberry regards her as if she is an ally, holds back his surprise. But she stands closer to Roxy, letting him know she is with the family in this. "He didn't want people to treat him differently because he was gay," she says. "But if this happened because someone hated him for no other reason because he is gay, then someone has to speak out about it. That's not right. That's not fair. If that's the case, then I'll talk to anyone about Danny." She gathers her breath, reins in her caution, keeps the focus on Danny, not herself. "I'll tell them what a good friend he's been to me since he came to this town. Tell them they can call me. I run the B&B over on Spring Street. All kinds of people stay there. White. Black. Gay. Even a few foreigners. We let all kinds of people come visit this town. Some of them decide to live here, too. You tell anyone who wants to talk about Danny that they can call me. I'll tell them a few things or two. I'll be honest about it. Just like Danny would."

33

The crime shocks the town and the University. A small item appears in the daily newspaper of a student beaten and left to die on Skyline Mount, near the old cemetery of the Upper White Chapel. The student is not identified, nor are any clues provided of the assailants. On campus security guards are more visible on the quad. Students soon hear the victim was a freshman. Gossip spreads other details. One arrest already. The student left overnight tied to the fence.

There are cars parked on the path before Reverend Fletcher arrives at the chapel. He parks in the back, unlocks the back door. He has skipped his duties at the retirement home this morning. He has not slept the night. His eyes are puffy, his mind cloudy.

He goes to the south window of the chapel, looks down the slope. He cannot see the fence. Only the parked cars. There are four. Someone walks along the slope of the cemetery—a woman wearing jeans, canvas jacket. She carries a camera, a large camera case on her shoulder. He sees her position the chapel in the viewfinder of her camera. She changes the position of the camera. He imagines he hears the shutters clicking at a rapid pace.

In a few minutes the woman is inside the chapel, taking more pictures. He has retreated to his office in the back. He does not try to stop her taking pictures. It is a beautiful chapel. It is why people come here. Tourists here throughout the seasons. This is a chapel that has been photographed many times.

The photographer finds him in the office. She asks him

some questions about the chapel. When was it built? (This one, the wooden and brick structure, in 1850, before the Civil War. The first one was built on the site in 1689.) Why the red door? (He thinks it has been like that since the Civil War.) Is anyone famous buried in the cemetery? (On the north side, the Ogden family, who first owned the land here. The small white footstones are soldiers buried during the Civil War, when the chapel was used as a hospital.) What time was the boy found? He answers that he can only answer questions about the chapel, advises her to talk to the police about the student. She tries to get more information from him. (Any suspects? What evidence was found?) Again he tells her to contact the local police.

When she leaves he returns to the south window. Another car has arrived. Someone else is taking pictures. He remembers walking down the slope, his fear so thick it was like moving through water. The boy was motionless except with the wind moving through him. His hair. His shirt. Filling his lungs with pain.

He returns to his office, checks the chapel calendar. There are two wedding rehearsals at the end of the week. Two weddings on Saturday, back to back. On the answering machine is a message from the florist, Nancy Gambone. She heard that something happened at the chapel last night. Could he give her a call? He does not call her back. He gets his coat. Walks outside. He thinks about raking leaves even though it is not his job. Then decides the yellow and brown and red leaves seem to be in the right places. The way God would want it to be. He walks through the cemetery. Looks down at the slope. Then walks more through the cemetery.

Legend has it that the Indians made the place sacred. Buried their ancestors here. Called it Senechiaha, meaning small stones at big sky. Praising the beauty of the land. The generosity of the spirits who let them dwell here. The Indians burned the first chapel to the ground. The settlers were massacred. The chapel remained in ruins for more than thirty years. The next settlement was in the valley. Where the town and the University began. Another generation rebuilt the chapel. A place for locals, away from the University.

On the east slope he looks down at the river bed at the slope of the mountain, the water catching sunlight like tinsel. The stacks of the cement factory chug white clouds out into the sky. If he looks close enough, he can see cars moving along the roads.

At his feet lies buried the Meeteers, a Swedish family who perished in a town fire in 1763. Mother, father, two sons, one daughter. His emptiness begins to fill with misery. He looks away again, out against the slope. He sees someone approaching him. Someone with more questions. What does he say now? What role does God want him to play?

34

Wednesday

Already the myth has begun. A statement made by the sheriff—
or the chief of police—to a reporter—or perhaps a nurse at the
hospital to an intern—says the boy was found tied to the fence
like a scarecrow.

"A scarecrow?" someone else asks, maybe an editor, or a
student who works in a lab.

The deconstruction begins as quickly as the construction
starts. "Like his arms were outstretched? His legs spread-
eagle?"

The story spreads. It is bigger than the fire in the
kindergarten annex four years ago, or the scandal where the
mayor and two councilmen were accused of taking kickbacks
from a construction company. Stuart does not hear about the
beating until he reads an e-mail from Colin, another member of
the Caucus, who heard about it when the news spread through
the dormitory. He calls the police station to tell them what
he knows. That he saw Danny twice the day he was assaulted.
Once on campus to warn his about the rise in violence against
gays in this town. Another time at a campus meeting. "We
ate together afterwards," he said to the investigator on the
phone. "Why does someone have to get beaten or killed before
someone listens to us? I complained to the police last week
about this. This shouldn't have happened."

The investigators do not find him till noon. Two in uniform.
One with a gut, the other with a crewcut. The details they want
are not about the beating but about Danny. They ask him about
Danny's drinking habits, about any drugs he took and where
he got them, about the frequency of his sexual activity and

where he met his partners. Stuart plays coy on as much as he feels necessary. "Of course he has sex," Stuart answers. "He's a twenty year-old man. Everyone in this town has sex. Why are you trying to find something *wrong* with that? This attack happened because the state legislature has failed to pass a hate crimes bill, failed to offer gay men and lesbians protection under the laws. I have heard over and over that nothing like that happens here because someone is gay. Guess what? You're wrong. And I am letting everyone I know about this know that this state should be accountable for this crime."

The investigators try another tactic, ask Stuart to talk about himself. They see a well-groomed young man, a bit too smug with his education. He identifies himself as twenty-one, a senior, a psychology major from New Bern, North Carolina. They ask him for other details: his date of birth, what kind of car he drives. He says he has known Danny for three months, since orientation day when Danny appeared at the registration table in the student union inquiring about the theater productions the Ad Hoc players planned for this year. Danny was thinking about helping out after the first semester, once he got his bearings. He describes Danny as the type of guy who pays in cash rather than credit card, wore expensive clothes that didn't look expensive. He states he never saw him drunk. Then begins asking the officers questions. Are the suspects students? Townies? Did Danny know them before the beating?

The taller officer, the one with the gut, says the meeting might have taken place at a bar off campus. They hit Stuart with more questions? What bars did Danny go to? Did he have a habit of drinking?

After speaking with Stuart, the investigators (Hector Quintero and Adam Hardiman, age thirty and thirty-three, two years and seven years on the force, respectively) arrive at the 110 North Pine, the home address of David Grzelewski, the bartender on duty at the Starlite Bar and Grill the night the victim and suspects were believed to have met one another. The purpose of this visit is to interview David, follow up on information that has been previously obtained by one of the suspects and the manager of the bar, Karla Kellemaris, thirty-eight, the daughter of the owner, Steve Kellemaris.

David identifies himself as twenty-six, a resident of the town for eight years, a graduate of the University but a dropout of the law school. He has dark eyes, a thin body, and a head of wiry hair which he pulls back into a pony tail. He advises the investigators he has a somewhat limited knowledge regarding Danny. David says Danny had been to the bar a few times, and can't imagine he would have done anything to provoke his own death. He says Danny showed no sexual interest in him. "He wasn't a big parader," he says. "He wasn't trying to come on to you. I don't think he was the kind of kid making random advances." He believes the gay community here is reserved and respectable, mostly underground. He states he does not know of anyone that Danny might have been involved with sexually.

David identifies himself as straight and single, a lapsed Baptist. No girlfriend to speak of, since the last one, Jodi Ann Ridings, a girl who used to work at the University but didn't like him working at the club. He states that his shift at the club starts at 10 p.m. Goes to 4 a.m. Danny arrived at the bar at approximately 10:30 p.m. He states that the two guys he left the bar with arrived later, around 11:30 p.m.

He tells the investigators that he does not remember if the suspects had been to the bar before. He says the night in question they ordered a pitcher of beer and paid for it in coins. He states that their hands were dirty, dirt under their fingernails. He describes them as both short, one cute, the other with big ears. He identifies the suspects when investigators show him photographs. He says none of the three appeared drunk when they left the bar.

Next the investigators go to 2200 Old Union Highway, ask to speak to the one of the workers on the roofing project. They gather in the driveway, near the parked trucks. They speak to Moses Cassell, age thirty-two, African-American. Moses tells the investigators that he has worked for B.R. Construction & Roofing for two years. Says he knows the suspects from work only. Worked with them a couple of times on prior jobs. Says

135

he cannot provide any insights into their lives. "We never talked about their favorite movies, favorite music, shit like that." Moses says he found them to be pretty dull except when they were cranky on the job. "But most of the guys are here. Nobody likes this kind of work."

Moses is a big man with an educated voice, diction a little too perfect, would say it comes from Bible reading and church if he were asked (which he is not). He tells the officers he has not seen the suspects in over two weeks. Moses says, "A.J. had a lot of anger, more that most kids. I could imagine him beating someone up, but not like that."

Moses says the suspects used foul language on the job. "But who doesn't." A.J. particularly was prone to start fights. "He loved to call people names. Wus. Faggot. Dickhead. Things like that."

Moses says he heard the suspects were big partiers, used drugs—crank mostly—but so do most of the kids in this town. He says he believes that A.J. was also involved in the sale of pharmaceutical type drugs that were stolen in some manner. Moses does not offer any more details when pressed. Other than to say he never saw any prescription bottles or other types of drugs in the suspect's possession. Then he adds that he overheard A.J. once brag to Rick, "That's the quickest amount I ever made."

Moses says he never bought any drugs from A.J. He does recall that when he was having chronic hand pain that A.J. gave him a pill to try because the Advil he had taken didn't work. He does not recall if the pill came from a prescription bottle or not. "It's not too bad if you use a nail gun," he says. "But if you use a hammer for eight hours a day you can't even turn a doorknob when you're through."

"Did you check the nails in the guy's hands?" Moses asks the investigators.

"Nails?" Officer Quintero responds.

"I heard they strung him up like Jesus," Moses says. "Don't understand why anyone would do shit like that. You should check the nails to see if they match the company ones."

35

Wednesday

"I had four phone calls from the police yesterday and a couple from some reporters already this morning," Risa says, following Leah up the stairs. Leah tries to keep her steps light, without breaking sound. She doesn't know why. Because it might be disrespectful, somehow.

"I went in and fed the cat last night, when I heard about it," Risa adds, when they reach the door. "It's just awful. Awful. Do they know who did this?"

"I don't think so," she answers.

She waits while Risa unlocks the door of Danny's apartment. Risa Wald is over thirty, pale-faced, wears black eyeglasses with thick lenses. She is dressed in loose fitting cotton clothes, her long, black hair braided, hanging behind her back. Risa and her husband are two of the University alumni who have remained in town after graduating, buying up properties like small apartment buildings and renovating them. "I'm sorry to surprise you like this but I was on my way back from the hospital. I was worried about his cat."

Chloe is at the door when Risa opens it. She runs out into the hall, stops, rubs against Leah's legs.

"The police were asking me if I had a picture of him," Risa says. "Why would I have a picture of him? I suppose we could look to see if there is something here."

"His aunt gave one to somebody at the hospital," she says. "I think they have that one. And some that the University gave them."

"This is such a shame," Risa says. She crouches to the floor, runs her hand across Chloe's back. Her braid flaps to her shoulder. "He seemed like such a good fella."

They exchange details on the crime when they reach the kitchen—Was he really beaten as badly as they said? Are they certain about the suspects? Squeezed between the phone and the refrigerator, Leah notices a small bulletin board. There is a picture of Danny and his younger brother Luke at a picnic table, taken, she thinks, when their family went camping at Yosemite. A postcard of a shirtless man, a small rainbow magnet, a headline cut out of a newspaper that reads, "BE NOT AFRAID." Next to it is a schedule of the movies playing this semester at the downstairs cinema of the student center, a list of phone numbers, including her own. And Pop's business card: *Pop's Class Act. Limousine for hire.*

Leah looks in the cabinets beneath the sink. The hinges squeak. An eerie, penetrating sound. It makes them stop, smile at each other awkwardly. There is a box of detergent, a roll of paper towels, and a bottle of whiskey, unopened—probably a gift from someone. Leah finds what she wants in a closet opposite the refrigerator. "There it is," she says. She lifts the cat carrier from the bottom of the closet, places it onto the counter.

"She's such a beautiful cat," Risa says. "Where did he find her?"

"She's one of Anne Herbert's cats," Leah answers. "One of the babies."

"She's gotten awfully big," Risa says. "You should take some of the food, too. And the bowls. It'll help her adjust to a new place if she's got her same bowls."

Leah lifts the bowls off the floor, rinses them in the sink. On the windowsill she notices a small ceramic figurine. It's the angel Naomi gave Danny when he moved into the apartment— for good luck. She remembers the story that he told them one night while they were watching TV in the common room—about the year he was an angel in the Christmas pageant at the church. He was five years old. His wings had fallen off on the drive to the church. Backstage he had started to cry because the wings were broken. His mother had tried to

138

pin them back on but they kept falling off. He kept crying more and more. Finally, she found a yardstick, broke it in half, taped and stapled pieces of an old choir robe to them. On stage, he carried the sticks beneath his arms until it was time to appear as the angel. He stretched his arms out over his head and the audience applauded. He was the biggest little angel they had ever had in the church.

Risa packs the cat food in a plastic sack she found beneath the sink. Leah catches Chloe, lifts her up, holds her against her chest. She hears her purring. Like a motor. Tells her she's safe. Loved. Everything will be all right.

Risa helps put her in the carrier. The phone rings. The two women tense. Look at each other. The cat moves deeper into the carrier. As if hiding. They let the phone ring six times. Then it stops. "It's like a ghost is here already," Risa says. She darts her eyes around the room. Her eyeglasses look like binoculars, zoomed in expecting one to appear.

Leah lifts the cat carrier off the counter, follows Risa out the door. Waits while she locks it.

Outside the day has grown bright, warmer. Gusts send little spikes of chill. The smell of the ground mixes with the smell of the tar of the parking lot. At Leah's car, Risa helps her put the carrier on the seat. The door creaks as it is shut. It is a longer, more tired creak than the cabinets. A creak with a squeal at the end. Leah smiles, says, "Someday, I'm gonna have to really get rid of this piece of junk."

"As long as it gets you where you need to go," Risa says.

"That's just what Naomi says," Leah answers.

They hug each other good-bye. Breakaway, hesitate, look at each other's eyes, not ready to depart company. Leah feels tired, too agitated to drive home, fall asleep, explain things to Naomi just yet. "Risa, do you know much about him?" she asks.

"Probably not as much as you do," she answers. "I know he is a good boy. He could be high strung sometimes. Most of these college kids are. They have to let steam off. Long as they don't damage the apartment, what do I care? I had one tenant downstairs complain that she heard people coming and going late at night. She's a secretary. Works at the bank. I told her it's an apartment house, not a prison. That's why everyone has keys, so they can come and go as they please. We don't have any curfews. It's not a dormitory. I told her I heard she had a few late nights as well. That shut her up. It's not me to say if his life is good or bad. I suppose he got into this problem because of drugs. Kids today just don't know how to handle all of it. They don't realize they're frying themselves."

"Did you know that he did drugs?" Leah asks. She is surprised that Risa is so open with her suspicion. Risa is a new age parent, raising her two daughters as vegetarians. She usually doesn't talk about the odd habits of others. Too sensitive of her own.

"No," she says. "Not really. I never thought he did. Not like he was strung out or anything. I heard through a reporter—from the University paper—she thought it was probably a drug sale gone bad."

"I don't think it was drugs," Leah says. "It was something else, you know. Because he was different and all. Did you know he was different?"

"Different?" She laughs, smiles. "You could just listen to him talk and you'd think he was a bit queer. It's obvious. Or at least to you and me. He was a lot more polite than some of the other fellas in this town. This ain't because of that, is it?"

"I'm not sure," she says. "Maybe."

"Well, that boy wasn't big enough to hurt a fly," she says. "Any man who beat up a boy that size should feel like a disgrace."

Leah smiles. She feels drained. It crosses her mind that Risa might think this conversation odd. She knows Leah and Naomi are partners. Naomi sometimes shows up to the same yoga class as Risa. Leah has heard that Risa experimented with a lot of partners when she was at the University, before she met her husband, Elliott. Naomi has come back from classes with tales, remarks, innuendoes. "His parents will be here soon," Leah says. "I'm sure they'll call you to come by. We're putting them up in one of the guest rooms."

"I'll give them a key if they want," she says. "Come to think of it, his mom was writing me checks for the rent. You tell her I'll have a key made for her. And I'll tell her what a great boy her son is."

36

His mother believes fate made this happen, that this is a wake up call to stop acting like a punk, that his planets are misaligned, that God wants him to do other things with his life.

Troy does not believe in God, nor of fate supplying him with a destiny. He is too young. He believes he is invincible, like young people do. He does not think of himself as a punk. (*Not his style, man.*) He is only bored with authority, waiting to grow up. (*This place sucks.*) He thinks it is merely bad luck that brought him to the street that night. Wrong place. Wrong time. (*Fuckin' shit.*) Blame is for others. Not him. His head wound does not wake him up. It only makes him angry. He wants revenge. (*I'm gonna waste that fuckin' dude.*)

Something else will make him change, the point where he sees his life beginning.

This is how it happens: He is ready to check out. He is dressed in jeans, sweatshirt, boots, waiting to be released from the hospital. His mother is in one chair, holding his dirty clothes, folded neatly in her lap as if they are clean. He is in another chair, elbows on knees, staring at the door. His head is bandaged. His coat is on the hospital bed. A wheelchair has been brought into the room. A doctor enters through the door. This is when he thinks he will be told he can go home. Instead, the doctor clears his throat, says there is one more thing.

The patient stands up from his chair. It is a wobbly stand, tinted with frustration because he is unable to control his body's movements. "What is it?" he asks the doctor.

The doctor nods, closes the door of the room, his hand falls into his lab coat, rubs against a key chain, says, "The gun you were hit with was believed to be involved in another incident."

"I already know that," he answers. His voice is annoyed, restless. He wants this to be over. He wants to be doing other things. Out there. Not here.

"They've run some tests on the victim," the doctors says. "One of them was a blood test to detect antibodies for HIV. That patient has tested positive."

Troy sits down. The fight has gone out of him. His mother takes a deep breath, clasps her hands dramatically together in an I-told-you-so manner. "You sure, man?" he asks. His voice is different, changed. Frightened. His eyes are small, inward.

The doctor nods, takes a step to change his position. He wishes he had brought a clipboard to deflect his eyes. But he has nothing. He rattles his keys, finds coins deeper in the pocket, looks over at the boy's mother, says, "The police are not sure of the timing of the incidents, but it's my advice that you should start a drug program in case you were exposed to any of the blood. The police have reported that there was blood on the gun, possibly before you were attacked." And then, after a pause. "Because of the uncertainty."

The doctor looks away from the mother. Her expression is too pained. He says to the patient, the young boy of seventeen, "There have been tests done that show that high doses of medication very early in infection can sometimes stop the virus. The treatment is to try, in case you have been exposed to HIV, to stop the replication before it infects the cells, like putting out a brush fire before it gets out of control."

The boy nods. The doctor says a nurse will start him on the medication now. He should stay on it for four weeks. Then have his blood tested.

When the doctor leaves the room, the boy's frustration makes him react. He stands, paces a few steps. He stops, kicks the side of the hospital bed, yells, "Fuck!" with a deeper force than he ever has before. He is older now. He does this four more times: *"Fuck! Fuck! Fuck! Fuck!"*

37

Wednesday

The file grows thicker. The circle widens. The district attorney wants details. A lawyer is called, consulted. The mayor is briefed. Another witness comes forward from the bar: a doorman, a student at the University, ready to identify anyone, willing to talk. The details continue to unfold. Discarded bloody clothes have been recovered from a dumpster. Three arrests have been made; one suspect remains at large. Kelly has been released on bail. No one has confessed to the crime. All there is is a boy wounded, critical, facing his life, waiting for his family to arrive.

The story mushrooms, grows branches, spores like a fungus, an infection spreading. Someone looks into the suspicion of drugs. Were they dealing? Was he buying? What do the blood tests reveal? Anything suspicious? What about reports from the ER? Any signs of drugs? Another person questions if the boy was raped.

A lawyer arranges a postponement of A.J.'s robbery sentencing, pending the outcome of these more serious charges. These charges are debated, discussed. Hinges on the student's survival. And the search for the second assailant continues.

This is what happens: phones ring, information is requested or dispatched. It is a hard crime not to take personally.

Teddy is in his office when the phone rings. Basement, county courthouse, full of file cabinets, bulletin board with charts, photographs of victims. Head of a buck hangs on one wall. Antlers, wet-looking nose. A cigarette burns in the ashtray, a coffee pot is nearby. On his desk are photos of the crime scene. In plastic bags are fragments of rope, a carpet fragment, Danny's credit card, and watch in one bag. In another his student ID, dry cleaning slip, and bank card.

Teddy has been reviewing the case notes. No evidence of meth found in the truck, the apartment, the trailer. His brow is creased, lines at the sides of his eyes look like spokes of a wheel. He runs his hand over his scalp. It pauses there. The heat of his hand reaches his skull. He is trying to concentrate but his mind floats through options. He does not want to be interrupted. He reads a line, rereads it. Tries to think the motive through.

The call interrupts him. It is not the first call of the day. Nor the worst he will take. "It's Ray," he hears when he answers the phone. His stomach contracts, a bitter liquid rises into his chest. He says, hello, that's he's been meaning to call. He cannot disguise his voice to show that he is not hiding something. The doorman has identified A.J. with the college boy at the bar.

"Can't you do somethin' about getting bail set?" Ray asks. "Can't you tell them Kelly's due, that he should be out because of that?"

"I'm doing the best I can," Teddy says. "It was hard enough to get her out. Ray, you should know the evidence doesn't look good. We're looking at some serious charges here. Anything you can tell me that you might know could help."

Ray doesn't answer at first. There is a silence on his end of the line. He is in the kitchen, on a cordless phone. He is pacing. A wave of static hisses, then he says, "Such as?" His tone is suspicious, bitter.

Now it is Teddy's turn to wait. He taps a pencil against the folder, digs the eraser against the manila, leaves a pink streak, lets it drop to the desk. His hands find the bottom of his lip. He pushes his knuckles up to the underside of mustache, rubs them back and forth, like a brush. "Drugs," he says. "Were they doing drugs that night? Do you know that? Was A.J. doing any drugs that you know of?"

Ray stops pacing. Exasperation makes him light-headed. He stands so that he can see Marybeth and Kelly sitting in another room. "This isn't gonna help him," he answers. "You know that, Teddy. How is that going to help him?"

"Were they dealing drugs at all, Ray?" Teddy continues. He puts it out there. Let's his voice show that there is some concern. He has a report from A.J.'s boss that he and Rick were dealing crank, pot, a few other things, but he doesn't tell Ray that, keeps the info to himself. "Do you know if they were doing this regular-like? Did he ever try to sell you drugs? Anyone you know?"

"You don't understand, Teddy," Ray says. He paces again. His tone is determined. "This thing is out of control. I've got people calling me from places I've never heard. I've got people digging up dirt on us. Trying to find out how much money we make, why A.J.'s mom was in the hospital, how she died. Teddy, you got to put a stop to this."

"I don't have control over that," he says. "They have their ways of finding out information. All I can do is all I've promised you that I can do. Help A.J. and Kelly get a fair and honest treatment. I can't do that if people aren't talking. You're not telling me anything at all about A.J. Far as I know, you might even be helping the other one hide out instead of getting him to come in. And A.J.'s not talking to anyone anymore. Not to me. Not to a lawyer. Not to you. Nobody's gonna get through this unless somebody does some serious talking."

"Teddy, we've been friends a long time. We go back. This isn't right."

"I'll do my best for you and your family, Ray," he says. "That's all I can promise. But it looks like the facts will have to speak for themselves since no one's talking. Why don't you get A.J. to do some talking? That's gonna be best for everyone. Kelly included."

38

Wednesday

The light reveals the bareness of the front lawn. A beam cuts straight across the browning grass, across a child's red toy bucket and shovel, bends up a hedge. When a brown minivan parks at a curb, a woman opens the front door of the house from the inside. Marcie is in jeans and a sweatshirt. She is not a pretty woman but the sort who might age well, probably won't get fat. A stately look: brown hair cut to accent her long neck, lessen the thickness to the lower part of her face, the wide jaw. A four year-old boy stands at her side. His hair is still blond, eyes too big for his body, something is crusted on his cheek.

A man gets out of the police car. He is short, wide, looks like he could bench press more than two hundred pounds. He wears a white shirt, leather jacket, dark tie. He walks across the leafy landscape toward the woman in serious strides, his bald scalp catching the light.

"Hey Frank," the woman says. She knows the man. He is from the county police station, runs the show there. She is local. Off duty. "I was just trying to clean up after this one."

"Hey, Jesse," the man says.

She opens the door for him. He steps inside. From another room her mother looks in.

"Hey, Sara," he says to the older of the two women. "You don't mind if Marcie and I do some talking for a moment."

"She on her own time now, Frankie," Sara says. "Don't keep her too long."

"Jesse, go play with Nana," she says. Jesse tugs at his mother's pants, then goes to his grandmother.

"You want some coffee?" she asks.

"I already had three cups today," he answers. "Too much for me, ya know."

"I hear ya," she answers.

She sits on the sofa. He continues to stand. The house seems barren, as if something is missing. A plain covered couch. A lamp with a glass globe. A daddy-long legs crawling in the corner of the carpeted floor. "It's about the boy, isn't it?" she asks. She was the first officer on the scene. The one who cut him from the fence.

"It is, Marcie," he answers.

The light from outside bends into the room. The wind blows through a tree, causing the yellow undersides of leaves to change the pattern on the floor. "I heard it on the news," she says. "I didn't know nothing about him being gay. You think he's gonna live?"

"They don't expect it," he answers.

"I did the report as detailed as I could remember," she says. "It should all be there. I'm not interested in making any kind of statement in the media or nothin'."

"You don't have to do that," he says. "Listen, Marcie. It's about the boy." He hesitates. His skin changes color, thickens, reddens. Light sweat at the lip. He has lost his confidence. "The hospital ran some tests last night. They found the young man was HIV-positive He has the virus that causes AIDS."

She does not respond. At first she is blinded. This news is not expected. Not at all. Blood rushes swiftly inside her, creating blackness. She sees things being taken away from her: her job, her house, her health, Jesse. Who will take care of him? Who will be there for him? The scene replays in her mind. Her hands touching the boy's face at the fence. His chest. Cutting him loose.

"Were you wearing gloves?" he asks.

She doesn't answer him. She feels naked, exposed. She folds her arms across her breasts. She knows her job puts her on-the-line. Things are risky. She is trained for that. But this is afterward. At home. It doesn't seem right. She is healthy, shaken. She hears Jesse, her mom, moving in the kitchen. Something scuttles across the linoleum floor. Jesse's blue truck. The wheels scraping. She waits to hear the sound again.

"Marcie?"

"Not at first," she says.

"Have you been tested before?" the man asks.

It takes her time to respond. Things move slow. She waits for distraction. "No," she says. "There was no reason."

"I'll drive you down to the hospital," he says. "The doc knows you're gonna come in. They want to put you on medication, just in case."

"Who else knows this?" she asks.

"No one," he answers. "I'll keep it out of the report."

39

Wednesday

He has started the morning with a headache. The night was not kind to him. From the shadows of the trailer park, Rick watched Chase and the baby taken away in a police car. Kelly no longer answered the phone. A.J. was no longer at the hospital. He hid in a hanger near the railroad tracks. The old hat factory, north part of town. Every noise startled him: the tin roof shifting, the backfire of a carburetor from a car on a road, even the sound of his own breathing. Sleep came to him only in moments. Dreams haunted him, visions of the college boy tied to the fence post, A.J.'s brutal blows to the boy's neck, the college boy's whispered "please." He struggled with what to do. His options are small and dwindling: continue to hide and run, wait to be found, turn himself in. This is all A.J.'s fault. Everything has gone wrong because of A.J.

Tired, he walks into town. He lights a cigarette, his next to last. He touches the scab at his lip, pushes it till he feels the pain. He wishes he was out of here. Somewhere warmer. The beach. He smokes, continues to blame A.J., as if he were a witness himself. Not part of the situation. The nicotine makes him want more. He wants to get high. He searches his pocket for a loose pill, anything. He turns up nothing. He walks, messes with his lip some more.

He stops at a fast food place where he worked when he was in high school. He's got to keep his energy going. He orders a burrito and a soda, eats at a table outside, taunting the town. He dares it to recognize him, arrest him, bring him to justice. He is surprised that people pass him without notice. His headache lessens. He feels better. He studies the bright red and yellow logo on the napkin, the waxy paper cup in his grasp. A squad car passes on the road outside the restaurant. He watches it, expecting it to turn around, come back to him. He tenses himself, ready to run, forcing his headache back to the surface. The car continues on its path away from him. His invisibility gives him the courage to move on, dare the next place, the next person. He decides he likes his freedom. He thinks he can no longer stay in this town. He begins to plan his escape.

He finishes his burrito and soda and leaves the tray outside on the table for someone else to clean up. He walks toward town, still hungry, tired.

He enters the grocery store on Old Union. He takes a shopping cart, heads down the first aisle. Stops at the fruit. Moist cold air rises around him. Smell of insulation. He sticks his head in over the oranges, feels the cold. He wants an apple. Picks one out. Lays it in the top shelf of the cart.

He continues down the aisle, past the lettuce, salad dressings, jars of mayonnaise. He fills the cart with other items: bread, soup cans, pasta mixes. He stops in the aisle where knives hang on hooks above the shelves. He takes the largest one off the hook. He doesn't place it in the cart. Instead, he unwraps it from the cardboard and plastic, lays it in the top shelf of the cart. The blood in his head is pounding. He feels himself sweating. He wants to stop, can't.

He wheels the cart down an aisle in such an awkward way a little girl standing on tiptoe to reach a cereal box notices. Her mother moves her cart aside to let him pass. He continues down the aisle to the check-out counters. There are seven register spots but only two cashiers on duty. He chooses the one closest to the exit. A tanned woman in a white smock nods hello to him as he wheels the cart into her station.

"Listen, honey, I got a problem," he says. His voice is raspy, brittle. "Why don't you give me the cash you got and we won't have any trouble here."

Her eyes widen. She is about fifty, he thinks, and doesn't look too frightened by him. She looks at his lip, will remember him because of it. Then looks down at the knife he is holding in his hand which is resting on the top shelf of the cart.

"Gotta ring somethin' up to open the register," she says. "You want to hand me something?"

He reaches for a box of doughnuts from the cart. "No funny business," he says.

She takes the box, scans the bar code on the side. She pops the register open, chooses a few bills.

"All of it," he says.

She empties the tray, hands him the bills. He stuffs them in the front pocket of his jeans.

"Bag it," he says, nodding to the doughnuts.

He picks the apple out of the cart, shoves the cart out of his way, slips the apple into the bag she has pushed toward him.

"And a pack of lights," he says.

This surprises her. That he wants more. Doesn't leave so quickly. She reaches for a pack of cigarettes, lifts it out of the shelf, puts it on the counter.

He swipes it up with his free hand, the one which had been holding the bag, sticks the pack in his back pocket, lifts up the bag and leaves. He walks quickly toward the exit, the knife at his side. On his right he notices a heavy set man in a white shirt and tie moving toward him. He thinks it must be the manager. He walks faster. The automatic doors open. He bolts outside to the parking lot. Above, plastic flags snap in the wind.

He starts to run, hears someone shout, "Hey!" He turns down McCoy, crosses to the east side. He makes it to Gatewood, tosses the knife into a bush. He continues walking, on the fringes of the University, till he reaches the east side, hides in a spot behind the rear of a gas station just before the Interstate exit. He sits down beside a dumpster, counts the money in his pocket. Seventy-nine dollars. He opens the box, eats a doughnut. Then another, ignoring the apple, the cigarettes still in his back pocket.

He heads back out to the street. Traffic comes and goes. He walks about a half-mile, past the car franchises, crosses the road. He checks to see if Baffer's truck is in the motel parking lot. It's there. Red Chevy, banged in fender, left tail light cracked, bumper sticker of a green marijuana leaf.

He walks into the office, asks the girl behind the counter what room Baffer's in today. Her face is pockmarked. Meth under the skin. She says he's upstairs. 215. Like always.

He jumps the stairs two at a time. Knocks on the door.

Another girl opens the door. Her eyes are wide, nervous. She is thin, breasts don't fill her bra.

"Heard you're in some deep shit," Baffer says when he is inside the room. It is warm, moist, like a damp armpit. Baffer is lying on the bed, smoking. Tattoos travel under his T-shirt like snakes. "Looks like that girl of yours gave you a nasty love bite."

"Thought you could front me an eight ball," he says.

"No can do, little man."

He hates being talked to this way. Thinks about bashing Baffer's head in. Decides against it. "Thought I could travel some stuff for you if you need it," he says. "Trying to get out of town."

"You didn't bring any pigs with you?" Baffer asks. "Anybody on your tail?"

"Nope," he says.

"Come back tonight," Baffer says. "I got a guy cookin' up some stuff."

"I was hoping to get out of here earlier," he says.

"That's what they all want," Baffer answers.

He shoves his hands in his pockets. Brings out some bills. "Let me just get something in case I'm not back later. You got a bag here?"

Baffer nods to the girl. She opens the bureau drawer. Brings out a bag. Her head flicks, jerks back and forth like she hears a noise. "Shit," she yells. It sounds like a spit.

Baffer jumps up off the bed, reaches for a gun, goes to the window. He pulls back the curtain. Looks out at the parking lot.

When he's satisfied it's clear the girl takes Rick's money. He shoves the bag in his pocket. Baffer tells him to get lost.

Outside, he takes the stairs down two at a time. He looks

at the sweatshirt he is wearing. It is blue with a white logo. He knows he will have to change soon. Will be part of the report. Right now his head aches. He wants to rest. Or smoke. Can't decide which.

He crouches behind the motel dumpster so that he can't be seen. He leans his head back, thinks about running. The smell is overpowering—sweet, syrupy, something sticky. He needs the headache to disappear. He slows his breathing, closes his eyes.

The wind finds him first. A cold, evil breeze. He opens his eyes in time to recognize the sound of footsteps. There is no chance to run. A policeman is in front of him, gun pointed at his head. Another is headed up the stairs.

He stands, feels oddly thankful. Now he can tell someone about A.J. This is all because of A.J. None of this is his fault. A.J. got this mess started.

40

Monday

He sees Stuart while he is crossing the quad. Stuart is a tall guy with spiky reddish-brown hair, round face, and flat nose, not much shape of a body, thinks he looks tougher than he is. Stuart is a business school major and a control freak. He is business manager of the Investment Club, chairman of the Caucus, president of the Ad Hoc Players. His obsession (beyond making money) is musical comedy. He wishes the University had a real drama school, not the amateurish student-run organization that does two productions a year. (But if it did, he would most likely be voted out of control. Too many people dislike him. Or worry that he is manipulative.) Danny met Stuart during orientation week when they had a conversation about why the University never did any Stephen Sondheim musicals.

"I'm getting tickets to the show at the Arena next month," Stuart says when they stop beside the memorial for alumni lost during the Civil War. "Interested in going?"

He's a bit wary of Stuart, a guy who wants to know everyone's secret. He leans against the base of the memorial, a pedestal inscribed with names beneath a statue of two soldiers arm-in-arm, nicknamed by the campus paper as "Gus and Sam." "It's not my favorite show," he says. "I guess if you can't find anyone else to go with you, I'll go."

"That's an awfully passive-aggressive yes," Stuart says. He steps into the shadow of statue in order not to squint.

Danny hates being called that. Passive-aggressive. "It's such a silly show," he says. He doesn't know Stuart that well, and is not too interested in knowing him better.

"I thought I might get a couple of guys to go," Stuart says. "We could go to a club afterwards. Even stay over if I can find a decent weekend rate."

"That sounds possible," Danny says. He thinks about telling Stuart about the trip he made last weekend to Richmond. But he holds himself back. Stuart always comes up with a story himself, like a trump.

"Maybe Walt and Jim Easely."

"Jim Easley?" Danny says. His lips flatten out while he changes his mind.

"Why not Jim?"

He doesn't want to say anything bad about Jim to Stuart. It is more about the two of them together—Jim and Stuart—that make him uneasy. "He's so intense," Danny says. Jim is a heavy smoker. There's something dark about him as well. Danny can't really put his finger on it. Doesn't want to either. "And he doesn't really get along with Walt."

"Your homophobia is showing," Stuart says. "Nobody gets along with Walt."

Stuart's remark is light-hearted, but its tone annoys Danny. "That's not true," Danny says. He becomes more defensive, adds, "Just because I am gay does not mean that I have to like everyone else that is gay. I'm allowed to have opinions. Same thing goes for Walt."

"And you both wouldn't be queens-for-a-day if you didn't," Stuart answers. He laughs as if he has won the argument. "But we're all in the same boat, honey, and it's full of a lot of holes that need patching. You coming to the Caucus tonight?"

The Caucus is the campus gay organization, about thirty members, all students, in a University community of more than fifteen thousand people. "Probably not," Danny answers. "I'm supposed to go to the movies with Walt."

"Walt's turning into a pretty bad influence on you, I see," Stuart answers. His expression turns sour: he juts out his chin. "What good is there having a group like this on campus if no one's going to participate? You heard what happened to Colin?"

"Colin?"

"The biology student. The blond guy with the body."

"What happened?"

"Some frat boys were harassing him last weekend outside the library," Stuart says. "They scared him so bad he wouldn't tell security."

"Was he hurt?"

"No, no, they didn't hit him. Just yelled at him while he walked back to the dorm. He was so shaken he's thinking about dropping out next week. We really need him to help out. The more of us the safer we all are."

"Maybe it's not such a good idea," Danny says. Next week the group is planning Gay Awareness events. This weekend they are to start the events with marching in the homecoming parade. Danny hadn't planned to do it if Gary is coming. He remembers he still has to e-mail Gary. Now he's not sure again if Gary should come. Would Gary march in the parade too? Or would he have to convince him to do it? And is it worth the effort? Or just forget about both? Relax, study, not worry about anything.

"You have to come to this meeting tonight," Stuart says. "If one of us looks like a fool next week then we all look like fools. You have to be there."

Danny feels an uneasiness overcoming him. Coming out never seems to stop. A sudden rush to make decisions when he's not ready. He adjusts his knapsack on his back, the straps cutting into his skin, and stands. "Sure," he says, shoving his hand into his pants pocket and shrugging. "But if I don't make it you can sign me up to help."

41

Something about this crime has made it different. The beating? The fence? A handsome young man? The victim abandoned? Suffering overnight? Crucified beside a church?

These are the things that are noticed. Newspapers request photographs. What they get is an image of a boyish man, turned sideways toward the camera. He has a half-knowing smile, long bangs of blond hair. Attractive as any mother's son. It is shown on newscasts, posted on Web sites. Information travels swiftly. It strikes at the heart of disbelief.

The photo provokes more questions. Something larger is expected to explain the crime, as though it no longer happens at a specific place and moment. Reporters are hungry for the facts and more facts. Details of the victim's sexuality are disclosed in a phone call between the sheriff's office and a local reporter. The news makes its way over the wire reports, fax machines. It becomes part of the story, just like the news.

And more questions are asked. The town is scrutinized. Many residents will say they have never even met a gay person before. The word will have a foreign sound to it, part of another language. It will be stuck in the throat of many: Queer. Gay. *Home-O-Sex-U-Awl.* One resident, a thirty-four year-old secretary in the Chemistry department at the University, will joke that this place is so behind-the-times, "there ain't even a decent shopping mall."

By three o'clock there are more than fifty people in Room 17A of the University medical center. Reporters, cameramen, staff. It is full of suspicion. Cords snake around chairs, looking for outlets. Duct tape tears in long strips, patches in microphones. Lamps atop camera cases flip on, flood the room, go off. A podium has been set up at one end of the room. Folding chairs have been moved, rearranged. Dark bags, knapsacks, duffel bags find their way into corners. Everyone has a piece of equipment to test.

Donald Carberry approaches the podium, tests the microphone with a tap. Thump, thump, thump hits the back wall. A hollow sound. His face is washed with light. More light. It makes him squint, till his pupils adjust. Someone reaches out another microphone toward his face. He is surprised how quickly it has descended on the hospital. How many people have shown up to make this a part of the day's news. People from other places. Some who don't belong here. Or so he thinks.

He had expected the college boy to die last evening when a staff doctor called him at home with details of the admittance. He had expected to simply recount the facts this morning to a few phone callers—a reporter from the college paper, another from the town newspaper, maybe someone from Richmond or Washington. A student found at an off-student site. Suspects not associated with the University. But by noon he was aware the situation was escalating. Last night, a local radio station had announced a college boy had been found beaten and tied to a wooden fence by the chapel. As if he were crucified. A wire service had then picked up the item. By 11 p.m. it was mentioned on the evening news in Washington.

He taps the microphone again, this time to get the room to fall quiet. Thump. Thump. Thump. The hollow sound hits the back wall. He straightens his posture. The noise lessens. A cell phone rings. Someone answers, leaves the room.

He had expected to announce only the college boy's death. The doctor who had called him at home said the boy would most likely not live through the night. He had gotten to the office early this morning and already there was a call about the patient's sexuality. These were things he knew he could not answer, could not discuss, were improper to comment on. He had avoided returning the call to the reporter from the college newspaper. But when the sheriff's office had issued a statement to the radio station that one arrest had been made and another suspect was in custody, he knew he could no longer hide. The news was traveling too fast. He was being asked for details. And more details. Everyone wanted a story.

He says into the microphone, "Danny came to us by ambulance Tuesday evening after he was discovered at an off-campus site. He was admitted in critical condition at approximately 6:45 p.m. When he arrived, he was unresponsive and breathing support was provided."

His voice remains steady, impassive. Medical training has given him distance, detachment. He sounds like a newscaster. His voice is low-toned, no accent.

"He is in the surgical-neuro intensive care unit. Respiratory support continues to be provided. He remains on a ventilator. Danny's major injuries upon arrival consisted of hypothermia and a fracture behind his head to just in front of the right ear. This has caused bleeding in the brain, as well as pressure on the brain. There were also approximately a dozen small lacerations around his head, face, and neck. Since his arrival at the hospital his temperature has fluctuated, ranging from 98 to 106 degrees. We have had difficulty controlling his temperature.

"Members of the family and his close friends are at his bedside. His parents and brother are currently on their way to the hospital. We will not provide any additional information on the patient until his parents are present at the hospital. Thank you."

He does not wait to see if there are any questions. He leaves the room from the side door, his feet stepping into a long rectangular shadow. He doesn't anticipate this going on, answering questions. He doesn't worry about the displeasure he leaves behind. In the room. He has not revealed the patient's sexuality. The information about the patient's blood remains confidential. It is the parents' decision what to discuss, what to disclose. The parents will arrive soon. It is up to them. And besides, the boy is not expected to live. This will all be over before it begins.

42

Wednesday

Nine hundred miles away from the victim, the suspects, the police station, the hospital, the University and the town, a girl, seven, feeds a sheet of paper into a fax machine. She has hazel eyes, long brown hair pinned behind her ears, a hand-me-down dress with a pattern of blue cornflowers. Above her, a magazine article about a college student's crusade against "necking" on campus, hangs in a photo frame on the wall, suspended by a nail that was tapped into paneling more than thirty years ago. Beside it hangs a framed law degree. There are four other children in the room. Ages ten, twelve, eight, nine. Boy, girl, girl, boy. Like her, they look foolish trying to look professional. The twelve year-old girl is printing out e-mails from a computer. The other three children are huddled around a photocopier, watching paper shoot out into a tray.

A tall, gray-haired man strides into the room dressed in lycra shorts and a windbreaker. He looks like an old hawk searching for his next meal: big nose, small, dark eyes, hunch of a back. He tells one of the children at the photocopier, the nine year-old boy named Justin, to go tell his grandmother that he is ready now for his Vitamin C cocktail, a concoction of Vitamin C, diet soda, water. The boy runs from the room. The grandfather takes his chair behind the old steel desk, cardboard chips placed beneath the right front leg to keep it level. He sits there alert, ready to attack anything that moves beyond his control. His fingers are long, bony, freckled with age spots. They fidget in front of him like spiders.

This is the working office of the Eastgate Baptist Church. The grandfather, Reverend Abraham White, has his congregation of children and grandchildren send more than two hundred faxes and e-mails a day. They are sent to public officials and the media warning them that God hates homosexuals and that they are doomed to Hell. His reasoning is that God does not hate them because they are homosexuals; instead, they are homosexuals because God hates them. But his messages and warnings are more bluntly worded. "*God hates Fags*," he writes, prints, types, yells. He calls them fags because the word is used in the Bible, a contraction for "faggots" (short sticks of wood that burn very quickly). A metaphor chosen by the Holy Ghost to describe a group of people who burn in their lust toward one another and who fuel god's wrath.

Homosexuals are not his only concern. According to the Reverend most Christians are Christians by name only and should be ashamed. They are cowardly, lukewarm, confused of Christ's Word. They have substituted their own pathetic ideas for God's clear commandments. All have sinned, come short of the glory of God. If any man says he has not sinned, the Reverend calls him a liar. Every person at the moment of birth utterly deserves to go straight to Hell. Wickedness makes the sinner as heavy as lead, swiftly sinking into the bottomless gulf.

His messages and meanings put him at odds with everyone except his family of believers. His God is a hateful God. The Bible preaches hate. For every verse about God's mercy, love, compassion, there are two verses about His vengeance, hatred, wrath. The maudlin, kissy-pooh, feel-good, touchy-feely preachers today are only damning this world to Hell. His mission is to warn people that they will soon face God, that unless they repent, they will perish in Hell. And he is not content to send out his messages from his office by machines invented by sinners. He feels he must take his crusade to the streets, warning passersby that the only righteousness God recognizes is the righteousness that he gives.

The Reverend is writing a new fax when a man in his late thirties enters the room. He is the Reverend's son, Jonathan, father of the seven year-old girl and nine year-old boy. Like his father he is tall, beak-nosed, beady-eyed. His appearance seems more streamlined, finished, like a shark. He carries a piece of paper in his hand, close to his chest. "Have you noticed the reports about the college boy that was beaten?" he asks his father.

The Reverend looks up from his desk, nods, "No." He takes a piece of paper that Jonathan offers him to read. There is a moment of silence in the room, silent except for the children pressing fax buttons, keys being hit on a computer keyboard, while the Reverend reads the news.

He jumps up from his chair before he has finished. "We'll need to start making signs right away," the Reverend says. His eyes are bright, on fire. A darkness burns in them. Leaps across the room, finds an alliance in his son's. "Keep them simple," he adds. He rubs his hands together, like a villain in a fairy tale. "Something to make everyone annoyed. Something like: 'Danny Burns in Hell.' And make sure we use his picture."

43

Wednesday

Marcie goes outside to get Jesse's pail. The cold startles her. She looks down the street at the children playing outside. The grass next door is still green but the tree is empty of leaves. A dog barks down the street. She takes the pail inside, finds her car keys, leaves the house, the door clicking shut behind her.

She sighs as she unlocks her car. Her stomach cramps. She waits for it to disappear. The dog continues barking. She hears a far-away humming. Traffic. Or the agitation at her heart. She hears a bird's cry, looks up. She hears it again, more faintly. The bird is not visible.

She wants privacy, a place beyond eyes of others. She wants a cigarette, too, even though she stopped almost six years ago. Those days when she'd enjoyed a cigarette and a drink. Jesse's birth changed that. Joe's leaving changed things more.

She starts the car, backs out of the driveway, catching her image in a mirror. She hardly recognizes the girl she was. So much of her has disappeared. The brown of her hair, dingy, like an eroded beach. Her eyelids look heavier, darker, as if she needs sleep. Her libido changed long ago. She only half regrets the way she'd been, how carelessly available she must have seemed when she first met Joe.

Those early times with him had been difficult. Not loving him. She'd been tempted to see whatever guy asked her out. She was young, reckless. And could get away with it. She found a job at the University right after high school, but hated being trapped in an office. She wanted to be out in the world, not locked in an office. She wanted to be talking with people, not to a phone. Her brother had told her about the opening on the police force. Which is where she met Joe.

Joe promised to give up his own recklessness if she wanted to settle down quick. He wanted her to quit dating other guys. Get married. Wanted her off the force. At home. Raising kids. The only compromise she made was to love him. She kept her job. But he didn't keep his own promise. In less than a year, he was out the door. The thought of a family, fidelity, responsibility, scared him more than it did her.

These days she seems indifferent to love—making love—found it ironic that the doctor who told her only hours ago that she'd been exposed to the virus also told her to use precautions with her lovers. *What lovers?* she thought. *Does he know something I don't?* Men did not seem to see her anymore. Particularly her co-workers. She has become one of the guys. Outside of work her life revolves around Jesse, her mom, her cat. The truth is she would rather have the cigarettes returned instead of temptation. Lust abandoned her long ago.

She turns onto Upper Chapel. The car seems to be taking over from her. She can't remember what the inside of the chapel looks like. She glances down the path as she passes by the turnoff. Notices cars parked there. She feels a pressure to release something. Not to confess, not to ask forgiveness or mercy. Only to ask God to make sure her own son will come to no harm. That He will look after him if she's not around. She parks her car in the chapel parking lot. Notices another car there. Thinks it must be the Reverend's.

Her stomach cramps again as she locks the door. A sickness enters her throat. The doctor told her the medicine she must take may give her diarrhea, make her light-headed. She takes the steps to the front door slowly. If she didn't know better she would think this was morning sickness. But it's not. She knows better.

Inside, the church feels cold, vacant. She rubs her hands slowly together when she sits. The pews are worn and greasy, hymn books on ledges. The timbers strain to hold faith inside. She wears a scarf around her head, not sure if it is right or not. Because it hides her hair, makes her jaw look wide, it makes her look odd, not feminine at all. She takes a seat in the back of the chapel, turns to the left to watch sunlight stream in from the window to the altar.

She still carries with her the vision of discovering the college boy on the fence. The rusty color of his face, the straw-like blond hair. She hadn't anticipated the chill and the silence and the bleakness of the church carrying her thoughts deeper. Did he feel the rope cutting into his wrists? How long had he been conscious? Had he watched his blood drop from his face to the ground? Did the pain travel swiftly or linger in the wounds and welts of his body?

It's not that she is afraid to die herself. She is a police officer, after all. She is supposed to understand mortality. Especially her own.

Now, in the chapel, she thinks about others. Eddie had been her first friend to die. They had met twenty years ago when his family moved next door. They had played together. He had been a sickly boy. Or so her mother had told her. One day he got an infection. Then he was in the hospital. She never saw him after that. She never got a chance to say good-bye.

She never got to say good-bye to Gordon either. One day he was at work. The next he was killed in an accident on the Interstate. That was about seven years ago. When she had first joined the force. She didn't like these abrupt transformations.

And then there are the others. Not the ones she knows. The ones she knows of. She is not the first person to ever be exposed to a virus. This virus. But it is what has sent her back to the church today. All those others—cut off from their lives so soon. She wants to be around to see her son's graduation from high school, cry at his wedding. Things are closing into a tunnel now. She doesn't want to be treated differently. She doesn't want people to look at her differently. She wants to keep her job. She wants to keep her family. She wants to see her son grow up. Keep all this. *Now. Somehow.*

She stands up abruptly. Leaves the chapel. She needs to find somewhere to escape herself. Zigzagging down the front steps she heads to where she parked her car. A gust of wind whips around the corner of the building, carries scraps of dust up in a whirlpool. It makes her look to the south. Toward the fence. Even now she can't forget the boy. Let the image of him alone.

44

Wednesday

The town lies within the fringes of the Bible Belt. A combination of Dutch, Irish, English, and Germans first settled the land. By the turn of the twentieth century there were twenty-two churches within the town's borders. Two Roman Catholic, but the rest mostly Baptist or Methodist. The growing University diversified the population, adding Presbyterians and Episcopalians. On campus, a Jewish group uses a conference room in the student center to hold their weekly temple services. Gospel choirs in the old Southern churches along South Main Street still draw faculty and staff because they offer a good show.

Marcie's own religion is the reduced rituals of Christianity—a visit to church at Easter and Christmas. Grace before meals to teach her son the quality of gratitude. Prayers at Thanksgiving. Which is why she approaches the Reverend when she sees him walking through the cemetery behind the Upper White Chapel. She feels a need to find a deeper spirituality within herself.

They meet on the hill. The chapel is in the background. Wind blows her hair. His hands are in gloves. Because of the beauty around her, the wind, it strikes her that she might have entered the scene of a movie.

"There have been people here all day," he says. From where he stands he can see flowers at the fence that someone has left.

"I don't understand this," she says. "Why does this mean so much to them? Why does everyone need to know this story?"

He does not answer her right away. The hills to the west are blue. His eyes are dilated. Something about her lifts him.

She looks down to the river, the valley. "I'm not sure we should intervene," he says.

"Why?" she answers. "Why do you say that? Is this part of some plan?"

"A plan?" he asks.

"Some kind of plan from God? Is this supposed to shake us up? I've had enough shit in my life that I don't need this to make me change for the better."

"No, of course not," he says. "God tests us all the time."

They walk together higher up the hill. He wants to hold her hand, put his arm around her, offer her protection. But he holds himself back. She senses his compassion. It softens her. Makes her less strident.

"I don't understand this," she says. "Why am I a part of this?"

"God is not so easy with the answers," he answers.

Again she stops walking. She casts her eyes around—at the cemetery, at the fence, at the church.

"There is something disturbing about this place." she says. She has moved into a memory. "Even before all this."

"No, you're wrong," he says. "It is not the place."

"I was in school here," she says. "Miss Thompson ran the kindergarten here. When Reverend Drake ran the chapel. We used to play over there." She points to the north slope, where the annex building used to be. "It seemed like such a magical place. Half the kids in the valley went to kindergarten here. Before the fire. It seems so ironic now."

"Ironic?" he asks. "How?"

"You haven't heard? One of the boys that beat him. He was her grandson. Lois Thompson's grandson. It's like they chose this place for a reason."

He does not answer her. This news startles him. There is more story to this than he wants to know. But he wants to know this story anyway. "It must be a coincidence," he says. "Why would he bring him here deliberately? To a church?"

"There's always been something creepy about this place," she says. "Like it's too pretty to believe."

45

Wednesday

She has been crying since the phone calls. First an officer, then a doctor, then her sister. She had called Paul first, after the officer phoned, then managed to leave a message for her youngest son Luke in San Francisco, telling him to call as soon as possible.

She had calmed herself by concentrating on the details ahead of her, even though she felt rushed, disorganized. She had to pack, ask Suzanne, her neighbor, to watch the cat and check the mail. She had to make sure they brought enough clothes—for how long? No one was sure. The doctor had said that her son would not regain consciousness. But he was uncertain how much longer he would live. She thought of him in the hospital room, waiting for her to arrive, and she stopped to cry again. She was overcome with helplessness. She thought she would never stop, never be able to function normally again. Then, as easily as she began crying, she dried the tears with the back of her hand, recounted the details to her sister on the phone, then hung up, wondering where she had stored her large suitcase.

Now, in the limo that has picked them up at the airport, she steadies herself as the driver talks with Paul. He tells her husband what a polite boy her son was—he had used the car service only last weekend for a trip out of town. Luke sits by the window, silent, looking at the mountains at the edges of the horizon, the sun low, like a burning coin. She does the same, looking out at the gray cement, silent, thinking she had finally gotten her family out of this place, only to be pulled back by another tragedy. She looks away when the limo startles a flock of crows picking at road kill, her eyes following them toward the telephone lines, the weight of their bodies not even making the wires sway.

She had grown up here. So had Paul. They had started dating in high school, then lived together when he started at the University, despite her mother's objections. She was glad when they finally moved away, when Paul got a job outside Portland. She was ready to leave this place behind; her parents divorcing when she was fifteen had not been an easy pill to swallow. She felt that she and her sister had been part of some melodramatic script. A bad soap opera. First, her father's affair. Then his leaving home. His remarriage and his new wife's suicide after a miscarriage. Her father died a year later in a freak car accident, a patrolman said he had fallen asleep behind the wheel. Then her mother announced that she had cancer not long after Danny was born. Roxy, her sister, had tried to help their mother through the illness. But it had been swift, unmerciful. Roxy moved away too, not long after their mother's death. "Too many memories," her sister told her one night on the phone. "I had to get away from that shit, too."

At Leah's, she waits in the car while Paul and Luke take the luggage inside. She runs through a list of the details she needs to know. What made him go out on a school night? Didn't he know better? Why did they beat him? Leave him there in the night? What are his chances to regain consciousness? To speak? Walk? Understand what someone is saying? She is embarrassed by the sudden rush of thoughts when Leah comes out to the car. She recognizes her immediately as the older girl who used to work in the stables and wore her long brown hair clipped back from her face with silver barrettes. She seems shorter to her now, heavier, more colorless with her silver hair and pale skin, not at all like the dark-eyed athlete at the barn she used to be. She is also struck even harder by the memory of what a poor rider she was herself. She had been terrified of the horses. Unlike her sister, unlike her other friends, she had only wanted to get as far away as she could from the creatures.

Leah hugs her through an open window of the limo, says

that now it all comes back to her. "You were the little girl who was always too scared to braid her pony's mane. Your daddy wanted you to be such a good rider, too. Your sister was always much better at it."

She watches Leah's eyes well up with tears. She shakes her head back and forth and continues, "I don't know what to say, darlin'. This has taken all of us by surprise."

She refuses Leah's offer of something to eat before they go. She wants to get to the hospital as soon as possible. Paul and Luke return with bags of food that Leah has made for them, in case they get hungry, as though there were no other places in the world to eat. Or the thought that they would need them.

On the drive to the hospital bits and pieces of her past float back to her. She recognizes the old railroad station house and buildings which housed the canning factory. The BP station on the Old Union highway is now a Texaco, but a convenience store has been added to the lot. She recognizes the Baptist Church on Market, but the triangular building is new. The shops on Main Street are different but the University buildings are familiar when they reach Clifton Road. She recognizes the old limestone law school but the hospital is larger. It is a high rise medical center now, a compartmentalized structure of red brick and circular glass walls that fold into one another.

Roxy is waiting for her in the lobby. They hug. She wipes away her sister's tears. "Oh, baby," she says to Roxy. "It'll be okay. We'll find a way through this."

They walk a few steps together, arms around each other's backs. They separate as she hugs Wayne. Paul shakes hands. Soon, they are waiting for an elevator.

Her first thought when she arrives on the floor is she feels his presence already. Then she is struck by the amount of flowers—daffodils, daisies, roses—red and yellow. Flowers line the hallway, sit on tables, counters—all sorts of flowers and plants—carnations, orchids, baby's breaths, ferns. Even a potted jade tree with yellow ribbon tied around its tiny trunk. Flowers that she feels must have been trucked in from other places—plants that must have begun journeys before her own had been set in motion. Why are there so many flowers? What has happened here?

Paul's parents are waiting outside the hospital room. As they make their way down the hall, she thinks of how much they have aged in the last five years. His father's hair is completely white; his face fattened with jowls. His mother has become plump, round, her eyes now small, fleshy slits where they were once bright.

They stop and there are more hugs, more words of disbelief exchanged. They dote on Luke. Ask him if he's grown taller.

She wants to continue on. As she approaches the door of his room, she feels as if someone is pressing their hands against her chest, warning her not to come in—so different from the lightness she felt a moment ago. She stops walking, her purse drops to the floor. She tries to regulate her breathing. Tears well up in her eyes. She feels herself flush; blood settles in her cheeks, forehead, ears. She thinks she is being too dramatic, but what she feels is truthful. "I can't go in there yet," she says, and backs away from the door.

She bends her body, as if she is having abdominal pains, and covers her face with her hands. She begins to cry. Helplessness overwhelms her. "I can't let him see me this upset," she says. She tries to reach for her purse but can't. Paul retrieves it for her, takes her by the shoulder, walks her to a window in the hallway.

The view is of the side hospital parking lot. The lot where the limo is still parked. She sees Pop, the limo driver, leaning against a car, smoking a cigarette. She sees him talking with a group of people who have surrounded him. One man appears to have a camera positioned on his shoulder, another carries a long pole. Suddenly, a bright light is switched on, casting Pop into an eerie colorlessness. She turns to her husband, asks, "Who are these people? Why are they here? Does this have anything to do with Danny? Does this have something to do with our son?"

46

Wednesday

He checks his e-mail when he gets home. There is a message from his friend Jon checking on dinner next week, a message from Andrew, his college roommate who now lives in Atlanta, describing the leather crowd at the Eagle over the weekend, and plenty of spam: "Sexy, horny, barely legal teens," "Did you get my pix?" and "Stop getting booted off line." Nothing from Danny.

He signs off the computer and goes to the kitchen. What could have changed his mind? He said he would e-mail plans for the weekend. Nothing. Nothing at all. No answer to the e-mail he sent Monday. Nothing from the one he sent Tuesday.

He pulls the bottle of wine he opened last night from the refrigerator. Pours himself a glass. He'll let it go, but he can't help be disappointed. They've been chatting on-line for almost a month now. Every time he plans to visit him, Danny gets cold feet. He wonders if he's being scammed. If Danny is not Danny at all but a teenage girl playing a prank, someone who lives in Utah. Or Vermont. Or Mississippi. That it's all just a game. A disappointing game. So much for romance.

This is what he knows about Danny: He likes the country better than the city, wants to become involved in local politics, wants to meet the right guy. He took some time off after high school to get his shit together. He worked for a while at a counseling center, but quit to return to school. He's majoring in political science. He is short (five feet, two inches), thin, blondish-brown hair, blue eyes. Wears braces. Has a cat named Chloe. Goes by the nickname DBS2020 on-line.

This is what he wrote: He is an ophthalmologist. Lives

in D.C. He is not as short (five feet, seven inches), not stocky but not sleek (157 pounds), a bit older (twelve years more than Danny). Black hair, brown eyes. He likes movies, biking, Sinatra records. Hates the partisanship of the Capitol, and had a boyfriend for four years who wouldn't make any kind of commitment. Wears glasses, Clark Kent style, to hide his bushy eyebrows. Figured out pretty early in life that he was gay. Goes by the nickname Eyeful.

They didn't chat about sex. Instead, they talked about wanting relationships, needing to grow up and learn different things, what was wrong with religion today, the way it excludes gays. By the end of their first week of e-mails, Danny wrote that he was really going to like Gary because he hadn't hit on him. They spoke on the phone twice for almost an hour each time. Danny made the calls using a phone card his mother had sent him. His voice was softer, higher, than he expected. But also more sincere. Shy. He wasn't a girl somewhere in Utah. Or Ohio or Vermont. He wasn't a figment of the imagination. Or a scam. Nobody would have wasted that much time trying to be honest to a stranger.

They talked about a sitcom on TV, then about skiing of all things. Gary wanted to learn to ski. Danny said the idea of going that fast scared him. (Though he had water skied once. And liked it.)

They agreed to meet as friends. No pressure on the first date. Danny invited Gary up for weekend. Homecoming weekend at the University. He could stay over if he wanted. On the couch. As a friend. No pressure. Just to meet one another.

Something must have scared him away. Maybe it was midterms. Maybe he's been studying and forgotten to call. When Gary was in college he would disappear for hours in the basement of his dorm, incommunicado with the world in order to pass a test or finish a paper.

He takes the chicken breast from the freezer and defrosts it in the microwave. Heats up the oven. Takes a sip of the wine. While the microwave is going he turns on the TV. Changes the channel to the news. He hopes the TV will distract him—he is still annoyed. He takes out the chicken, seasons it, places it in the oven.

From the refrigerator he takes out a plastic container. He breaks off pieces of lettuce. Rinses them under water in the sink. Finds the tomato and cucumber he bought over the weekend. Finds a knife, cutting board. He rinses the tomato and cucumber. He thinks how effortless it would be to cook for two. With Jerry—the guy he dated for four years—he always cooked. Liked to experiment. Now it just seems to be rote, functional. Sometimes empty.

Something makes him turn and listen to the news. Something about a University student being beaten. The name of the University catches him first, then the student's. It can't be the same person, he thinks.

First there is disbelief. Then he stops making the salad.

He goes back to the computer in his bedroom and logs on. He checks his e-mail messages again. There is nothing from Danny. He doesn't log off. Or return to the salad.

He begins searching for more news.

47

Wednesday

On the plane he'd thought about the apartment they rented on Sanderson right after they were married. Basement, paid in cash every month. The landlady, an older, lonely woman, would call downstairs in the afternoon to see if Julie wanted a cup of coffee. He'd been thrown back into many memories on this trip. More than the common man must endure, or so he thinks. He loved living in that apartment. He would come home from afternoon classes and they would make love on top of the sagging mattress and frame, as soft and fluid as a water bed.

He'd thought about his son on the flight too. Danny, on the rug they'd bought because the floor was always cold. And the puppy they had gotten when he was three months old. He thought about Luke as a baby, the way Danny always wanted to hold him in his arms. He remembers the first Halloween he took them door to door to collect candy: Danny as a pirate with a cape; Luke fidgeting with the black patch over his eye.

So it was not hard for him to recall a few memories about Fancy Gap Trail when his father told him that this was where Danny had been found. The chapel, the cemetery, the fence, the dirt path. They were sitting together in the small waiting area at the end of the hospital floor. He knew immediately when his father relayed the news that he would be the one who would have to tell his wife. He had left her behind in Danny's room. She had taken a seat next to the bed, watching him try to breathe.

He'd absorbed the facts as boldly as he could. He did not cry. But this news now reached him like a kick in the stomach.

Julie had wanted them to be married at the chapel. They had gone to talk to the minister, got an estimate of the costs for the chapel and a reception in the annex before they decided that it was more important to put their money toward tuition and rent instead of an elaborate wedding. They had been married at city hall. They'd paid the justice in cash at the ceremony. At times, lost in his memories, he felt he had disappointed her right from the start. No engagement ring. No wedding in the chapel. The cold basement apartment. But they were also happy memories. For both of them.

"You two used to go up there quite a bit, didn't you?" his father asks.

"A lot when we were dating," he answers. "Does Julie know this?" he asks his father. He does not question his father about who the attackers were. Nor why they brought his son there. The news about the place is too disturbing. It is enough to make him return to his wife.

"Not unless your mother done told her," his father answers, looking down the hall where they have left the women. "But I'm sure she was waiting for you to tell her."

"As if there was not enough to think about," he says, not to his father, not to anyone, really, but to himself. He stands and twists his body so that he can step around where his father has thrown his legs out to relax.

"Paul, it can wait," his father says. "I'd let it wait."

"No," he answers and walks away. And again to himself. "She'd only be upset that I knew this and she didn't."

48

Monday

A maple tree has left a puddle of red leaves beside the east wing of the Chemistry building. Stuart leaves him when they reach the path to the student center. "Remember, see you there," Stuart says.

The tone of Stuart's voice reminds him of Mark. He stands in front of the building, looks at where the Love Bandit tagged the stones, then walks away. His mind goes elsewhere, away from the campus. It is the memory of Mark that walks with him. He wouldn't be here if it weren't for Mark. Mark saved his life, helped him when he was floundering, when he didn't want to go on. "There are two ways you can live your life," Mark had said. "You can go somewhere safe. Or you can go somewhere that challenges you."

The last he had heard was that Mark was improving, the new "cocktail" of drugs were working to counteract the virus. At the beginning of the summer he had sent Danny an e-mail— "gaining weight, even have a little tummy, now."

He walks across campus toward the library again. The sky above is big, full of clouds. He imagines the darkness Mark must have felt at the end—the fight to breathe, to continue to live. Mark was never a quitter. He was always optimistic, said it was the best way to navigate the difficult days.

Fall surrounds him as he hikes the small hill to the library. Yellow, gold, amber leaves. The maples adding a dash of red. He's always thought the library looked like some kind of medieval castle—or a monastery where monks were scribbling away at copying manuscripts. It towers over the rest of the campus—only the bell tower on the quad rises higher.

In the library he takes the elevator to the second floor. He walks through the stacks without looking at the books. He goes to the restroom in the south section. It is empty inside. He goes into a stall. Closes the door. Hangs his coat and knapsack on the back. His fear rises. It makes him depressed. He tries to calm himself by unbuckling his pants, sitting on the toilet, touching his dick. He fondles himself till the blood thickens, makes him hard. He's fine till he hears the door open, someone walk inside.

This is what he remembers: The smell of wet fabric, musty, mixed with a sweet gasoline odor. The sound of his voice going into a high-pitched plea, "No, don't, no, that hurts." The pressure against his back. The fights for breaths. The burning pain erupting inside his bowels, the raspy growl of "nice ass." The shame he felt for not being able to defend himself.

One hand moves to his forehead while the other continues to stroke. He touches where the small trail of scabs had formed. He wants to move on. Away from this memory. It haunts him as much as his desire to connect. To feel good about sex. Having sex. Wanting sex.

He hears the restroom door open again. Another set of shoes. A voice: deep, whispery. He stretches his eye through the crack of the stall. Sees denim, the hem of a jacket. He imagines hearing a zipper move, breathing become deeper. He stares ahead, watching, even if there is nothing he can see.

This is what happened: He had finished studying at the library and was walking across campus to the dorms. He was seventeen. It was fall, Seattle, three weeks after classes had started. It was a little after nine, people were still around. The weather was warm, the air heavy. Water thickened leaves, dampened the roads, sidewalks. A light breeze was blowing. Nothing ominous.

He was sleepy as he walked toward his room. He wasn't paying attention. The van backed up and the driver smiled at him, said that he and his friend were having trouble locating a street. Could he help them find it on the map.

He said, "Sure," and the passenger got out of the van. He

was a tall guy, balding, with a big stomach. A tattoo fading on his forearm. Said, "the map's in the back."

He walked with the man to the back of the van, waited while the guy opened the door. He tried to hide his reaction when he realized that there wasn't any map. Then it occurred to him that the man had picked up a gun.

The man waved the gun at him, said, "Why don't you get inside?"

His first impulse was to run, but he was frozen into place, his mind shouting at itself: *Why me? Why me?* Just as he shook his head "No" and was turning away, the man grabbed him by the arm and the gun was against his back. Next, the man grabbed the crotch of his pants, lifted him off the ground with a force that shoved him into the van. His forehead scraped against the metal siding, pain shot through his skull like a headache.

His next thought was that he was being robbed. He tried to remember how much was in his wallet. Then, out of the darkness, he saw the white of the mattress in the back of the van. The driver turned and flashed a strange smile. The other guy, the big one, had crawled into the back of the van behind him. He was lifted again, this time by the waist of his pants. He landed on the edge of the mattress, face down, the smell flying into his body like a jolt of lightening.

His hand stops stroking. Both hands are now against his head, his eyes bowed to the floor. Mark had been raped, too. Had said that it was not his fault. He'd not done anything wrong, either. "Wrong place, wrong time. It happens. I can't beat myself up for that, you know. Not when there are better things that I can control. Like why I smoke too much."

He hears water running down the sink. The click-click-click of the paper towel dispenser. The footsteps go out the restroom door. He is alone again. The silence moves into him.

Mark had taught him that there was nothing to be ashamed about. "Yes, you can be angry you were raped. You can say you didn't enjoy it, didn't bring it about. But should that mean that you don't like sex? Don't want sex? No. You cannot let that action rule your life. It took me a long time to disassociate one event from the other. That I had a gay consciousness before I was raped."

He stands and pulls up his pants. His dick is thick, but not hard. He twists it into his underwear. Zips up. Buckles up. Goes out of the stall to the sink. Washes his hands, rinses his face, pulls the paper towels out—click-click-click, dries his face in front of the mirror.

The blood had scared him most.

He had woken up on the side of the road. It was still dark, his clothes wet from the grass, dew. He reacted with a force that surprised him. He stood up, felt the pain shoot through his body, and ran across campus.

They made him wait in the infirmary. That was the beginning. The seed of humiliation. The nurse did not believe him. He could not even remember the color of the van. The type of shoes the man wore. He started to cry. He felt too emotional, out of control. When he repeated his story to a security guard, his response was, "Why didn't you just run? The guy wouldn't have shot you."

It wasn't his fault. He didn't know that then. He spent the next three days hiding in his dorm room. There did not seem to be a moment where he felt safe. And then he became sick. Vomiting, fevers, chills. In a week he had moved home. He hid in his bedroom, thought about killing himself.

That was how he met Mark.

He studies his face in the mirror, thinks how things changed inside of him. He decides he will not go downstairs to study. His head is splitting. His headache is growing. Since the rape his headaches have seemed to grow the more relaxed his body feels. Veins at his temple begin hammering—thump, thump, thump—a nerve-pinching band of pain closes around his forehead. Sometimes he continues to function this way, his voice growing loud and rapid, his senses unnaturally keen, until he can't even paint a smile across his face.

He decides he needs some kind of relief. He'll walk home and take a pill. Or maybe a nap. He wants to push himself but not too much. He doesn't want to give up again.

Thoughts of Mark follow him across the campus, down Clifton, around the block. The raspy laugh. The cough to clear phlegm caught in his throat. The tap-tap-tap against his wrist to check the amount of cigarettes left in his pack.

At the apartment, he chases a pill down with a glass of water in the bathroom, then calls Walt and cancels the movie for tonight, saying he isn't feeling well. Walt offers a concerned response but he answers, "Maybe just a beginning of a cold," not wanting to clue him into his mounting depression, his other problems. He warns Walt that Stuart is on the rag, upset that they were not planning to go to the Caucus meeting that night.

When he hangs up, he lays down on the sofa, wanting to nap, wondering why he can't shake Mark from his mind, why the headache makes him feel as if his body is burning. Chloe joins him on the sofa. He strokes her neck, listens to her purr. Maybe this is the beginning of a cold, not the beginning of the end. He closes his eyes, hoping to think of something else, letting a blank, white space fill up his thoughts.

49

Wednesday

Music is always playing at the Starlite—Dwight Yoakum. Clint Black. Shania Twain. Patsy Cline. Which is why he likes this place better than Sloppy Joe's or Backhaven. Or the other bars on Market Street. The Starlite is crowded tonight. Regulars who haven't been here for a while. Reporters who made it past the doorman. Others new. Or nosy. He is here tonight because of Danny, too. He's guilty, curious. Two days ago he turned twenty-two; he's the one who introduced Danny to the Starlite.

The Starlite is nothing more than a fixed-up barn. One of the sheds of the old farmer's market. Still has its tin roof. There's a bar near the entrance, circular, always someone propped up on their elbows. The rest of the room is a dance floor. A small stage for either a DJ or a band.

The women in the Starlite have a tough, fleshy look. Dark roots, light hair. The college guys show up in sweatshirts and jeans. So do the college girls. The local guys in the Starlite seem more Western than Southern, more macho than redneck, more dressed up for a night on the town: narrow jeans, rawhide belts, boots with pointed toes, Stetsons instead of baseball caps. Most of the time they show up on weekends with a date wanting to dance. But the rest of the week they're here as fair game. He told Danny this was part of the primp factor. A dressed up guy is usually a lot more easy-going than a frat boy, will consider doing anything if you last till closing.

The Starlite is his favorite pick-up place in town. This is what he told Danny a few months ago when they met at the Blue Moon, the adult bookstore on the outskirts of town. He didn't tell the police that yesterday when he was questioned. He was vague, upset, didn't want to be part of a police report.

And Danny was a friend. A good listener. They were supposed to get together for his birthday to see a movie. He didn't think Danny had it in him to go cruising these bars by himself. Without him. That's what hurt him hardest when he heard the news. That Danny went out without him.

His name is Walt. He's from Winchester, Tennessee. He's a senior, history major. Wants to take a year off after graduation to travel, then go back to study architecture. Maybe here at the University. Maybe Princeton. If he can get in. If he can keep all this stuff out of his record.

That's the advice he gave Danny. Keep it off the record. He told Danny it was best not to do the gay stuff on campus. Stay away from the Caucus. Anything where they could add your name to a list. Sodomy is illegal in this state. A felony. By admitting you are gay, you are in effect admitting to serious criminal behavior. A few years ago—when Walt was a freshman—the biggest story on campus was a sting operation in which six men were arrested in Jackson Park, the triangle of grass and shrubs that's opposite the old Opera House on South Main. They weren't arrested for having sex but for *talking* about having sex with an undercover cop. The six were charged with soliciting a felony, which in this state is *itself* a felony. One of the six was a student who was expelled. Which was why the Caucus was formed in the first place. To make this stuff more visible. So there wouldn't be all the harassment.

"It's a double standard," he told Danny. "They want to be a gay group but they don't call themselves that. The minute they applied for funding from the student council there was a request for names. Besides, all those guys are interested in are pretty boys. It's bad enough when you get the cold shoulder, but it's just fucked up when they won't take you serious because you don't look like a gym rat."

Walt is not a pretty boy. Nor a gym rat. Just under six feet he's got a pug face, big mouth, something of an overbite. An attribute he told Danny comes in handy a lot. "Has its

185

advantages," he told Danny. "Specially down at the Blue Moon."

He met Danny in the parking lot of the Blue Moon. August. It was humid, just after a rain. Danny was sitting in his big old car. Didn't look old enough to drive. When Walt approached the car, said hello to Danny through the open window, Danny shyly said he was just getting up the nerve to go inside.

They didn't have sex that day. Danny wasn't Walt's type. (He preferred cowboys, working class guys, truckers that stopped at the Blue Moon.) But he did show Danny around. Showed him the magazine racks, the adult toys, the shelf of lubricants, where to buy tokens for the booths, how to catch a guy's interest even if he was looking at a girlie mag. He told Danny about all the gay places he knew of in town or at the University. The cruisy toilets in the library. Jackson Park. The best bars on Market Street. Told him all about guys he went home with from the Starlite.

He tries to catch the bartender's eye. He wants a drink. Lots of drinks tonight. He's not interested in scoring. He's too upset about Danny. Danny was an easy friend. The best thing Walt liked about him. He was someone he could call up and go see a movie with. Which pissed him off that Danny didn't call. That he canceled. Blew him off.

The bartender has a dark hooded look made silly by a ponytail. He's talking with a guy wearing a cap and a long floppy coat, looks like a media guy. Reporter. Or TV producer. Walt wonders if the two of them will score with each other tonight. If the guy will stick around till the bartender is off duty. Probably not. The bartender probably thinks he's straight. Himself. Not the reporter. They're probably talking about Danny. Lots of people have been talking about Danny tonight.

He could tell them a thing or too. The one time he had sex with Danny was about a month ago. They had gone out to eat. Been drinking. Danny always picked up the tab. That was just his way of showing he had a good time. So he gave Danny a blow job. In the car. And Walt wanted to satisfy his curiosity. See if what he thought might be true: little boy with a big dick.

And it was. Let them put that in the paper, he thinks. Let them try to get that out of him. Not on the record. Nothing's gonna be on his record.

The bartender comes over. Asks Walt what he's drinking. Walt orders a beer. Draft. He reaches for his wallet when the bartender returns with the drink. "Guy over there's buying for you," he says. The bartender points to the reporter, the guy in the cap and the floppy jacket.

"What he want to do that for?" Walt asks. He's usually the one who has to buy the round of drinks.

"I told him I'd seen you in here with that guy who got all beat up," the bartender says.

"You must have me mixed up with somebody else," Walt says. He's decided to leave. Go to another bar now. "Don't know him. Don't know who you're talking about."

50

Thursday

"Danny's parents arrived at 7 p.m. Wednesday and are now at his bed side," Donald Carberry tells the room of reporters. There are more than the day before. The lights from the camera crew are so bright that he cannot look up from his paper. He wears a white hospital jacket over his blue shirt and patterned tie. He creases his brow as he reads, "The parents and other family members who are present strongly request no interviews with the media and they ask that their privacy is respected.

"The following statement is from Danny's parents:

'First of all, we want to thank the American public for their kind thoughts about Danny and their fond wishes for his speedy recovery. We appreciate your prayers and good will, and we know they are something Danny would appreciate, too.'"

He makes a dramatic pause here. He looks up from the paper, blinded. His mouth forms a small frown, which becomes a sad pout. His wife had told him to soften up, play it more emotional in front of the camera. This was a chance to be noticed by the hospital, the University, to move up. He appeared too condescending the first time. Isn't it clear that the media is on the side of the boy?

"'Danny is a very special person, and everyone can learn important lessons from his life. All of us who know Danny see him as he is, a very kind and gentle soul. He is a strong believer in humanity and human rights. He is a trusting person who takes everybody at face value and he does not see the bad side of anyone.

'His one intolerance is when people don't accept others as they are. He has always strongly felt that all people are the same—regardless of their sexual preference, race or religion.

'We know he believes that all of us are part of the same family called Humanity, and each and every one of us should treat all people with respect and dignity, and that each of us has the right to live a full and rewarding life. That is one lesson which we are very certain he would share with you, if he could.'"

Again he lifts his head away from the paper. He opens his mouth, as if his voice is caught in his throat. He offers a small cough. Then again the frown, the pout, the creased brow. It is still an act; he is not truly moved. "'Danny also feels strongly about family. He is a loving son, brother, nephew, and grandson who has made our own lives much richer and fuller than what we would have experienced without him.

'Danny's life has often been a struggle in one way or another. He was born prematurely, and he struggled to survive as an infant. He is physically short in stature but we believe he is a giant when it comes to respecting the worth of others. We know that he thinks if he can make one person's life better in this world, then he has succeeded. That is a measure of success which Danny has always pursued.

'Danny very much enjoys the outdoors and camping, and he has always loved acting in the theater—he started acting in community theater at the age of five. Acting and the theater arts are skills at which Danny excels.

'He knows he's not the best athlete in the world but he has a very competitive spirit. One time he participated in the state games. He had a respectable finish in a running competition and then he decided to compete in a swimming event. He did this even though he knew he would likely finish last. Which he did. Afterwards, he acknowledged to us that he knew his chances of winning were far from good but he wasn't going to let that stop him from trying. That's Danny's lesson for all of us—it's a lesson that we hope everyone takes to heart.'"

The camera lights have made him start to sweat. He looks

uncomfortable, because he is hot. He uses it to his advantage. He takes a handkerchief and dabs his temple, where the sweat runs down the side of his face. He uses the moment to wipe his eyes. Then he looks down at the paper again, reads: "'Danny loves it here in this town and at the University. We feel that, if he was giving this statement himself, he would emphasize he does not want the horrible actions of a few very disturbed individuals to mar the fine reputations of the town or the University.

'Finally, we would like to thank the sheriff's department and the University hospital for their very professional efforts on Danny's behalf.

'We also have a special request for the members of the media. Danny is very much in need of his family at this time, and we ask that you respect our privacy, as well as Danny's so we can concentrate all of our efforts, thoughts, and love on our son.

'Thank you very much.'"

51

Thursday

Lois Thompson is the kind of woman who talks and talks. She also frets, frowns, wags her finger at appropriate inappropriate times. She is sixty-seven years old, a great-grandmother. She has always been an old soul. Even while she was entertaining children.

She answers the door holding a baby in her arms. "Reverend, it's good to see you," she says. "Come on in. I'll make you a cup of coffee."

They have met several times before. Perhaps at a wedding, a church potluck. For a while she visited the chapel to look around, remember. She leads him into a kitchen full of warm smells. It is decorated with crafts—hand-made baskets, clay pots, macramé planters—things her students made for her years before. She sits the baby down in a crib that is in front of a sliding glass door. "Just finished feeding this one something," she says. "Chase's boy," she adds, nods in the direction of the baby. "I'm lookin' after him for now."

There is a touch of the bird about her, or a baby chick: big eyes, pale skin, mouth full of teeth, light, vivacious, thick, white hair that springs up like a crest. She leaves the baby in the chair to go to the stove. She turns on the burner, checks the level of the water in her coffee pot. "You're not writing a story for anyone, are you Reverend?"

"Of course not Lois," he answers. The way she says it makes him realize that there could be another story. Something deeper. Something not known. Something that no one is talking about. Something hidden.

"It's a messy thing," she says. "Them kids are good. I've had reporters chasing me since yesterday. A camera crew came and filmed the outside of the house. *The outside of my house!* It's a bit intrusive. And people calling. Wanting to help out. I have to take the phone off the hook to let the baby sleep."

"Yes, I tried calling," he says. "Are you okay?"

"We're doin' fine," she answers. He knows that means there is a struggle here.

"He's a cute one," the Reverend says. "How old?"

"Four months."

"And how are they doing?" he asks.

She breaths in deeply. Her chest cage heightens, but her sigh flattens it out. "I raised both of them kids, you know. Rick when his mother went on, bless her heart. And Chase when she used to show up here after school some times. All worked up about her daddy or somethin' like that."

They drink the coffee in the living room. The furnishings are more examples of Lois's teaching career—pillows bearing embroidered legends such as "My Favorite Teacher," "The Heart is the Home," and "You are My Shining Star." Photos of classes of children hang on one wall. On the table where she places her coffee cup is a bronzed handprint, next to a set of bronzed baby shoes. Lois mentions to the Reverend that she's trying to get her husband to use this room more. The sofa is new. Beige, with reclining features. There are photos lined on the fireplace mantle. Lois and her husband from a cruise. Cindy. Chase and the baby. Rick in his boy scout uniform. A yellowed portrait of another boy, black and white, in profile. And others.

She is the only daughter of an immigrant Irish carpenter and his wife who made their way down from Boston. Lois first went to Skyline Mount with her father on his days off from Sutton Lumber Company, when the mill was located where Clifton intersects the railroad. When she was eighteen, she met and married Hugh Thompson, a pious and strong-willed student at the University. She raised two children in the house on Sancton Street—Cindy and her younger brother, Hugh, Jr., who ran away to Canada to escape facing drug charges when police discovered the marijuana plants he was growing in the basement apartment he rented on South Main. Hugh turned out alright, though. Married a good woman who gave him two sons. Both boys have two kids, boy and girl each.

Lois talks briefly with the Reverend about the growing troubles at the chapel while she settles into a more comfortable position at the edge of the new recliner to better hear his voice. The Reverend admits there is a lot of activity out by the cemetery and the fence. She shakes her head, says, "I don't agree with most of the mothering instincts in this town, you know. I got into a lot of trouble for opening my mouth when I ran the kindergarten. Especially when a kid showed up with a bruise under her eye. That always set me off. That place up there just seemed to invite trouble. I just dreaded every Halloween. Kids would roll the cemetery with toilet paper and set off firecrackers. It was a scary place sometimes."

He mentions that last year one of the University fraternity's held their initiation in the cemetery without his knowledge. He found out after the fact. He made the school pay a fine and filed a police report.

Lois first started teaching Bible classes on Sundays when her own children were young, and, once they both had started Clifton Elementary, she began to offer daily Bible classes for the toddlers of working couples who lived in the valley and could transport them to the annex building in back of the Upper White Chapel. Questions about Lois's teaching skills never arose until the one-two punch of Cindy's drunk driving accident and Hugh Jr.'s flight to Canada. Both children had come of age during the turbulent Vietnam years. Lois always believed that Rick had escaped the family's rebellious Irish streak.

"Do you still keep in touch with Reverend Drake?" he asks, when he finishes his coffee.

"Reverend Drake?" she says, her expression turning hard. "Why no. No, there at the end, we had a bit of a disagreement. When they decided not to rebuild the kindergarten after the fire. I heard he's over in Wolverton county now, though. Works at the youth center."

"I was going through some chapel records yesterday and I found that Rick was working there as a volunteer when he was senior. Is that something that could help him? Maybe we could get Reverend Drake to speak on his behalf."

She holds her coffee cup in midair, as if she is about to let it crash to the floor. Her eyes are wide, full of blinks. "There was more to Reverend Drake's leaving than the fire," she says. "We should leave it at that, Reverend."

He doesn't, of course. He feels as responsible for the student's beating as he imagines Reverend Drake must have felt about the fire. And then it occurs to him. "He wasn't involved in the fire, was he, Lois? Rick? Did he have something to do with the fire?"

Her mouth opens. She struggles with sounds. Finally, she says, "No. I don't think so. They never found out who set the fire."

He doesn't relent now. Even though he knows he has stepped on sore territory. "Then why not ask Reverend Drake to speak about your grandson?"

She fidgets with her cup. It clinks and taps against the saucer. She lifts her head as if to listen for the baby crying. "Reverend Drake was not altogether honorable," she says. "He used to pay some boys for favors." She places the coffee cup on a side table, as if she is worried about the strength of her grip. "*Favors*," she emphasizes. "Rick was one of those boys. No one ever wrote any of the accusations up," she adds. "I always thought it was just another one of Rick's exaggerations, you know. The way he could blow a story out of proportion. But it wasn't this time. It was enough to make the Reverend decide to leave town when it got out after the fire. And he did so honorably. I'm a good Christian woman, Mr. Fletcher, but there are times I wish he hadn't escaped so easily."

52

Thursday

In his room the machines continue their pings and hummings. The sound does not carry out into the hall. Instead, the hallway remains quiet, punctured only by the whirring sound of a cart moving slowly down the hall or the click-click-click of the steps of someone headed for the water fountain. People come and go from the room to speak to his mother and father. Their voices rise and fall in hushed, whispered tones, their postures stooped as though they know they are intruding on moments where they don't belong. His doctors confer in small groups away from the family. They question their ethics, compassion: Are we doing the right thing? Should we be doing anything at all?

A cycle of events has begun that few believe can be reversed, even if he does regain consciousness, which all of his physicians doubt. Sepsis has set off a chain of reactions to the heart, lungs, blood vessels, kidney, and liver. His circulation has slowed. Blood pools in pockets of his dormant body. Toxins invade his tissues, the cells incapable of extracting sufficient oxygen from hemoglobin. His liver restrains his immune system; his damaged kidney no longer properly filters. One physician suggests they declare him legally dead, the heart will stop soon once the artificial supports can be withdrawn. Other staff members on the floor begin to avoid the family—particularly his mother and father—not wanting to witness the inevitable and sad decline.

A few doors down from his room a television set is turned on. A tumble of sounds occasionally fall out into the hall though the level of sound is no more than that of a radio broadcast dimmed to provide distraction for an insomniac.

In that room a white male patient, age sixty-seven, named Ned Spears, has been admitted for a kidney stone. His frame is too big for the bed, his body is a mass of wiry, gray curls. His left hand, thick, dry, and callused, surrounds a remote control. He is watching the evening news. In a surreal moment he witnesses the newscaster, a man with thick, black hair that looks too evenly colored, stand in front of the hospital where he lies recuperating. "Even the President today condemned the tragic and brutal beating of the twenty year-old University student in this community of less than thirty-thousand," the newscaster says. In a press conference earlier at the White House, the President urged Congress to enact the Hate Crimes Prevention Act."

The screen cuts to the President standing in front of a podium and a microphone. He is wearing a dark suit, white shirt, red tie. His eyes narrow as he speaks, "Just this year there have been a number of recent tragedies across our country that involve hate crimes. Our Federal laws already punish some crimes committed against people on the basis of race or religion or national origin, but we should do more. This crucial legislation would strengthen and expand the ability of the Justice Department to prosecute hate crimes by removing needless jurisdictional requirements for existing crimes and give Federal prosecutors the power to prosecute hate crimes committed because of the victim's sexual orientation, gender, or disability. All Americans deserve protection from hate."

As the news program cuts back to the reporter in front of the hospital, Ned Spears' wife, Helen, walks to the window of his room. She is better dressed than usual, but not quite in her church clothes, a beige-patterned dress wrinkled from sitting. She wears a pink sweater around her shoulders, light makeup on her eyes, cheeks. She looks down at the lawn and the parking lot. She sees the news van with the network's logo on it but cannot see if the newscaster is reporting live. She counts the vans in the lot. Seven, eight, nine, more than a dozen. A nurse's aide has told her that it would take a miracle for that boy to survive. "Eighteen hours hanging on a fence," the aide said. "Can you imagine that?"

"I can't even lift my arms up for a few minutes without them aching," she replied. "And nobody's done punched me in the stomach none either."

She returns to her chair by her husband's bed but their eyes don't connect. She doesn't know what to say to him. Her throat feels tight; the sharp, chemical disinfectant smell in the room makes her nauseous. Somehow all this news has made her feel guilty about taking up space. She feels their troubles are much less than others right now.

53

Monday

He dreams he is unable to wake. His eyes open but are too heavy to stay awake. He dreams he is dreaming he is unable to lift his body up. There is a heaviness to him. Light registers. But he cannot move. When Chloe jumps off of the couch he wakes. He realizes he has been sweating despite the chill in the room. He looks at the clock. He has been asleep for only a few minutes. But there it is again. Something he can't escape. This is the baggage that he carries. The dream that he cannot move. That he is conscious and cannot control his body. That it is his fault that he cannot move.

He didn't leave a note. He could not tell his story again. His mother found him unconscious in his bed. They pumped his stomach, a social worker visited, a counselor from the college called. He would no longer talk about what had happened. Convinced that no one believed him.

At the hospital his mother made him see a psychiatrist. The depression was alarming. He had not told her the cause. But she knew what had happened. It hadn't been difficult to find out. The police questioning. The school calling. But he hadn't told her about the way he felt. The way things were. He was not there yet himself.

He discussed his options, medication, with a therapist. He voluntarily admitted himself into St. Clare's, not wanting to give up hope, but without enough energy to continue on his own. He wanted to die as much as he wanted to move ahead. He was put into a room with a guy named Jacob. He was tall, thin, always singing under his breath. It made him more depressed. Just when he was about to give up again he met Mark.

At first he found Mark repulsive. Too flamboyant. His thinning hair was dyed a strange, reddish color. He looked like he wore make-up. He walked with a cane and was always trying to camp. There was a remark to everything. An opinion. Advice. Or the proper way to do something.

But he soon found himself drawn to listening to Mark talk. The nasal New York accent filled up his mind, made him distracted, amused. "I had a therapist who suggested I begin each day by crying a little," Mark told him one morning. "So I still do. I get up every morning and cry. Sometimes I imagine I'm holding Andy's head in my lap and we're crying together. I do it so I can get it out of me and feel other things. Sometimes it works and sometimes it doesn't."

Mark had been recommended by a therapist. He volunteered at the rape crisis center. His own story was full of horrors. "I went to the hospital after I was raped," he said. "There were so many questions coming at me I wanted to scream. I was convinced I was a terrible person, that I should have been able to avoid being attacked in the first place. They made me feel like shit. I sat there humiliated, naked, while a doctor swabbed every opening in my body. A few days later I called a rape center because I needed someone to talk to. This woman on the phone got real angry with me, told me I was lying, that I was probably jerking off while I was talking to her. That's when I really got angry. I called back and yelled at her. I was ready for a fight. Of course I understand it all now. Nobody believes that this can happen to a guy. But it can."

They met in the mornings before Mark started his shift at the center on the other side of town. They drank coffee together, talked about other things before they talked about the thing that defined them. Sometimes only Mark talked. He said a lot of things about Andy, his lover who had died two years before. "I was lucky Andy came along," he said. "Even though he was a mess. You think I'm cranky, you should've heard him. He had a truck driver's mouth but he was a real pussycat at heart."

They met at the pride parade in Manhattan. Mark was dressed in a bikini and a feather and sequin headdress. "I had a fabulous body back then," he said. "But I was going through a phase where if I had sex with someone I would freak out if he tried to touch my face. I had been hit in the head when I was raped. Andy was working at a kissing booth at a fair at the end of Christopher Street. I thought he was cute so I bought a bunch of kisses from him. Made him kiss my face."

"Did he know what had happened?" Danny asked.

"No," Mark said. "Not at first. I had to get to trust him. Then I told him. Once he found out I had a few secrets he wanted to know about all about them. And tell me his."

"What kind of secrets?" Danny said.

"Fantasies," Mark said. "What kind of guys he found attractive. How much he wanted us to do a three-way. He was more talk than anything else. The one time I arranged a three-way he backed out. He was mortified. He couldn't go through it."

Some mornings Mark talked about the "old places." They would walk outside together to the parking lot so Mark could smoke a cigarette. He'd talk about those places where he met guys—backrooms of clubs in the Village, the Hudson River piers, a downtown dance club—places before he and Andy moved to Seattle together a decade ago. "This doesn't bother you, does it?" Mark asked him. "My talking about my sex life?"

"No," he answered. "I understand your psychology."

Mark's eyebrows wiggled like caterpillars. "What? You mean you think because I'm talking about sex in front of you I'm trying to make you feel more comfortable about it."

"Something like that," he said.

"Well, I just want you to know we can talk about sex if you want to," Mark added. "I love talking about sex."

He gets up off the sofa, goes to the bathroom, takes a piss, flushes. He thinks about sex. Thinks about meeting someone. Like the guy at the language lab. He plays out a few positions in his mind. Then looks at himself in the mirror. Wishes the braces away. Wishes he felt better about himself. He opens the cabinet and finds the pill he wants. Cups his hand under the water and washes the pill down in one swallow. Mark knew he had to talk about it. That's why he was there. To get him talking.

And one day he talked about Craig. Being attracted to him. The tumble. The confusion. It came out in a blurt when he noticed a visitor to the floor, someone he thought was attractive. He finally thought of Mark as a friend, not a case worker. Or a therapy. "I don't know what to feel," he said to Mark in a rush of emotion as he watched the guy talk with a patient. "If I told my parents about this it would just upset them. I've made them upset enough already. They think I'm going crazy. I'm not going crazy. I just don't want to upset them."

"They must know you're struggling with it," Mark said. "The sooner you tell them the sooner they'll be more comfortable with it."

"Oh, they'll never be comfortable with it," he said. "If I tell them I'll be in here the rest of my life." He laughed at the thought of it. At himself, locked up for years, silently pining away after visitors.

"Well, it's a good sign that you want to get out," Mark said. "It's a step in the right direction."

That was the day he realized he was in better shape than others. He began helping in the cafeteria. He volunteered to help others walk on the lawn. By the end of the second month he was ready to leave.

But he stayed on. Took a job as an assistant. Moved out of the dorm-like space into an upstairs room in the administration building. He would have stayed on longer except his parents felt he should not abandon the possibility of college. He started a class, once a week on Wednesday nights, at a community college, now able to drive a car again. By the end of the semester he felt strong enough to move out of St. Clare's. He re-applied to the University. And sent applications to a few other schools, including his father's alma matter. Which is where he landed.

Here. On stronger feet, but tougher soil.

But he told them first. Before he left home again. He wanted them to know that things were different for him. And it wasn't a choice. It was the way things were.

He walks into the bedroom. Boots up the computer. Logs on to the Internet. He doesn't check his e-mail. Doesn't write his dad a note. His mind is cloudy. Upset over Mark. He doesn't want to think about school. Grades. Trying to meet someone. He types in a URL. Looks at photos. Goes to a link. Checks out another Web page. He fills his mind with enough fantasies so he does not have to think about himself.

His mother knew before he told her. They had never discussed the rape. But she had met Mark several times at St. Clare's. She said she always thought he might be gay. Though it was not what she wanted. She suggested he live at home. Somewhere he felt safe. Maybe things would be different. He could postpone going to college a little bit longer.

"That's not going to work," he said. "I can't go through this being afraid."

He opens some links on a picture post, studies the bodies— the positions of mouths, arms, cocks. He looks through maybe fifteen pictures and then decides he is wasting time. He decides he feels better. In the bathroom he washes his face, dries himself on a towel, remembers he needs to do laundry if Gary is coming. He realizes that he has not e-mailed Gary or his dad. The thought of it makes him weary. He finds his jacket before this overwhelms him. The best thing now is to be out of the apartment.

54

Thursday

The room is four walls, white, plaster flaking where moisture has invaded, warmed, and dried. The floor is beige linoleum tiles full of scuff marks, black and brown from boots, wooden chairs, the metal legs of the table in the room. It is chilly, a musty smell hangs in the air. The lighting is fluorescent, artificial, heartless. On the table top sits a microphone, wires that lead to a tape recorder, and an ash tray.

"We went to Joe's first," he says. "Sloppy Joe's. That's the place on Market." He doesn't attempt to lean into the microphone. The orange jumpsuit he wears is the brightest thing in the room. It highlights the redness in his eyes, only half-open because he feels heavy, tired. "We had a pitcher of beer there, then Rick said he wanted to go somewhere else."

"The beer was all you had?" Teddy asks. He sits across the table from the suspect. His hands rest on the table top. A pencil and a notepad are in front of him but he doesn't write anything down. A lawyer sits next to his client. Kurt Vong. He is in a dark suit, hair slicked back. There is a sharpness to him that his client does not have. Another man stands watching at the door. The town prosecutor. Cal. Cal Marram. Like Teddy, there is a lumpiness to him. Bald, mustache, something of a gut. Wears a jacket, tie.

"To drink, yeah," A.J. answers. "We ran out of crank that morning."

"Crank?" Teddy asks.

"Yeah," A.J. answers. "We used up a bag the day before. Toked it."

"You had nothing other than the beers?" Teddy asks.

"Yeah," A.J. answers. "We had a pitcher at the Starlite, too."

"So you weren't looking for any drugs?" Teddy asks.

"Sure, we were looking," A.J. says. His eyes swivel, then steady. "We're always looking. But we were both broke. Rick had spent what he had at Joe's. We barely had enough money to get the pitcher at the Starlite."

"What time did you arrive at the Starlite?" Teddy asks.

"It was about 11:30," the suspect answers. "I didn't have any money on me except some change. We paid for the pitcher with change. Rick did."

"So you walked into the Starlite. Got a pitcher. Saw you didn't have any money. And decided to rob someone." Teddy says. "Because you needed some money?"

The lawyer does not offer an objection. His expression is tense. Wavy lines in forehead. Flat lips. A meeting before this one he agreed to let his client talk. Confess. Tell his side of the story.

"No. Not at first," he says.

"What happened first?"

"We played a game of pool," A.J. says. "We didn't even know anything about the guy. We were just shootin'. Rick wanted a cigarette so he asked a couple of guys at the bar. The queer dude had one. They talked a bit before I came over."

"So he introduced himself to you?" Teddy asks.

"I got his name," A.J. replies.

"Did the college boy—did Danny offer you any drugs?"

"Nope," A.J. answers. "If he'd had anything like that we'd probably wouldn't be here."

"Here," Teddy says. "In this room."

"Yeah," A.J. answers. "We were strung out because we were coming down from the crank. From the night before."

"So all you had were the beers. A pitcher at Joe's. A pitcher at the Starlite."

"That's it," A.J. says. "That's what I said before."

"So you had a lot to drink. Two pitchers. You were drunk then?"

"On a pitcher?" A.J. laughs. "Don't think so."

"So you wanted some more," Teddy says. "So you and your friend, Rick, decide to hit on someone to get some more beer."

"No," A.J. answers. "Not beer. We wanted the money."

"You wanted money," Teddy says. "But not for beer. Drugs, maybe? So you could score some drugs?"

"Maybe," A.J. says. "Or maybe another pitcher. We weren't sure. We'd been cranked up since Friday night. We sorta wanted to come down a bit."

"So when you met Danny at the bar," Teddy says. "Did he identify himself as homosexual to you?"

"Well, he looked like fag to me," he answers. "From the way he was talking and stuff."

"What do you mean?" Teddy asks. "That he looked feminine?"

"Yeah," he answers. "He looked like a sissy boy."

"And that's when you decided to rob him," Teddy asks.

"No," he answers. "We went to the head. Rick said we could give him a ride home and jack him then."

"So it was Rick's idea to rob him?"

"That's what I said."

"And he left the bar with you because you were giving him a ride home?"

"That's what I said."

"Did you give him any indication that you were homosexual?" Teddy asks him.

"I ain't queer," he answers quickly, an edge in his voice. His eyes are wider now, a blackness to the pupils, as if it is drawing in anger. "You know that."

"But did he think you were?"

His eyes shift a bit uneasy. He looks for something to alight on, to deflect his expression, but there is nothing in the room except the suit by the door, staring down at him. He casts his eyes uneasily at the table. "He might have. Rick was being flirty."

"Flirty?"

"Dancing a bit," he says. "The music was playing. Rick was sort of dancing as he smoked. Like he was showing off for the guy or something."

"And it was sexual?"

"Depends on how you look at it?"

"So he thought you were a homosexual?"

"He was askin' Rick if he'd been to a place in Richmond," he says. "Said he'd gone there over the weekend. He said it was a place for queers."

"He used that word—queer?" Teddy asks.

"No, he said 'gay.' He said it was a gay club. He started talking about the music they played there."

"And your friend, how did he respond?"

"He played it real cool," he says. "Said he wanted to go there sometime and check it out. The queer guy said he'd go with him, if Rick wanted."

"And did he?" Teddy continues.

"He was being friendly with him," A.J. answers. "He was leading the guy on. That's when he asked the faggot if he wanted a ride home."

"Danny?"

"Him."

"And then what happened?" Teddy asks.

"We left together," he says. "Walked out to the car."

"And where were you headed?"

"Rick was driving," he answers. "I let Rick pick the spot."

"So Rick was driving your uncle's truck?"

"That's the way it was," he answers. His voice is again steady, unrattled, sleepy.

"And that left you free to beat the guy?" Teddy asks.

There is a pause, as if A.J. is aware that he is offering a confession. He tilts his head toward his lawyer, then back. "I didn't do anything to him till he grabbed me."

"He grabbed you?"

"That's right," A.J. answers.

"Where did he grab you?"

"He sort of ran his hand along my thigh,"

he says. "And he was close to my crotch."

Teddy is surprised by the answer, but tries not to show it. He thinks the suspect is taunting him, mocking him. That this part was rehearsed with the lawyer. "And this was when you hit him?"

"He was coming on to me," he answers. "I let him know I wasn't that way."

"And then what happened?"

"He tried it again. Said 'please.' I gave him a good punch. That's when I took his wallet."

"And Rick was driving during this."

"That's right," he answers. "He was sort of laughing. That's when we pulled over and drug him out of the car."

"Did he try to defend himself?"

"Well, yeah," A.J. says, as if it is the dumbest question he has been asked all day. "But he won't much of a fighter. Too much a girl. He kept saying 'please, please,' real soft like. Like a sissy would."

"And that made you angry?"

"He was coming on to me," A.J. says, his voice rising. "He was all over me."

"I think my client has established that he panicked," the lawyer says. It is the first thing he has said, except for clearing his throat when he arrived to the room. He folds his hands across the table, an edge of a lip pulled up into a smile.

Teddy returns to A.J. "And your friend, what was his reaction?"

"He was laughing at first," A.J. says.

Teddy looks down at the pad, thinks a moment, then asks, "How long were you out there—at the fence?"

"Maybe ten minutes," A.J. says. "Seems like longer."

"Did he ask you to stop?"

"Well, yeah, he was getting the shit beat of him," he answers. He gives a little laugh. Then decides it is the wrong thing to do, turns his head toward his lawyer, then back. "I wanted to take him home but Rick got a rope from the truck and said to tie him up to the fence and leave him there." He thinks some more about his story, then continues. "It was like someone else was doing it. I don't know what was going on with me." He looks over at the detective, searching out his eyes for the first time since he entered the room. "He's bad off, isn't he, Mr. DeWitt? Is he gonna die for sure?"

"I think so," Teddy answers. He doesn't give A.J. the satisfaction of returning his gaze.

A.J.'s expression changes. His cheeks flush, then the corner of his lip turns downward, into a pout, like a bad boy mad that he got caught. "I didn't mean to kill him. I can't believe it happened. I just blacked out. I felt possessed. You know, he was coming on to me."

"Is that why you were afraid of him, A.J.? Because he made you think you were gay?"

"I ain't gay."

"You beat him and took his money and his coat," Teddy says. "Because he made you scared about yourself. Is that why you took his shoes? Because he scared you?" Teddy asks.

"His shoes?" he answers. His voice is rusty. Like it is a stupid question. "Don't know. When is this ending? This is making my head hurt, you know. I don't know why we took the shoes. You should ask Rick. Rick was behind all this. Why haven't you asked Rick all these questions?"

55

Thursday

Bob Kadden, the Dean of Students, becomes the University's best asset. Dean Kadden, a former halfback who attended the University on a football scholarship, gathers students on the quad, talks with the media. Twenty-five years at University has made him an institution. (He jokes he has weathered better than most buildings on campus. He considers himself a real charmer: good head of hair, great smile, a penchant for athletic jackets and windbreakers.)

"Doesn't it seem like this kind of elitist environment is ripe to breed hate?" a reporter asks the Dean during a break between classes. She is thirty-three, single, from a news bureau in D.C., part of a group of eight following the Dean around campus. Two men holding cameras. Three other reporters and two photographers.

Students gather where the Dean and his followers have stopped in front of the Alumni House portico. He lightly punches a favorite student in the arm before addressing the reporter, aware his background remains the red bricks and white columns. "We pride ourselves on being an educated and diverse community," he says. "This year minorities made up one-fourth of our freshman class. We have students from seventeen different countries attending the ten different schools of the University. We are looking forward to kicking off our annual homecoming weekend tomorrow and we'll be welcoming our alumni back from across the country. We even know of a graduate coming back from as far away as Italy. We're excited that our football team has been having a winning season this year and we're looking for our boys to whomp some tail on

Saturday. We've had a long standing rivalry with State."

His language does not go overlooked. But the Dean's charisma softens the impact. Hate from a handsome face does not alarm. In fact, the students react as if they are at a pep rally. Only the female reporter, Patricia Lipson, is perturbed. She wants a harder edge to show. She calls his bluff. "Don't you think, Dean Kadden, in light of the recent beating, that the University should consider postponing these kind of festivities?

He answers quickly. Again with a smile. "Nothing could match the sorrow and revulsion we feel for this attack. It is almost as sad, however, to see individuals and groups around the country react to this event by stereotyping an entire community, as if the University were responsible for this kind of behavior, which we are not."

The Dean keeps the group moving across campus. He points out the exterior renovation of the Foreign Studies building, the new language labs in the basement, explains the history of the bell tower and the reason for the design of a medieval library as the whims of big money donors.

Geoff and Holly meet by accident when they are both drawn into the Dean's orbit when he passes through the quad. She is on her way to the cafeteria. Geoff is headed to check his mail at the student union. Their bodies cast shadows on the lawn. His is long, broad-shouldered, his head short and square, like Frankenstein. Hers is slender, tinier, like a fairy.

"They talked about me on CNN and CBS yesterday," he says.

"That doesn't mean it's okay," she answers.

He understands her change in attitude. "I didn't do anything yesterday," he says. "There's too much security around everywhere. They're looking for trouble."

Holly has long straight brown hair, streaked with blond. Her hazel eyes turn cat-like when she looks at him—big, round, yellowish with dark centers. Her clothes—white T-shirt, bright green sweater, jeans, seem to drape her bony body, hang in place. She stretches her neck, like a ballerina.

210

Her hair is knotted in the back today. She asks him if he knew the boy who was beaten. He answers he knew him only from the language lab, that he was nice. Always polite. He says, "I guess you can never tell about someone."

"What is that supposed to mean?" she asks.

"You know," he says. "That they have a dark side."

"A dark side?" she replies. "Because he was gay?"

"Listen," he says. His tone is rougher, defensive. "I don't know anything about those kinds of guys."

"But he was a nice guy," she says. "You just said so."

"But I didn't know him. What kind of guy he was. I never met a gay guy before. I didn't know he was gay."

"Did you hear the way those boys treated him? They beat him up and tied him to a fence and just left him."

"But they were doing drugs," he says. "That's what I heard."

"What makes you so judgmental?" she asks. Her tone is defensive. Smarter. "I've seen you smoke a joint, too. It's not like the guy was out defacing property and then claiming it was for the good of the community because it raised people's consciousness."

He stands tall in front of her. His chest swells, somewhere between anger and desire. "Holly," he says. "You're blowing this all out of proportion. I'm sorry that guy got beat up. But I didn't do it. You can't make me into a heartless son-of-a-bitch. It has nothing to do with us. I was just doing it for you."

"You can't keep doing it, Geoff," she says. "You think you're such a hot shot getting away with it."

"You know I don't think that."

"You're going to get in trouble. Sooner or later you're going to get caught. And they are going to come down hard. You could be expelled. You could go to jail." Her face is scrunched. She has worked herself up close to tears. "You don't even know what it means."

"I do, too."

"I asked you to stop," she says. "That means nothing to you."

"I'll stop," he says. "I'll stop if you want me to."

56

A green pick-up truck comes up behind him and stays there. Everyone in this town drives a truck or a mini-van. Depends on the neighborhood and income. University or not. Pop slows down, hoping the truck will pass, but doesn't. He grips the wheel until his fingers hurt, then signals for the next turn. The truck follows him down the gravely path. He drives slowly, not wanting to ruin the shocks or the silver finish of the limo. The pickup tails him, riding his bumper. There is no room to pass. He says to the guy riding beside him in the front seat that the spot is up there, on the hill, just at the end of the cemetery. The guy responds, surprised, "This is it? This is where he was found? This isn't remote at all. You can still see the University from here."

He drives the limo past the part of the fence where strangers have placed flowers. "Just got to turn around so I can park better," he says.

He pulls to the side to let the truck pass. There are two other cars parked along the shoulder of the gravel road. A black Mustang and a gray BMW.

"You don't mind if I get out right here, do you?" the reporter asks. He is twenty-eight years-old, city boy, impatient. His name is Arnie Darrow. He writes for a gay newspaper in Texas. When Pop met him earlier, he said he grew up in Loma Alta. So he knows something about what the college boy was going through out here.

Pop lets the reporter out of the car. He watches the guy approach the fence as if he were scared of what he might find. Like the body was still there. Pop thinks the sneakers, long coat, notebook, pen held behind his ear seem out of place on the landscape. This guy is indifferent, even though he professes compassion. Something about him makes him ruder than the others. Stuck up, his nose in the air, as if he's better than everyone else. Like he knows it all already. Life. Things about life. Wait till he learns what it is really like.

Pop drives slowly along the path, listening to the pebbles crunch beneath the tires. He turns the limo around in a wide gully about two hundred feet further down the lane. The ground is muddy. Wheels churn up grass, dirt. He drives back, parks the limo at the base of small hill, behind the Mustang.

His wife says there is something wrong with him giving tours to people wanting to see the fence where Danny was found. They've even gotten into arguments about it. He says he doesn't get paid for it. He talks about the boy. "What's so bad about telling people what a good guy he was?" he asked her. He was a good tipper. A good customer. A polite guy.

"I can't put my finger on it but there's something disrespectful to it," she said.

He told her he talks about the other boys, too. He knew Rick's mom. And Lois. He's been hunting with Ray, A.J.'s uncle. He told her he tries to get them to see the whole picture. That this was just a bad moment in a good town.

She says he just likes to hear himself talk. So far he's been interviewed for CNN, Court TV, MSNBC, CBS Evening News, 20/20. He's been quoted in the *Richmond Times-Dispatch*, the University student paper, *The New York Times*. He's talked to a bunch of gay reporters. She asked him why he doesn't just take a lawn chair and six-pack of beer out to the fence and set up shop. She can't even stand to hear the phone ring now. He sort of agrees with her—it's gotten that it rings every five minutes with someone wanting to know something about one of the boys that no one else knows. Which is why he only takes calls on the limo phone. Which is why he's told his wife that when this blows over they'll take a trip somewhere. So when they come back things will be normal again.

For a man in his sixties Pop is not as agile as he ought to

be. He stands by the limo while the reporter looks at the fence, rubbing his wrist. A burning pain bothers him. Happens every time the seasons start to change. His hair turned silver twenty years ago. Now that he's not working in front of the ovens all the time, he's become a better dresser: jeans, cowboy boots, bolero ties. His face is full of deep, dry wrinkles. A smoker's face. Someone who has seen something.

The fence is old, assembled from split pine, held together by wire. The police have removed the section where Danny was tied. For evidence. A pale yellow light shoots across the graves as the clouds shift overhead. The sun has broken through. It gilds the top of the tombstones, settles on the fence.

On the section that's missing, flower stems have been pushed into the grooves, tied together with garbage bag ties or rubber bands, whatever the person had at the moment. Every crevice near the missing section is filled with bouquets, notes, stray tokens. On the grass, small yellow stones have been arranged to form a cross. Another cross, wood, painted white, has been decorated with a cut out picture of a long-haired Jesus, and leans against the post. Tacked to another cross on the ground is a swatch of fabric in rainbow-colored stripes.

He's heard a lot of the college kids are coming out here. To check it out. See if it's true. What they say. They've been likening the place to a spiritual shrine, a place for pilgrimages. One fella said it reminded him of Golgotha. Pop can't see it happening. Not here. Not in this town. Not because he's not religious. It's never been a place for an easy life here. This is a place of sky and ground and hard work. Which is why all those boys got into trouble. All of them. Not just the two punks. The college boy, too. He doesn't tell anyone this. None of them appreciated the value of hard work. Which is why his wife is getting so bent out of shape. They've always worked hard in this town to survive. Job after job after job. He can't afford to retire. That's what no one is talking about. That's the story he wants to hear. That this is a town of honest, hard-working people who can't afford to stop working.

At the fence Arnie watches an insect begin its journey

over the cross. His instinct is to squash it, a habit of killing whatever crawls in his city apartment. He looks at the dust on his sneakers, holds himself back. A woman moves into his field of view. He forgot there are other people at the fence. Three others. Two men. And this woman. Somehow he feels that she has no right to be here—this is his tragedy, not hers. He feels her presence is usurping its meaning. The sanctity of a shrine. A gay shrine. There's not many of these around, you know. He writes the thought down in his notebook, thinking he will try to make sense of it later. When he looks up, three birds skirt across the sky. He twists his head, watches them settle on a telephone wire behind him.

He remembers the time he was chased in the hallway at school, the time his notebook was yanked out of his hand, tossed to the floor. He remembers hiding from the taunts, the burning stings that were the truth before he could accept it himself. He remembers the time he was punched in the eye outside a bar in Houston, falling to the ground and then struggling to right himself. He remembers the searing pain. Not that night. The next day. The stitches. The swollen flesh. The humiliation.

He walks back to Pop and the limo. He is about to speak when Pop says, "The first time I met him was in town. He had called me on the phone in the car and asked about me to drive him and a friend to a club in Richmond that night. But he said, 'I got to meet you first.' So I drove to where he was. He was walking home from campus. I cranked the window down and he walked right up and introduced himself and said he was gay and did I have a problem with that. I told him I only had a problem if he didn't pay me for my work. He said that wouldn't happen and it didn't. He reached into his wallet and paid me right there on the spot. He was a nice fella. So was his friends. Some of the people I've driven around in this town think they deserve the royal treatment without paying for it. Just because life gave them a bummer they deserve some luxury and being pampered."

57

Thursday

The cameraman places the camera on his shoulder. As he settles the weight, he realizes he is hungry. He tries to push the urge away. They won't be here much longer. Even though the assignment is running late.

His name is Burt Goodman. He is Jewish, thirty-two years old, married five years, has one kid—a girl who is four. He is standing outside the Eastgate Baptist Church. He focuses the camera lens on the Reverend's face, zooms in and out, tries to get the steeple in the frame of the picture, then decides against it. He's had enough of this guy. But he keeps his opinion to himself. Tries to be professional. Unlike the Reverend. Who can't help let anyone know what his opinion is even if he is trying to mask it as the will of God.

He knows he doesn't have it as bad as she does. The reporter. Sandra Whey. She is black, slender, not even thirty. Wants to be a network anchor someday, so she says. Since they got out of the news van, the Reverend has pelted her with comments. He has even made her read a passage from the Bible, made Burt film him holding the Good Book in front of the church.

"This boy will go to Hell because he was out trolling for anonymous sex," the Reverend tells Sandra. Burt moves the camera away from her face, trying not to capture her wincing. "His parents did not bring him up in the nature and admonition of the Lord or he would not have been trolling for perverted sex partners in a cheap bar."

"Reverend, there have been complaints that your pickets and demonstrations are hateful and uncompassionate," Sandra says. "How do you respond to this, particularly when many politicians are decrying the violence of this particular case and calling for hate crime legislation to be enacted on a Federal level?"

"According to your standards I am hateful and uncompassionate," the Reverend says. "But according to mine I am not. It would be mean and uncompassionate of me to keep my mouth shut and not warn you, too. But these sodomites want to force you by law to support their filth. They want to shut you up by law when they hate what you say. They would be perfectly happy to make it a crime to preach my church's message that 'God hates fags' under the guise of 'hate speech' legislation. This is the only sin to which America is seriously contemplating giving civil rights. Imagine embezzlers, murderers or rapists demanding that they be given protection, not punishment, by law because of their wrongful deeds. You'd find it amazing."

"Reverend, don't you think it's a bit insensitive that you have already announced that you intend to picket this student's funeral?" Sandra asks. "He's still alive, fighting for breath."

"This boy will certainly die and it is our mission to let people know that they must repent while they are living," the Reverend answers. "This boy will go to Hell when he dies. As I understand it, he is in a coma and is not expected to regain consciousness. There is absolutely not one shred of evidence that this boy ever repented."

Burt cuts the camera and removes it from his shoulder. "That's it," he says. "Out of tape."

"Did you get it?" the Reverend asks. There is too much eagerness in his voice. "Do you want to shoot it again?"

"It's in the can," Burt answers. He turns his back toward the minister.

Sandra shakes the minister's hand, helps Burt roll up the cords of the microphones. She is aware of the Reverend still beside her, towering over her, watching her moves.

"We can bring out the pickets if you want," he says. "It would give you more visuals."

"We've got plenty," Sandra says. "Thanks so much for your

time. I know how busy you are."

Burt returns to the vans. Puts the equipment, camera in the back. He watches Sandra trying to break away from the Reverend. He opens the driver's door, starts the van, waits.

Sandra opens the van door a few minutes later. She adjusts the coat around her legs, pats her hair. Inside the van, as they are pulling away, she looks at her image in the mirror on the back of the overhead visor. "I would never have done this if I didn't believe the network would pick this up," she says. "He always has good quotes. Even if he gives me the creeps."

"You don't have to account to me on this," Burt says. "Only yourself on this one."

58

Thursday

This is what she has accepted: Her son will die. Not that she didn't know he would die, nor that this is his first brush with death. But she knows he will now die before she does. In his room, she wonders if she could make a pact with God. If they could change places. If she could be the struggling one. If he could have the healthy body.

She has asked that the hospital respect their privacy. No visitors other than family and Leah. No reporters on the floor. No phone calls put through to the room. But her request—only one of many—has not softened her mood. She wants a list of things she must expect now. How is the infection spreading? Is he in any pain? If they remove the breathing support what happens next? How long will his breathing continue? Could he hear something? Could his mind recognize her voice?

She moves her hand from his wrist to touch her cheek. The waiting is what bothers her most. She does not want to think about the moments ahead. She feels flushed, knows her cheeks are red. She wonders how much fault this is of hers. Letting him leave home. Letting him choose this place. If his life was difficult because of something she could have controlled. Or altered. Or have done something different to prevent this.

Then it occurs to her that he was born in this hospital. Not this part—the old wing at the back of the lobby—the section that was here when she and Paul were students. She had had a bothersome pregnancy from the tenth week on, erratic contractions which ice water and lying down barely seemed to relieve. In her sixth month she had headaches that went away shortly after they came; occasional black spots appeared in her vision. She was persistently tired, as though she had the ending of a flu she couldn't quite seem to shake.

At her thirty-week checkup, a nurse told her her blood pressure was abnormally high. What was her name? Martha. Martha Ann Cooper. How odd that she could remember *that*. When the doctor appeared in the examination room, he discovered she was dilated three centimeters. She was sent to the hospital. An ultrasound discovered that the baby had quit growing at approximately twenty-eight weeks. Very little fluid surrounded him. They placed her on magnesium sulfate to prevent seizures, hooked her up to fluids and oxygen. She couldn't control her panic, even after Paul had arrived.

That evening, the hospital staff started an epidural. She became disoriented. But her chaotic feeling was soon replaced by the sensation of seeming outside of her own body, as if she were watching everything going on around her. She watched the contractions on the monitor beside the bed in mostly a daze. She wanted tests to check the acidity of the baby's blood. She had thought, then, that science had progressed too far—that they knew too many things about the process of birthing (instead of letting it happen as God should will it to be). This was when she made her first prayer about Danny. More of a bargain than a prayer, really, asking Him to save the baby and take her in his place. Save her child. Let her go instead.

The next morning, the baby's heart rate fell. An emergency cesarean was done. Danny was born weighing two pounds and eight ounces.

He was taken away from her, put on a respirator. He had brocnopulmonary dysplasia, respiratory distress syndrome, apnea of prematurity, bradycardia, necrotizing entercolitis, anemia, and a bacterial infection. She was sent to another floor. Away from him. Her platelets had dropped. Her liver and kidneys were not functioning as they were supposed to function. She spent the next three days hazy, recovering, relying on Paul to quell her panic, to tell her what was happening to her son. She did not ask God for help again. Instead, she promised herself that if she survived, if the baby survived, she would never let things get out of her control again.

Did her abandonment of God create a child full of problems? Or had she asked too much of Him? Had she not spent enough time thanking Him for what he had provided her? She looked at the pregnancy as the cause of many facts—the unusual rashes he got as a baby, the allergies from fruits, nuts. When Danny was seven and struggling in school, she sent him to specialists to diagnose his vision, only to discover he was dyslexic. She blamed herself, the premature childbirth. Even when he came down with normal childhood diseases—measles, chickenpox, flu after flu, season after season—her difficult pregnancy was its cause.

She blamed herself when he broke his leg. (His bones were brittle—that was because of her, wasn't it?) When, at sixteen, he seemed to stop growing and his younger brother became taller, she was again the cause.

And she blamed herself when he was raped. It was because he was so small, unable to fight back, wasn't it? That was her fault too. She blamed herself for his depression, his suicide attempt. She blamed herself when he told her he was gay, even though she had sensed it long before he had admitted it to her—from the way he reacted when girls got crushes on him. She had hoped it was confusion because of the rape, or at worse, an adolescent phase he was passing through, something he would outgrow. But in her heart she knew it was true. Did she cause this too? Was this from her?

And now this. Had they not prepared him better to face the world? Or had she taught him to be too trusting. Too hopeful? Was this her fault too?

She returns her hand to his wrist, squeezes it. "Just relax," she says. "I'm right here." But her face turns slightly away as the sour, dying smell of his body reaches her. She replays what a doctor said when they arrived: *It is doubtful if he will regain consciousness.*

"So what you're telling us is that even if he survives—there is still this?" she said.

"There is medication that could help him—a combination

of drugs—but we don't advise it now, at this moment," the doctor answered. "We don't think his system is strong enough to tolerate those drugs. We're also assuming he wasn't on this medication before, that he did not know about this. About being positive. It doesn't show up in the blood work we've run."

She strokes his skin as if a light brush were at the tips of her fingers. She thinks only of those things they will never discuss together. Things she will not know of her son. Things he will not experience. She wonders if God would listen to her now. Give her a miracle. Or save him the suffering. If he must die now, please take him soon, she prays. Don't let him suffer, Lord. Please, God, take him in your arms if he suffers.

59

Monday

The day feels lighter without the backpack, the umbrella, the headache. The sky has become a deep blue sheet. He stops at the campus bookstore, reads an article in *The Nation* about think tanks, then wanders down the textbook aisle, checks out the books for the next semester of Political Theory.

He spends a few minutes looking at the index of a textbook, then wanders through the bookstore, stopping in front of the magazine racks. He flips through the current issue of *Men's Fitness*, but feels a bit uncomfortable doing it in public, looks at *People*, then decides he'll read the free copy in the Rathskellar, the coffee-house in the basement of the student center. He leaves the bookstore, stops by the post office first to see if there is any more mail (none), then buys a cup of coffee (decaf cappuccino) and sits at a table and reads *Rolling Stone* instead.

At six, he goes back outside, walks across the quad. The sky is darker, velvety, not yet night. The meeting room for the Caucus is on the second floor in a building on the east campus, away from the student center because of worries over harassment. There are about fifteen people tonight—excited, talkative, uncertain, curious. Walt does not show up.

Stuart begins the meeting with outlining the plans for the Gay Awareness activities. Stuart is from Chicago, was out before he arrived on campus. It gives him an air of superiority. He outlines the event on Saturday: the homecoming parade. There is some discussion on safety. Stuart cautions that being out also opens them up for harassment. Particularly when out by yourself. He repeats the story of what happened to Colin (who is also not present at the meeting).

Stuart asks for volunteers to come Thursday night to help make a banner to march behind in the homecoming parade. This is the first year the organization will march in the parade. He mentions that a wooden pole which had belonged to a sorority was donated after last year's parade. He mentions that someone will need to buy fabric.

There is some discussion on what the banner should say. Danny raises his left hand, following Roberts Rules of Order, which Stuart tries to use to govern (even though he has never read the document).

Danny: "Mr. Chairman, don't you think it is a bit hypocritical for us to be planning a Gay Awareness Week when we call ourselves The Caucus? I propose that we use the name Gay and Lesbian Caucus so people will know why we are marching."

Stuart (surprised by the boldness): "We have a motion to change the name of the group. Should we vote on this or table it for another meeting?"

Danny: "I think we should vote on it now."

Stuart: "You can't second your own motion."

Shelly, a graduate student from Gettysburg: "I'll second it. But I think we need to make the name more inclusive. Not just gay and lesbian. What about transgender and transsexual?"

Danny: "And bisexuals."

Stuart (trying to remain composed, in charge): "I hate names that have all those letters in front."

Shelly: "Then what about Queer? What about The Queer Caucus?"

Stuart: "It's such a derogatory term. Like faggot." (He tries to stall the discussion.)

Danny (raising hand again, but speaking at the same time): "But if we appropriate it, then it's not negative. I propose that we call ourselves the Queer Caucus so that people will know why we are sponsoring a Coming Out week."

Shelly: "I second it."

Stuart (trying not to look steamrolled): "Alright, we have a vote for the floor. All in favor of calling the organization Queer

Caucus raise your hand."

Stuart is surprised by the response. The members present vote for the name change. Another discussion follows. This one on whether the banner should be a rainbow design, in keeping with the national movement of using several colors to show diversity. One student in the back, a girl with shortly cropped hair and dark eyeglasses, reminds the group that they are not in New York or Washington, D.C. or Chicago but a small University town. She adds that it would also be very difficult to sew a banner like that. Some of those present have not fully committed themselves to marching out in the open, announcing themselves, coming out beyond the small world of this room.

More discussion follows. It is agreed that a white banner will be made, but different colors will be used in the lettering.

The meeting continues with comments about other activities: A National Coming Out Day booth in the student center. On Tuesday of next week, a speaker from New York will be on campus. Part of a program co-sponsored by the library and the education department. Stuart asks for volunteers to usher at the lecture.

After the meeting Danny stands behind the table in the back, pouring sodas. He meets a girl named Michelle, who shyly tells him this is her first meeting. He hands her a diet soda, introduces himself. She lingers by the table, as if it will protect her. She tells him she is a freshman, eighteen, from Arkansas and a Methodist. She does not tell him how uncertain she is, needing to make a few baby steps first before she makes a bigger leap. Danny introduces her to Stuart and Shelly.

The group filters down to seven people. Danny throws out the paper cups, napkins. Recaps the soda. Gives the left-overs to Stuart and Shelly. Shelly asks him if he wants to walk across the street to the Wooden Nickel to get something to eat. When they leave there are four of them now: Stuart, Shelly, Michelle, and Danny.

The Nickel stands on the site of the town's first trading post, long before the University was built, before the farmers market was opened at Clifton and the railroad. A candlelit refuge for bohemians, liberals, and other town misfits, the owner, Jimmy Lee Hunter, purchased the restaurant more than two decades ago when a fast food chain was making eyes at the property.

In the back booth of the restaurant, the Caucus's favorite hang-out spot, Michelle orders a hamburger because she has not eaten anything since this morning. Her stomach was nervous till now. She did not know what to expect from the meeting. Shelly gets soup. Stuart and Danny split a slice of cherry pie.

Danny talks about a trip he made last weekend to a club in Richmond. He describes the music for Stuart, the types of guys who were there. He whispers to Stuart about what was happening in the backroom. The girls point their chins toward their necks, stare at their napkins till the food arrives. They pretend they are comfortable with the notion of guys talking about sex with other guys. But they are not. They do not know that it is a way for Danny to look important to his friend.

When Danny finishes his story, the conversation breaks down into pairs. Shelly asks Michelle if she is out to her parents. Michelle's response is uncertain. She says, "My mom found a poem I wrote to another girl a few years ago—a love note. But we never talked about it. Somewhere in the conversation Danny tells Stuart that he might go out tonight. He asks Stuart if he wants to go to a bar together. Danny confesses to feeling horny. He's always feeling horny. This makes Stuart laugh. The girls react with smiles, stretching their necks, stopping their own conversation.

Stuart declines the invitation, telling Danny he's fighting off a cold. He wants to stay in tonight. "Everyone's getting sick," Shelly says. "Must be the weather."

Danny asks Shelly and Michelle if they want to go to a bar tonight—just to get a drink—or to dance. Danny says to Michelle: "I love to dance. It works off a lot of frustration. But there's not a place for guys here. Unless you go with a girl. Two guys and a girl can get away with it, without too many people talking."

Shelly says tonight's not good for her, even though she

briefly entertains the idea of going out. Michelle says she's worried about a test tomorrow. She talks about how much time her studying has been taking. She wants to go pre-med. But Chemistry is giving her a lot of problems. She has to study. She won't party till the weekend.

After they are finished eating they split the bill. Outside it is dark, the air unusually still. Stuart and Shelly walk to where they parked their cars. Michelle walks with Danny down Clifton toward the student dorms. Danny kicks the dry leaves at his feet as he walks, says autumn is his favorite time of the year. The way everything is so layered with colors. At Sanderson, he asks her again if she wants to go out later.

She appears interested but answers, "No thanks. I'll take a rain check for another night."

He says, "That's cool."

They part at the corner. He crosses the street. She heads toward the dorm.

60

Thursday

There are more questions about the college boy. More questions. More details to recall. His head feels as if it will explode.

"Why did you decide to rob the boy?" the prosecutor asks. They are in the white room. A lawyer and a court reporter are present. Three people wait for his answers.

"He looked like an easy target," Rick says. His voice sounds rough. As though he hasn't slept for days. He has not shaved. He can feel the oil and dirt on his face. Dust in his nose. He is so tired he would like to claw his eyes out. He thought this would be over by now. That he would have reached some kind of relief. That he could sleep.

"Why did you pick him?" the prosecutor asks.

He studies the man's white shirt, the pattern on the gray tie, the hands placed on the table. He wonders why his lawyer says nothing. Like he's in on something. "He looked like he had money," he answers.

"So you were going to rob him?"

"Yeah."

"Did you know the boy was gay?"

He doesn't like the sound of the prosecutor's voice. It is harsh, clipped, accusatory. He wants someone to know that. "Not at first," he answers. It was easy to figure out once we were talking to him."

"How is that?"

"He used his hands a lot," he answers. "His voice sounded like a homo's."

"How is that?"

228

"High, like a sissy."

"So you decided to rob him because he was gay," the prosecutor asks.

"No," he answers. "Because he looked like he had money. It was A.J.'s idea."

The lawyer reacts by lifting his eyebrows. He writes something down on a pad of paper. It makes the suspect turn, shift in his chair. The orange jump suit he wears scratches, thick with starch.

"A.J. had the plan for the robbery?" the prosecutor asks.

"Yeah," he answers. "We went to the john. A.J. said for me to drive, he'd take care of getting the guy's wallet and watch."

"His watch?"

"He had a gold watch on," he answers. "It looked expensive."

"And you offered him a ride home?" he asks.

"Yeah," he answers.

The prosecutor pauses his line of questioning. He takes a sip from the coffee cup on the table in front of him, then looks up at the door, as though he is expecting someone to enter. He is fifty, balding. There is gray in his mustache. He is married, father of two girls. For a long time he lived and worked in other places. (But never lost his country twang. He sounds more like a preacher than most preachers in this town.) He came back six years ago to be the town prosecutor. He has spent the day catching up on this case, was silent during the other perpetrator's confession. "Did you give him any indication that you were homosexual?" he asks. His name is Cal Marram. He is gathering material, evidence, statements to use in a trial somewhere down the road. A long road for him. And for the town.

"He was talking about being gay," he answers. "Going dancing. I was just being friendly."

"Friendly?"

"I wasn't hittin' on him because he was gay," he says. He wishes he had slept. If he had slept he could think his answers through. Everything seems to be repeating now. Nothing seems finished, relieved. His brain seems heavy, like a wet sponge. "And I wasn't beatin' the shit out of him either," he adds. His tone is annoyed, irritated. "That was A.J. A.J. was beating him."

Marram waits for the suspect to calm down. "So he goes to the truck with the two of you. You're driving?"

"Yeah."

"Why were you driving?"

"It was part of A.J.'s plan. A.J. thought this up."

The lawyer remains silent. His pen scribbles, makes a light noise. His hair remains in place. A slick, oily helmet.

"The college guy is in the center of the seat," Marram says. "A.J. is by the other door?"

"Yeah."

Again the prosecutor looks up at the door, as though someone was watching him. He looks back at the suspect and asks, "What happened next, Rick?"

"A.J. told the guy we were jackin' him. He threw a couple of punches and the guy doubled over. That's when he reached in and got the guy's wallet."

"A.J. made the first move?"

"That's right."

The prosecutor turns to the lawyer, watches him write more on his pad. It makes the suspect feel uneasy, uncertain. He looks at the court reporter. She is overweight, fleshy rings at her neck. Eyebrows black, glossy, like covered with Vaseline. Her fingers have paused in the air. Rick flips his gaze to the table, studies the scratches on the surface, thinks about why he has no interest in the woman.

"The boy—Danny—did he make any type of sexual advance?" Marram asks.

"To me? Nope."

"Or to A.J.?"

"None that I saw," he answers. "Once I pulled out of the parking lot, A.J. went right at the guy."

"Hitting him?"

"Yeah."

"And he asked you to stop?"

"A.J.," Rick says. "A.J. was hitting him."

"Were you and A.J. doing any drugs that night?" Marram asks.

"We had a beer," Rick says. "That's all."

"Had you done drugs at all that day?"

"No," he answers. "We had tried to get some from one of A.J.'s dealers but we didn't have the money for it."

"So you didn't get any drugs?"

"Nope."

"But you had been doing drugs?"

"Yeah."

"Did the college boy—Danny—did he try and sell you any drugs?"

"Nope," he answers. "I bummed a cigarette off him. That's all."

"Just a cigarette?"

"His last one."

"Why did you stop on Upper Chapel Road?" the prosecutor asks. "By the fence?"

"I used to go there as a kid," he answers. "With my granny. It's her place. Her church."

"So you knew the place," he asks.

"I didn't know A.J. was going to beat him like that."

"Did the boy try to defend himself?"

"Yeah," he answers. "But more like he was trying to get away."

"Away?"

The prosecutor's tone makes him think that things might work out after all. As if he will get out of this. That this was A.J.'s mess. "Run away," he says. "Escape." The moment comes back to him. Catching the college boy by the coat. The tackle. His face pressed against his neck. The blood. The memories now make him dizzy. "That's when I caught him. I wanted to let him go after that. He was pretty bad off. A.J. wasn't through with him yet. He wanted me to tie him up to the fence."

"And you did?"

He doesn't answer at first. At first, the scene plays again in his mind. Thump. Thump. Thump. He lifts his eyes toward the prosecutor. He knows that his cooperation in the crime will not go unpunished. He struggles with his own defeat. "I told him that we should go," he says. "That's when he hit me in the lip with the gun. That's when it changed. That's when I knew we were in deep shit."

61

Thursday

"Everybody has an interest in this story," Teddy says to Reverend Fletcher.

They are seated in Teddy's office. Basement of the court house building. More papers on his desk. The Reverend sits with his hands folded in his lap. His soul is heavy, full of subtext. He thinks two cases might be linked. The fire, five years ago. The beating of the student.

"Frankly, I don't have the manpower to pursue this hunch of yours," Teddy says. "Though it is an interesting one. And to tell you the truth, the boys have confessed. I have confessions from both of them. This case is pretty much wrapped up. I will write up your statements and put them in the file. In case they need to be looked at further. But if you ask me, God handed this one to us."

"God?" the Reverend answers.

"I've never worked a case like this where there was so much evidence around, out in the open," he says. "It was like, here it is guys, work it out. It's almost like it pissed off God, and he said, 'Oh well, come here, let me walk you over here—walk you over there, be sure to pick up all this—don't forget to pick up that.' This case has been easy as making mud—it's just all the other shit we've had to contend with. You know, I'm sure you've seen 'em all down at the chapel. All these activists trying to pass this place off as the capital of hate."

"It makes me wonder if we've ignored things too long," the Reverend says. "Doesn't it disturb you that maybe there are people in your community you are unable to protect?"

He gives the Reverend a sour look, doesn't like it being

insinuated that he's forgetting part of his job.

"I'd like to think that we offer protection for everyone," he says. "But like I said—everybody's got their issue on this one. No matter what I do on this case, somebody's gonna think it wasn't enough. I've got activists jumping down my neck trying to find out if the boy was raped or not. There's a homosexual organization in New York that wants to build a shrine on Skyline Mount. Every minister in the valley thinks the chapel should be torn down. I got a state senator and a town councilman on my neck, asking me every two minutes what's happening with this investigation. What's happening is what we're all forgetting about—that this poor guy is still clinging to life. And if he does make it—he's got a whole lot of medical issues to deal with. I've got reporters ready to release the medical information on the victim. The defense attorney is ready to use it as a motive. He's thinking about calling a press conference to announce that the guy was HIV-positive and that his client has been compromised. Nothing is confidential on this case. If all that gets out—which it will at some point—I've got trouble here. I've got officers who are struggling with a host of extra issues because of this case. It's like, God's going to make one part of this easy and another part of it a challenge."

"So you think this is all the work of God's hand?" the Reverend asks. His mind is back at the chapel, the cemetery, seeing the boy tied to the fence. "This is part of a plan?"

"He's certainly trying to tell us something," Teddy says. "What it is, I'm not entirely sure."

62

Thursday

Michelle arrives early, starts working on the banner by herself. She lays out the fabric on the table she had picked up from Stuart's apartment earlier in the day—a large bolt of white cotton with a satiny sheen which is water repellent, in case it rains. She has already cut the lettering out from swatches of different colored fabrics. She had found the stencils in a storage locker at the student union and had walked into town yesterday, asked the owner of the fabric store if she had any scraps to donate to the project. At first she had only told the woman—Alice Tanner—that she was making a banner for the homecoming parade. Mrs. Tanner had given her a few squares and scraps and had started asking her what sorority it was for. Michelle was afraid of revealing too much of herself or the nature of her project to the owner, for fear of the donation being rescinded. But it was Mrs. Tanner who approached the subject of Danny first, with a shaking of her head, saying, "Isn't it awful about that boy. Did you know him at all? Was he a friend of yours?"

She answered that she had known him and had seen him a few hours before the beating.

"I can't imagine that kind of anger," Mrs. Tanner said. "I read that they beat his skull in. That just gives me the shivers. No one deserves that kind of beating. Even when I read about it happening in the Middle East or Northern Ireland, I just don't think it's right. I just can't believe it could happen here. It's just too barbaric."

Then, Michelle confessed that the banner she was making was to offer him support. "I thought a few of us would march behind it," she said. "To show that we care about what happens in this town." At that point she was prepared to pay for the fabric, for the privilege of telling someone that she knew Danny, that he was her friend and the grim facts had moved her too, made her want to speak out against this kind of behavior. Mrs. Tanner responded by touching other bolts, saying, "Hon, I could give you some of this, too. You take what you need to make a beautiful sign."

Now, in the room on campus, Michelle lays the lettering out in their sequence to spell the message she had thought of. She knew she was changing things, that she was proceeding ahead with her own initiative and not by group method, but she felt strong enough to convince anyone that this was the direction to take.

Shelly is the next to arrive and, as she leans over to read the banner's message, she offers no hint of displeasure with Michelle's alteration. Her only reaction is a business-like one. "Do you think we should glue them on or sew them on?" she asks Michelle.

They debate on the pros and cons of gluing or stitching. They decide, for the sake of time, to glue the letters to the fabric. Colin, a biology major, is the next to arrive. He tells the two girls that he has come to help, even though he is not on the committee. "I heard someone on the news say that this wasn't a gay issue," he says. "Of course it's a gay issue. And then I heard about that guy—the God Hates Fags minister—deciding to come here, and it makes me pissed that he would try to do something like that. I don't understand why someone could feel that way—why wouldn't he just want to stay home and cry? Or pray? If he's coming here I'm going to be waiting for him. I can't believe this is happening."

In the next hour more and more students arrive to help. The room fills with conversations—Michelle hugs a girl whom she has never met before because she has entered crying, saying, "It could have been me. It could have been any of us. None of us are safe here." By the time of the last arrivals, the banner is completed. The mood is defensive, angry, everyone wondering how could this happen. Here. Where they live.

Michelle finds she is now the strength of support, the rock of determination needed to convince others that they must be who they are and not be afraid to show it. She smiles, talks about the banner, the fabric, and soon she begins asking what time they will assemble for the parade.

Stuart arrives almost fifteen minutes later. He says there's an impromptu vigil planned outside the hospital. In his hands he carries a box of white candles—donated by a minister of a church over in Rodneysville—which was why Stuart was so late. Soon, everyone is holding a candle and a small paper circle to reflect the light. The banner is folded and stored. Michelle follows a river of people out of the building and across campus to the hospital.

63

They try to rehearse as if nothing has changed since they were last together. But it is surprising to each of them how, in just a week, things can change so abruptly—that their town, their home, can become synonymous with hate. That they can be afraid to drive their car alone. That they must look over their shoulders and watch their back. That wherever they go, someone is probing into them deeper, trying to understand why hate is here. As if it is nowhere else.

Leah watches Naomi try to keep the tempo at the piano. Her cheeks are flushed. Strands of hair at her neck are damp. Dr. Graham, the choir director, pushes the beat. "Keep up," he yells at her, above the sound of the choir. They are off key. The alto section is a half-note off, the bass a beat behind. Leah thinks the music is too difficult for the choir—they are not like the University musicians—they are amateurs, volunteers, members of the choir for years, like herself. Dr. Graham is an amateur musician, too, a member of the University's history faculty, not a professional musician. She remembers what Danny said when he first heard the choir at Sunday services. "They're much more ambitious than when I was a kid here," he said. "And a lot noisier."

They rehearse the song for another ten minutes, trying to get the bass section to learn a sequence of notes. Then Dr. Graham says they must stop. There are some new songs that they need to rehearse.

The announcement surprises Leah, even though she knows why it was made. And had expected it. She had spoken to Dr. Graham earlier in the day—at the request of Danny's parents.

238

If Danny dies, which he most certainly will, his mother wants the funeral services to be held at this church—the church she was baptized in, the church her son was baptized in. In the last day, his parents have had to discuss impossible things: Do they talk to reporters? Do they set up a memorial fund? Do they keep him on life support? Do they bury him here or in Seattle? Where, exactly, should his final home be?

When Leah was at the hospital this morning, Julie mentioned the music that Danny might have wanted. "Something popular, that's for sure," she said. "He wasn't a big fan of church music, you know. Maybe he would like you to choose something. What would you like?"

This bothered Leah. She didn't feel it was her place to choose. She tried to imagine herself singing in a choir at Danny's funeral and shuddered the thought away.

"I once heard his junior high choir sing that Simon and Garfunkel song," Julie said. "When we lived in Portland. That might be nice. 'Bridge Over Troubled Water.' Something like that."

Leah gave a list of ten songs to Dr. Graham, hoping there might be an arrangement to one or two of them. At their weekly rehearsal that night, Dr. Graham passes out copies of a choral arrangement of "Bridge Over Troubled Waters." Margie, the alto sitting beside Leah, begins crying before Naomi begins the introduction on the keyboard. Leah notices that Dr. Graham's eyes have teared up as well.

"I know that this has been an emotional week for all of us," he says, again stopping Naomi. "We have all been put under a microscope. There has been a special request for us to sing a few different songs sometime in the future. One thing we will have to do with this song is to keep our courage together. We have to be strong in this song because others will not be. Your emotion in this song must be strength."

He starts directing the beat. Naomi begins at the piano. The chorus starts: first, the tenors. Then the altos. When the sopranos and bass arrive, they are louder, firmer, a unified sound. Leah thinks it's the best they've sounded in the fortysomething years she's been in this choir. But she doesn't want anyone to hear them this way. She doesn't want any of this to keep happening.

64

Thursday

Walking home after work Gary stops at the bookstore on Connecticut Avenue, looks through the titles of the magazines in the back of the store. He picks one up, looks at the photos, replaces it in the rack. He looks to the ground to see if the new issue of the free weekly newspaper is out. It is not. On the bulletin board above the stack of papers he notices a note: Candlelight Vigil, 8 p.m. He reads the name of the church. He's walked by that building many times and never been inside. He can't even remember the last time he was inside a church. Not since he moved to D.C., that's for sure. On his way out of the store he thinks he wants a nap more than he wants to sit in church. He didn't sleep well the night before, the news too disturbing. He kept playing the details over and over, that it couldn't be the same guy, that this had happened to someone else.

At home he places his briefcase on the table, lies down on the couch without taking off his shoes or clothes. He doesn't even loosen his tie. Only the glasses come off. Plop, on the coffee table. The day has exhausted him. It's been harder to concentrate. He had more patients than he expected.

He thinks about turning on the TV but he can't bear the sound. Or any more news. All day long he has chased the updates. Is he still in a coma? Was anyone arrested? How did the beating happen?

He closes his eyes and falls asleep. He doesn't dream. It is a deep, blank sleep. When he wakes he notices it is a quarter past seven. He looks out the window behind the couch. Notices it is dark. His head is cloudy, thick, in spite of feeling rested.

Weight has settled into his shoulders. He stands and steadies himself. Walks to the kitchen, pours himself a glass of water.

He looks at his watch. He thinks he could make it. It would be good for him to be out. He takes off his coat and tie, throws them on the back of a chair. He rinses his face at the sink, takes a sweater from the closet, finds a jacket. In front of the mirror he squints to clear the hardness from his face. Runs his hands through his hair. Cleans his glasses. Then heads out the door.

At the church they are passing out small, white candles and paper reflectors at the entrance. He takes one and walks down the aisle, not too far, chooses a pew in the back. There are maybe fifty people seated in the church, but more are finding their way inside. The church is full of arches, thick, white candles on an altar of dark, carved wood. A blood red carpet covers the floor. Stained glass windows of New Testament scenes line the sides. An organist is playing, the windy sound filling the room. It is too much church for him. But if prayer can help then prayer is what he will do.

He looks through a hymn book while he waits for the service to begin. He thinks about the time before he was gay—before he identified himself as gay—the way even the thought of a man could disturb him—the dilated iris, the quickened heartbeat, the trace of sweat—all because of an attraction. A surge of confusion and lust. The bent of his desire had bitten him in his late teens. He wonders if it was easier then—the not accepting of himself. He wonders if because he now admits that he is gay that he is also more afraid of being alone.

The row he sits in fills up with men. A few wiggle out of their coats when they are seated. Someone stands up, fold his jacket, places it on his lap. He senses individuals and colors. Some like blue. Others brown. Short, buzzed cropped hair still in fashion.

There are hymns and prayers, kneeling and standing, voices singing, the organ drowning out all sound. His mind wanders to the windows during the reading of scriptures. Fake daylight comes from behind each pane. More dust than color.

Toward the end of the service, ushers stand in the center aisle, light the candles of those seated at the end of the pew. Flames are passed from person to person. A guy in a flannel shirt passes the light to him. He passes it to a woman on his left. The chandelier lights are dimmed. Another prayer is said; another hymn is sung. The candles are blown out. The service ends.

He follows the guy in the flannel shirt down the main aisle toward the exit. He waits his turn to return his extinguished candle to a box. He is disappointed in the service. He has not reached any kind of internal resolution. He doesn't feel better. But he doesn't feel worse. He feels incomplete. Something remains unfinished.

He notices a bright light as he heads through the lobby to the large wooden doors of the exit. The guy in the flannel shirt is now wearing a quilted vest. Yellow. They are side by side at one point, waiting to leave the church. The guy gives him a smile. He returns it, hears someone ahead say, "You can't just do that. This is not a place for that." On the steps, a camera crew is filming people exiting the church. Instead of taking the front exit, he heads for a side door. The guy in the yellow jacket does the same. They are again side by side, both waiting to exit.

"I'm Scott," the guy says, nodding and smiling again to him.

He smiles, says his name. "Gary."

"You're a friend of Jon's, aren't you?" Scott asks. "I think I've seen you at the gym."

"Yes," he answers. "I thought you looked familiar, too."

Scott has a pretty face: full lips, pale skin, wide eyes, small ears. He'd be too pretty were it not for receding hairline, heavy Adam's apple. And the voice. Deep, nasal, full of hormones. Cuts right through to the chest. They talk about the service as they wait to exit. Gary reaches the stairs outside first, slows his walk so that Scott can catch up. He doesn't know why he does it. It is cold out. Breath condenses into white air. He thinks Scott will vanish the moment they reach the street, thinks he is part of the group of guys who were seated in his row and who will head their own way once they regroup on the sidewalk. Instead, Scott walks with him up the sidewalk toward the street corner. They talk some more. About whether the college boy will live. Scott's voice hits Gary's ribs, swirls around in his lungs, makes him too giddy for such a serious subject.

But he does not confess his friendship with Danny. It's not that he wants to keep it secret. He's not ready to admit it's the same guy. Or ready to admit that if it isn't, once again, he's been dumped.

Scott says some nights in this neighborhood it can be pretty rough—teenagers driving by, throwing bottles. "That's what you get living in the ghetto," he says.

"And a pricey one at that," Gary adds.

They talk some more about the way real estate prices have gotten higher, about the favorite neighborhood restaurant a block away that went out of business when the landlord tripled the rent. Then there is a break in conversation. A point where the subject should change but they are both aware they are still standing together at the corner.

"I'm parked over there," Scott says.

Gary looks over Scott's shoulder, into the dark.

"You want to get together for dinner some time?" Scott asks.

"Sure," Gary answers. "What's your schedule like?"

"What about tomorrow?" he asks. "Are you free tomorrow?"

Gary wants to respond that he's been free for quite a while, but he answers, instead, "That sounds good."

They exchange phone numbers. Gary has a pen in his coat pocket. Scott has the program from the vigil folded in his back pocket.

65

Friday

He will not know of the vigils, more than thirty of them held around the country. He will not know of the shock that permeates the University, the town, bleeds across the nation. He will not know of strangers crying over his injuries. He will not know that his mother vomited when she saw a story about him on the news for the first time, thinking he was being exploited.

He will not know that in a classroom students will be allowed to publicly express their objection to this crime. He will not know that even as they do so, a man in Arizona, thousands of miles away, will write to his local paper calling him an "unfortunate person" who should have "stuck with his own kind and kept it under his hat." He will not know that an organization in Washington, D.C.—a gay political fund-raising group—has sent field investigators to the town to dissect this crime. He will not know that the University president does not support hate crimes, does not plan to propose insurance benefits to same-sex partners, and will restrict media access as the scrutiny becomes tougher, calling upon a public relations firm in New York City to help keep their image clean in this crisis.

He will not know of the messages or e-mails or flowers that arrive at the hospital. He will not know of the intersection of his friends with his family, of the police with his parents, of the argument between his mother and his aunt when a request comes from *20/20* for an interview.

He does not know that the myth continues, widening, shaping itself on its own. He will not know that his shoes, his coat, his watch, his student ID have now been sealed and stored away as future evidence. He will not know that the gun used to attack him will be photographed, sketched, weighed (three pounds, four ounces). He will not know that the gun did not belong to his attacker's uncle, but was acquired in a drug trade a few days before it was used. He will not know that his writing instructor has released the contents of his essay on capital punishment to the student newspaper, that it will be picked up by the Associated Press, Bloomberg News, and National Public Radio. He will not know that in their search for more news, the news itself will become invented. One reporter will ask another, "Did you hear that he was burned, too?" He will not know that another reporter repeated the assumption and that another reporter reported it as fact. He will not know about the debate over whether his hands were found outstretched or behind his back, will not know that one source says that his hands were nailed to the fence.

He will not know of the minister who makes his way to the place where he lies struggling to attack him further—his life, his lifestyle, even his upbringing. He will not know that Leah struggles with a way to handle her own concerns and disbelief. He will not know that Gary thinks about what might have been. He will not know of the lists his mother has created—a list of songs, a list of friends, a list of people she will need to thank.

He will not know he is in the presence of many thoughts. His life still exists on a smaller level. A cellular struggle. Where nature knows no distinction between what is good and what has been evil.

66

Friday

"My father is addicted to hate," he says. He is thirty-nine years old. His name is Sol. Short for Solomon. He has his father's height. His forehead. His nose. He sits in the chair, sweating from the bright, overhead lights of the television studio. He doesn't want to be here but he can no longer keep quiet. It's time to for him to fight back. "Living in that house was like being in a war zone. My father was very violent. One Christmas, my brother and I were beaten with the handle of a mallet more than two hundred times. My sister was locked in her room and given only water to drink for four days. My mother was abused. My father was also addicted to amphetamines. I'm not trying to hurt my father. But I'm not trying to save him either. This is no way for a minister to act."

Now this news filters out through the media. Into the papers. On the Internet. Over the radio. Hate is a topic that cannot be overlooked. Why do we hate? What causes hate? When does the moment of fear and loathing become hate? And why is it so fascinating? Why do people watch it? Listen to it? Read these stories? What is the attraction of hate—its repulsion? Its violence? The fear it causes?

In Washington, D.C., an intern for a Senator photocopies an essay about why states should pass hate crimes legislation. In San Diego, a journalist begins an opinion piece defending hatred because he himself would like to retain the right to hate those he does not appreciate. In Missouri, a woman tells her sister that there should be severe punishment for those who commit hate crimes because it sends a message that such behavior is unacceptable. In Dallas, a lawyer discusses the necessity of gun control with a colleague. Isn't this all related as well? he asks.

Throughout the day more and more politicians will call for a war on hate. They will talk to reporters, hold press conferences, deliver sound bytes to be sent out across the news. They will denounce hate. Battle hate. Fight hate. All the while unaware of their own violent rhetoric. *Hate* hate.

On the Internet a petition will be circulated, a statewide drive calling for the passage of a hate crimes law. At 2242 Valley Road in Alpharetta, a suburb of Atlanta, a woman will write her local newspaper: "The murder or death of anyone is tragic, but listening to all the media coverage of this crime and then to have other murders go unmentioned, I feel a taste of bitterness and anger over the whole situation. Now I am hearing all the talk for legislation to make penalties for hate crimes harsher than others are. I have difficulty understanding this mentality. Aren't all murders born out of hate?"

Hate is everywhere, another reporter will write. Reasonable and unreasonable. Rational and irrational. Its shadows and shades are labeled and categorized, held up for scrutiny, examination, discussion, and argument. One writer will even detail the blunt and subtle shades of hate: There is hate that fears and hate that merely feels contempt. There is hate that exudes power and hate that comes from powerlessness. There is hate that is revenge and hate that is envy. There is hate that was love and hate that is an expression of love. There is hate of the other and hate that reminds us of ourselves. There is the oppressor's hate and the victim's hate. There is hate that burns slowly and hate that fades. There is hate that comes from knowledge and hate that comes from ignorance. There is obsessive hate and hysterical hate. There is hate that kills and hate that merely wounds.

Reverend White will offer a quick response to his son's allegations of being addicted to hate. He does not hide behind a public relations campaign or an institutional profile. He is his church. He is the voice of his God. From a cell phone the Reverend tells a local reporter, "Crying 'judge not lest you be judged' or 'let he who is without sin cast the first stone' is a favorite tactic among fags and so-called wimpy Christians, just like it was among the ancient sodomites. Children are besieged by their own lusts and foreign ideas. That boy wanted to enjoy the pleasures of sin and that was why he was punished, just like any child should be for choosing the path of sin. I feel sorry for him because he is not bound for the promised land. God hates him as much as he hates God. Yes, he is still my son, but he will spend his eternity burning in Hell."

67

Friday

And so another myth begins. This one of bad luck. Misfortunes. It starts when the town newspaper runs a story about the unfortunate history of Skyline Mount.

In the article, a history professor at the University explains the chapel's use during the Civil War as a hospital for wounded Confederate soldiers, run by Dr. Harvey Baker, who was not officially on one side or the other. When slaves brought word to Dr. Baker that Federal troops were on their way to arrest him, the doctor barricaded himself and the patients inside the chapel. Six Bluecoats charged through the chapel door and fired shots. The doctor and three others were killed. The dark stains on the chapel floor are believed to be from their blood. It was the only war casualty on town property, and in 1926, the United Daughters of the Confederacy erected a stone memorial to the doctor in the cemetery behind the chapel. The inscription on the stone reads, "Cowards die many times, the brave but once." According to the professor, Dr. Howard J. Maltin, the pastor of the Chapel had the front door painted red for the marker's unveiling. Since then it has remained that color as an unknown tribute to the doctor and the soldiers.

"The doctor was a young man, never married," Dr. Maltin says in the article. "Not more than thirty-five according to the accounts of the time."

"I really think that place is haunted," Nancy Gambone, a town florist, is also quoted as saying about the chapel. "I've been at wedding rehearsals there when the lights just go out for no reason at all. Makes that place real sort of spooky."

Even Parker Mahonen, the woman who owns a portion of the southwestern corner of the Mount, the area where the fence is located where the beaten student was found, is quoted about the poor soils and the bad crops her family had before they turned to raising show horses. "The birds are relentless in that area by the cemetery. Like they're waiting for something to happen."

The story is reported and embellished. A radio announcer adds items about University students being hazed in the cemetery. A call-in listener adds details about the kindergarten fire five years ago, even though no one was killed or injured. "They never did find the person who did that," the woman says. "I think that place is just bad luck."

68

Friday

"I don't think it will happen," Marcie says. "They would never tear down the chapel."

Reverend Fletcher doesn't recognize her at first. His thoughts are elsewhere. "I heard that a councilman is already proposing that the University take over the property," he says when he looks at her instead of the courthouse doors. "Put some kind of observation tower there. Fence the area all in."

Their meeting is out of chance. He is carrying the paper beneath his arm, waiting for the doors to open for seating for the arraignment. She is dressed in her uniform, standing in the hallway with several other officers.

"They wouldn't do it," she says. "A lot of people have some good memories of that place too. My ex-husband and I used to go there when we were dating. There used to be a lane in front of the annex. You could park there and look out over the valley. It was a big make-out spot. Very romantic. I'm surprised that they never put up a sign that said it was Lovers Lane."

"Kids still park up there," he says. "But mostly in summer. I've heard there's a lot of other popular parking spots in the valley now."

"What spots are those?" she asks. She offers him a smile, the first time in days she has used those facial muscles. "I'll have to tell the night shift."

He laughs, says he can't reveal inside information, he's sworn to secrecy by a bunch of soon-to-be brides. Their conversation stops when the courtroom doors are opened and a crowd forms in front of a guard trying to stop a camera crew from entering the room.

"Are you on duty today?" he asks her.

"Not officially," she says. "Some of the people at the station thought I should be here for this. I'm taking some time off."

His face clouds, his mind travels back to the fence, the boy on the ground, blood on the officer's hands, her wiping them against her pants, Teddy's confession about the boy's blood. "Are things okay?" he asks.

She tries to answer him, but can't bring herself to tell him a lie. She casts her eyes down to her feet.

"I can listen if you need someone," he says. "I'm not giving any stories out to the press."

She smiles again, nods without speaking. The crowd headed into the courtroom soon pulls them apart. But only physically. They each remain in the other's thoughts.

69

Friday

Chase enters the courtroom crying. She is wearing the orange jumpsuit she must wear at the county detention center. Her feet and hands are shackled, linked together by chains that clink as she moves. Her hair partially hides her head but her disgrace still shows. She wants to look for Granny and the baby in the room, but she can't bring herself outside her shame. Instead, she buries her chin against her chest, cries some more.

She takes a seat in the row beside A.J. Rick is on the other side of him. Kelly is led into the room by another officer, sits on the bench beside her. They are all wearing orange jumpsuits. She is the only one crying. She can hear Kelly's heavy breathing. It makes her think of her own baby again. She turns her head to look behind her back, out into the courtroom, aware that a photographer is capturing her confusion.

The crowd surprises her. There are video cameras in the back of the room, mounted on tripods. Every seat is taken by men and women holding tape recorders or notepads. A young woman with pink hair a few rows back wears a button that reads, "Straight but not Narrow." She spots Granny two rows behind her, notices that the baby is not with her. Their eyes lock. She sees that Granny's eyes are red, as though she has been crying too.

The courtroom stands when the judge enters. She hears A.J. mutter something under his breath, like "this should be a joke." She wishes she was seated next to Rick, so she could take his hand. She is only here because she wanted to help him. None of this is her fault. Is it? Is it a crime to protect someone you love?

The judge reads from a document in front of him. There is a table of lawyers in front of their row. For a crime she is supposed to be involved in, she realizes how little details she knows as the facts find their way to her—the college boy "struck in the head with a pistol," "beaten again while he begged for his life."

More facts come with numbers attached. A.J. and Rick met the college boy at a bar where the college boy "confided he was gay." (Item number four.) The subjects deceived the college boy into "leaving with them in their vehicle to a remote area outside of town." (Item number five.) Number six reveals "the subjects took the victim's credit card, wallet containing cash, his shoes, and other items."

Her own involvement does not arrive until item number fifteen. She cries hearing her name launched into the courtroom, her attempts to hide Rick's clothing, confuse the police. She cries until she hears the judge reach item number eighteen, describing Kelly's alibi attempt for Rick. This is news to her. The whole time, the hours she has spent in the detention center, no one has told her this. Her face drains of blood, then it refills bright red.

She tries to look around A.J. at Rick, but he is staring blankly ahead. A.J. does not register the charges that his wife and Rick were having an affair.

Anger and indignation rise into her throat. She feels she must respond. She turns to Kelly, but her eyes drop to the large orange covered mound of her stomach. Air catches in her throat. She begins to cough, crying at the same time.

Kelly does not look at her. She bows her own head against her chest and cries. "Whose baby do you think this is?" she says in a whisper to Chase. "I always loved him. I loved him before you even met him."

70

Friday

Ray stops by his car when a reporter yells after him. He listens to the question, watches the sneakers of the reporter swing beneath the hem of the long overcoat. The feelings of a man have not altogether deserted him. He fights to contain his anger, answers, "Why is this so important to you? My answer."

The reporter says, "It's important to see how both families are doing in this." He is out of breath from chasing after A.J.'s uncle. He stands with his hand on his hip, one shoulder lower than another. He reaches for a notebook from a pocket of the coat.

Ray sucks in the last smoke of his cigarette, flicks it to the ground. "How we are doing in this?" he answers. He thinks the reporter's gestures into his coat are suspicious. "What do you care? You're only after a story."

"No one feels good about what's happened," the reporter says. "I can at least put that in my story. I think it's important to understand how people are handling this."

He is a man with a temper; tenacious, faithful. The events have shaken him so that he doesn't understand himself. "I don't need to talk to anyone from the press," Ray says. He unlocks the door of his car. Opens it, stands behind it, as if using it as a shield. "The press is the problem here. The news has taken this and blown it totally out of proportion. If this wasn't about a homosexual, you wouldn't be interested in my opinion. You're trying to make a special case about this and that's not what it's about. Had this been a heterosexual guy these two boys decided to take out and rob, this never would have made the national news. Now you've got them guilty before there's even a trial."

"I know it's been a difficult time," the reporter says. "For all the families."

"What's your name?" the uncle asks.

"Arnie," the reporter answers.

"Arnie?" the uncle repeats. "So who is this for? Who wants to know this?"

"A paper in Texas," Arnie answers. He does not offer any more details. The kind of papers. The readership. His own opinion in this matter.

"I've never even been to Texas," Ray says. "Why would anyone care there?"

"This happens everywhere," Arnie explains. "People need to understand why this happens and why it hurts everyone."

"Everyone?" Ray replies. His brow creases. "This hasn't happened to everyone. This has happened to us. This has been the worst week of my life. Write that down. Why don't you write about what it's like to have your family's name linked to hate. I've lived in this town all my life and I can't go anywhere without people turning cold to me. Try writing about that kind of hate."

"Did you have a chance to talk to your nephew after the arraignment?" Arnie asks.

"I did," Ray answers. "But I don't think it's appropriate to discuss with anyone outside the family."

"Did he say anything about being sorry?"

"What is the point in this?" Ray asks. His voice is tired, tense. He feels its scratchiness. "You guys just don't stop. Go chase another story. I don't have any understanding of what happened that night."

71

Friday

The beating continues to shape the news. An article on a cheating incident in two Organic Chemistry classes, which would ordinarily create a front page headline in the campus newspaper, is buried to a small item in a general news roundup column inside. William Schacht, a nineteen year-old student reporter, leaked about the Administration's proposal to drop spring break in order to finish classes a week earlier, bypasses the tip in order to write an editorial about the University's neglect to include sexual orientation as a protected category in its equal employment policy.

On campus—in the classrooms, the carrels of the library, the steps of the quad, the paths that snake in and around the quadrangles—the mood is brighter if still reverentially subdued. Overnight, white canvas tenting has been erected for alumni gatherings. A barbecue for the Business School alumni. A reception for the Law School. Five, ten, twenty-five year class reunions beneath an archway of gold and blue balloons at the south end of the quad.

At noon, a campus tradition offers another respite from the prevailing uneasiness. The frat boys kick off the homecoming festivities with the annual "running of the bulls." Students, dressed in animals costumes as the University mascot, Rocky the Bull, charge through the quad followed by as many fans waving blue-and-gold pennants as can keep up with the rowdy boys. Parties begin when the bulls reach sorority row. Clifton Street is blocked off for a street fair and carnival.

Throughout campus the arriving alumni are aware of the recent news. They ask questions of professors, deans, student council members, dormitory monitors—anyone willing to give them an ear, seeking what they call the "truth," the "real story behind the attack." More theories are proposed to offer an understanding to the crime—the "townies" versus the "college boys," the "educated" versus the "overlooked." One student even tests the waters with the notion that Danny was the Love Bandit—two days have passed since the last building was tagged. He doesn't stop to do the math, however, to figure out that the hospital was tagged the night Danny was admitted. But the idea is repeated, circulated; soon it is debated how he managed to keep this secret hidden.

"Did you know him?" is another repeated question. "He was in my class," "I saw him at a game," "He knows a girl in my dorm," are a few responses. Others are more guarded with their friendships. Walt refuses to talk to reporters who still roam campus looking for more depth to their stories; his denial of the beating has turned to anger, flashes of depression keep him absent from classes. He doesn't confess to anyone he told Danny about the guys he could pick up at the Starlite.

Andrea has taken a harder stance on herself as well. She has spent the day reading, her mind transforming words into images, thoughts. She knew the paper on C.S. Lewis would present her with problems. Not because of the spiritual nature of the work she had chosen. Nor because the subject was pain and suffering. She knew it would be Danny's friendship that would make coming to terms with *The Problem with Pain* a bit harder.

"What do we learn when we imagine suffering?" she writes on her yellow pad of paper, hidden away in her dorm room covered with art museum posters—reproductions of Monet's water lilies, Haring's dancing figures, Warhol's soup can, and Pollock's splattered paint. What happens is her imagination soars as her thoughts fail to become written words, sending her to the fence that night—struggling with Danny's bruises and welts, the broken bones of his spine, his shattered ribs, his prolonged discomfort, what it must have been like to watch your own blood pool at your feet.

259

"Suffering imagined is as painful as it is real," she will eventually write, strike out the phrase, write again at the bottom of a page of notes.

Stuart will also reach this insight today. Stuart—who prides himself on being quickly reactive against hate, defensive of justice above and over laws or the system—will falter emotionally when he visits Danny's hospital room, when he meets Danny's parents and grandparents, when he offers to answer the e-mails being sent to the hospital wishing Danny a speedy recovery.

Suffering will transform him. He will soften, cry, even though he will do it while he is alone. He will also look inward at himself, will wonder if the soul suffers even after the body no longer registers pain. Pain will startle him throughout the day. At one point he will check his hands to see if they are red, covered with blood, to see if he is to blame in any of this. He hates what has happened to his friend; he wants vengeance with a speedy trial. Knowing this will not happen makes him suffer even more.

72

Friday

By afternoon, town is crowded. The double-whammy of the arraignment and the University street fair create a traffic jam at Clifton and Market. Amy Mayumi, Clifton Elementary's crossing guard, is summoned to help divert traffic toward the Old Union Highway, animatedly waving her bright orange signs to keep an emergency lane open. Cars park along the steep bank of grass which runs beside the railroad tracks once the vacant lot is full where the old Sutton Lumber warehouse was located. Children headed toward the fair look at those loaded with balloons and stuffed animals on their way home. Larger hands grasp tiny palms. Eyes widen with anticipation.

The media is present to capture every nuance, playing up the juxtaposition—a town and University community celebrating while a young man still struggles to survive. Were it not for the heavy rocking gusts of the wind this might be all overlooked. But the brittle flurries give an almost cartoonish glee to the battle with the weather—it rattles the plastic apron around the booths, sends a stack of leaflets skyward like confetti. Henry Crockett, the fifty-two year-old chief of the volunteer fire department, chases his cap down an aisle, laughing, telling his wife it's the most exercise he's had in a year. Behind him, a mother asks a photographer—a middle-aged woman wearing a vest of mini-pockets—not to photograph her daughter as her blond hair whips skyward into a cone similar to the cotton candy in her hand.

Reverend Fletcher crosses paths again with Marcie Piccolo at the fair. He is on his way to find Nancy Gambone, the florist, to ask her about the quotes she gave to the newspaper—why she thinks the chapel might be haunted. To see if she really believes herself. If there is such a thing as restless spirits. If she believes that. And perhaps to see if she can convince him as well.

Marcie has changed into jeans and a jacket, is headed toward the pharmacy to get medicine—not for herself this time but for her son. When she left home this morning he was running a slight fever and her worries over him mingle with the unsteadiness of her own predicament. She walks down an aisle of booths thinking she might find something else to bring back for Jesse—to lift his spirits—but a scowl has settled across her face. She is absorbed in her own story—in the midst of a crowd of sorority girls giggling as they turn their backs against a fast breeze—and doesn't see the Reverend until he approaches her, touches her elbow.

"I didn't mean to startle you," he says.

"No, no," she answers. She uses her hand to shield her eyes from whirl of dirt. "I was just somewhere else." She tries to counter her tension with a smile, but it makes her feel phony, uneasy, not at all comfortable with herself.

"Did you eat?" he asks. "Let's get out of the wind."

She lifts her head toward him, as if she needs to find more air. She hadn't thought about food at all today, at least not for herself, and the thought of it now and the sharp recognition of sausages burning in a booth nearby make her realize she is hungry. She looks down at her watch and answers, "Sure," thinking she needs to get outside of herself, into someone else's life for a few minutes.

"We could go to the café," he says and they begin walking in that direction. She's fine for a few steps and then she stops, shakes her head, but can't bring herself to tell him what is on her mind. She feels like screaming. She wants to connect with him but feels that her life is being taken away from her just as the opportunity presents itself. And then the misery of Joe falls upon her—his leaving, if she were at fault.

He walks without noticing her falter, then recognizes it, stops, but she is again beside him. He is aware only of her hesitation, not entirely conscious of its motivations, a squall is also stirring inside his own head as he reaches to stop the wind from flapping his jacket. He has noticed now her similarities to his wife—the way she pushes her hair back on her head, the way she coughs to clear her throat, the bony joints of her fingers and the tiny wrist. He thinks that it is too odd that he is drawn to her, that in all this misfortune storming around them that this is what he now observes. He wants to tell her this but can't. "It's just some food," he says, trying to feel non-chalant holding the door of the café open for her. His heart is racing. His voice is out of his throat and clogging his ears. "It'll do you good," he adds, when they reach the door of Perkins Café. "When was the last time you were here?"

Perkins Café has been around longer than most of its steady customers—a lunch counter, a few tables and booths, the town's best known secret, loved more for its Southern home cooking than its decor (grits, country-fried steak, peanut pie). "We've been swamped all week," the owner and regular waitress Betty Lee Perkins tells the Reverend when he enters. "Between the alumni and the tragedy, I've been doing double shifts. And we can't get that young fella over there to leave your favorite booth. Everybody wants to hear what he has to say. Been a line to talk to him all day."

In the booth is a young man wearing a navy blue cap, twisted backwards. He is dark-skinned (mixed parents, one black, another Hispanic), has thick eyebrows and lips, lots of wiry energy. His name is Jamey. He was the fourth guy at the Hogan Street altercation. He sits opposite a thin, tired-looking woman with short black hair, a reporter for a daily paper in Atlanta, whose hand lingers between a tape recorder and a cup of tea. "Those two dudes were fucked up, that's for sure," Jamey says to his listener. "But ya gotta know there's another story to this shit. Something that nobody's really talking about."

There is a sense of history in the dinner—not just because of the framed black-and-white photographs of the University and the town that hang on the wall. Many customers expect this will be the place that something memorable will happen next. The next thing people will be reading about, talking about, arguing about in the newspaper or in court. A few customers recognize either the Reverend or Marcie, and this sends the conversations to a slight higher pitch; speculation about their meeting sends a buzz through the place—*the one who runs the chapel and the one who found him.* When the front door of the diner opens again and the wind rattles the window blinds, a nervous laughter erupts, as if the whole place has been spooked.

They keep their conversation aloof, out of their thoughts. They talk about the menu, Betty Lee Perkins, the fact that the courthouse could use a new paint job. "I could get fat," Reverend Fletcher says when his food arrives.

Marcie mentions she tries to watch her weight, so her uniform doesn't feel uncomfortable. "Do you do a lot of cooking for yourself?" she asks him.

"No," he answers and his mind drifts elsewhere. "My eating habits are really bad."

73

They meet at the waiting area at the end of the hall. Leah has brought more food (though no one has an appetite or thinks it looks bad to be eating outside his room). Roxy has decided she doesn't want a cigarette, her mouth still ashy from the last one. On the table are the day's papers. Headlines about the beating, the struggle, the history of Skyline Mount.

"Do you miss the stables?" Roxy asks. "Julie said you don't ride anymore." She looks at the plate of brownies Leah has brought, picks off a sliver of a walnut from the top one.

Leah folds the tinfoil that covered the plate into a tiny square. "I stopped when I got married," she says. "I go up there maybe once a year now to see Parker, help her out with horses. When she does a show. Some of the girls who compete stay at the house."

There is a silence between them now. They are both thrown back to memories. The soft, sandy path of Fancy Gap. The slopes of wildflowers. The horses grazing in the pasture behind Parker Mahonen's barn.

The barn was a fifteen-minute walk from the old chapel, down a dirt road that led past a grassy paddock. Skyline Mount was full of dirt paths for horses which was why it was so popular. All the girls at Brannert Day wanted to ride at Parker Mahonen's place so they could go out on the trails. It was classy Southern, not mountain trash. Roxy started wanting a pony when she was three or four, went through a phase of wanting to be a vet. Her favorite memories are hanging out in the aisle, tacking her horse up, kissing him on the nose.

"I always wondered what happened to Sashay," she says.

That was the horse she rode every day after school. After her parents separated her mother had taken an extra job so that she could continue riding. But when the divorce was final the horse was sold. Her riding stopped.

"Parker doesn't keep many horses on her own any more," Leah says. "Most of them are boarders now. She's too old to care for them herself."

Leah had grown to hate the Mahonen barn. She thought it had made her mean-spirited, not like herself. Too much like Parker. Parker could reduce girls to tears. "Pathetic," Parker would yell at a girl in the ring. "Arch your back. Pick up your ass." The only thing Leah enjoyed were the times she could ride on her own. Out on the trails. And the more girls that came to the barn the harder it got. It was too much responsibility. And very little pay. Parker thought Leah should work there for nothing just because of the prestige.

"She's still pretty rough on the girls," Leah says. "Now she says that they aren't aggressive enough. We were doing four foot jumps when I was there. She has to beg them to do two foot ones. They're so squeamish now."

Roxy nods, takes a pinch of the brownie now. She looks out the window, drifts away again. Sometimes two or three girls would go out together onto Fancy Gap. They'd canter, walk, canter, take the pasture at full speed. At the cemetery the trail would head back toward the barn. But they were never ready to head back. Instead, they would walk the horses up the slope to look at the view of the valley. It comes back to her now—the river, the cement factory, the cluster of University buildings like a small city. The fence was always there. Something she never noticed at the edge of the cemetery. She was always looking forward in those days. Never behind her.

74

Friday

He carries the white of the bandages out of the room. Down the hall. To the elevator. The image of his brother continues to confuse him. A part of Luke wishes Danny would die, make it easier. Let them begin to move on. Start to heal.

He feels the car keys in his pockets. He needs air. Needs to get away. He refused to answer his father when he was asked whether they should keep his brother on life support. It wasn't his decision to make. He did not want to play God.

They'd never talked about a lot. His brother was opinionated, always trying to give him advice. Play the older brother. In spite of the fact he was too naïve, too trusting to ever be outright suspicious of anything. Or anyone. Even after all that had happened to him. He was always surprised to find himself the younger brother, watching his older brother's back, even though Danny always tried to lead the way. When the family went camping together Danny always had to walk at the front of the path. When they went driving together, Danny was always deciding what route they would take, even if he wasn't at the wheel.

He finds the rental car in the parking lot. The day is cold, windy. The sky cloudy. The outside air is refreshing, not processed, like inside the hospital, He breathes in and out, remembering the mechanical sound of his brother's breathing, the shloop-shloop-shloop of the machine. This can't continue, he thinks. It's hurting them all too much. This is not how he wants to remember his brother.

His brother had always been the one with the bad karma. He'd even said so himself. He said if a piano was falling from the sky, the wind would blow it so it would land on him, and nobody else.

"What would you want?" his father asked him that morning. His dad wasn't dropping the subject. It seemed too morbid to him. To be thinking like this. About life, death. The power to change one or the other.

"Not to have to think about it," he answered. He is eighteen years-old. He sees himself on his father's face, wonders if that's the person he wants to be. He didn't continue the conversation, afraid he'd be thought of as a monster.

"But we have to think about this," his father said. "Because we have to make a decision for Danny."

"It's not like he's going to be in a wheelchair," he answered. "It's not like he just can't hear. Or he just can't see. Or he can't use his hands."

"I don't like making these decisions any more than you do," his mother said. "But we have to do it. What's best for your brother."

In the parking lot he starts the car, backs out of the parking space, drives out of the lot, past the media vans parked by the road. She did not want any of the family to attend the arraignment. She wanted Luke to remain at the hospital, in case something happened. "Something has happened," he said. "That's why we're all here."

The town is unfamiliar to him. He's been away for more than ten years. Memories only surface to him—the swing set in the back yard, the Indian rug on his bedroom floor, his brother leaving the house on his bike, leaving him alone.

He twists his body so he can reach into his pocket as he drives. He checks the address he wrote down at the hospital. His mother handed him the keys this morning, said he could stay there if he wanted to, if he needed his own space. They did not know how long. No one could say how long. There is no kind of timetable for this.

It was another morbid moment. Or so he thinks. She doesn't understand anything that's going on. It makes him upset. To see her like this. To watch hiis brother dying. Suffering.

He wishes he were back at school. This has interrupted his life. Changed his life now too. He thinks he will have to call someone tomorrow. Arrange for incompletes. He left so quickly he did not take any books with him. There's not even studying to distract him. All he has to do with his time is just wait. Wait. Wait.

He finds the building and parks in the lot in the back. It takes two tries to open the front door. He climbs the steps slowly, cautiously, as if he expects someone to stop him, ask him who he is and why he is here.

He unlocks the apartment door. It creaks open, just like a horror movie. Inside the air is warm, stale, a radiator by the window hisses quietly. He sets the keys down and hears them settle with a clink-clink. He is spooked but he does not leave. Someone will have to empty his brother's apartment, box things up, send them to Washington. Or to a charity. Someone will have to do all this. He knows it will not be them. He will have to make the decisions here. That is what his brother would want. To spare them. Spare mom and dad. He looks around the rooms, not touching anything, just looking. So this is it. He does not sit. He just stands. Looks more but not deeper. Where to start? *When* to start? Then he realizes he is hungry. He hasn't eaten anything substantial in days.

75

Monday

He stands at the corner of Sanderson and Clifton. It has a familiar darkness to it. The pavilion design of the History Building, about six floors high, rising above a flat square-shaped parking lot. He tries not to let it spook him. It is nothing like before. He is safer here. More in control. He knows how to ask for help. Knows how to think his way through things.

He watches Michelle head across Sanderson, books cradled beneath her right arm. He thinks about calling Walt to see if he wants to go out for a drink. But he's already canceled him once today; he'd find it strange that he had changed his mind.

Insects circle the flood lights which illuminate the History building's wings. He watches them dance in front of the light, thinks they look like dust motes, then thinks maybe more like a light flurry of snow. He walks along the sidewalk, pauses in the light of a lamp, stands motionless beneath it. It drenches him from head to toe. He imagines his blood cells dancing like insects. He stands with his hands in his pockets, watching the University go on without him, as if he is a ghost who has returned to the scene of the crime. He sees three guys in sweatshirts and jeans; the silhouette of the University buildings, a girl galloping into the pool of another light, her hair in a ponytail swaying behind her. Their lack of concern for him does not create a gloominess; it simply makes him realize that all people are lonely at some point in their lives.

He decides to walk back to the student center. Maybe he'll check what movies are playing this weekend. In case Gary visits. Mark had not told him how hard it would be to meet someone. Hard if you were not tall, good-looking, well-built

270

or well-hung. Or if you weren't just out prowling for sex. He could go to the library for quick sex. He'd even heard about the truck stop just outside of town. But that isn't what he wants. Not now. Not tonight. Tonight, he wants a date. Someone to talk to. Someone to hold hands with, care about what he is thinking. Intimacy. Affection. And sex. Someone to make plans with. Maybe that is too hard to find here. Maybe he should have stayed in Seattle. Or moved to a bigger city. Los Angeles. San Francisco. New York. Where there's more support.

Maybe that's what he should write about for his assignment. About how rare love is in this town. Queer love. How difficult it is to find for someone like him. Maybe he should write about how easy it is the suck a dick of a stranger on the second floor of the library but how hard it is to get the guy's name and phone number and go out on a date. In public. To be out, open, romantically gay in a small town like this.

Maybe that's what he should write about. What a fallacy gay pride is. How millions of men and women around the world march down the streets in the big cities so they can be out and open, yet just as many sneak around in dark bars and anonymous chat rooms. And worse—in a small town like this—a small, liberal, educated University town—relegated to a mere handful of people desperately searching out others for some kind of spiritual-sexual connection. Pride. How proud are they really here? They couldn't even call themselves gay. Just The Caucus. Where is the sexuality in that?

Mark had taken him to his first openly gay event—a concert of the gay choir in Seattle. It had been a changing moment for him—seeing men on stage singing about, well, singing about loving other men. He had almost collapsed from the sheer exhilaration of it. The desire to be part of that community. He had started volunteering after that. First, for the Chicken Soup Brigade, helping AIDS patients with food and transportation. And then he became more social, political—helping out with voter registration, ushering for services at the gay church. Always thinking: This is the way to make it, to meet someone, to give his life direction.

A van passes him. He watches it stop at the light. There was a time when he was always looking over his shoulder. Every van was suspect. He thought he was still being chased. Thought the guys would find him again. Hunt him down. Pitch him inside. Into the darkness. Here he was away from that. The fear. But now he found that it was a tradeoff. Strength in return for isolation.

Mark had said, "Sometimes something good happens out of bad things." It was still a long process. After the rape—the first guy he had met for sex—a volunteer he had meet at a social gathering held after the Sunday services of the gay church he had started to attend—he hadn't been able to get the image of the back of the van out of his mind. It was a disappointment. They had chased each other's eyes across the room. They had left the party together—walked down Fifth Street to the guy's apartment. It was dark inside the bedroom. The guy had tried to make it feel more special. They had shared a drink first. Made small talk. Candles were lit in the bedroom. But he hadn't been able to get aroused. It felt dirty, forced. He felt defeated and ashamed; somehow it seemed sacrilegious to him to meet like that. At home, he scrubbed his teeth for hours to try and get rid of the salty taste, stayed even longer in the shower trying to relieve his tension. When he told Mark about the event his advice had been to go out and do it again. Sex should not scare him. It should be fun, pleasurable, not something he should shy away from. "It's only something natural," Mark said. "Just try masturbating together next time. Till you get used to the way it feels when someone touches you. How they feel and smell and taste. Don't be in such a hurry. Enjoy it. There's nothing wrong with being a bit hedonistic."

Sex, sex, sex. That's what it all comes down to. Straight or gay. Man was no different than any other species in the animal kingdom. He was friends with Mark simply because of sex. The desire to understand it. He was friends with Walt and Stuart because of sex, too. The curiosity of sex. The desire to find sex. Sex, sex, sex. It was a part of the real world. Real people were having sex. But if it was something everyone wanted, why was it such a difficult part of life?

He had seen a therapist, a doctor, another therapist because of sex. He took pills to calm him because of sex, more pills to fight off the depression sex caused him. Even before the rape he had known what he wanted. It seemed to telescope into such a simple answer. Sex. That was his desire. To have it, find it, keep it without guilt. Or shame.

But not exactly. There was something else at work. He tried to put this into words for Mark. "It's over so quickly," he said. "You dream about someone and you fantasize about someone and then you meet and it's over in just a few minutes. I want someone to stick around."

He looks at his shoes, the light from the street lamp bounces off of them. The wind stirs. He listens to the sound. He thinks of a warmer place. The beach. Or even in bed, cradled in someone's arms. This was what he wants: Someone to share his time with. A boyfriend. A lover. A partner. "It has to happen to some people," he said to Mark. "Why would there be such an uproar over gay marriages if they didn't exist for *someone*?"

"You can't be too anxious about it," Mark said. "That won't work. It's true what they say. When you're not expecting to meet someone, you will. You're young. No need to rush into something. There's a lot of stuff to learn. You've got plenty of time to play around."

Play around. It seemed such a strange thing to think about when he felt so serious about things. *Play around.*

He studies the way the light reflects off the tip of his shoes, thinking about being barefoot in the sand. "You've got plenty of time," Mark had said. "I didn't fall in love till I was long out of my twenties."

76

Friday

Ethan dribbles the ball. Shoots. Does a lay-up. Dribbles. Bounces it against the brick wall of the house. He sweats beneath his arms, the back of his neck, a trickle at his forehead. But his fingers stay cold. Like the tip of his nose.

This is what he remembers: He was thirteen, fourteen maybe. It was a rainy day. Weekend. Probably Sunday. He had fought with his mother because she said his stereo was too loud. He was driving her crazy with that music.

When the rain stopped he found his jacket, the denim one with the ripped collar, went outside, shot baskets in the driveway, his hands wet, grimy after a few dribbles. After a while he was bored and decided to go to the house they were building on the empty lot at the end of the block.

Beams had been added in the last few days. No roof, just framing for future gypsum board, bricks, nails. The house smelled of wet wood.

That was where he found A.J. On the steps leading to the basement, behind him the cement walls stained with moisture. He was smoking, a magazine on the step below him, folded open.

He started to walk away when A.J. asked, "Want a hit?"

"Can't," he said. "My dad would get me."

"No worse than ice cream," A.J. said. "He let you eat ice cream, don't he?"

"I'm not supposed to smoke," he said, his eyes traveling toward a picture in the magazine.

"Stunt your growth?" A.J. said. It was sort of a joke. He was already taller than A.J. was. By about six inches.

A.J. noticed he was looking at the magazine. "Your dad have any of these around?"

His eyes met A.J.'s and then went back to the magazine. He offered no answer, just his wild, excited, dilated eyes.

"Bet you've never seen a pussy," A.J. said. "Here, take a look."

He felt a worrisome vertigo, sat down on the step above A.J. He had been experiencing erections in class, safely hidden beneath his jeans. Everything seemed to have a sexual tone to it. He leaned down and picked up the magazine, sat on the step above A.J., looked at the picture of a naked girl. She was lying on a large bed. Pink satin sheets. She had nothing on except a thin gold bracelet on her wrist. Another one on her ankle. Her breasts were large and pink, except for the nipples. He was hard before he flipped the page to look at another photo.

"You ever seen one?" A.J. asked.

"At the store," he answered. "The one on Sanderson."

"No, stupid," A.J. said. "A real pussy."

Again he doesn't answer. Holds his tongue. His dick is still hard, strains against his jeans.

"Bet you're still a virgin," A.J. said. "You do get hard, don't you?"

He flicks his eyes away from A.J. Back to the magazine. He knew it got hard, but thought it was something it did all by itself.

"You ever beat off?" A.J. asked.

When he didn't answer A.J. again, A.J. said, "Nah, bet you don't. You're probably too much of a geek."

"I've done it before," he finally answered, not fully convinced what, exactly, he should have done.

"You think about girls or guys when you beat off?"

He was silent for another moment, taking in the photograph in the magazine, then answered, "Both."

"Woo, dude," A.J. answered. "A switch hitter. Cool."

He was pleased that the answer seemed to satisfy A.J.

"You like having a mouth around your dick?" A.J. asked.

He played it cool now, like he was older than he was. "Sure," he answered.

"Want me to suck you off?" A.J. asked. "Only thing is you owe me a favor if I need one."

"What kind of favor? he asked.

"Don't know till I need it."

"Okay," he answered.

He unzipped his jeans, slid them around his hips to let them bunch up beneath his knees. A.J. shifted so that he was on his knees on the step below him. He watched, hypnotized, as A.J. reached in his underwear and lifted his dick out. The sensation was warm and slick when his dick disappeared into A.J.'s mouth. Then the realization gripped him that something was going to happen—though he didn't know what. He tried to control his breathing but he became short of breath. He pulled his dick out of A.J.'s mouth, took a deep breath of air and let out a moan. A.J. smiled as he watched a creamy fluid squirt out of Ethan's dick.

"I'll take that favor now," A.J. said. His jeans were already down around his knees and he was standing up on the step. He pulled down his underwear so that his dick popped out. It had a bright red head, like it was angry.

"Go on," he said. "Just like I did it."

He bounces the basketball against the brick wall, trying to keep a rhythm going. His mom comes outside, tells him to stop it, she's trying to talk on the phone. He throws the basketball into the garage, asks if he can use the car. She gives him the keys. Tells him to be home before supper.

He drives to the school parking lot, doesn't see anyone he knows, so he drives down Market Street, parks in the back lot of the cement factory where no one goes. He met A.J. a few more times, always repaying a favor with another favor. When the house was finished they went once to the wooded area behind A.J.'s uncle's house. That was when A.J. said they couldn't do it anymore because he was doing it with someone else. "Guy up on Skyline Mount," A.J. said. "He pays to suck us off."

The air is sharp in his nostrils. With the engine off the cold settles back into the car. Deep into the plastic. The folds of his clothes. He leans his head back against the car seat, slips his hand beneath his jeans and fondles himself where it is warm. He's hard before he knows it. His head is full of thoughts. Some about A.J. Some about other things. He's always horny. Fighting to understand it. There's a lot of guys in his mind now. He thinks mostly about guys.

77

Friday

Luke has found eggs and bread. Sausage in the freezer. Spent the time cooking instead of looking through the apartment. A smoky haze hovers above the stove from the sausage, the sizzle of the meat louder than the radio he has turned on. His cooking is interrupted by a knock at the front door. It makes his heart beat fast.

"Who is it?" he asks.

"Arnie," a voice answers. "I'm a friend of Danny's."

His head is edgy, thick with hunger, full of smells from the food. He is not sure how to answer. He stands by the door until the voice starts again. "He borrowed some notes from me. I thought I might get them back. I know it's a bad time. But there are mid-terms next week."

He unlocks the door, cracks it open, says, "Sorry. I was just busy in the kitchen."

"I know this must be a terrible time, and all," the guy says. He is dark-eyed. Wears a scarf and a hat. Long coat. Rubs his hands together to keep them warm. "You must be his brother."

The shake hands. The door opens wider and Arnie steps into the apartment, smells the sausage in the kitchen. The brother is taller than was expected. Same face, color of eyes. More freckles. Wears a sweatshirt. His eyes flash around quickly, taking in size of the kitchen: the number of chairs at the table (four), the coffee pot on the stove (green), the plate of eggs and toast, the picture hanging on the wall (travel poster: Key West).

"What kind of notes?" Luke asks.

"They were in a spiral binder," he says. "I'd recognize it if I saw it."

Luke opens the refrigerator, says, "Go ahead. Look around."

He stays within hearing distance, surprised the brother doesn't even suspect he is not a student. "I'm sorry about what happened to your brother and all," he says. He thinks this sounds empty, phony, not like a student at all. He adds, "I hope they hang those guys."

Luke does not answer. Arnie continues to move through the apartment, noting the color of the sofa (sorta like milk chocolate), the magazines on the coffee table (*Time, Details*), the ashtray by the window (black, empty, only the trace of ashes). He reaches into his pocket, writes down "smoker." It is too warm in the apartment; he thinks about asking if it is like this always but doesn't. Might reveal the fact that he hasn't been here before. He looks at a manila folder on a bookshelf. Picks it up, thumbs through it, handwriting flat, leans to the right, letters written quickly. He walks to the doorway, notices a collection of blue glass bottles sitting on a bookshelf. "This must be hitting your family pretty hard," he says.

"Yeah," Luke answers.

There is no sound of footsteps coming toward him. His eyes roam more. "You missing school because of this?"

"Yeah," Luke says. "Hopefully, I won't be too far behind when I get back."

"You're in California, aren't you?"

"Yeah. Pre-law if I ever get there."

"It's great that you know what you want to do," he says. "I'm still trying to decide. You like California?"

"Yeah, it's cool."

"I got a brother that lives in San Francisco," he says. "Lot better than this place. Were you and your brother close?" He realizes he has stepped over a line. Asked too many questions. Needing too many answers. He doesn't wait for an answer. Instead, he says, "You know, it's been hard to go to class this week. I see people just start crying when it hits them. When they start thinking about this. Sitting next to me. They just break out into tears and all. Leave the room. It's strange. Then you walk home and see it on TV."

"I don't understand the fascination with it," Luke says. He walks to the end of the hallway, stands looking into the room at Arnie. "What makes this so special? The need to know every detail. Someone called up where my parents are staying and asked if my brother had a Bible. If he had brought a Bible with him when he moved here. They're trying to turn him into a martyr."

"People look for some kind of explanation," he says. "Why it happened. Like there is a meaning to that kind of suffering."

"He just had a lot of bad luck," Luke says, turning back to the kitchen. "Bad luck karma. He even said so."

"Danny?" Arnie says. He steps into the hall so that he can see Luke in the kitchen. "Danny thought he had bad luck?"

"All the time," he answers. "We went on a camping trip last summer. The whole family. Danny got drunk at a bar. Some guy punched him in the lip. Said he was coming on to him. That wasn't like him at all."

"Did he have a drinking problem?"

"No, don't think so. Except he would have a drink when he wasn't supposed to. That was real stupid of him."

"When he wasn't supposed to?"

"Anti-depressants," Luke says. "He's been on them for a while. I shouldn't be telling you all this. Did you see the notebook?"

"No," he answers. "Not yet. He might have given it to this girl in our class. It was getting passed around a lot. You don't mind if I use the bathroom before I go? Don't know if I can hold it till I get back to campus."

"Sure," Luke says. "It's on the right."

In the bathroom he runs the water, cracks open the medicine cabinets. Notes the names of medication on the bottles, the dates they were prescribed, the names of doctors. He takes one of the bottles off the shelf and puts it into his pocket. He looks at the brand of deodorant, the type of toothpaste. He turns off the water. Flushes the toilet. Before he steps out of the bathroom he hears the phone ring. He stands still, waiting to hear one side of the conversation if Luke answers the line.

Luke's voice is muffled, does not carry through the tile. Arnie opens the bathroom door. Walks down to the kitchen. Just catches Luke hanging up.

"Everything okay?" Arnie asks.

"No, not really," Luke answers. "My mom. She wants me back at the hospital."

He doesn't ask another question, hoping Luke will confide in him easily enough now, thinking he is a family friend. "They've decided not to keep him on life support."

He doesn't answer. He goes to the door, opens it. "I'm sorry," he says, feeling like an intruder. "I should go. Get out of your way." He offers his hand to Luke. They shake, end up in an awkward hug. "I'm really sorry," he adds, breaking away.

He waits to see if Luke breaks into tears. When he doesn't Arnie turns away and mumbles "thanks" and then stops, turns back. "You need any help?" he asks. His voice is light, full of air. "I could go with you if you want."

It is a genuine request. An outsider wanting to know what it is like inside. Even if there is a motive it is not known now. By either side. The sincerity is what registers.

"No thanks," Luke answers. "I just want to get out of here."

"I know," Arnie answers. He nods, feels himself overcome with emotion. He turns and heads down the stairs. Outside, in the cold air, he fishes the prescription bottle out of his pocket. He reads the label, breathes the air in deeply, wonders what he should do about this part of the story.

78

Friday

They meet for dinner outside the restaurant. Scott is there first. They shake hands, take seats, order drinks from a waiter. The restaurant is a series of small rooms with small tables. There are candles lit on each table. Gary thinks Scott is more attractive than the waiter. Scott is wearing a black sweater, clingy, makes his face look younger, his body intimidating. Gary wears cologne, not his usual scent. Something different. He wants this to work.

They talk about the college boy. He is still in a coma. The suspects were arraigned this morning. Gary has heard that there is another vigil at the University this evening. And another one at a different church. They swap details that they know or have heard since yesterday. Gary says that the two guys were connected to another beating, which is how they were caught. Scott has heard that Reverend White has announced that he is going to protest—he told a reporter today that he was just waiting for the college boy to die and go to Hell.

The restaurant is Italian. Scott orders penne. Gary orders a chicken dish, even though he knows it's something he could prepare on his own. He feels light-headed from the wine he ordered. But happy. (And silently guilty.) Scott keeps the conversation moving, talking about his job drafting blueprints for an architect.

This is what he knows about Scott (from Jon, his friend, on the phone, earlier in the day): He hasn't had a steady boyfriend in over three years. (His mother died; his brother tested positive; his dates find him too needy.) He's sexy but dull. Obsessive about his body. (His legs are in great shape; his waist is under thirty.)

After dinner they decide to see a movie. They ride in Scott's car, a Honda Accord, to a mall where a multiplex cinema is located. Gary is still light-headed, ready to be affectionate. He wants to kiss Scott but holds back. They park the car, walk inside the mall, window shop for a few minutes, buy tickets at the booth. Dutch. They take seats together in a back row. When the light goes down, Scott reaches for Gary's hand. This surprises Gary; he adjusts his posture so that he is comfortable.

The movie doesn't entertain him. It is a satire about a Utopian community under a bubble. He finds the laughs forced. His mind drifts elsewhere—to Scott's hand, to the details of the college boy, to a patient who hasn't paid his bill. At one point he breaks into a sweat. His breathing becomes forced. He thinks something is wrong but he doesn't leave. The moment passes. The movie ends.

After the movie they walk back to Scott's car. Scott asks Gary if he wants to come over to his apartment for a drink. Gary understands it is an invitation for sex. He breaks out into a light sweat again.

"This is always awkward," Scott says. He has stopped by the car door. Passenger side. Next to Gary. "I can't do this without being honest. You should know I'm positive." He casts his eyes to the ground and then rapidly adds. "I'm not sick or anything."

The news is unexpected, takes Gary by surprise. His first response is to tell Scott that he is not the first guy he's slept with. Positive or not. But he holds the thought back, thinks it would sound crummy, impersonal. Instead, he answers, "It's okay." He keeps the moment simple. Then reaches up and presses his hand against Scott's neck. Their eyes meet. Scott reaches around him and unlocks the car door.

Scott parallel parks a block away from his building. They walk together down the street. It is dark, leafy, idyllic. As cold as the night before. Scott lives on the fourth floor. They ride in the elevator standing in separate corners.

They begin kissing as soon as Scott unlocks the door. Gary feels rushed, anxious, but he slows himself, running his hands along Scott's back. Scott presses forward, lifts the ends of Gary's shirt out of his pants, slips his hands beneath Gary's shirt, along his chest. The touch of his skin makes Gary gasp, but he continues kissing, breathing, holding Scott.

Scott breaks away, takes Gary by the hand. They walk through the apartment. Gary glimpses details: a framed poster of a lighthouse, a bookcase with seashells. They stop in the bedroom and kiss again at the foot of the bed.

Gary now lifts the edges of Scott's shirt out of his pants. He runs his fingers along Scott's skin. There is a coolness to the bedroom. They close in for warmth. He finds Scott's muscles shaping his grip. Scott breaks away, smiles, sits on the edge of the bed, unlaces his boots. Gary sits beside him, unties his shoes, then takes off his glasses, places them on the windowsill.

Before they kiss again, Scott helps Gary take his shirt off. He tosses it toward a chair. It misses, lands on the floor. He laughs, says "sorry," the voice playful. Scott takes his own shirt off, tosses it toward the chair. It lands a little further into the room, still misses the chair.

They draw together again and begin kissing. They shift their weight so that they are now lying on the bed. Scott positions Gary on his back, lies above him. He breaks away this time to help Gary remove his pants. They land on the floor, the belt buckle thunks against the wood floor. Scott takes off his jeans. Gary doesn't hear the sound they make. They are again against each other. Both in underwear. Kissing, feeling each other.

At points they giggle, laugh like boys. At other times they are serious, gasping, moaning. They both reach orgasms twice, separated by moments of lying in each other's arms. Everything is kept safe.

Gary has forgotten about Danny until he rises out of the bed to dress.

"Do you want to stay?" Scott asks. His voice is level, not needy. An easy invitation to continue. The room is full of intimacy. Deep, like a pool.

"I have patients tomorrow morning," Gary says. "Otherwise I would."

Scott watches Gary dress. He moves like a shadow through the room, lifting off clothing from the floor, holding them toward the light that drifts into the room from another place. "Want me to turn on the light?" he asks.

Gary shakes his head, "No." "This is fine," he says. When he is dressed he sits on the edge of the bed, kisses Scott again.

"Want me to drive you back?" Scott asks.

"I'm just a few blocks away," Gary answers. "Will I see you again?" he asks.

"Sure," Scott answers. He bows his head to his chest, his smile slips up toward his ears. "I'd like that."

"What are you doing tomorrow night?" Gary asks. He regrets the question the moment it is out there, in the room, waiting for an answer. Makes him seem too needy himself.

"Getting together with you," Scott answers.

It is smooth. This feeling. Gary likes it as much as Scott does. They kiss again. Gary lets himself out of Scott's apartment. He takes the walk back to his apartment slowly. The sounds of his footsteps echo back romantically.

Confusion surfaces when he unlocks his own door. He boots up his computer, checks his e-mail messages. Nothing from Danny. He logs off, walks into the den. He turns on the television and lies down on the couch. This is how the news will come to him.

79

Friday

There is a shift in the air. His blood pressure begins to drop. A magnetic feeling enters the room; as if his heart has broken open. As if another natural process of chemical reactions has begun within his body.

In the room, in his bed, he reaches toward another level of consciousness: his neural repatternings are transforming him into pure spirit, energy. What is unreal becomes real. What was inessential becomes essential. What is a part finds integration.

His mother notices the change first, then his father. Their eyes grow wider, recognizing the alteration. His mother feels sorrow and relief. His father is aware of the reason for this change. Peace is arriving.

He is a voyager, pulled into a dark void between heaven and earth. The darkness races along, swiftly, becoming a tunnel. He feels the wind but not the air. Slowly he sees a small point of light. It grows brighter and brighter. He sees figures within the light. Silhouettes that disappear, leaving only one figure. The face comes into view and he thinks it is Mark. He doesn't wonder why it is Mark. He knows he is there to meet him. The light grows stronger, brighter. Mark has come to show him the way. He notices his hands are white, like the light. He feels nothing but motion. As if he has become the light itself.

He is not afraid to die. Death is not a final experience for him. What he experiences is more like a floating joy. Bliss. Rapture. A sense of pervasive love. He is aware of some sort of border that must be crossed. He follows the figure of Mark deeper into the light. As if he has moved deeper into himself.

At 7:06 p.m. his physical body will stop breathing. His mother will notice the absence of his next breath even before the pulsing sound of a machine stops. She will stand and move in closer to his body. His father will move in beside her. His brother, waiting outside the room, will know it's time to return. Even though they have expected this, waited hours and days for it to happen, his death will still strike them as sudden.

The news of his death will be filtered through the hospital first. Staff on the floor where his room is located will become aware quickly. Others throughout the building will hear the news as people come and go by the elevator. Yasmin Bhasin, a nurse on duty on the floor above his, will call her sister in Atlanta who has a gay son in Los Angeles and tell her that the college boy has died. Peck Hsu, a work-study sophomore who is on duty as a maintenance worker, will overhear the phone conversation and shake his head in disbelief as he unlocks a storage closet.

Jarod Mann, the patient's overseeing physician, will notify Donald Carberry of the death. Carberry, still in his office, will walk down the hall to visit with the parents, trying to contain his emotion. True or false. True that this is now coming to a close. False, that it hasn't affected him in some way. What changed him was witnessing how the family struggled with this news, with the details of the beating. The gruesome facts. The damage to the boy's body.

He will return to his office and call the police station, leave messages before writing the facts for the press. He will stop and start several times, using his hand to clear his eyes, wondering how to play his own feelings in front of the cameras. At 10:03 p.m. he will deliver a statement to the press: "Danny's family expressed gratitude that they did not have to make a decision about removing life support. They said that like the good, caring son he was, he removed from them the guilt and stress of making that decision."

He wears a hospital lab coat this time. A blue shirt. A dark tie. His hair is neatly parted. He is not wearing any make-up. His tears are real. They do not run down his eyes. They stay there. Gathering. It is not an act.

"Funeral arrangements are pending, and we will announce those arrangements on our Web site. Please do not call the hospital for this information The family did release the following statement, 'We would like to thank the hospital for their kindness, professionalism, sympathy, and respect for the needs of our family under this stressful time. We will always be grateful for their concern for Danny.'

"The family again asked me to express their sincere gratitude to the entire world for the overwhelming response for their son. During the last twenty-four hours we have received thousands of e-mails from every continent. Our Web site, which normally receives a few hundred hits a day, received thousands of hits today. We will continue to forward the family any e-mail we receive. The family has asked that no flowers be sent. Donations may be made to a memorial fund established in Danny's name. That information is also on the hospital's Web site."

He looks at the camera now. Away from his notes. His nose is red, as if itchy. "His mother says, 'Go home, give your kids a hug, and don't let a day go by without telling them you love them.'"

The news will travel outside the hospital by reporters talking on cell-phones or faxing their notes back to their offices. The wires will pick up the news. It will reach the Internet. E-mails, in sympathy, will be sent to the hospital. Messages will be posted in chat rooms. Pages of tributes will begin to be designed. Cal Marram, the town prosecutor, will hear the news by phone at home before he receives Carberry's message left at his desk. A police officer on duty at the county correction center will deliver the news first to A.J. in his cell, then to Rick. They will not react with words. Rick will turn his back, hug his waist. A.J. will give a smile when a guard tosses him the line, "Hey, Dopey, the queer you knocked up just kicked the bucket."

It will be another hour before the news is taken to Chase and Kelly. Michelle will hear the news when she leaves the library after spending an hour reading an article which had been put on reserve by her history professor. She will walk across the campus shaken, thinking of Danny. Again she will be struck by another what if: What if she had agreed to go with him to the bar that evening? Could she have done something to prevent this from happening? Did God give her a test and she fail? Or what if this was supposed to happen? What if this is what God expected it to be?

When she returns to her dorm room she sits in the dark, thinks about her words before turning on the lamp and reaching for the phone. Her mother answers the line and Michelle explains that a friend of hers has died; she knew the boy who was beaten. She might have been one of the last to see him alive. She allows her mother to express a phrase of condolence and then Michelle says, "I was going to wait until Thanksgiving break to explain this to you. But I think you should know it now. Before you see it on the news."

She takes a breath before proceeding further. "I'm not in any trouble," she says. "But I think you should know how I feel about some things."

80

Friday

The rain wakes him, or what he thinks might be the rain. It could have been the sound of a commercial on the TV, the remote control tumbling to the floor when he shifted his position on the couch, or perhaps the branches of the cottonwood brushing against the window.

Sleep has never been kind to him since he lost his family. Sometimes he dreams about the flood. Sometimes he just sees the surface of water, gray like marble, calm as a table, from the deck of the house that night. It was a beautiful place. No one expected a tragedy to happen.

Janet had never wanted him to work for the church. But she never complained once he had made the decision. He knew it meant that they relied too much on the kindness of other people. The pot-luck dinners in homes other than their own, the hand-me-down chairs and sofas that would decorate the parsonage, the gifts of free theater tickets or movie passes. That weekend was just such a gift. The invitation was spontaneous, a church member was not using his beach house for a few days, did the Reverend and his family want to spend some time there?

It was one of the few favors she was comfortable with. Because it meant that they could be alone, just the family, together. The three of them—Janet, their three year-old son Mitchell, and himself. It was a three-hour drive but they had no trouble finding the house. The weather was a warm October day. They got to the house early, had a barbecue on the deck, felt the wet, salty air from the ocean seep into their clothes.

He turns the TV off and the room falls silent. He feels

lonely, walks to the window to see if it is raining. Nothing, it must have been the TV. He looks at the ring of leaves that circle the ground at the trunk of the old oak. He notices a leaf tremble, hop a few steps, settle on top of another. It makes him remember what Marcie said at lunch that afternoon. That she didn't believe in ghosts. What kind of a practical woman could she be if she were to believe in ghosts? But she wanted to know again about God. What about God? Was what was happening because of God? Was God punishing them for something or expecting them to learn a lesson from all this?

God? God? Where is God? The storm had moved in quickly that night. The rain was hard against the roof of the beach house, sounding like a rapid fire of bullets. There had been no calls for evacuation on the news before they had gone to bed. It was only a rain storm. But then the ocean moved forward with a force that shook their foundation. The house was the first to be swept out to sea.

They had managed in those first few moments of sluggish consciousness to plan their escape. In the dark he tied a sheet around his waist and hers—he would swim toward shore and she would hold herself and the baby afloat with a framed poster they had grabbed from the wall. But a wave suddenly flooded the room. The sheet, wet, tore and he found himself searching as hard as he was struggling to survive.

It happened so quickly there was not even a chance to remember her expression. Instead, panic overwhelmed him as he struggled to escape the crumbling room. So this is dying, he thought, the water cold, the rain still coming down hard. And then he remembered that he couldn't die, couldn't drown—he had a sermon to deliver on Sunday, and a meeting after services with a couple who wanted to be married, and a youth Bible-study class that night. He couldn't drown now.

He watches the leaves beneath the old tree swirl into a funnel as the wind rises, twists around the yard. He had been counseled for depression, given a prescription after worries over suicide. "Don't abandon God," another minister told him. How could he thank God for sparing his life when it took the

291

lives of his wife and child?

He hears a wall crack as the wind shifts the house into a new position. He knows, at that moment, that something has changed the night. He's not sure exactly how or why he knows it but he knows it has happened. Maybe it is because of God. Or perhaps it is a ghost or a spirit passing through the room, letting him know of something which will later reveal itself to him. But he senses news will come to him shortly. He knows that someone is now searching him out. He is not surprised when, in a few minutes, he will move away from the window to answer the phone. He knows he is now needed. God has moved him deeper into the story.

81

Friday

They were together when they heard the news. They had spent the afternoon shopping—Holly had wanted to find a warmer sweater and they had walked to a few stores in town. Afterwards, they had stopped for a bite at the Rathskellar before going to the movie. *Planet of the Apes*, at the student cinema.

Geoff had liked the movie better than she did. He was the bigger fan of science fiction. They had gotten popcorn and sodas, taken seats in the back row. She sat with his arm draped around her shoulder. He tilted his head in an awkward position to see around the guy in front of them. Whenever he sensed her mind wandering, he leaned over and kissed her neck. Or cheek. He had seen the movie before. That was not what was important to him.

They heard he had died on their way out of the movie room. She noticed a girl tilt her head down, lift up her palms to her face. She knew before anyone even said anything that that was what had happened, before she heard someone say, "They're meeting about canceling the rest of homecoming."

She didn't cry herself. She'd been upset for days. She had felt that this would happen. That this was the course, the path that would unfold. To survive would mean he wouldn't be alive. She can't imagine that. Doesn't want to imagine it. She had prayed he wouldn't suffer.

In the lobby Geoff took her hand and they walked to the food court. He ordered an ice cream. She sat with him at a table while he ate. She heard the news bouncing around, watching people's expressions change as they discovered the fact that Danny had died. While he licks his ice cream she says, "It's so sad."

He nods, licks, eats. He hopes this is the end of this story. That it won't consume them forever. That the next story that happens won't feel as tragic. Won't cast as sour a mood.

When he is finished eating they walk across campus holding hands. They walk to the stadium where they watch a bonfire blazing. There are about three hundred students, many dressed in blue-and-gold sweatshirts or knit caps. Their faces are licked by the amber light of the fire. They watch the flames rise up into the night, listen to the logs and twigs and leaves crackling. Songs and chants interrupt them. The mood is youthful, memorable. The fire shows faces far back: round, pale, smooth, bearded. The scene is captured by seven camera crews roaming in and out of the crowd. The camera lights are intrusive. Some guys yell, "Get the fuck away." Several couples turn away from the camera, unhappy that the spell of the bonfire has been broken. No one wants to be caught crying. Except one girl. She cries for the cameras to see. The crews are upon her like cheetahs after a kill.

What could be a violent moment withdraws because the girl runs away. The crews chase her, bored by the passivity of the crowd at the bonfire. Holly and Geoff stay till the cold overwhelms her. Then he walks her back across campus. Outside her dorm, they kiss for a few minutes till the cold air makes them break away. He says he will call her tomorrow morning. They'll go to the parade together if it's still on.

Upstairs in her room she feels restless. Her roommate is not around. The hallways are full of groups of girls dressed in nightgowns, robes. Some clutching tissues. She does not want to cry. Not that she doesn't feel sad.

She looks through the bottom drawer of her bureau and finds the stencil she had made the night she tagged the men's dorm. She rubs her fingers over it. Feels the slick residue of the dried paint.

She finds the can of red spray paint still in the top of her closet where she left it. She shakes it to see how much is left. Plenty.

She waits a few minutes and then calls Geoff. There is

surprise in his voice when he comes to the phone. She says she has an idea. For the parade. She hears his hesitation, then says, "I think it will work. I can get some girls here to help me."

"How much are you gonna tell them?" he asks. There is concern in his voice. He has left this behind and now she has reopened it.

"Nothing," she answers. "I'll just say it's my idea. I just don't want you to be mad at me. Or think I'm two faced."

"I like your face," he says. "Both of them."

This makes her laugh. She says she will meet him at Clifton and Main before the parade begins. She'll be the one handing out the arm bands.

82

Friday

There is no beauty in the darkness. Nor in human death. Or so he has come to believe. Which is why Reverend Fletcher has returned to the fence. He sits cross-legged on the ground, looking out at the trail. He imagines what the boy might have seen. In the darkness. The flood of darkness at his feet. *They took his shoes, Lord. What do I make of that?*

There is nothing before him but dirt, pebbles, darkness, cold air. *What do I make of this, Lord? What am I supposed to learn? What do I make of this death?*

He imagines the beating: the weight of a gun slapped against a face, a neck, a back. Bones cracked, bloody hands. Boot kicks in the stomach, the groin. Ribs broken. The struggle to get away. Rope tied around wrists. The knots burning into the flesh. The searing pain of being stranded here. Unable to move. Unable to call for help. *What must I find here to use? That death can come before it's due?*

He wonders if this is God's way of getting his attention. If this is God's way of making him listen up, getting him to look around, to understand what it is to live. *God I am listening. What should I hear?*

The wind moves around him. The only sound of the night. He hears it move through the branches of the trees, the blades of grass on the slope, then the sudden change of direction and a sound like flapping wings.

He feels the cold seep beneath his clothes. Is this what the boy felt? The cold? The abandonment? There is no beauty in the darkness. Only fear. Fear is the curse of darkness. If there is any reason for this place to be haunted, there is reason for it to be now. A boy murdered. For what? Twenty dollars? A pair of shoes? A coat too small for anyone else to wear?

He wonders if this is God's way of using death in the same way He uses beauty? To get attention? To get through to the thickheaded? To make someone understand human love? Fear human hate? Or does He use fear to make us feel alive? To make us want to embrace the fullness of opportunity? Or to make us repent? Pray for forgiveness. To admit our sins and shortcomings. Or to test our faith?

He feels a heaviness residing in his forehead. He struggles with sleep. He fights exhaustion. He thinks about what his own son might be like if he had survived. A boy coming into his teens. Struggling with identity, issues, decisions for the future. He looks back at Janet, thinks about how she felt in his arms. The way she smelled. The touch of her skin. He takes a deep breath of air. The cold air stings the membranes of his lungs. He is ready to move on, go forward with his life.

My faith is strong, Lord. I thank you for my life, my will to continue, to want to love again. Let me learn what I must from this death. Give me the opportunity to teach the living that life must go on. That death does not slaughter faith. Faith is the strongest thing a man can know. Death cannot kill faith. Death cannot kill what never dies.

83

Saturday

The October light is thin, diluted by clouds, but the town winds itself up again for another day. The factory is astir; the machines begin. A store is unlocked, opened. Then another, and another. Gates are unlocked. Signs turned around to say "Welcome." It is tempting to believe that the town is wholly indifferent to the tragedy it has encompassed. As though nobody cares about a young man's death. As if the media which has descended upon the town can be overlooked, ignored because that is not the norm of their lives, the way things really are here, after all.

But the day moves on. People arrive in town. A cold wind carries sounds like howls. For every ten people there seems to be a reporter, a newsman, someone holding a microphone or a note pad. Trucks arrive and trailers are hitched to their bumpers that will later carry the floats down the street for the homecoming parade. The band assembles in a lot behind the gas station. The minutes pass, the sun bleeds through the clouds intermittently, catching the flash of a shiny metal button of a uniform, the glass pane of a window, the hood of a car.

They join the parade when the last float turns off Main onto Clifton. There are twelve of them. Michelle holds the banner she helped make. It reads: "In honor of Danny. The University Queer Caucus." She expects that people will be horrified or terrified by their presence. Especially in such a small town. She thinks they might be egged. Called names. But she is wrong. After the first block, twenty more people have joined the group, marching behind the banner toward the stadium.

Every block they pass she sees people clapping, smiling. Someone has made "L-O-V-E" armbands and there are clusters of people wearing them on their sleeves, a little girl uses one as a headband.

She looks behind her, sees the crowd growing larger and larger with every block. It is not just women. There are men, boys, guys from the University, as well. There are people holding hands. Mothers and fathers have joined them in their march, as if they have waded into a shallow river, tentative but purposeful in order to cross to the other side.

She tries to not let hypocrisy overcome her, that if Danny were alive they would not be getting this kind of reception. So she goes with the moment, looking at the sign someone has made that reads, "Straight but not Stupid," and another one that says, "Is This What Equality Feels Like?" Ahead, someone has draped a banner from a second story window: "Hate and Violence Are Not Our Way of Life."

Now this human river brings from one side of the street to the other, diagonally, a girl in patent leather boots and a brown coat. Then a young man in a maroon overcoat. Then an elderly man using a cane. Then a mother carrying a young baby against her hip. By the time the parade reaches Clifton, there are almost two hundred people marching behind the banner Michelle has spent hours of her own life to create.

The sight is ordinary enough. People following a parade. Marching behind a banner. But what is strange and wondrous is the rhythmical order and purpose that the followers have invested into it, the fact that the growing crowd of marchers has the power to communicate something to ease the individual mind of strain. In order to say: Not here. Not again.

The crowd behind the banner continues to grow as the march moves toward the stadium. Michelle is awed, overwhelmed, empowered by such support. But she is not without her sadness. In a way, she's glad it's come to this. The community united. Even if from a terrible, tragic loss. This is what the suffering has brought. Something has changed here. She feels certain of it.

This is what it feels like for her to march: her feet ache, especially where her ankle bears the weight of her body. She grows warm and clammy from the heavy jacket she has worn. She feels a light sweat against her back, wonders if she will get sick from a chill. At times a cold wind forces someone to stop, squint, pull a coat tighter. But Michelle does not stop this moment for anything. Why does life work this way? she asks herself. What must she learn to keep this feeling with her?

84

Saturday

Teddy hears the car turn into the driveway. The wheels roll to a stop. The motor shut off. He looks at his watch. He walks to the window. Looks out at the driveway. Sees his son walk toward the kitchen door. He is not even wearing a jacket. Still dressed in the black T-shirt and jeans he had on the day before.

The screen door slams. They meet in the kitchen. His wife is arranging things in the refrigerator. They have finished dinner.

"I've got something to tell you," his son says. "You better sit down."

"We'll stand," he says. His first thought is it is about drugs. His son's eyes are red, scratchy-looking. He thinks it's about the drugs even though there's been no arrest, no warning. Someone on the force would have told him. Would have called. Then he thinks it might be trouble with a girl. That's what this is about. Trouble with a girl.

"I'm gay," his son says. His ears are now red. His cheeks are flushed. Inkblot flushed. Patterns like a Rorschach test. He doesn't push away the hair that falls over his eyes.

Emma reacts first, bows her head toward the counter, emits a gasp. "Are you sure?" she asks.

"Yes," he answers. He folds his arms across his chest, tightens his body. He is as tall as his father. Has her chin, her eyes. But his nose. His large body. His big feet.

"How do you know this?" Teddy asks. His words are slow to come. He cannot say the word "gay." Even after all that has happened, he cannot say, "How do you know you're *gay*?"

"I just do, dad," his son answers.

"How long have you known?" he asks. He feels blood rise into his neck, settle into his cheeks, ears, travel into a semi-circle and meet in his forehead. He creases his brow, juts out his lip, mustache. His fists dig into his pants pockets.

"A long time."

"Maybe it's just a phase," she says. "Maybe you're not sure."

"I'm sure," the boy says. "I know I'm sure." He starts to walk away, the statement done. The conversation over.

"Have you told anyone else?" he asks. He walks toward his son. Stops, not wanting to be intimidating.

"No," his son says. "Not really."

"What does that mean?" His voice registers more contempt than concern. He is sure his son is lying.

"It means I have friends," the boy says. "I've talked to them about this. Not anyone else."

Again his son tries to leave the room, but is stopped with another question. "This doesn't have something to do with the college boy that was killed, does it?" he asks. "Or about A.J.?"

"Yes," his son says. "And no."

"What does that mean?" he asks. Again his voice is full of contempt. But also layered with fear.

"It means it just made it more important to me. It made me realize that I can't keep this a secret anymore," the boy says. "Not after all this."

He doesn't try to stop him now. He looks at his wife, asks, "Did you know any of this?"

"No," she answers. Her eyes are teary. The tip of her nose red. "Not really. Not anything other than wondering."

Teddy moves slowly through the den, the hall, stops at his son's bedroom door, stares at the faces of the rock band in the poster taped to the door, the yellow lettering spelling out K-I-S-S. He thinks about something he might have done wrong, not encouraged, for this to happen. He knocks on the bedroom door, just below the poster, feeling strange, like he has walked into an episode of *The Twilight Zone*. He's never knocked on a door in his house before.

"Yeah?" his son answers.

Teddy pushes the door open, looks into the room. It could be any boy's room. Full of books, clothes on the floor. The trophy Ethan won in junior high for basketball. "Your health. Is it okay?"

He notices his son's face relax. "Yeah," the boy answers. "It's fine."

"I can pay for you to talk to someone if you want," he says.

"I've talked to plenty of people, Dad," the boy answers.

He nods. "You know it's going to be a hard path, Ethan," he says. "We'll help you through whatever you have to go through."

He watches his son's face redden. The boy turns away from him, reaches for a Walkman on the bed, then says. "It's true what they're saying about the chapel," he says. "A lot of things used to go on up there."

"You want to tell me what you know?" he asks. He sounds more like a policeman than a father at this point. He shifts his weight, softens his voice. "Tell me when you're ready," he adds. He waits before he closes the door. Nothing is finished. Everything begins from here.

85

Saturday

By three p.m. they begin talking about the weather. They have been on the road eight hours. Jonathan expects the trip to be another three. Maybe four. The children are growing restless in the back of the bus. They need to stop for gas. To let the children use the restroom. And they need to talk about the weather.

The Reverend doesn't foresee a problem. A lesser person will lose his nerve against a challenge. Triumph over hardship is proof of holiness. Since a boy he'd learned to put his discomfort to good use. Excessive fluids of the body were signs of evil—sneezing, vomiting, sperm, too much urine. The urge of the bladder must first be resisted. The ache must be endured. The children must learn this. He must pass this knowledge on. It will distance them from the common man, the evils of the soul.

He is not a man who is tired and disappointed. God has drawn him to this mission for a purpose. By the time he was thirteen he knew religion was simply a series of dull rituals. God was not in hymns and sermons. God was not found in prayers. By his late teens he learned he'd found a stage beyond prayer. His every step and sound were direct from God. He no longer looked for answers, clues or signals from God. He did not weep with confusion. He did not question that his mission was right. He no longer asked God what for and why. The sky was not harsh and colorless to him. He was not a tourist waiting for hospitality to arrive. He was not waiting to find a burning bush. He no longer took the easy path of questions, but instead, found the harder, stronger one of answers. His was a path of harsh winds and light that shivered.

His son reminds him that the storm is sweeping down from the north, that the news on the radio says it could immobilize the region with more than a foot of snow. They are driving right into it. So far, it has only been cold and clear, the sun so bright that Jonathan, driving, has needed to wear sunglasses.

He says he will compromise. Show them he is not an abusive man like some of his children claim. (This he has learned as a necessity to survive as an adult, or at least as the head of his family.) They will stop in Nashville. They'll hold a press conference in Nashville. Outside the bus. In front of a station. (So his compromise is not really a compromise. It is merely manipulation, disguised.) He asks Jackie, his daughter, if she knows a reporter in Nashville. She says she had contact with a segment producer about two years ago but thinks she has moved on. Is in Atlanta now.

He asks her for the cell phone. He dials information and asks for the telephone number of a TV station. He repeats it for Jackie to write down. She reads it back to him as he dials the number. The line breaks into static, then comes into focus. He asks the operator for the news assignment desk.

When he gets a producer on the phone he says, "This is Reverend Abraham White. I am about forty minutes outside of Nashville. I've got a few things I want to say that I think your viewers might want to hear."

86

Saturday

"I'm not sure what to say," Paul says to her. He is seated in the chair by the window. A yellow pad of paper rests on his knees. His fist is twisted around a pen. "What do you say at a moment like this?"

She doesn't answer. She blows her nose, the sound is full of mucous. She twists the tissue into a knot into her fist. She is half-lying on the bed, her feet stretched downward to the floor. Chloe, Danny's cat, has found his way to their room. He sits near her waist, on the edge of the bed.

"I don't know," Julie says. Her voice is wavy, full of fluid. She is still wearing her dress. Her hair is teased, full. She looks like a doll thrown to the floor. "Say what you feel."

"That I hope those bastards fry," he answers. "That I have as much hate and contempt for them as they did Danny?"

She reaches for another tissues. Blows. Twists. Her feet still dangle. "I don't think revenge is the answer for any of us."

He does not hear her. He has moved to a thought about his son as a little boy, about four—the way he hated to follow his father into the men's room at the church, as if he were afraid of the toilets, thinking they were white goblins because of the flushing water.

"You could talk about why you don't understand the way people hate," she says.

"I'm not sure I know what a hate crime is," he answers. He tries to write this down but his mind stops him, is full of other questions. Is it a crime because someone hates someone or is it the crime that makes someone hate its result? Before his grip lessens on the pen another memory floats to surface: Danny's first football game. He was seven. He was on the field. He caught the ball. A pass. But stopped running because he thought he had done what he was supposed to do. He was tackled by the entire opposing team. He never played football again. It was a funny image. And frightening. Full of consequences.

"You never wanted him to play football, did you?" he asks her.

She lifts her eyes in surprise. It is a strange comment for him. "No," she answers. She strokes the back of the cat. "It was too violent for him. He was too small for that."

He nods, gives her a flat smile, looks down at his paper. He noticed it first when his son was five. The morning he put training wheels on the bike, the unsettling way he squirmed, squealed. Did he fail to teach his son to be a man, not act like a girl? It happened over and over—the piano lessons, the flashy clothes he wanted to wear to school, the way he danced in his room when he thought no one was paying him any attention. When they were. They talked about him late at night. In bed. She said he would grow out of it. Not into it. But it was nothing he knew how to stop.

Another image floats into the room. The hospital bed. The white bandages around his forehead. He writes on the paper: *This is not how I want to remember my son.* Then another thought overcomes him: his son, tied to a fence, beaten, bloody. He looks up, searches for her eyes. They are closed. Her hand at her head. Melodramatic. "Did you think of him as gay?" he asks her. He is forty-two, more gray hair than brown, though he does not think of himself as old. Not even middle-aged. He smells of deodorant, after-shave. His complexion is ruddy, more farmer than executive. He prefers to be outside. Not cooped up. "After all that?"

"Yes," she says. "I worried more."

He writes again: *I still don't fully understand homosexuality. I guess I never will, because I'm not gay. But there is no real reason for parents to refuse to accept a gay son or lesbian daughter. Isn't the life of a son or daughter worth more than that?*

He stops. Another memory overcomes him. The school play. The hyper way Danny delivered his lines. They should have known then. Why did they not do something earlier? Could they have prevented this?

"You don't think he knew, do you?" he asks her.

"He was tested last year," she answers. "He said he was careful. He would have told us if he knew. Don't you think?"

"We didn't ask about a lot of things," he answers. "There was a lot we didn't want to know."

The phone rings in another room. She opens her eyes. Her hand falls to her side. She lifts her head. Looks up. There are voices coming through the walls, up from the floor.

"I can't answer any more questions," she says. "When will this stop?"

He doesn't answer. He looks out the window but there is nothing he wants to see. He looks down again at the yellow pad. Thinks of how strange the pen feels in his hand. He writes again. *This will never stop. This will haunt us the rest of our lives.*

87

Saturday

"Do you have any blue eye shadow?" Kelly asks the make-up lady. "It'll bring out my eyes."

The woman, heavy-set, about forty-five with blond-streaked hair, pushes back the sleeves of her sweatshirt, says, "Sure, hon. If that's what you want."

She looks at herself in the mirror and thinks about adding rouge, too. Something to make her face look longer, not so round and heavy. "I love this base you put on," she says. "It has a real beauty queen look to it."

The woman smiles. It is a weak smile. She finds the make-up kit in a tray, searches for a brush, says, "Close your eyes, hon. I'll put some on you."

Kelly closes her eyes, feels the spongy brush touch her eyelid. She feels the baby move, push against her spine, makes it unbearable to sit still. She shifts her weight to one side. It is more uncomfortable. She shifts back, tries another position. She thinks she is being punished. It is not funny. She opens her eyes and coughs. "Sorry," she says.

The pain makes her sweat. She feels claustrophobic. The make-up room is no bigger than a closet, hot with all the bright lights. The woman reaches for a tissue and dabs the moisture off her face. She smiles at Kelly. Like she deserves the attention. Because of all she's been through. All that's happening now.

"When you due, hon?" the woman asks.

"Soon," she says. "About six weeks."

"We'll, you certainly got a lot of stories for him. It's a boy?"

"Don't know," she answers. "I didn't want to know."

In the mirror she sees a man walk into the room, look at her in the mirror. He is dressed in a blue button-down shirt, khaki pants, carries a yellow pad of paper under his arm. He introduces himself. He says he is the pre-interviewer, wants to go over a few questions. He sits in a chair beside her. She is slightly higher than him. It makes her think she is special. Like a real beauty queen being interviewed by the media.

"I never met the guy," she answers his first question. "So I can't talk too much about him." She shakes her hair, likes the way it waves around her head. She glances over at herself in the mirror. Makes a note to tell the woman she wants a darker lipstick too. Her lips are her best feature. Or so she thinks.

The man frowns at her, asks her about another detail. "I don't know about the drugs," she says. "He wasn't around for a few days."

The man looks down at his list. He runs through some other questions that the interviewer might ask. He doesn't wait for her answers. He clicks his ball point pen rapidly, leaves the room.

The woman adds lipstick, then removes her paper bib. She stands, brushes her skirt. She follows a policeman out of the make-up room to the television set. She shakes her hair, fluffs it as she walks. She moves slowly because of the baby. She pretends that the electronic bracelet on her ankle is a piece of jewelry. She sees an end to all this soon.

The interviewer greets her. Shakes her hand. Kelly stretches her neck, says the set looks "neat," and adds that it's "cool that she got to come to the station to do this."

She thinks the interviewer is wearing too much make-up. The woman is about thirty. Wears blond bangs, a red suit. The make-up doesn't hide the wrinkles at her eyes, the small white hairs at her lip. Kelly wonders if this shows up on TV. Maybe on the giant new ones.

She stands to let the sound man run a microphone up the inside of her dress. Winks at him that it's okay, you know, nothing's gonna happen between them. She's a pregnant lady, after all.

Again she says her due date. "About six weeks," she says to the interviewer.

It starts before she is ready. It happens so quick. The light on her left is so bright she cannot look in that direction. She feels the baby move again. She shifts in her seat. She says she is "mad at myself" for being involved in this. She answers that she didn't bother to search for the college boy because she didn't know him. "He was a story to me," she says. "Not something real. And when I did get involved, I was protecting someone I loved. I don't see anything wrong with that. Anyone would do it that way. I think anyone would do the same thing that I did. Does it bother me now—thinking that I could have helped him somehow? If they found him earlier? Of course it does. I'm the one who has to live with that every day. Wondering if I could have made a difference."

88

Saturday

"I heard he died," Marcie says. Her eyes are teary, red. She moves with an effort but not as much, as if she has learned something about herself in the last few days. "I had some kind of hope he wouldn't."

She has found Reverend Fletcher in the cemetery behind the chapel. He looks down the hill, around her, at the small crowd at the fence, then back at her. "Yes," he answers. "I heard last night."

"They are already petitioning to have the trial somewhere else," she says. "In another county. Away from here."

"That might be wise," he says. "People have become very sensitive to all this attention." They walk a few steps and he realizes that they have entered the perimeter of the cemetery. "I've spoken to his father about a memorial service here," he says. "But it doesn't seem right, you know. Here, of all places. The service will be at one of the larger churches in the valley. The one his mother belonged to since she was a girl." They walk a few more steps, and then consciously, or unconsciously, something makes them hold hands, as if they had become lovers. A passerby would think this unremarkable, however, more likely it was merely a minister attending to a congregant's concern, but there is more chemistry at work here, and they both are sensitive to this.

"They'll have another service in Seattle," he says. "They've made arrangements there."

"What about here?" she asks. "Will there be something here? At the chapel?"

"I'm not sure we should draw more attention to this place,"

he says. "It's why I've asked that there not be any vigils here."

Behind him, he hears the sound of wheels moving across gravel. He turns and sees a silver limo in the parking lot behind the chapel. Their hands drop away from one another, as if they have been caught in the act of something that should not be witnessed. But they walk together back toward the chapel. The wind blows her scarf. His eyes turn skyward, at the dark assembling clouds.

89

Saturday

The scene is dramatic. He could not ask for God to make it any better. A storm is swelling above him. Gray-bottomed clouds blow violently to the east. The sun has lost its strength. He wears a white scarf that tosses back and forth against his black coat, flaps against his chest, shoulders, twists around his neck. His hair refuses to stay in place. "Americans are headed into foul weather if they do not give in to God," he says. He is in front of the bus. His arm is around his daughter's shoulder, her hair whipping across her face. The youngest child, Ruthie, his granddaughter, stands in front of him, tries to hold back a wave to the camera, but is distracted by the way her own scarf travels over her mouth. Their breaths break into small clouds in front of their faces. His skin is pale, washed out by the camera lights, the gray sky.

"My family cares about the family of America," he says. "My church adheres to the teachings of the Bible," he says. "I teach against all forms of sin—fornication, adultery, sodomy. These sins—particularly sodomy—are at the forefront of the foul climate that is overtaking our nation. Leviticus says that 'If a man also lie with mankind, as he lieth with a woman, both of them have committed an abomination: they shall surely be put to death. Their blood shall be upon them. And ye shall not walk in the manners of the nation, which I cast out before you: for they committed all these things, and therefore I abhorred them.'"

He squeezes his daughter closer to his side. She looks up at him, pushes hair away from her face, smiles as if the weather around her is painful to endure. Her jaw drops, the white of her teeth make his skin look more pale. "I do not make this up," he says. "This is the temperature of God. Who changed the climate of God into something unbearable? I did not do that. I have not changed God's climate. Homosexuals are filthy, lawless, brute beasts who have no shame. That is God's climate. That is what God forecasts. If this does not stop we are headed into even more uncertain weather."

His daughter turns to the camera, widens her smile. "Our church is against this sodomy," she says. Her voice is level but loud. She worries the wind is drowning her out. She raises her voice louder. "This perversion that is not natural. It is not God's way. We did not start the homosexual movement. We did not put this movement on the front page of every major newspaper. We are not the ones marching up and down the streets demanding that people accept and respect us for our sins. My father and I are appalled by this."

He breaks in, finishing her thought. "When God has turned his back on a people, sodomites rule the land. America is overcast by perversity. Our national support of perversity is bringing God's wrath upon us. This storm is only one of many more to come. Only by an abundance of mercy will God forebear the utter destruction of this country. That is why we focus on this issue in our ministry at this time in our journey. We must let America know of the even worse climate that is yet to come."

90

Saturday

Leah finds him at his house on Elden Street. Graham invites her in. She kisses him on the cheek, then kisses his partner, Wilson, when he comes down the stairs to see who is at the door. She follows the two men through the living room and into the kitchen, mentions how bad traffic is in town because of the homecoming game. She sits at a table in a glass enclosed atrium filled with clay potted plants.

"It's beautiful," she says, looking at the plants around her. "It must take hours watering them."

"It keeps us from yelling at each other," Wilson says.

"Nagging each other, you mean," Graham adds.

Wilson is stick thin, his skin leathery from smoking, working outdoors. Graham is the hefty one, the one who likes to cook and talk. He starts in about the news about the boy, her friend. The charges upgraded since his death. The decision of the pastor to hold the funeral services on Sunday, before the regular church services.

Wilson pours a cup of coffee for Leah, shows her the cactus he brought back from a trip to Arizona. He wants to change the subject. Gay talk bothers him. Unless it is camp.

Graham is the sensitive one. He sits at the table, draws more information out of Leah: What she knew of Danny, the fact that he used to sing in the church choir when he was a boy. Leah tells them about the Christmas pageant, the way his mother created angel wings out of yardsticks and fabric. Wilson hovers around the conversation, not sitting, not participating. Listening. The story makes Graham smile, pull Leah's hand toward him.

Leah tells them about the council vote, the demonstrations, the minister traveling to picket the funeral, the way she feels certain the news crews will be at the church.

"Reverend Denison's not going to let them inside," Dr. Graham says. It is as much a question as a statement. His eyes are wide, concerned. He doesn't like disruption either.

"No, of course not," she answers. "But they'll be there. Outside the church. That's the thing his mother hates so much. The intrusion. She wants to keep this private."

"I don't blame her," Wilson says. He is standing by the sliding glass door. "There was a camera crew at the gas station yesterday. *The gas station.* They were filming someone pumping gas. Why? Why pumping gas? They were asking a guy how he felt about homosexuals." His face turns red with the last word, as if he is uncomfortable with its sound in his throat. "It's gotten where we can't do anything without someone looking over our shoulder. Nothing's safe, here. It's got me worried, you know. This could have happened to any of us. It's not safe for us in this town."

"Stop being such a scaredy-cat," Graham says. "Who wants to bother two old queens? It's not like we're prowling the rest stops and toilets. Unless you haven't been telling me a few things, dear."

"Not funny," Wilson says. "We might not be out there flaunting our business but we are two old men living together in a town where a lot of men aren't doing that. I've lived in this town most of my life. This town is not a gay haven."

"I'm not going to be afraid to go out my door," Graham says. "And we're not rubbing our lives in anyone noses. We're just living our lives like we want to. We're part of this town whether they like us or not."

"But it's gonna change now," Wilson says. "People are going to be looking harder at us."

"And I'm not going to change," Graham says. "Are you?" he asks Leah. "Are you and Naomi going to change?"

Leah shakes her head, "No." Her eyes are wide, caught in the crossfire. She feels a sense of shame because she will not.

Nor will Naomi.

"I'm not going around wearing a pink triangle," he says. "But I want to keep the option to do it. It's my right. It's our right."

"You're awfully sanctimonious," Wilson says. "You won't even walk into a store with a rainbow flag unless it's in another town."

"And that's my choice," he answers. "That's the way I want to do it. I don't need Miss Busy-body next door staring through our windows trying to see how we live our life."

"Sounds like a double standard, if you ask me," Wilson says.

"She has no right to know my privacy," Graham says. "Which is why this whole thing just makes me miserable. That boy was killed. That's a disgrace to this town. That everyone has to know about what he did during sex is none of their business. His parents must be going crazy. I know I would if I had to listen to your sex life on TV," he says to Wilson.

"From what I've heard he was pretty open with his mother," Wilson says. "About things."

"That was his prerogative," Graham says. "My mother would drop dead at the word 'dick' used in that way."

"Your mother would cluck at anything," Wilson answers. "She still won't call me by my name." He looks at Leah and adds, "Refers to me as 'your friend.'"

"We don't need to be bringing my mother into this," Graham says. "Or his. She didn't change her mind on the music, did she?"

"No," Leah answers. "Not really."

"What does that mean?" Graham asks. "She wants us to do another song?"

"No," Leah says. "I wanted to talk to you about something. About an idea."

"What?" both men say at once.

"It's not about the music," she says. "It's about keeping this private. For the family. Danny's friends."

She begins to explain her idea of the choir standing on the

steps of the church when the family arrives, unfolding wings from their sleeves, raising their arms into the air to block out the demonstrations, the camera crews, from their view. Dr. Graham politely listens to her describe how the wings can be made easily. She and Naomi could make enough for ten choir members by tonight.

"It's not our place to be activists," Graham says. "It's a beautiful idea, but I don't think Reverend Denison will allow it."

"He's agreeable to it as long as you make sure to oversee it," she says. She thinks he will be hurt by the idea that she has already proposed the idea to the minister. But he's not. He's too busy eyeing Wilson's reaction.

"I bet Hart and Margie would do it too," Graham says. "Maybe six, seven of us."

"What about the police?" Wilson asks.

"As long as we keep it on the church steps and make it part of services, we don't need a permit," Leah says. "I checked with Reverend Denison about it."

"But we should certainly sing something," Graham says. "It should be something peaceful. Inspirational. Something that won't make people want to fight."

"You're gonna drag the piano out onto the steps, too?" Wilson asks. "Are you nuts?"

"This is going to drive you crazy," Graham says to Wilson. "So just let go of it. We have to be who we are supposed to be in this. This is our *moment*." He presses his chin against his neck, smiles dramatically, his hands reach up to his side. "A cappella. Just voices. Voices of angels. We'll be angels. Angels in white robes."

"Angels?" Wilson asks. He is troubled at the thought.

"What would you rather us be, dear?" Graham answers. "Fairies? Fairies in rainbow outfits?"

91

Saturday

She recognizes the red door right away. The limo drives past the chapel, parks in the parking lot on the north side. On the slope.

"Why?" Paul asks. "Why do you want to come here?"

They sit together in the back seat of the limo. Pop does not turn to talk to them. He leaves them alone. But listens.

"We used to park here, remember?" Julie says. "At night. After the library."

"Of course I remember," he answers. His voice is level, calm. He does not want to be thrown back to more memories.

"It's my best memory of this place," she says. "I remember I used to look out at the lights in the valley and think what it would be like to live somewhere else. Even if it was just another house."

"Did you want to get out and walk around?" he asks her.

"I think so," she says.

They get out of the limo. They walk to the edge of the parking lot, do not step on the grass, look out at the valley. The sky is low, gray, full of wind. She turns her back to the view, looks at him.

"You remember that picnic we had," she says. "Not far from the cemetery."

He says, "I figured it out, too. I did the math. I think it hit me probably Thursday."

"I'm not certain," she says. "But it's possible. The time adds up."

They walk to the ruins of the old annex. The wind blows her hair around in a silly manner. She keeps a hand next to the side of her head, stopping her hair from whipping against her eyes.

"You remember we had his second birthday in the annex," he says.

"We should talk to Lois before we leave," she says. "To let her know we remember. She must be going through a lot, too."

They turn when they hear footsteps on the gravel. Reverend Fletcher approaches them, introduces himself to the parents, then introduces the woman who stands slightly behind him, looking at her shoes, her face reddening from the chill in the air, embarrassment, or both.

"I'm so sorry about your son," Marcie says, moves forward to the parents. "I was the officer who responded to Reverend Fletcher's call that night."

Julie draws forward to her, kisses her on the cheek as if they are old friends reunited. "Thank you for everything," she says. "We appreciate everything you tried to do."

"Your son has left an impression on all of us," Reverend Fletcher says. "God has given his life a meaning none of us ever expected, nor would any of us have chosen for him."

"My son was not a saint," Julie says. There is no bitterness in her voice. Only the flat tone of fact. "I've heard about the things they are leaving at the fence."

"Yes," he answers. "Let me show you the fence."

She does not follow him at first. But Paul walks beside the Reverend so she follows a few paces behind, in stride with Marcie. The women walk close together. As if to keep warm. As they pass the front of the chapel Julie does not mention the dream about the red door to anyone. She walks silently, clasping the top flaps of her coat together.

92

Saturday

He confesses over dinner. Not at first. At first he listens to how Scott spent his day—the morning trip to the gym, the afternoon search for a replacement bulb for his grandmother's chandelier. Then he describes two patients he saw. A man in his fifties with a toupee. And a woman with a facelift wanting information on laser surgery. Something he wouldn't advise her to consider.

And then Scott takes over the conversation. He talks about his younger brother, who also tested positive last year. "It was a big wake up call," Scott says. "For both of us. We were big party boys. We thought it was neat that we were brothers and both gay."

Scott talks about how he's changed since then. If he goes to a club he won't do drugs. Usually leaves early. Gary says he goes to a bar maybe once every two months. "I end up just getting drunk," he says. "And I don't like that hangover feeling the next day. It's wasted time."

While they are waiting for the check, Gary says, "There's something I should tell you." He watches Scott's eyes widen, ready for the worst case. "It's something strange. Not strange, but it's left me feeling odd. I've been chatting with a guy on the Internet for almost two months. I met him on-line on a Saturday morning. His name was Danny and he was a college student."

Scott relaxes his posture but his expression takes on one of amazement. He asks, "Did you meet him?"

"No," Gary answers. "We talked on the phone twice. He sounded like a nice guy. We made a date to meet this weekend.

To go to a homecoming football game at his school. I was going to drive out there. He was supposed to e-mail me at the beginning of the week—to send me details on where to meet him."

"And they never came," Scott says.

"It could be that he just got cold feet, and is blowing me off," Gary says.

Scott doesn't answer quickly now. He lets the details sink in. "Did he send you his picture?"

Gary nods, answers, "Yes."

"So it's the same guy?" Scott asks.

Gary nods, answers, "I think so. I can't be certain. I never got his last name. Or his phone number. He called me."

Scott's hands rest on the table, his eyes cast downward. "I had a guy keep blowing me off that way about a year ago. He'd find me on line and chat and say to meet him at so-and-so and then never show up. It was frustrating. I finally just put a block on him. I know how you feel. Even though this sounds too weird of a coincidence."

"I'm not certain what I should do," Gary says. "When I got home last night, there it was, on the news. It's just I feel I should tell someone it happened, so I don't think I made it all up."

"I understand," Scott says. He offers a little laugh, to lighten the mood. "It could drive you crazy with all the wondering. The what if."

"I don't know, I feel like I've failed some kind of test," Gary says. "Like I wasn't there for him. Like I should have been there."

"If it was him," Scott says.

"If it was him," Gary agrees. Now he laughs and tries to lighten the mood. "But according to some people we are going to rot in Hell, you know."

"Eternity in Hell," Scott answers. "They already have our names stitched in the uniforms."

"I mean, I thought about contacting the police," Gary says. "But what do I tell them? That I got e-mails from someone who might have been Danny?"

"Just bypass the police and go directly to the press," Scott says. "It looks like what everyone else is doing."

"It makes it seem like a game," Gary says. "But it's not."

The waiter brings the bill to the table. They split the check evenly. They put on their coats and walk out to the parking lot. It is colder than the night before. Their steps are faster.

Later, in bed, in a more intimate position, Gary says to Scott, "It doesn't scare me at all. It should. It could happen right here. In this neighborhood, too. It just seems so unreal. Even because it's so close to home."

"There was a piece on the news today how people are leaving flowers at the fence," Scott says. "I heard someone at the gym talking about driving out there. The funeral's tomorrow morning."

"Why would he do that?" Gary asks. "Drive out there? For someone he didn't know."

"Because it happened," Scott says. "Because it could happen anywhere."

93

Saturday

He arrives with a fury, like a tunnel of wind ready to destroy a carnival. The mood of the University has shifted. The homecoming game has been won (27-14). The Blue-and-Gold ball has started in the Archive Pavilion. On fraternity row, Saturday night kegs and house bands keep the pitch rowdy. In town, the Market Street bars are noisy. Alumni celebrating. Visitors unwinding from the tension of the week. In the air something seems resolved. Even though it is not.

The weather is not with him this time. The night is still, broken up only by celebration. This, too, Reverend White uses to his advantage. The camera crews find his bus parked in front of the Blue Moon. The red neon sign behind him flashes XXX. Cars, trucks, jeeps drive in and out of the lot.

"I have come here to warn the nation about the homosexual agenda," he says. There are three crews filming. Two national. One local. Their lights blind him but he uses his discomfort as an advantage. Once again his family surround him. The smallest children in the front. His hands on his grandson's shoulders. "Homosexuality is by definition not healthy and wholesome. Fags live filthy, unhealthy, dangerous, unhappy, and violent lives. They historically account for the bulk of syphilis, gonorrhea, and hepatitis in America. Fags are responsible for spreading AIDS in the United States, and then creating violent groups like Act Up to complain about it. Their sexual practices include urinating on each other; they are infected with intestinal parasites like worms and amoebae. They prey on our children because they can't reproduce naturally. They recruit our children. They molest our children. They turn our children away from Christianity. Are your children safe? Listen to what my children say."

Justin, the smallest boy, speaks first. "Fags are scary," he says. "They scare God too." Then the girl, Ruthie, adds, "God says fags are sinners. They will always live in Hell."

"I am here to preach the word of God to this crooked and perverse generation," the Reverend says. "It is my solemn job to preach this gospel to every creature and warm them to flee from the wrath to come. Christianity is not a game. Be not deceived. Fornicators, thieves, idolaters, adulterers, faggots will not inherit the kingdom of God."

94

Saturday

It is late. There is a card game in the east block. The ceilings are peeling. The floors are wet. A powerful smell of urine fills the air. Four men gamble at a table. Chips are playing cards torn into quarters. Already, he has a nickname. Dopey. He's punched in the arm. Paid attention to. He can even smile, laugh, brag about anything. He's won enough for a joint, a pack of batteries, and a devil dog.

He is smaller than the other three. 145 pounds. 5'6". Tiny arms. Tiny chest. No definition to his body. Just the big ears, slopey eyes. He wins this hand with two aces. The other three react with barnyard noises. Aaiiiiieeee. Woof, woof, woof! One guy, Marco, says Dopey's king of the hill. The king! The king! He raises his fists in the air. Woofs some more. Marco is shirtless, wears a net cap. Sent here for stabbing his girlfriend's brother. Tuba, locked up for robbing a car, says, Dopey's making more inside than he ever did outside on the street. Sparky, the fourth, has silver caps. He watches Dopey gather up his chips, says, "You gonna have enough to spend a night with Peaches." He grins, sticks out his tongue. Wiggles it.

"Peaches?" he asks.

"Oh, man, Peaches is the best," Marco says. "She's the best piece in this place."

Peaches is male by gender. Female by occupation. She is forty-three, coffee-skinned, been convicted more than eighty times. She's back in protective custody because her trick did not understand that she was borrowing his car, not stealing it. She costs twenty-five dollars, always likes a tip.

"There's always some kind of way to work it off if you can't pay the tip," Sparky says. Wiggles his tongue again.

The irony does not find him. Not now. That will come later. Right now he is Dopey, King of the Hill. He does not know that the joint he won came inside through a balloon shoved up a greased rectum. He does not know that one day he will be king, another he might be queen. He does not know that everything is worth something here. Nothing goes to waste. Even his ass.

Right now he brags about being on TV, says a reporter chased after him at the hearing, wanted a quote.

"You the man," Marco says. "You the man!"

After this hand, the card game breaks up. He cashes out. Has enough to buy a picture of a naked blond. Playboy bunny type. Big hooters. "The dream machine," Sparky says.

Back in his cell he looks at the picture. The model is bent over, facing away from the camera. He lays it on the edge of the bed. He thinks about the model instead of other things. Not his past. Not the college boy. Rick. The AZT he's had to start taking. The time with his cousin. The other guys. Not even Kelly.

What he thinks about is winning. Maybe some cigarettes. Matches. Another joint. And tape. He needs something to hang her to the wall.

95

Sunday

They will talk about the weather first—those who were there that day—how the snow fell through the gray sky in large, white flakes, melting as soon as it touched something—a shoulder of a coat, the top of an umbrella, the sidewalk in front of the church—leaving dark, wet stains so that it seemed as if tears had fallen from Heaven.

Heaven was on many people's minds that day, not just because it was Sunday, a day of prayer and contemplation. The Reverend White had arrived early with the nine members of his congregation—four grandchildren, two sons, their wives, and the minister's wife—and taken the spot where the two police officers, Larry English and Chris Santini, had instructed them. The congregation chanted, "God hate fags," carried signs that read: "Fags Die, God Laughs," "No Fags in Heaven," "AIDS Cures Fags." The youngest child, eight year-old Jennifer, carried a sign that said, "Danny Burns in Hell"—flames colorfully drawn in red and yellow ink at the bottom edge.

Her grandfather, the Reverend, was called by his own spirit that day. Beneath his coat he wore a bullet proof vest, as he always does at demonstrations. In his left hand, clutching it to the chest of his coat, he held the Bible his father had given to him when he was seven. His eyes were turned toward a camera crew, preaching directly to the lens, warning everyone of the "black clouds of God's wrath which are now hanging directly over our heads."

Gabe Garcia, an officer from Richmond, led a German shepherd named Molly around the congregation, sniffing for bombs. SWAT teams were sent from as far as Washington,

D.C. Police were stationed on rooftops, at intersections, beside barricades. Even before the Reverend arrived late last night the City Council, alarmed by the increasing visibility of the town in the news, had voted to ban all protesters from demonstrating within fifty feet of the funeral. Molly found nothing ominous to the contingent from Eastgate Baptist, though Officer Stuart felt trouble was brewing as the dog sniffed the area in front of the street barricades, the wind freezing his cheeks.

"We've never faced this before," Richard Bertoglio, a town councilman, said to a reporter from CNN, not far from the Eastgate congregation. "It's sad that we have to do this—that the sanctity of a funeral is not upheld. One of the things we're trying to do, besides protecting those who want to protest on both sides, is protecting the family and relatives to allow them to breathe in peace."

But everyone was aware of the crowds and the protests. Just like the snow. When they remember the day they remember the commotion, the surreal, war-like landscape, the sniffing dog, the Hellish posters, flags hung around town at half mast, the trees, wet and black. No one had seen anything like this before. Not in this town. Not here.

The Reverend continued his assault for all to hear. "The wrath of God is like great waters that are damned," he shouted. "They increase more and more and rise higher and higher, till the stream can no longer be stopped and God will let His might loose on all who have not repented. Your guilt rises every day. There is nothing but the mere pleasure of God that holds the waters back. If God should withdraw His hand from the flood-gate, it would immediately fly open. The fiery floods of the wrath of God will rush forth with inconceivable fury."

The Reverend Joel Sheldon, fifty-seven, a conservative Baptist minister, had left his congregation in Washington, D.C. in order to speak to reporters that Reverend White's message was not that of God's. He stood with his hands deep in his pockets, hiding his clenched fists, his publicist beside him. "The church does not preach a message of hate," he said to a thirty-five year-old reporter from MSNBC, a woman who had flown in from Atlanta to cover the breaking news. "Homosexuality is a sin, but gays—like alcoholics and criminals—can be saved."

Reverend Fletcher had only driven across town. He had circled the church several times searching for a parking space, finding something almost a mile away. The sight of Reverend White and his posters sickened him. He could not overlook this horror, this travesty that was occurring in God's name. "How do you know he went to Hell?" he shouted at Reverend White when he had arrived at the demonstration. This was the only point their paths crossed. Two men of faith. Two men sent on different journeys by the same God.

"I'm sure as anything this boy is in Hell," Jonathan, the minister's son, answered for his father.

"Who gave you the right to condemn him?" asked Reverend Fletcher. He tried to contain his animosity, to act like a minister, a man of God, but his voice was strident, as if he were in the pulpit. "Did you know him?"

"I didn't need to," Jonathan said. "All faggots are in Hell. Jesus does not want those people in Heaven."

Reverend White approached and began chanting, "Shill, shill, shill," at the Reverend Fletcher.

"I would like to see if Christ were standing here today how Christ would judge you," Reverend Fletcher said, his voice now carrying above the chants.

"Shill," Jonathan yelled back.

The chant was taken up by the entire congregation now, even the youngest child. "Shill, shill, shill, shill," they yelled, till the Reverend Fletcher left defeated, red-faced.

By nine o'clock, an hour before the service was to begin, more than three hundred people had arrived at the church. They stood behind barricades that lined the sidewalk, huddled close in the heavy winter coats they wore, umbrellas lifted toward the gray sky to shield them from the falling snow.

Arnie Darrow had arrived by then. He stood behind the barricades, watching, not making any notes, till he could no longer resist and began to write his thoughts down.

Michelle had walked over from campus with Colin and

two other members from the Gay Caucus. They watched the Eastgate congregation for a few minutes, horrified by the noise and accusations, and decided to watch from the barricades on the other side of the steps.

Teddy DeWitt stood on the sides for a while, watching the crowd swell seven deep behind the barricades, thinking about how his own son now fit into this picture, what he needed to do before the day was over. He stayed there until a few minutes before the service began, looked at his watch, then made his way to the church. As he climbed the steps to the church, the choir, in long white robes, filed out of the church and stood on the stairs, their backs to the barricades and demonstrators. Leah and Naomi were among the choir members. Wilson and Graham were not. Softly the choir began to sing, "Amazing Grace," their voices lifting with the lyrics till others began to join in. The spectacle made Teddy shake his head in disbelief, that even the church could play to the media, till he turned and saw the dark cars of the funeral procession making their way down the street.

Pop had volunteered to drive the family to the church in his limo. Luke sat up front. Danny's parents sat in the back with Roxy and Wayne. Julie looked at the snow landing against the glass and melting, aware of how slowly the limo was taking the corners. The morning had left her feeling incomplete, unfinished. There was too much activity. She wished these moments would end soon. She wanted to be alone.

She did not put the sunglasses on until the limo slowed in front of the church, the darkened view left her disoriented. Pop opened the door for her. She was aware, as she stepped out of the limo, of people dressed in white robes and singing. She felt, oddly, so out of place, as if she were a starlet arriving at a movie premiere in her hometown. Paul took her by the elbow and they began walking up the steps of the church. Luke led the way.

Slowly the members of the choir began to stretch their arms out, revealing in their grasps long white sticks draped with white fabric. As they stretched them out and over their heads they looked like angel's wings, their singing continuing, "but now am found," shielding the family from noticing the protests across the street. Julie never saw Reverend White or his family. Nor did Paul. But they both noticed the word "Love" stenciled with red paint on the sidewalk before the church, before ascending the stairs.

Marcie Piccolo saw their arrival. She was on duty that day. She had volunteered because the force needed help. She was stationed in front of the barricades on Howe Street, so she had a clear view of the front of the church. She had watched the choir file out of the great wood doors, down the steps, lift their arms into giant wingspans. After the family filed its way into the church, she noticed a black bird, hidden in the eaves above the door, near the roof, out of the falling snow. At first she thought there was a nest of some kind there, and didn't give it any more thought, watching the choir process back inside the church. But when she looked back again, she noticed that the dark bird was really a white one made darker by the shade of the eaves. Years later, she would tell her children that that was the moment she knew she was okay, that no harm had come to her for helping the boy. That once the family and the choir was inside the church the bird took flight, out into the snow. White against white. Sorrow against faith.

Inside the church, his mother will remember shaking hands, hugging people she had only begun to know this week. Donald Carberry and his wife, Sharon; Dr. Gardner and his wife; Bob Kadden; Stuart Gray and other members of the Gay Caucus who had helped the family with errands. The service began with a procession of the choir, shaking off the snow and dampness, still singing "Amazing Grace."

His father was the first to speak. "There is an image seared upon my mind when I reflect on Danny on that wooden fence," he said. "However, I have found a different image to replace that with and that is the image of another man, almost two thousand years ago. When I concentrate on the Son of God being crucified, only then can I be released from the bitterness and anger that I feel."

She agreed to make only a small statement at the funeral.

"I am sure Danny feels your love," she said from the pulpit of the church. She felt strange being in front of so many people talking about her son. She could not contain her tears. "My son was just a young man in search of himself. Thank you all for being here to help Danny take one more step toward his goals and dreams."

There were others who spoke at the funeral that day. The President of the University, the town's mayor, a state senator's wife. But what they remember, those inside the church, was the scene which continued outside it: the protests, the camera crews, the umbrellas, the snow.

They left the church through the back—the family followed a minister through a door behind the altar, down a flight of stairs, out a back door where Pop and the other cars were waiting to take them to the airport, where Danny's body would be buried in a Seattle cemetery. The casket was led down the aisle and outside the large, carved wooden doors. The crowd watched the snow fall on the casket as it was loaded into the waiting hearse. It was not a quiet moment. The chants continued, "Danny in Hell. Danny in Hell. Danny in Hell."

96

Sunday

Teddy finds the house easily. It is a two family unit, a slender set of stairs lead to a second floor entrance. When he parks his Jeep at the curb two men are on the upstairs landing, locking a door. They are both dressed in similar hunting jackets. One older, with graying hair and glasses. The other younger, young enough to be his son.

He meets them when they reach dark green Volvo parked outside the garage. He feels as if he has played out this scene before but never noticed the details. "We've met a few times," he says, stretches his hand out for a friendly shake. "Back when you were over at the chapel."

"Yes, of course," the older man says. He offers his hand and the two men shake. The younger man, a teenager, really, stands on the other side of the car, waiting for the door to be unlocked. "We're just on our way out." The older man hits a button on his key ring and a choo-ching sends the latches open. The boy settles in the car seat, waiting, glancing at the two men talking.

"I'm sorry to hear about all that stuff happening up there," the older man says. "That poor boy. There was a reporter around two days ago but I wouldn't talk to him. Said it was none of my concern now."

"It's a bit of mess, yes," he says. He still hates this chit-chat. This aw-shucks routine he has to do to get to the information he wants. "One of the boys we've charged used to work with you at the chapel. I was wondering if you could tell me a few things about him, Reverend Drake."

"I'd be glad to come down to the station and talk to you,"

the Reverend says. "Maybe one day next week?"

"We could either talk here or you can come down to the station with me now," he says. He does not use his tone as a threat. It is more authoritative, letting the man know that he wants information now, not later.

"Rick, right?" the man says. He tries to hide his annoyance but it leaks beneath his expression, senses the young man in the car leaning down to see what the delay is. "Yes, I heard about him. I don't know much about him, of course. More about Lois, his grandmother. We worked there every day together. I'd always come over and lead the kids in prayer. Rick worked a few months on the grounds. One spring, I think. Only a few months. He was a good worker. When he wasn't working on the grounds he helped his grandmother out in the classroom. He loved to tell the kids some tall tales, as I recall. He could get real excited doing that."

"There's been a bit of talk about linking all this to the fire that was there a few years ago," he says. "Did you ever have any reason to suspect Rick in that?"

"Rick?" he answers. "Why no. No. The fire was after he left. All the investigators determined the electrical wiring was so old and it was never brought up to code."

"Yes, I know that," he says. "I looked through the files yesterday. But I thought you might have a hunch. Was there a reason behind his leaving the church? Why you didn't keep him on? He was there such a short time. A lot of the boys who worked for you there were there for just a short time."

The man's face reddens. He looks away to keep his composure. "There were several boys working there in the summer. There always was. Rick didn't do that fire. I don't think he had that in him. Not then at least. He was a good, honest boy. It's hard to believe he's even involved in this."

"You knew him pretty well then," he says. The way he meets the man's eyes, the sound of his voice, now registers his meaning, his hunt for other clues.

"I don't know what you mean by that."

"Only that some people have started talking," he says.

"Looking into the boy's past."

"I don't know what you mean by that," the older man says again. "What has he said? Has he said something?"

"Do you know any boys who might have been involved in starting that fire? Any boy who might have had a reason to want to set the building on fire while you were there?"

"I'm not sure I understand what you are suggesting?"

"Some boys have started talking, Reverend," he says. "We're looking into what might have caused someone to set fire to the annex building a few years ago."

"Nothing," the man answers. "It was an accident. The boys had nothing to do with the fire."

"Then why are they talking about it now?" he asks.

"I don't know what they're saying," the man answers.

"They're talking now," he says. "That's the important thing."

97

Sunday

He will not see the snow. But he will feel the cold, his arms numb. He will rub the skin, thump the veins. He will become itchy, restless. He will stand, walk, sit. Time will stretch out, his enemy.

He will imagine spiders, moving across the floor of his cell, up the walls, clinging to the corners, looking down at him. They weave a frail, quivering sound, a voice bubbling up from the floor, running weakly into his body. *Ee ooo ssss emmm. Ee ooo ssss emmm.* The voices will have no meaning, the sounds are not words. They exist only to haunt him. Prevent him from solitude.

He will not kill himself, though fear of death surrounds him. He is afraid of closing his eyes, afraid of sleep, afraid of being vulnerable. He will not shower, afraid of someone attacking him. He looks over his shoulder when he pisses. Even though he is alone. Isolated. Separated. His ass is marked. Or so he has been warned.

That's what the spiders sing. His ass is marked. His ass is marked. He will rise from the bed. Walk the cell. Talk to himself. When he tires he will sit down. Then lie so that he can see the door. Make sure the spiders know he is alert. Watching them watch him.

His eyes will close for a second. Out of exhaustion. When he wakes he finds himself erect. This will bother him. Thinks it is part of the plan. He will think about the blood. On his hands. His coat. The shoes.

He will grow harder till he must touch himself. This registers pleasure. He will close his eyes. Tries to think of a

338

woman. Chase. Kelly. *Ee ooo ssss emmm. Ee ooo ssss emmm.*

The college boy will be there instead. In his thoughts. *Thump. Thump. Thump.* He touches himself to forget. Strokes himself so that pleasure eases his brain. He touches his balls. Kneads them. Cups them. Imagines a mouth around his dick. Like before. Like it happened before at the church. A.J.'s laugh splits his memory. The spiders chant. *Ee ooo ssss emmm. Ee ooo ssss emmm.* The college boy's face is pressed against his neck.

He continues this way until his body tightens, his ass squeezes. He wipes himself dry on the mattress. He looks at the spiders looking at him. Thinks about being alone. They're trying to make him mad. *Ee ooo ssss emmm. Ee ooo ssss emmm.*

98

Monday

He looks at his watch. It is 10:08 when he leaves the student center. Outside, on the street, he knows he should have worn a warmer jacket, but he didn't want to carry around his winter coat all day. He's not ready to admit the weather is changing. Winter is headed this way.

It is only a few minutes' walk to the bar. Leah has warned him about walking the streets alone so late at night. "It might be a small town, hon, but there's still a bunch of no-goods looking for trouble," she said. He doesn't heed her advice, telling himself he needs to conquer *some* of his fears. One of them walking alone. At night. (But he does try to stick to the well-lighted paths. Places where other people might also be walking.)

He shoves his hands into the pockets of the coat, pulls the flaps closer together to prevent the wind seeping into his clothes. He should have worn a sweater to break the chill. Or a hat. Or a scarf. But they would only bring more attention to himself. He wants to be noticed for the right reasons, not the wrong ones.

He listens to his steps along the pavement. He tries to make them into a rhythm. A two-step rhythm. He decides he's never going to meet someone studying. He can't spend his life in front of a book. Time is too precious to him now.

He takes Clifton Avenue and walks along the perimeter of the campus. He wishes he could have convinced someone at the meeting to come along tonight. He feels better finally, the best he's felt all day. Relaxed. Stress free. When he feels this good he usually wants to dance. He's too shy to dance alone.

Especially in a mixed place. Straight guys would know right away he was gay—as if they couldn't sniff it out already. He could have shielded himself behind Michelle or Leah if they had decided to come along. He wishes the town had its own gay bar. He wonders what they would call it if they did—something academic or something country? The Library? The Bootrack? He wonders if the town politicians would even allow such a place. Probably not. It would only stir up trouble. "The only good faggot is a dead one," he could hear them saying. No one has ever complained about the billboard on Hogan Street, the one that someone painted with graffiti to read, "Shoot a gay or two." Leah had told him the reason why: "The minute someone complained about it they would be called homo lovers. Who in this town could live with a reputation like that?"

He thinks again about moving away from here. Would he have better luck finding a boyfriend in a larger city? Maybe. Maybe not. Big cities overwhelm him, make it clear he's not exactly like those gay men, either. He has faith that he'll meet the right guy someday, even if it doesn't happen tonight, in this town.

"The first thing you have to do is to think of it as your home," Mark said, when they said goodbye in Seattle last summer. "That'll help make things easier. You'll see."

Home. So this is my home now. This is where I must find myself. Where all things revolve around. Where comfort and challenge keep me alive. Wanting to be alive.

When he reaches the path that leads to the stadium, he begins to outline his day tomorrow. A habit he picked up from his mother. He will call her to apologize about the money. He will study for the French test in the morning before class. He will finally get up the nerve to speak to the guy in the language lab. He needs to buy groceries, too. Cat food for Chloe. More milk. Bread. Maybe bagels if Gary comes for the weekend.

Gary. Maybe there's a possibility there. Maybe that could work out. He will call him tomorrow. Or e-mail him when he gets home tonight. If it's not too late. If he's alone. And not too tired. Things could work out with Gary. He's not like other guys. Different. Wants something too. He mentioned he was willing to compromise. Nobody's perfect. Relationships are all about working together to make it continue.

The sidewalks disappear when he reaches Market Street. He walks along the edge of road instead of trying to navigate one parking lot to another, cuts across the street at a gas station. He takes a deep breath of air when a car passes behind him, walks closer to a row of parked cars in order not to be hit. He decides to skip Sloppy Joe's and go to the Starlite instead—the parking lot looks more crowded. Maybe there are more people at the Starlite. Then he remembers what Walt told him when they talked a few days ago on the phone—that he always has luck meeting guys at the Starlite.

When he reaches for the door handle he wonders what he'll say if he sees Walt inside the bar. He'll buy him a drink, say he felt better, tried calling him before he set out. Maybe he'll explain to Walt why he feels so lonely, confused here. Walt might understand more than he gives him credit for. They could be a better friends. He shouldn't overlook Walt either.

99

Sunday

The hearse carrying the casket takes the Interstate route to the airport. Pop makes one final stop with his limousine before leaving town.

This is why another rumor, another myth, another story persists.

The snow continues. It covers the branches of the maples, the leaves that have not yet turned and fallen, the needles of the pines. The road begins to lighten, except where tire tracks still darken the cement. The family gathers in the old cemetery behind the chapel. Julie, Paul, Luke, Roxy, Wayne. The boy's grandparents. Leah and Naomi. Marcie Piccolo is with the Reverend.

"Tragedies like this have a way of grabbing hold of us and shaking us up and telling us that we should not forget what has happened," Reverend Fletcher says. He carries a Bible in his hand, clasped against his side. He wears a black suit. His shoes are already muddy from the services in town. "For those of us who survive disasters it often becomes the defining moment of our lives. Tragedies have a way of making us consider the brevity of life and to reassess our purpose on earth. Some will say that this is the wrath of God. Others will question how could God allow this to happen. But the true nature of God is not in the tragedies we experience but in the peace that follows. The comfort God brings as we bury our dead."

Paul holds out his arms toward Julie. In his hands is a small white box. Julie takes the first handful of ashes and casts them to the ground. Next, Paul takes a fistful and throws it in the same direction as his wife. Luke follows, then Roxy, Wayne, the others.

They scatter his ashes: son, brother, grandson, friend. There was no body in the casket. It was a way to present closure to the town, the media, others outside the family circle.

There is closure here too, but not final closure. They will return to this spot many times. The myth will continue to grow. People will revisit this story many times. It will mean different things to different people.

The snow will be part of the story. How it fell and fell. Later that day, eight hundred people will gather for a service on the University quadrangle in memory of a fellow student, the snow still falling, making the candle lights wave and blink in the dark.

In Washington, D.C., twelve hundred people will gather at the steps of the Lincoln Memorial, which is where Gary and Scott can be found. It will snow there too. In Richmond, three hundred people will assemble. It will be without snow, though cold. In Nashville, the two hundred present will be more vocal than the others around the nation. They will chant "We will not be silenced" before singing their own version of "Amazing Grace."

And there will be more snow that night. In the morning the fence will still be there, coated with a soft, romantic dusting. Its part in the tragedy will not soon be forgotten either. Many will continue to seek it out. Many will struggle with God's meaning here.

100

Monday

The air is muddy with smoke and music. A Ronnie Milsap song is playing when A.J. and Rick enter the bar. After showing their IDs to the guy by the door—a big guy with a big stomach wearing a black T-shirt and jeans—they hang out by the door for a moment, their hands looped into the pockets of their jeans, their eyes searching through the room.

Inside, there are guys in working clothes, a few women with teased or dyed hair. Most of the crowd looks like college kids. Girls in sweatshirts squeezed into a booth around a pitcher of beer. Guys looking bored, watching the dance floor, or the bartender, or at the buck head in front of the DJ's booth, waiting for it to blow smoke between the nostrils.

They leave the door and walk back to the pool table. Two frat boys have just finished. A.J. hands a stick to Rick. Keeps one for himself. He chalks the tip. Rick racks the balls.

A.J. breaks. The balls scatter. He tries a shot, misses. He reaches into his shirt pocket, gets a cigarette. Lights it. His hands are dirty, callused. They were working on Rick's car earlier. Trying to replace engine parts. He digs his hand into his jeans pocket and comes up with coins. He lays the coins on the pool table, making Rick stop lining up his shot.

"Let's get a pitcher," A.J. says. "How much you got?"

"Just change," Rick says.

A.J. looks away from the table out into the room, looking for someone to hit up for money. Someone they know. He digs into his other pocket, comes up with more change. "How much you got?"

They count the change. They have enough for a cheap

pitcher. A dime left over. No tip for the bartender. Rick scoops up the coins in his hands. They are dirty, too. Dirtier than A.J.'s. He was the one working on the car. A.J. was fiddlin' around with things. Tossing a new wrench up in the air, watching it drop head first, trying to catch it. Till it made him paranoid. Thought he saw it squirm when it hit the ground.

At the bar they wedge into the empty space between a greaser and a college boy. The college boy is neatly dressed. Blue blazer, khaki's, expensive shirt. He looks like a kid. Face still young. He smiles and nods at Rick as they wait for the bartender to bring the pitcher and glasses. A.J. leaves with the pitcher while Rick dumps the change on the counter. He senses the bartender's disgust. He doesn't wait while it's counted. He takes the glasses, nods to the college boy, heads back to the pool table.

Rick shoots while A.J. drinks. He makes a shot. Then another. Then misses. A.J. chalks his cue, aims. The game continues till Rick wins. They begin another. Rick sways his shoulders to the music while A.J. shoots. He's happy he's winning.

They play until they run out of beer. A.J. scans the room again for someone to hit up. No one here tonight that he knows. Rick decides he needs to piss. A.J. follows him to the john. As they pass the bar, A.J. notices the college boy looking at Rick.

In the restroom, A.J. asks Rick if he knows the guy at the bar.

"Who?" Rick answers.

"The pretty boy in the blue blazer," he answers.

"Nah," Rick says.

"I bet we could hit him up," A.J. says. "I saw him looking real friendly at you."

"What's that supposed to mean?" Rick asks. He hates it when A.J. starts this. Guys wanting to jump his bones 'cause he's got a good face.

"Try and get him to buy us a beer," A.J. says.

"Why don't you?"

"'Cause I saw him lookin' at you."

Rick pushes A.J. away. Heads toward the sink. He washes his hands. "Okay then," A.J. says. He is behind Rick. Looking at him in the mirror. "You get him outside and I'll jump him. Get his wallet. We can go to Baffer's and get another bag."

"Why don't we just try to rob the fuckin' Red Lobster again?" Rick says. "So we can see if they're going to send us to jail this time."

"Just get him outside and into the truck," he says. "I'll do the rest."

"I got to mellow out," Rick says. "Did we eat today? I got to eat something."

"So we go get something to eat," he says. "Or drink."

Back in the bar they stand against a wall, hands in pockets, looking bored. Rick leaves the wall, walks along the aisle behind the bar, approaches the college boy. The college boy is shaking out a cigarette from a pack. "You got an extra one?" Rick asks when the college boy notices him passing. "One for the road?"

"My last one," the college boy answers. His voice is light, full of syllables and vowels, like he's almost drunk.

"Don't want to take your last one," Rick says. He senses A.J. behind him. It makes his skin prickle. "We're just on our way out."

The college boy looks at A.J. Smiles. "Well, you guys will have to share it. I can bum another later from someone, if I want." He hands the cigarette and matches to Rick. Watches him light it. Then he asks, "Where you guys goin' to next?"

"Maybe back to Joe's," A.J. says. His eyes look eager, hungry. "Music's better."

"Yeah," the college boy says. "But I like to watch the dancing here."

"Music's not too bad here," Rick says. "It rocks on the weekend when they have a live band."

"But nobody dances on the weekend here," the college boy answers. There is a slight whine to his voice. "The place is too crowded. I went to this club in Richmond last weekend where they've got a room just for dancing. Not some fenced off little spot."

"What place?" A.J. asks.

The college boy tells him the name of the club. A.J. nods. Rick says, "I went there once in high school. The sound system is great. A lot of gay guys were there dancing."

"It's mostly gay now," the college boy says.

This information filters in quicker to Rick than to A.J. Rick says, "I'll have to go dancin' with you sometime." A.J.'s eyes widen. Then narrow. He realizes for certain the college boy is queer. He wants to take a step away. But remains in place. His face breaks a light sweat.

Rick drops the cigarette on the floor, grounds it out with his boot. He dances a bit to the music, as if he's showing off. He says to A.J., "Maybe we should go dancin' tonight. I could go for some dancin'." His voice is lighter.

A.J. doesn't respond. He is frozen in place. Rick says to the college boy, "You want to come dancin' with us tonight?" He touches the college boy at the elbow. To make a connection.

"Better not," the college boy answers. "I've got a test tomorrow. It's been a long day. I ended up going to a meeting I hadn't expected to go to. They're going to do a gay awareness week on campus next week. You guys should come."

A.J. doesn't answer. He looks at his feet. Rick is still dancing. He says, "My old man would kill me if he found out. Wouldn't he, A.J.?"

A.J. shuffles his foot, looks at the floor. The lies are confusing him.

"The best thing that happened was when my parents found out," the college boy says. "It made it much easier to go on from there."

Rick does a fancy step, shakes his head, repeats his lie, "I could never tell my old man about being gay. He'd beat me to shit."

The college boy introduces himself, states his name, shakes hands. A.J. and Rick do not give their names away. Rick only repeats the college boy's name with a smile, saying, "Hey,

Danny. Nice to meet ya."

Danny says he is a freshman at the University and that a friend told him this bar was one of the better gay-friendly places near campus.

A.J. tenses up again, says through his teeth, "Yeah, it's great that we have a place like this to hang out."

There is a slight pause, then Danny asks, "Are you guys boyfriends?"

A.J. freezes. Blood rushes to his face, like embarrassment. Rick answers, "Naah. We're just good friends. Don't go for the same types."

"Yeah," Danny answers. "I know how it is."

"Well, we're gonna check out another place," Rick says. "You sure you don't want to come get another drink or something?"

Danny feels a connection with the dark-eyed guy. Thinks he's cute. Even the guy with the big ears looks nice. Bashful. He knows he should go back home. Study. Sleep. Call a few people—Walt, Stuart. E-mail Gary, his dad. But he's really undecided, kind of itchy, so he says, "I better not. But if you guys are heading down Clifton I could use a ride back to my apartment."

"We can drop you off," the dark-eyed one says to Danny. He looks at his friend, the one with the big ears to make sure it is alright, get his okay, like he's the one driving.

The big-eared guy breaks his stance. "Yeah," he answers. "We're going by there. No problem."

Danny follows the two guys through the bar, smiles at the doorman as he leaves the bar. Outside, a gust of wind hits him as he walks across the parking lot, as if warning him to hurry inside somewhere. He senses the heaviness of the air, the climbing humidity, the rising level of a storm. He remembers the forecast he heard earlier: a cold front moving from the north, a wind shift from the south. Possibly snow by the weekend if the temperature drops.

Ahead, one guy throws a set of keys to another, a gesture Danny interprets as a sign of comfortable friendship. The keys catch the neon light as they float through the air, clink when they land in the palm of the other guy's hand.

The sound, the arc of light, the idea of friends out with each other make Danny exhilarated. He hurries ahead, not to seek shelter from the cold, but happy with hope. Hope keeps him going. Hope is his faith.

Author's Note

This is a work of fiction. Portions of this novel were inspired by the events surrounding several hate crimes against gay men, including the murder of Matthew Shepard. While details from news sources and court transcripts have been used in some instances, their presentation, attributes, and specifics have been altered, re-arranged, or fictionalized for this novel. The characters and their actions depicted herein are fictitious.

I am indebted to the many readers of the drafts of this manuscript, and whose comments helped shaped the final novel, particularly my friends and fellow writers Anne H. Wood and Brian Keesling. I am particularly indebted to the details which were uncovered by the reporters, journalists, and activists during the Shepard investigation and trials, and to items, ideas, and concepts set forth originally in articles by Andrew Sullivan, Melanie Thernstrom, and JoAnn Wypijewski, and in comprehensive works by Beth Loffreda, Max Ember, and Moisés Kaufman and the Tectonic Theater Project. I am also indebted to the works of Kathleen Dowling Singh, Sherwin B. Nuland, Virginia Woolf, Truman Capote, Jim Crace, Michael Scarce, Gary Indiana, and Peter J. Gomes, which were used as touchstones in the writing of this novel.

Jameson Currier

Jameson Currier is the author of six novels: *Where the Rainbow Ends; The Wolf at the Door; The Third Buddha; What Comes Around; The Forever Marathon;* and *A Gathering Storm;* four collections of short fiction: *Dancing on the Moon; Desire, Lust, Passion, Sex; Still Dancing: New and Selected Stories;* and *The Haunted Heart and Other Tales;* and a memoir, *Until My Heart Stops.* His short fiction has appeared in many literary magazines and Web sites, including *OutsiderInk, Velvet Mafia, Blithe House Quarterly, Absinthe Literary Review, Confrontation, Rainbow Curve, Christopher Street, Harrington Gay Men's Fiction Quarterly,* and the anthologies *Men on Men 5, Best American Gay Fiction 3, Certain Voices, Boyfriends from Hell, Men Seeking Men, Mammoth Book of New Gay Erotica, Best Gay Erotica, Best American Erotica, Best Gay Romance, Best Gay Stories, Circa 2000, Rebel Yell, I Do/I Don't, Where the Boys Are, Nine Hundred & Sixty-Nine, Wilde Stories, Unspeakable Horror, Art from Art,* and *Making Literature Matter.* His AIDS-themed short stories have also been translated into French by Anne-Laure Hubert and published as *Les Fantômes,* and he is the author of the documentary film, *Living Proof: HIV and the Pursuit of Happiness.* His reviews, essays, interviews, and articles on AIDS and gay culture have been published in many national and local publications, including *The Washington Post, The Los Angeles Times, Newsday, The Dallas Morning News, The St. Louis Post-Dispatch, The Minneapolis Star-Tribune, The Philadelphia Inquirer Magazine, Lambda Book Report, The Harvard Gay and Lesbian Review, Dallas Voice, The Washington Blade, Southern Voice, Metrosource, Bay Area Reporter, Frontiers, Ten Percent, The New York*

Native, The New York Blade, Out, and *Body Positive.* In 2010 he founded Chelsea Station Editions, an independent press devoted to gay literature. Among the authors the press has published are debut writers Dan Lopez, Gil Cole, Michael Graves, J.R. Greenwell, Jeffrey Luscombe, Craig Moreau, David Pratt, and William Sterling Walker, and veterans Felice Picano, Walter Holland, Charles Silverstein, Wesley Gibson, Tom Cardamone, Craig Cotter, and Jon Marans. In 2013, he edited two original anthologies: *With: New Gay Fiction* and *Between: New Gay Poetry.* The press also serves as the home for Mr. Currier's own writings which now span a career of more than four decades. Books published by the press have been honored by the Lambda Literary Foundation, the American Library Association GLBTRT Roundtable, the Saints and Sinners Literary Festival, the Gaylactic Spectrum Awards Foundation, and the Rainbow Book Awards. In 2011, Mr. Currier launched the literary magazine *Chelsea Station,* which has published the works of more than a hundred writers, and in 2014 he re-launched the magazine as an online site. Mr. Currier is a member of the Board of Directors of the Arch and Bruce Brown Foundation, a recipient of a fellowship from New York Foundation for the Arts, and has been a judge for many literary competitions. A native of the South, he currently resides in New York.

CPSIA information can be obtained
at www.ICGtesting.com
Printed in the USA
LVOW01s0034230816
501376LV00037B/2300/P